Xenophon
The Education of Cyrus

A volume in the series
Agora Editions

General Editor: Thomas L. Pangle
Founding Editor: Allan Bloom

A full list of titles in the series appears at
the end of the book.

Xenophon
The Education of Cyrus

*Translated and
Annotated by*
WAYNE AMBLER

CORNELL UNIVERSITY PRESS

ITHACA AND LONDON

First published 2001 by Cornell University Press
First printing, Cornell Paperbacks, 2001

Printed in the United States of America

Library of Congress Cataloging-in-Publication Data

Xenophon.
    [Cyropaedia. English]
    The education of Cyrus / Xenophon ; translated and annotated by
Wayne Ambler.
      p. cm.—(Agora paperback editions)
(Includes bibliographical references and index.
ISBN-13: 978-0-8014-3818-9 (cloth : alk. paper)
ISBN-10: 0-8014-3818-7 (cloth : alk. paper)
ISBN-13: 978-0-8014-8750-7 (pbk. : alk. paper)
ISBN-10: 0-8014-8750-1 (pbk. : alk. paper)
    1. Cyrus, King of Persia, d. 529 B.C.—Fiction. 2.
Iran—History—To 640—Fiction.   I. Ambler, Wayne, II. Title. III.
Series.
    PA4495.C5 A44 2001
    883'.01—dc21
                                           2001001416

1 3 5 7 9 Cloth printing 10 8 6 4 2
7 9 Paperback printing 10 8 6

To the memory of my father

Contents

◈ *The Education of Cyrus* ◈
Xenophon

Translator's Note

That Xenophon is a thinker of the first rank is definitely not the dominant view in the academy today. Nevertheless, a growing literature takes note of his more distinguished earlier reputation and argues that Xenophon's often unassuming and apparently naive prose is in fact a carefully chosen vehicle for reflections with profound political and ethical implications.[1] Open-minded readers of *The Education of Cyrus* will naturally want to put this view to the test, and this translation is intended to help them do so.

I have been guided by the view that Xenophon's treatment of philosophical issues is worthy of the most serious study. As he often touches on such issues obliquely and through the associations of his terminology, I have taken pains to convey as accurately as possible everything that might help readers to encounter his thought, even though doing so complicates the task of translating into familiar English idiom. I do not claim to have achieved full accuracy nor do I deny that the literary qualities of the *Education* would themselves be worthy of careful study. Instead, I state my aim in order to explain

---

[1] The best introduction to the recent secondary literature on the *Education* is Christopher Nadon, "From Republic to Empire: Political Revolution and the Common Good in Xenophon's *Education of Cyrus*," *American Political Science Review* 90 (June 1996): 361–74. For an extended consideration and brilliant analysis of the *Education* as a whole, see Christopher Nadon, *Xenophon's Prince: Republic and Empire in the "Cyropaedia"* (Berkeley: University of California Press, 2001). For a guide to the literature that takes Xenophon seriously as a philosophic thinker, see Amy L. Bonnette, "Translator's Note," in Xenophon, *Memorabilia*, trans. Amy L. Bonnette (Ithaca: Cornell University Press, 1994), xxvii–xxviii.

why this translation differs from its two most recent predecessors and to help readers to make better use of it.[2]

Translating a text that might convey important knowledge or even wisdom increases the translator's responsibility to translate accurately. In the name of fidelity to Xenophon's Greek text, I have tried to translate as consistently as possible the words that are most directly related to the major issues of the work. An example of one such issue is whether what is *kalon* is also *agathon*, whether what is noble is also good. When and in what ways is it also good for someone to perform noble actions? Is it good in substantial ways, or only for the sake of appearances? Do the gods directly or indirectly protect or reward those who act nobly? Are there other foundations for an ethics of noble self-sacrifice? If there are actions that may be good without being noble, what sort are most worthy of serious attention? Only partly because the *Education* is more like a novel than a treatise, Xenophon raises but does not answer questions of this sort directly, and yet many episodes in the work shed light upon them (e.g., 1.5.7–10, 2.2.23–24, 6.3.36, 6.4.6, 7.1.42, 7.3.11, 8.1.30). A consistent translation of *kalon* allows readers to see and follow the moral, political, and theological questions raised by noble self-sacrifice, thus enabling them to grapple with them with a reduced measure of distortion by the translator. For such reasons I have sought consistency wherever possible, especially for words like *kalon* that are so important for the central themes of the work.

A glossary and notes will help interested readers to see a bit more of the Greek that lies behind the English translation, and they indicate as well certain of the more important cases in which I have not found it possible to translate with strict consistency. In the important case of *kalon*, for example, the Greek word has a wider range of meanings than does the English "noble," so strict consistency would lead us to use the English "noble," where the Greek *kalon* may mean merely "fine" or "okay," without any important difference from "good" (e.g., 4.1.1). Since *kalon* can also mean "beautiful" or "handsome" (e.g., 1.3.2, 5.1.8), such consistency would also mean speaking of good-looking people

---

[2] Xenophon, *Cyropaedia*, trans. Walter Miller (Cambridge: Harvard University Press, 1914); Xenophon, *The Education of Cyrus*, trans. H. G. Dakyns (London: Everyman's Library, 1914; reissued 1992).

as "noble." In short, the consistent translation of a single word can be misleading, just as inconsistency can keep readers from seeing the richness of an author's use of a particular word.

Although I have stopped well short of the strictest possible consistency, I have striven for it wherever it did not run counter to the sense of the Greek. If the result sometimes sounds a bit odd, it is often the result of an attempt to give the reader a better chance to understand the text. It is also true that Xenophon himself seemed not to have minded sounding a bit odd in certain places, as when he speaks of a just chariot needing to have just horses to pull it (2.2.26). What is more, it would be more than surprising if a book written over two thousand years ago contained nothing that at first glance seemed strange to us. I have in any event not taken it to be my goal to make the book conform to a preconceived notion of the author's intention nor to place the reader's ease above all.

I have translated the Greek text published by the Sociéte d'édition "Les Belles Lettres," and I have noted my few departures from it.[3]

I have kept the notes to a minimum. Readers new to the *Education* should bear in mind that many of the events and issues in this book recall passages from other works of Xenophon and acquire added importance when considered together with them. Bruell and Nadon are of special help in guiding study of the *Education* in the context of Xenophon's writings as a whole.[4]

The deficiencies in what follows are evidence of my own, but I am fortunate in being the beneficiary of much helpful advice. I am especially indebted to Robert Bartlett, Amy Bonnette Nendza, Scott Crider, Alexander Alderman, and Chris Lynch for their suggestions about the translation, and to Peter Heyne, Connie Baumgartner, and Catherine Ambler for proofreading and help with the glossary. The National Endowment for the Humanities helped support this project with a summer grant. For my appreciation of Xenophon I am indebted to Chris Bruell.

---

[3] Xénophon, *Cyropédie*, vols. I–II ed. Marcel Bizos, vol. III, ed. Édouard Delebecque (Paris: Belles Lettres, 1971–78).

[4] Christopher Bruell, "Xenophon," in *The History of Political Philosophy*, ed. Leo Strauss and Joseph Cropsey (Chicago: University of Chicago Press, 1987), 90–107; Nadon, "From Republic to Empire," 361–74.

Xenophon's *Education of Cyrus*

Xenophon's *Education of Cyrus* offers its own introduction, one that helps turn the reader's attention to the core issues of the book. It states a problem and proposes a solution, or at least a way of arriving at a solution. The problem is that because it is very difficult for human beings to rule over other human beings, political instability is a constant fact of life. But it turns out that there was once a certain Cyrus who was a successful ruler on a vast scale. Xenophon's own introduction culminates in the bold suggestion that by studying what Cyrus did and how he did it, we can arrive at knowledge of how to rule and, thereby, of how to overcome the problem of political instability (1.1.3).

Xenophon underscores our need for this science of rule by briefly reminding the reader of the grave problems we suffer in its absence. No form of government endures as it would wish; many collapse with breathtaking speed. This instability seems not to be the result of bad circumstances or bad luck. Contrary to Alexander Hamilton's opening argument in *Federalist No. 9*, which also raises this issue, it is not a problem only or especially for "the petty republics of Greece and Italy." It seems to be inherent in political life: politics entails rule, and rule entails dividing a single species into two very different groups, rulers and ruled (1.1.2). For reasons that Xenophon does not elaborate at this point, but that are not hard to imagine, subjects are not content with this division and struggle to undo it. As Hamilton

A version of this essay appeared in *The World & I*, November 1992, 515–31. I am grateful for the publisher's permission to use it as the basis for this introduction.

emphasizes, democracy is not exempt from this problem. For if democracy is the rule by the people, then in practice "the people" does not mean everyone; it means especially the majority. To a minority, even to a minority of one, rule by the majority may often be preferable to the risks of anarchy or civil war, but why would it be preferable to rule by the minority? Like other regimes, democracy has built-in sources of instability that are likely to surface when opportunities present themselves. The opening observation of the *Education* remains intelligible across the centuries and at least as powerful as that of Madison in *Federalist No. 51*: Political rule by angels is not to be counted on, but rule by some human beings over others is highly problematic.

It appears that Xenophon, like Hamilton in *Federalist No. 9*, has sketched the problem of political instability not to show that it is insuperable but to prepare the proper reception for his solution. Both Hamilton and Xenophon locate the solution for the political problem in science or knowledge. Hamilton referred directly to a new science of politics; here is how Xenophon puts it:

> Now when we considered these things, we inclined to this judg-
> ment about them: It is easier, given his nature, for a human being
> to rule all the other kinds of animals than to rule human beings. But
> when we reflected that there was Cyrus, a Persian, who acquired
> very many people, very many cities, and very many nations, all
> obedient to himself, we were thus compelled to change our mind
> to the view that ruling human beings does not belong among those
> tasks that are impossible, or even among those that are difficult, if
> one does it with knowledge. (1.1.3)

Hamilton identified the new and promising elements of his political science as being the separation of powers, checks and balances, representative government, and an independent judiciary. Hamilton's new science sought especially to solve the problem of "domestic faction and insurrection," which he associated with democratic government in particular, but it also was alive to the usefulness of size and unity for defense. Embodied as it is in the empire he builds, Cyrus' solution is in one respect still more ambitious. For not only does the building of Cyrus' empire reduce Persia's domestic instability by breaking down the rigid lines of class that used to divide Persia into

opposed factions and increase security by enlarging Persia and reducing its neighbors, it also brings a general peace to a multinational
region so vast as to be in effect a world unto itself, set off by natural
boundaries (8.6.21). The *Education* responds not only to the problems
of domestic faction and self-defense but also to those of world peace.
It does so, of course, not by a strictly institutional approach but by
concentrating our hopes on a single ruler.

The *Education of Cyrus* thus begins with a brief but bleak observation that political life is inevitably beset by turmoil (even if civil turmoil is not the only political evil), but it does not lose its spirit in the
face of this daunting problem. Rather, it quickly offers the observation that Cyrus was a successful ruler on a vast scale and that we can
learn from him. And yet once Xenophon introduces the *Education* by
raising the problem of rule, the character of the book changes dra-
matically. Instead of an analytical account of the key elements of the
promised political science, the *Education* becomes a narration of
Cyrus' life in its entirety, and his work loses all resemblance to a treatise. Readers seeking a simple compendium of the techniques of
power will be disappointed, but the altered form of the *Education* has
much to recommend it: it is engaging (for the story of Cyrus' life acts
upon the reader's passions, as does a good novel), it is comprehen-
sive (for it studies the character and fundamental beliefs of the ruler,
for example, as well as the techniques of his success), and it is true to
the subtleties of ruling (for it does not trivialize the "lessons" of rule
by wrenching them out of the specific circumstances that must always
be considered in formulating a speech or a plan of action). It certainly
does not aspire to teach the historical truth about Cyrus the Great,
Persia, or the geography of Asia,[1] but—as Sir Philip Sidney wrote in
The Defense of Poesy—because he is imagined rather than historical,
and because he is imagined *well*, on the basis of nature, Xenophon's

---

[1] It has been noted by many and in detail that Xenophon's "Cyrus" is only loosely
based on the life of Cyrus the Great, that Xenophon's "Persia" resembles Sparta more
than Persia, and that the geography of Asia is adjusted to suit dramatic or didactic necessity. *The Education of Cyrus* does not aspire to be a history in the modern sense. See
Walter Miller, "Introduction," in Xenophon, *The Education of Cyrus*, trans. Miller (Cambridge: Harvard University Press, 1914), viii–x; Marcel Bizos, "Notice," in Xénophon,
Cyropédie (Paris: Belles Lettres, 1971), vi–xvi; Christopher Nadon, "From Republic to
Empire: Political Revolution and the Common Good in Xenophon's *Education of Cyrus*,"
American Political Science Review 90 (June 1996): 364.

Cyrus can "make many Cyruses, if they will learn aright why and how [his] maker made him."[2] These, at least, are the explicit and implicit claims of the introduction, claims to be tested on the basis of a patient reading.

Cyrus' Successes

One must be impressed by Cyrus' extraordinary successes and by the extraordinary character who seems to deserve them. Cyrus marches from one victory to another, and, no less important, he seems entitled to these victories by a host of attractive qualities. By making Cyrus at once so successful and so admirable as a human being, Xenophon seems to suggest not only that rule is possible but also that it is fully compatible with qualities we esteem—or even is their natural result. In addition to his ability to size up a situation on a battlefield, his daring, and his hard-earned equestrian skills, Cyrus displays such qualities as clemency, benevolence, generosity, and justice; these qualities are hard not to admire, and are especially important if we identify more with Cyrus' subjects than with Cyrus himself. For although Cyrus is introduced in light of the difficult but still limited problem of how to secure stability, for which mere obedience is sufficient, he emerges as an example of a ruler who is always keenly alive to his subjects' hopes and interests.

Throughout the first two-thirds of his book, Xenophon goes to surprising lengths to show how widespread are the blessings of Cyrus' successes. The general picture is of Cyrus bringing order into a world that is badly out of kilter. Although Xenophon does not dwell on human misery, he indicates the destructiveness of civil war (7.4.1, 3–6), the high costs of foolish attempts at aggrandizement (7.2.23–24), and many occasions on which a nation's wealth is hoarded or squandered by its rulers rather than employed for the general good (1.6.8). When Cyrus enters this world, he comes to light as a boon to his na-

---

[2] Sir Philip Sidney, "The Apology for Poetry," in *Critical Theory since Plato*, ed. Hazard Adams (New York: Harcourt Brace Jovanovich, 1971), 157–58.

tive Persia and to people everywhere. Let us consider a few of the
many beneficiaries of Cyrus' career.

In the political world of the *Education*, the Persian regime—which
is rather a consciously modified Sparta than a poor effort at describ-
ing historical Persia[3]—seems to be the one government that is not seriously disordered. Anything but a modern liberal regime, it is presented as a republic in which the citizens were responsible for
governing themselves by ruling and being ruled, as admirable for the
way the laws educated the citizens to a concern for the common good
and to the virtues through which this common good could be secured,
and as blessed by a king whose authority was limited in the interest
of republican government but whose wisdom knew no bounds. It
gradually emerges, however, that like its Spartan model, the Persian
republic compels a huge class of commoners to work and deprives
them of political rights.[4] And in the manner more of a Greek polis than
of the Persian nation known to historians, its small size and strict class
division left it vulnerable to attack by powerful neighbors. Finally, its
understanding of virtue, and hence its whole education, was flawed,
at least in Cyrus' judgment (1.5.9–11).

Cyrus does not simply bestow an empire upon Persia; he also
transforms Persia itself. Cyrus liberates the Persian underclass and
institutes a policy of rewarding all Persians on the basis of merit
(2.2.18–2.3.16). Lest the important consequences of this policy be
missed, Xenophon shows through the career of a commoner named
Pheraulas both that some commoners did possess remarkable gifts
and that Cyrus rewarded them generously (8.3.5–8, 35–50). Were it
not for Cyrus, Pheraulas and all like him would have been confined
to a life of hard labor, poverty, and political impotence. Even when
he was a boy, Cyrus seemed to grasp that Persian laws were
defective in their blindness to important individual differences
(1.3.16–17); Cyrus' victories thus not only advance himself and

---

[3] For an excellent discussion of how Persia is and is not modeled on Sparta, see
Nadon, *Xenophon's Prince*, 29–42.

[4] That "Persia" is a close oligarchy is first evident in 1.2.15. The narrowness of this
oligarchy and its foundation in the military might of the Peers becomes ever more clear
as we see how vast a pool of manpower the Commoners provide for Cyrus (1.5.5) and
how important is their learning the mode of fighting that had been reserved for the
Peers (2.1.9).

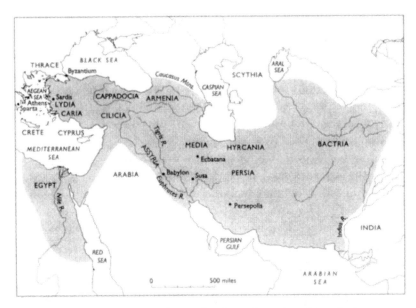

The Persian Empire under Cyrus the Great, based on historical sources.
(For Xenophon's summaries of the extent of Cyrus' empire, see 1.1.4
and 8.6.20–21.)

protect Persia, they also make Persia more just by establishing and
enforcing the principle of reward on the basis of individual merit.
And, of course, this principle has still other advantages as an engine
of enterprise.

But Cyrus does not reform only the Persian regime under which
he was born, he addresses all the grosser injustices of his world, including those of his allies. The initial stimulus for Cyrus' career is a
call from the neighboring Median monarchy for Persia's aid against
a threatened attack by an alliance led by Assyria. Cyaxares, the Median despot, who happens to be Cyrus' uncle, is a fool who is severe
with his subjects while reserving the soft life for himself. Since Cyrus
is as continent and demanding of himself as Cyaxares is licentious
and indulgent, and since he also possesses many other virtues of
good kings and generals, it is no surprise that the Median troops can
be brought to think of Cyrus as a natural king, as one born to lead;
and their loyalty to their legitimate king naturally suffers as a consequence (5.1.24–29). In the end, one must admire the cunning and

delicacy with which the deserving ruler replaces the undeserving, even with the latter's consent! For Cyrus himself seems to advance only in accord with the principle of merit that he extends to others. And why, Cyrus asks, should the principle of merit be clouded by questions of national origin (2.2.26)? An international empire can transcend the division of the world into separate jurisdictions, an artificial division that for no good reason brings blessings to some and deprives others of a decent chance for happiness. Thus, like their Persian allies, the Medes themselves, and especially the most deserving among them, also gain by Cyrus' advancement. As one of them says, compared with life under the despots of Media, going to war with Cyrus at one's side is like a banquet (6.1.9); and one cannot help but think it still the case today that military service in a foreign army would bring a better life for many than the lives of oppression they lead in their native lands, even in times of peace. The political world is woefully disordered, and one must be pleased as this Cyrus rearranges it. If he ends up at the top, it is not without deserving it.

Xenophon goes so far as to have some of Cyrus' defeated foes pay tribute to him and thus suggests that Cyrus' rule is advantageous even in the least likely cases. Cyrus' first major battle was against the king of Armenia, for example. After defeating him handily, he then achieved a moral victory that was no less complete than the military one: The king came to believe that he no longer had any right to possess his own property (3.1.35). Only through Cyrus' clemency was he spared death and overthrow, and the king ended up a grateful dependent instead of an enemy (though Cyrus did not fail to take the precaution of leaving behind a small occupying force [3.3.1, 3.1.27]). Moreover, since Cyrus took the opportunity to impose a mutually beneficial peace between the defeated Armenians and their troublesome neighbors, the Chaldaeans, he was hailed as follows by those he had just attacked and subdued:

> When he went down into the inhabited country, none of the Armenians remained inside, neither man nor woman, but in their pleasure at the peace all went out to meet him, and they carried or drove in herds whatever they had that was of value. And the Armenian was not annoyed with them, for he believed that Cyrus would be more pleased like this, with an honor bestowed by all.

> Finally, the Armenian's wife with her daughters and her younger
> son also went out to meet him, and along with other gifts she
> brought the gold that Cyrus previously had not been willing to
> take. (3.3.2)

It is thus with some reason that Cyrus can think of himself not so
much as having conquered an enemy as having made friends (3.1.31).

Even more striking in this regard is the case of Croesus the Lydian
king. It is true that after he has fallen into Cyrus' hands, Croesus is in
no position to grumble openly about what has happened to him, but
he is so detailed in his enthusiasm for becoming a subject of Cyrus
that I am led to think his sentiments are sincere. Croesus makes no
excuses for his defeat at Cyrus' hands: He simply says that he had
been flattered into thinking that he deserved the greatest victories and
was a worthy opponent of Cyrus. His defeats have taught him self-
knowledge,[5] and he now sees that he was no match for a man who,
among other things, exercised himself in the virtues his whole life
long (7.2.24). Croesus showed no aptitude for ruling (not to mention
considerable awkwardness in his dealings with the Oracle at Delphi
[7.2.15–25]). Cyrus is the more deserving ruler, and even Croesus has
come to realize this. When Cyrus pities Croesus, lets him keep his
family intact, and even allows him a comfortable living, Croesus declares that he will now lead the most blessedly happy life, for he is
free of political responsibilities (7.2.27). Cyrus often thinks of himself
as a benefactor, but in this case even he is amazed at the good spirits
of one he has defeated (7.2.29).

These examples help convey some sense of the distance between a
natural ruler like Cyrus and such mediocre and foolish leaders as continue to turn up in political life. His subjects' enthusiasm for his rule
also suggests that there are few casualties in his rise to power. It is
better for everyone that Cyrus should rule, it seems, and even some
of those whom he defeats come to believe it.

One may think that Xenophon has made Cyrus' rise to power too
easy by surrounding him with foolish and wicked rivals who leave
themselves wide open for attack. Perhaps, but it is not at all hard to

---

[5] This is one of several passages in which one is led to understand "the education
of Cyrus" as referring not only to what he learns but also to what he teaches others,
whether directly or indirectly.

think of rulers in our day who start wars before they have the weapons or troops needed to win them, who are led by vanity to seek authority they cannot exercise well, who are prone to grudges and national hatreds that forestall the attainment of benefits that they themselves might enjoy, and who simply try to amass as much personal wealth as they can—insensitive not only to the claims of virtue but even to the utility of not being hated. And although it is certainly not impossible to find subjects and citizens who have enjoyed important political blessings, in both ancient and modern history, sometimes for centuries, the shadow cast by the folly of men with power is never far from the scene. If rulers in *The Education of Cyrus* should seem even more incompetent and vulnerable to being overthrown than do those of actual history, they may seem so partly because Xenophon pits them against a Cyrus whose life is a constant meditation on how to take advantage of others' weaknesses. Bad rulers often have the apparent good fortune not to encounter good ones, but not in a world in which there is a Cyrus at large. If the *Education* could really educate another Cyrus, even if only "for the most part," it would be a book of unusual power.

But Cyrus' archenemy is the king of Assyria, and he is so wicked, and especially so envious, that he can never be expected to acknowledge the worth of anyone else, least of all someone of Cyrus' caliber. Having killed the son of a certain Gobryas simply because he appeared to be a superior hunter, and having castrated a nobleman named Gadatas simply because his concubine thought this nobleman to be attractive (4.6.3–5, 5.2.28), the Assyrian king made himself hated even by his more powerful subjects and thereby offered Cyrus useful opportunities to show himself an avenger of injustices. Cyrus' final victory is over the Assyrian's stronghold in Babylon, and it results in the king's execution at the hands of Gobryas and Gadatas. The Assyrian king is thus the limit case: not everyone profits from Cyrus' conquests, but he is so wicked a character that no reader can mourn his execution. The common good that assists and is brought out by Cyrus' coming to power may not benefit everyone, but those excluded still get what they deserve. Cyrus would not be so attractive if he were simply a man with remarkable gifts for amassing political power. He is admired because he also seems able to make a moral claim to this power and because he seems to

exercise it for the benefit of men generally.[6] To exaggerate for the
sake of making a point, one could say that whereas Plato's Socrates
argued that no real harm could come to a good man (even though
he might suffer such lesser or merely apparent evils as poverty, dishonor, and death), Xenophon's Cyrus goes further and appears to
demonstrate that the great man will be rewarded with every success. Better still, Cyrus' successes are good for everyone, or at least
for everyone who is at all deserving. The apparent promise of the
Education is not only that virtue is rewarded, but also that a great
ruler like Cyrus enables all decent people to share simultaneously
in these rewards. Politics need not be a dirty game, and it is not a
zero sum game either.

Surely the power of some such impressions has led to the view that
the last chapter of the *Education*, in which Cyrus' empire falls completely apart soon after his death, cannot have been written by
Xenophon and was not part of the original work.[7] How could it be
that a ruler whose virtues are so impressive, and whose empire is so
good for almost everyone, establishes nothing lasting in the end?
How could it be that after seeming to present Cyrus as a god among
men, or at least as an effective agent of the gods, Xenophon would
write a final chapter suggesting that Cyrus' whole career was built on
sand? To those who maintain that the final chapter cannot be au-
thentic, it must be conceded that it does weaken both the explicit
promise of a science of stable political rule—at least of such stability
as outlasts one's own life—and the promise implicit in Cyrus' career,
that the benefits conferred by the great ruler are not ephemeral.

But it is not only the conclusion of the *Education* that casts doubt on
Cyrus' accomplishments. Great rulers always *seem* impressive, and
in his faithful portrait of the ruler par excellence, Xenophon lets his
Cyrus enjoy this appearance. Nor is the appearance false in all respects, but we need to advance our account by noting that altogether

---

[6] The sequel will show the extent to which I consider this appearance to be false, but
it has had its influence. See Miller, Introduction to *Education of Cyrus*, xii: "[Xenophon's
Cyrus] has the same qualities of greatness, goodness, gentleness, and justice that are
given to him by the great prophets of Israel." See also Bodil Due, *The Cyropaedia:
Xenophon's Aims and Methods* (Aarhus: Aarhus University Press, 1989), 146: "Cyrus is
kind and considerate to his fellow human beings, he is full of piety and humility to-
wards the gods from the beginning to the end."

[7] *Education of Cyrus*, trans. Miller, vol. II, 438–39.

apart from the last chapter of the *Education*, both the desirability and the possibility of Cyrus' political science are more in question than is suggested by the general aura that surrounds Cyrus. Since the question of desirability eclipses the question of possibility, we focus on it.

Cyrus' Successes Reconsidered

Our impression that Cyrus' empire is generally beneficial and that he is morally commendable derives in part from the enthusiasm for Cyrus that is routinely expressed by various characters in the account of his rise to power. Cyrus is often praised to the skies in the *Education*, and he conquers the world with hardly a hint of criticism.[8] As we have noted, even some of his main victims seem to be among his admirers. Moreover, Xenophon began the book by calling Cyrus "worthy to be wondered at" and went on to have his Cyrus perform wonders, so the admiration expressed by the characters of the *Education* may seem to be confirmed by Xenophon himself.

But assessing Cyrus becomes somewhat more complicated when we notice that Cyrus is praised for quite different reasons and that he is sometimes praised mistakenly. Let us note first some of the ways in which Cyrus is celebrated and then how Xenophon shows some of Cyrus' admirers to be misguided.

Note in the first place that the problem described in Xenophon's introduction to the *Education* was instability, not injustice. Accordingly, Cyrus' success was measured by the extent of his domain, not by its justice or general beneficence (1.1). Fear was an important foundation of his rule (1.1.5). Although this foundation may recommend his rule to Machiavelli—for it *is* a token of strength and source of a certain stability—it should give pause to those who are moved by the hope of a peaceful world that is also just or at least in accord with the consent of the governed.[9] In light of the glowing successes

---

[8] For a few such hints, consider Aglaitadas in 2.2.14, Panthea in 7.3.10, and Hystaspas in 8.4.11–12.

[9] Niccolò Machiavelli, *The Prince* (Chicago: University of Chicago Press, 1998), chap. 17. For Machiavelli's interest in *The Education of Cyrus*, see chap. 14. See also Niccolò Machiavelli, *The Discourses on Livy* (Chicago: University of Chicago Press, 1996), III.20, III.23, III.39.

attributed to him in the body of the *Education*, it is striking to read again Xenophon's formulation of the problem in whose light Cyrus was introduced:

> We thought we saw all these herds more willing to obey their keepers than are human beings their rulers; for the herds go wherever their keepers direct them, they feed on whatever land their keepers drive them to, and they abstain from whatever lands their keepers turn them from. And as for such profits as arise from them, these they allow their keepers to use in whatever way they themselves wish. Nor have we ever perceived a herd uniting against its keeper, either so as not to obey or so as not to allow him to use the profits, but herds are more harsh toward all strangers than they are toward those who both rule over and benefit from them; on the other hand, human beings unite against none more than against those whom they perceive attempting to rule them. (1.1.2)

The model for rule in the light of which Cyrus is introduced is that of the herdsman who profits from his flocks in any way he wishes; the concern for obedience is strictly from the ruler's point of view. The image of the gain-seeking herdsman does not suggest that the ruler should treat his subjects well or that freedom for the ruled is of any importance. Whereas Hamilton's promised political science was explicit in its concern for "the principles of civil liberty" and for republican government, Xenophon's introduction makes no such claim for Cyrus' science. Indeed, he indicates both that Cyrus' subjects were not all willing to be subjects and that fear was a principal means by which Cyrus maintained his empire. Consider the following:

> He ruled these nations even though they did not speak the same language as either he himself or one another. Nevertheless, he was able to extend fear of himself to so much of the world that he intimidated all, and no one attempted anything against him; and he was able to implant in all so great a desire of gratifying him that they always thought it proper to be governed by his judgment. (1.1.5)

In light of the way Cyrus will come to be praised by others, the themes of justice, nobility, and beneficence are conspicuous by their absence from Xenophon's own introduction to Cyrus' accomplishment.

Whereas Xenophon seems to marvel only at the scope of Cyrus' sway, the characters in this philosophic novel often praise Cyrus by marveling at "the strength of his soul" (Hyrcanians, 4.2.14), by calling him a "benefactor" and "a good man" (Armenians, 3.3.4), by calling him "the noblest and best man" (Artabazus, 4.1.24), by speaking of his piety, moderation, and pity (Panthea, 6.1.47), and by speaking as Gadatas does in the following passage:

> "But I, by the gods," said Gadatas, "was coming in order to contemplate you again, how you appear in sight, you who have such a soul. You need from me now I know not what, nor did you promise me that you would do these things, nor have you experienced at my hands anything good, at least for yourself personally. But because I seemed to you to benefit your friends a bit, you helped me so enthusiastically that—although on my own I would be done for—I have been saved, thanks to you." (5.4.11)

Gadatas sees Cyrus' truly impressive rescue effort as being remarkable especially because Cyrus had no obligation to undertake it and had nothing to gain from it. Far from denying this, Cyrus seems to confirm the impression that his generosity is boundless by taking no special credit for the dramatic rescue he has just led; he instead suggests that what Gadatas has said of him should in fact be extended to all the troops, Persian and allied, who have come out in his defense. This noble gesture of sharing the credit does not deny but confirms Gadatas' view of Cyrus' generosity.

But Gadatas' view of Cyrus is false. Gadatas is right that Cyrus has no immediate need of running the risks of coming to his rescue; he could have safely stayed where he was and enjoyed the fruits of victories already won. But Cyrus is not guided by immediate needs; he has imperial ambitions, and devoted allies are essential for their fulfillment. He needs to acquire a reputation for going to great lengths to help allies and potential allies, as shown by Cyrus' own explanation of his reasons for going to Gadatas' rescue. After noting the justice and nobility of helping Gadatas, he adds,

> "But it seems to me that we would also be doing what is advantageous for ourselves. If it should be plain to everyone that we try to win victory over those who do evil by doing more evil to them, and

plain as well that we surpass our benefactors in good deeds, it is
likely that thanks to such actions many will wish to be our friends
and no one will desire to be our enemy." (5.3.31–32)

It is necessary to do favors to acquire political power, even if one
wants power for some reason other than to do favors. Cyrus recog-
nizes this necessity so clearly that, once one begins to look for it, it becomes visible in almost everything he does.

Of course the character of the favor varies with the person or group
he is trying to win over. He is so protective of the stunningly beautiful and utterly defenseless Panthea, for example, that she sees in Cyrus
an almost unbelievable model of piety, moderation, and pity. But we
hear Cyrus say out of her hearing that he is reserving her for a future
opportunity (5.1.17). Later, we see him cash in on his virtue or apparent virtue. By his posture of caring deeply for the happiness of the
beautiful Panthea, he gains for himself her husband's defection from
the Assyrian alliance (6.1.45–47), a powerful force of heavy chariots
(6.1.50–51), and an ally so devoted as to be willing to drive these chariots against the strongest part of the enemy's infantry, at the expense
of his life (6.3.35–36). On learning that her husband's courageous actions cost him his life, Panthea wonders about the wisdom of her and
her husband's noble response to their perceived debt to Cyrus (7.3.10).
Whatever else one may say about Cyrus' treatment of Panthea, it could
not have been better from the point of view of acquiring power.

Nor are Cyrus' favors like those of a knight errant; they are part of
a strategy of seeking useful "friends." Once he has sufficient strength,
he hunts for his friends from among the subjects and allies of his
enemy. Winning such a friend is not only an acquisition for Cyrus, it
is also a loss for his rivals, and it thus has a double effect. What is
more, a successful defection is an invitation to other disgruntled subjects to do likewise. Cyrus knows that the Assyrian alliance is full of
discontented followers. A credible force—or even a force that des-
perate hopes can make to seem credible—will rally them. The Hyrcanians, Gobryas, and Gadatas were all subjects of this sort, and aiding them brought Cyrus key defections and devoted followers.

But if Cyrus was sufficiently sensible to see that respecting a no-
blewoman's marriage might well be rewarded, and sufficiently sensible to seek new allies especially from among the forces of his actual

and potential enemies, his forte is in recognizing the lengths to which men will go for the sake of material gain, even if they prefer to be thought of as acting for higher motives. Adam Smith taught how to put the desire for individual gain at the service of the wealth of nations; Cyrus shows how to use it for the acquisition of empire. The following are among the more obvious applications of this principle. His speech beginning the campaign does not stress the need for defense against Assyria, which is the ostensible reason for going to war; rather, it argues to the Persians that their virtues are worthless unless they gain by them and that the opportunity for gain is now at hand (1.5.8–10). He increases the ardor of all Persian soldiers by breaking down class distinctions and promising rewards on the basis of individual merit (2.3.4, 16). He wins a following among the Medes not simply by displaying his extraordinary personal qualities and aptitude for leadership but especially by letting it be known that the Medes would gain by following him (4.2.10, end). But his most striking application of this principle is that he invites others, and most notably allies whom he needs to attach to his army, to take responsibility for safeguarding the considerable spoils his army accumulates. He thereby shows how much he trusts them, and proceeds to make high-toned speeches about the importance of trust, all the while letting them see, feel, and even revel in the bounteous fruits of their victories. But Cyrus trusts them not at all. As he explains it to his Persian troops, the more they steal from the common treasury, the more they will be attached to the common enterprise.

> "Moreover, there is still a lot of money in the camp, and I am not ignorant of the fact that it is possible for us to appropriate as much as we wish, even though it belongs in common to those who joined in taking it. But it does not seem to me to be a greater gain to take it than, by *appearing to be just* to them, to try to make them delight in us still more than they do now. It seems to me that we should commit even the distribution of the money to the Medes, Hyrcanians, and Tigranes, when they come back. And if they allocate somewhat less to us, to hold it a gain, for because of these gains, they will be more pleased to stay with us, for *greedily securing an extra advantage now would provide us wealth that is short-lived, but letting this go and acquiring instead that from which wealth naturally springs, this, as it seems to me, would have the power of providing ageless riches*

to us and ours. I think that even at home we practiced being superior to our stomachs and untimely gains so that we would be able to make advantageous use of this restraint if ever it should be needed. I do not see that we could display our education on an occasion greater than that now present." (4.2.42–45; emphasis added)

At this stage, he does not seek honest allies so much as enthusiastic ones, and he openly summons his Persian troops to cultivate the appearance of justice in order to secure allies, and through them, the fountain of wealth. The importance of apparent justice for lasting gain is one of the central principles taught by Cyrus' example, and the Persian education in continence is a marvelous foundation for apparent justice. What better ally is there than one that is remarkably capable of securing victory but seems unconcerned with enjoying its rewards? Yet one may now begin to guess how far the allies' hopes raised by such conduct will be met in the end.

We now have seen that several of the most extravagant celebrations of Cyrus' moral qualities turn out to be based on the failure to recognize that his extraordinary restraint in the short run is necessary as a means to the attainment of his empire in the long run. Once he has attained imperial power, Cyrus can treat everything valuable as his own. He took virtually nothing for himself and his Persians during the time he was building and extending the foundations of his power, and he was then the very model of austerity. But in the end he owns everything. Moreover, after he has reached this point, he confesses in a private conversation that he craves wealth and always desires more (8.2.20–22). Cyrus' self-restraint was but a foundation required by the vast scope of his desires. Although it certainly *seems* otherwise, even Cyaxares the libertine has some title to charge that Cyrus is uncontrolled in his pursuit of pleasure (4.1.14).

Conclusion

When we see Cyrus revealed in the end as an oriental despot, we may be tempted to say that the *Education* is the ultimate demonstration that power corrupts and that absolute power corrupts absolutely, for the distance Cyrus travels from Persian continence to Median sump-tuousness could not be greater. We would have to modify and strengthen this thesis, however, by noting that it was not so much power as the prospect of power that corrupted Cyrus. Perhaps in part because of his boyhood sojourn amidst Median luxury, Cyrus' cor-ruption occurred well before he became powerful; he was simply careful not to show too, too openly its depth and breadth.

It would also be no less correct to reverse the cliché and say that Cyrus' corruption empowers. His speech to his supporters before they leave Persia indicates that "what are believed to be the works of virtue" are useful only as a means of acquiring. Because it teaches that what is believed to be obligatory may not really be obligatory, and be-cause it helps one to focus on the goal of acquisition without distrac-tions or second thoughts, clever corruption empowers, and Cyrus' most clever corruption empowered absolutely. We would be entitled to say this, at least, once we established that Cyrus' view was wrong and hence deserved to be called corrupt. Xenophon's treatment of Socrates in his *Memorabilia*, and especially his discussion of whether Socrates was guilty of corrupting the youth, as the Athenians charged, would be no less helpful than the *Education* itself in determining whether and where Xenophon finds Cyrus' critique of Persian virtue to be misguided.

When we focus on the replacement of the old Persian republic, flawed though it was, by a vast despotism, the final dissolution of Cyrus' empire is less disturbing. Such enthusiasm as we felt for his rule while he was conferring benefits left and right vanishes when we see our hero turn despot in the end. His reflections on how a despot can secure his own personal safety and wealth are impressive. Where else can we read of the usefulness of using eunuchs as one's personal guards (7.5.58–65), of ways of sowing dissension among one's "friends" so as to fear them less (8.1.46–48, 8.2.26–28), of how to in-still fear by a half-secret system of universal surveillance (8.2.10), and of how huge military parades can rally supporters and intimidate enemies (8.3.5)? When Cyrus was eager to acquire allies, he wore fa-tigues and adorned himself with sweat, but after he had the world in his grasp, he turned to Median finery, even to the extent of eye shadow, cosmetics, and elevator shoes (2.4.1–8; 8.1.40–41). It is true that many benefited in the sense of becoming rich and powerful along with Cyrus, and men like Chrysantas and Pheraulas do reveal impressive political gifts that in some sense justify their rewards. But it becomes clear that Cyrus does not so much reward true merit as he rewards obedience and service to himself, and the number of peoples whom Cyrus liberates in the course of acquiring power is more than matched by those he subjugates once he has it. When we see that even the Persians, who are his greatest beneficiaries, now for the first time must prostrate themselves before Cyrus (8.3.14), it becomes impossible to think of Cyrus as having secured anyone's freedom. Whereas we were at first pleased to see a man of such apparent virtue as Cyrus' come to acquire political power and begin to set the world aright, we have come to doubt that Cyrus' virtues and benefactions are genuine. And although it is not a pretty sight, the dissolution of Cyrus' empire should neither shock nor cause dismay.

The collapse of Cyrus' rule returns us to the spectacle of political instability with which the *Education* began, and we are compelled anew to look for help as to how best to respond to this problem. Although the *Education* itself has much more to offer in this connection than has been touched on here, especially in the form of its quiet heroes, Cambyses and Tigranes, it should be noted that Xenophon's other works are also pertinent in this regard. In his *Memorabilia* and other Socratic writings, for example, we see a man whose entire mature life was spent amidst war, civil strife, and tyranny, and who nevertheless lived a life that Xenophon judged to be both best and most happy (*Mem.* 4.8.11): even if human wisdom is not able to teach a programmatic solution to the problem of political instability, it is able to teach how to live in light of this problem. And in his *Anabasis* we see Xenophon himself become a ruler and do so to the advantage of all concerned. Cyrus reduced more men to obedience than did anyone else, and Machiavelli testifies to the usefulness of his education about how to rule. But Xenophon puts this impressive accomplishment in the context of other achievements still more worthy of admiration and study.

Xenophon
The Education of Cyrus

BOOK I

ᨕ CHAPTER 1 ᨕ

(1) This reflection once occurred to us: How many democracies have been brought down by those who wished the governing to be done in some way other than under a democracy; how many monarchies and how many oligarchies have been overthrown by the people;[1] and how many who have tried to establish tyrannies have, some of them, been at once brought down completely, while others, if they have continued ruling for any time at all, are admired as wise and fortunate men. We thought we also observed many in their very own private households—some indeed having many servants, but others with only very few—and, nevertheless, they, the masters, were not able to keep even these few at all obedient for their use. (2) In addition to this we reflected also that cattlemen and horsemen are the rulers of cattle and horses, and that all those called keepers of animals could plausibly be believed to be the rulers of the animals in their charge. We thought we saw all these herds more willing to obey their keepers than are human beings[2] their rulers; for the herds go wherever their keepers direct them, they feed on whatever land their keepers drive them to, and they abstain from whatever lands their keepers turn them from. And as for such profits as arise from them, these they allow their keepers to use in whatever way they themselves wish. Nor have we ever perceived a herd uniting against its keeper, either so as not to obey or so as not to allow him to use the profits,

but herds are more harsh toward all others than they are toward those who both rule over and benefit from them; on the other hand, human beings unite against none more than against those whom they perceive attempting to rule them.

(3) Now when we considered these things, we inclined to this judgment about them: It is easier, given his nature, for a human being to rule all the other kinds of animals than to rule human beings. But when we reflected that there was Cyrus, a Persian, who acquired very many people, very many cities, and very many nations, all obedient to himself, we were thus compelled to change our mind to the view that ruling human beings does not belong among those tasks that are impossible, or even among those that are difficult, if one does it with knowledge.[3] We know that Cyrus, at any rate, was willingly obeyed by some, even though they were distant from him by a journey of many days; by others, distant by a journey even of months; by others, who had never yet seen him; and by others, who knew quite well that they would never see him. Nevertheless, they were willing to submit to him, (4) for so far did he excel other kings—both those who inherited rule from their forefathers and those who acquired it through their own efforts—that the Scythian king, even though there are very many Scythians, is unable to rule any additional nation, but would be content if he could continue ruling his own nation; and so would the Thracian king with the Thracians and the Illyrian king with the Illyrians. And it is like this also with as many other nations as we hear of; at least the nations of Europe are said to be still independent and detached from each other. But Cyrus, after finding the nations in Asia in just this independent condition, set out with a little army of Persians and became the leader of the Medes, who were willing that he do so, and over the Hyrcanians, who were also willing; and he subdued the Syrians, Assyrians, Arabians, Cappadocians, both the Phrygians,[4] the Lydians, Carians, Phoenicians, and Babylonians; he came to rule the Bactrians, Indians, and Cilicians, and similarly also the Sacians, Paphlagonians, and Magadidians, and very many other nations whose names one cannot even say. He ruled also over the Greeks who were in Asia, and, going down to the sea, over the Cyprians and Egyptians.[5] (5) He ruled these nations even though they did not speak the same language as either he himself or one another. Nevertheless, he was able to extend fear of himself to so much of the world that he

intimidated all, and no one attempted anything against him; and he was able to implant in all so great a desire of gratifying him that they always thought it proper to be governed by his judgment.[6] He attached to himself so many nations that it would be a task even to pass through them, no matter which direction one should begin to go from his royal[7] palace, whether toward the east, west, north, or south. (6) So on the grounds that this man was worthy of wonder,[8] we examined who he was by birth, what his nature was, and with what education he was brought up, such that he so excelled in ruling human beings. Whatever we have learned, therefore, and think we have perceived about him, we shall try to relate.

ᐯ᷉ CHAPTER 2 ᐯ᷉

(1) Now the father of Cyrus is said to have been Cambyses, king of the Persians; this Cambyses was of the race of the Perseidae, who were so named after Perseus.[9] His mother is agreed to have been Mandane. This Mandane was the daughter of Astyages, who became king of the Medes. As to his nature, even now Cyrus is still described in word and song by the barbarians as having been most beautiful in form and most benevolent in soul, most eager to learn, and most ambitious,[10] with the result that he endured every labor and faced every risk for the sake of being praised. (2) He is remembered, then, as having such a nature in body and soul.[11]

He was, moreover, educated in the laws of the Persians. These laws do not seem to begin where they begin in most cities, but by caring for the common good. For most cities allow each to educate his own children however he wants, and they allow the adults themselves to live however they please; then they enjoin them not to steal or plunder, not to use violence in entering a house, not to strike whomever it is unjust to strike, not to commit adultery, not to disobey a ruler, and similarly with other such matters. If someone transgresses one of these strictures, they punish him.

(3) But the Persian laws, starting earlier, take care that the citizens will not in the first place even be such as to desire any vile or shameful deed.[12] They exercise this care in the following way: They have a

so-called Free Square, where the king's palace and other government buildings have been built. From hence are banished to another place merchandise for sale and its sellers, their cries and their vulgarity, lest their confusion mingle with the good order of the educated. (4) This square by the government buildings is divided into four parts. One of these is for the boys, one for the youths, another for the mature men, another for those who are beyond the years of military service. It is required by law that these divisions attend their several places, the boys and the mature men at daybreak, the elders when it suits each of them, except for appointed days, when they are obliged to be present. The youths even sleep beside the government buildings with their light weapons, except the married youths; these are not sought after (unless it was previously required that they attend), although it is not noble for them to be absent often. (5) There are twelve rulers over each of these parts, for the Persians are divided into twelve tribes. Over the boys are chosen those of the elders who are thought to make the boys best; over the youths those of the mature men who are thought to render the youths best; and over the mature men those who are thought to render them especially ready to carry out the orders and exhortations of the greatest office.[13] Leaders of the elders are also chosen, and they lead so that these too perform their duties completely. In order that it may be more clear how they take care that the citizens be as good as possible, we will describe what each age group is ordered to do.

(6) The boys who go to school spend their time learning justice. It is said that they go for this purpose, as among us they go to learn their letters. Their rulers spend most of the day judging cases among them, for just as men do, of course, boys also accuse each other of theft, robbery, violence, deceit, calumny, and other such things as are likely; and they take vengeance on whomever they resolve to have done any of these injustices. (7) They punish also whomever they find to be bringing an unjust accusation. They also judge cases of ingratitude, an accusation for which human beings hate each other very much but very rarely adjudicate; and they punish severely whomever they judge not to have repaid a favor he was able to repay, for they think that those who are ungrateful would be especially uncaring also about gods, as well as about parents, fatherland, and friends; and shamelessness seems to follow especially upon ingratitude, and it

seems in turn to be the greatest leader to everything shameful. (8) They also teach the boys moderation.[14] It contributes greatly to their learning moderation that they see also their elders spending the whole day moderately.[15] They teach them also to obey the rulers. It contributes greatly to this too that they see their elders strictly obeying the rulers. They also teach continence in food and drink.[16] It contributes greatly also to this that they do not see their elders going off for food until the rulers dismiss them, and that the boys eat not with their mothers but with their teacher, and not before the rulers give the signal. They carry bread from home as their main food, greens as a relish, and a drinking cup so that if one is thirsty, he may draw up water from the river.[17] In addition to these things, they learn how to shoot a bow and to throw a spear. The boys do this until they are sixteen or seventeen years old; after this they enter among the youths.

(9) These youths spend their time in the following way. For ten years after they leave the class of the boys, they sleep around the government buildings, just as we said before, both for the city and for moderation, for this age seems especially in need of care. They present themselves to the rulers also during the day, in case they should need to use them for the community.[18] And whenever it is necessary, all remain around the government buildings; but when the king goes out for a hunt, he leads out half of the guard with him. And he does this many times during the month. Those who go out must have a bow and quiver, a scimitar[19] or small sword in a sheath, and, moreover, a light shield and two spears, one to throw and the other, if need be, to use close at hand.

(10) Here is why they take care that hunting be a matter of public concern, and why, just as he is also in war, the king is their leader, and he himself joins the hunt and also takes care that they do: It seems to them that hunting is the truest of the exercises that pertain to war. For it habituates them to rise at dawn and to endure cold and heat, it exercises them in marches and in running, and it is necessary both to shoot wild animals with the bow and to spear them whenever one comes close. It is necessary that, whenever one of the mightier wild animals turns up, as often happens, even the soul be whetted, for surely one must strike the wild animal that comes to close quarters and be on one's guard against the one that approaches. Consequently, it is not easy to find anything missing from hunting that is present in war.

(11) They go out on the hunt with a lunch that is larger, as is to be expected,[20] than that of the boys, but it is in other respects the same. They will not eat this lunch while hunting; and if it should be at all necessary to remain out to pursue the game, or if they are for any other reason willing to spend more time hunting, they eat their lunch for dinner and hunt again the next day until dinnertime, and they calculate that these two days are one, because they spent on them the food of only one day. This they do to habituate themselves, so that if it is at all necessary also in war, they are able to do the same thing. And as a relish, those of this age have whatever they catch on the hunt. If nothing else, there are greens. And if someone should think that they eat without pleasure when they have only greens with their bread, or drink without pleasure when they drink only water, let him remember how pleasant barley cake and bread are to those who hunger to eat, and how pleasant water is to one who thirsts to drink. (12) The tribes that remain behind spend their time concerned with shooting their bows and throwing their spears, and with the other things that they learned when they were boys; and they compete continuously against each other in these things. There are also public contests in them, and prizes are offered. In whichever tribe there are the most members who are most skillful, most manly, and most obedient, the citizens praise and honor not only their present ruler but also the one who educated them when they were boys. If there should be any need to post guards, to search for malefactors, to chase after robbers, or to do any other work that requires strength or speed, the magistrates make use of those of the youths who remain behind. This, then, is what the youths do.

But when they complete their ten years, they enter among the mature men. (13) From whenever they graduate, they spend the next twenty-five years in the following way. First, just as did the youths, they offer themselves to the magistrates[21] to be put to use if the community should be in need of such deeds as belong to men who have become prudent and yet are still powerful. If it should be necessary to go somewhere on a military expedition, those who have been educated in this way go on the expedition without taking their bows or their spears anymore, but with what are called weapons for close combat: a breastplate on their chest, a shield in their left hand (such as the Persians are painted as having), and a sword or scimitar in their right hand. And all the magistrates are drawn from this group except the teachers of the boys. When they have spent their twenty-five years and would be somewhat more than fifty years old, then they enter among those who are called the "elders" and really are.[22] (14) Now these elders no longer go on military expeditions outside of their own territory, but they remain at home and adjudicate all things common and private. They also judge capital cases as well as choose all magistrates. And if any of either the young or mature men should fall at all short of what is lawful, the several rulers of the tribes, or any other who wishes, show it, and the elders listen and pass judgment. Whoever is convicted spends the rest of his life in dishonor.

(15) In order that the whole Persian regime may be shown more clearly, I shall go back a little, for now, on account of what has been said above, it may be made clear quite concisely. The Persians are said to number about one hundred and twenty thousand. No one of them is barred by law from honors or political office, but it is permitted to all Persians to send their own children to the common[23] schools of justice. And yet only those who are able to raise their children without putting them to work do send them; those who are not able do not. Whoever is educated by the public teachers is permitted to spend his youth among the youths; to those who are not so educated, it is not permitted. To those in turn among the youths who spend their time fulfilling what is prescribed by law, it is permitted to be enrolled among the mature men and to share in political offices and honors. But those who do not pass their time among the youths do not enter among the mature men. Those who pass their time among the mature men without being censured become enrolled among the elders. Thus the elders are seated after having passed through everything noble. By using this regime, they think they may become the best.

(16) There remains even now evidence of their moderate diet and of their working off what they have taken in, for even now it is still shameful for them to spit and blow their noses, or to be detected passing gas, and it is also shameful to be detected going off somewhere to urinate or do some other such thing. They would not be able to act like this if they did not employ a moderate diet and expend their moisture through work, so that it goes off in another way. Now these

things we can say about all the Persians; but as for that[24] on account of which the argument began, we shall now relate the actions of Cyrus beginning from his boyhood.

ᴥ CHAPTER 3 ᴥ

(1) Cyrus was educated in this education until the age of twelve or a bit more, and he clearly surpassed all his agemates both in quickly learning what was necessary and in doing everything in a noble and manly way. But after this time Astyages sent for his daughter and her son, for he desired to see him because he heard that Cyrus was noble and good.[25] So Mandane herself went to her father and took her son Cyrus with her. (2) As soon as he arrived and Cyrus knew Astyages to be his mother's father, he immediately—since he was by nature an affectionate boy[26]—hugged him as one would have done if he had been raised with him and had been friendly with him for a long time. And he saw him adorned with eye shadow, rouge, and a wig—as was, of course, customary among the Medes (for all these things were Median: purple coats, cloaks, necklaces, and bracelets on their wrists; but among the Persians who are at home, their clothes are even now much more ordinary and their diet much cheaper). So seeing the adornment of his grandfather, he said while looking at him, "Mother, how handsome[27] my grandfather is!"

And when his mother asked him whom he thought more handsome, Astyages or his father, Cyrus then answered, "Of the Persians, my father is the most handsome by far; of the Medes, however, this grandfather of mine is by far the most handsome of those I have seen both in the streets and at court."

(3) Hugging him in return, the grandfather put a beautiful robe on him and honored and adorned him with necklaces and bracelets, and if ever he went out somewhere, he took him along on a horse with a golden bridle, in just the way he himself was accustomed to travel. Since he was a boy who loved beauty and honor,[28] Cyrus was pleased with the robe and exceedingly delighted at learning how to ride a horse. For among the Persians, it was very rare even to see a horse, because it is difficult to raise horses and difficult to ride them in so mountainous a country.

(4) When at dinner with his daughter and Cyrus, Astyages wished the boy to dine as pleasantly as possible so that he might yearn less for what he had left at home. He thus put before him fancy side dishes and all sorts of sauces and meats; and they say[29] that Cyrus said, "Grandfather, how many troubles you have at dinner, if it is necessary for you to stretch out your hands to all these little dishes and taste all these different sorts of meat!"

"What?" Astyages said. "Does it not seem to you that this dinner is much finer than that among the Persians?"[30]

To this Cyrus answered, "No, grandfather, for the road to satisfaction is much more simple and direct among us than among you, for bread and meat take us to it. You hurry to the same place as we do, yet only after wandering back and forth on many curves do you arrive with difficulty at the point we reached long ago."

(5) "But child," Astyages said, "we are not distressed to wander as we do. Taste them, and you too will realize that they are pleasant."

"And yet I see that even you, grandfather, are disgusted with these meats," he said.

And Astyages asked again, "And on what evidence do you say this, my child?"

"Because," he said, "I see that you too, whenever you touch your bread, do not wipe your hand on anything; but whenever you touch any of these, you wipe your hand on your napkin as if you were most distressed that it became soiled with them."

(6) To this Astyages said, "If you are so resolved, my child, feast at least upon these meats, so that you may go home a vigorous youth." As he was saying this, he had a great deal of meat brought to him, of both wild and tame animals.

When he saw all this meat, Cyrus said, "Are you giving me all this meat, grandfather, to use however I want?"

"Yes, my child, by Zeus I am," he said.

(7) Then Cyrus, taking the meat, distributed it to his grandfather's servants and said to each, "This is for you, because you teach me to ride with enthusiasm; for you, because you gave me a javelin, and now I have it; for you, because you serve my grandfather nobly; for you, because you honor my mother." He proceeded like this until he distributed all the meat that he received.

(8) "But to Sakas,[31] my cupbearer, whom I honor most," Astyages said, "do you give nothing?" Now Sakas happened to be handsome

and to have the honor of admitting those who sought Astyages and of excluding such as he did not think it opportune to admit.

And Cyrus answered rashly, as would a boy not yet afraid.[32] "Why, grandfather, do you honor him so?"

And Astyages replied jokingly, "Do you not see how nobly and gracefully he pours out my wine?" The cupbearers of these kings carry the cup with refinement, pour the wine cleanly, hand over the cup while holding it with three fingers, and present the cup in the way it is most easily grasped by the one who is about to drink.

(9) "Order Sakas to give me the cup, grandfather," he said, "that I too, by nobly pouring wine for you to drink, may win you over if I can." And he ordered him to give it. Cyrus, they say, taking the cup, rinsed it so well, as he had seen Sakas do, made such a serious face, and brought and presented it to his grandfather so gracefully that he afforded much laughter to his mother and Astyages. Cyrus himself laughed out loud, leaped up onto his grandfather, kissed him, and said, "Sakas, you are done for; I will cast you out of honor, for I will both pour the wine more nobly than you in other respects and I will not drink of the wine myself." Now the cupbearers of the kings, when they present the cup, draw out some of it with a small cup and, pouring it into their left hand, swallow it down, so that they might not profit if they have added poison.

(10) Upon this Astyages said jokingly, "Cyrus, since you imitated Sakas in other respects, why did you not swallow some of the wine?"

"Because, by Zeus," he said, "I was afraid there might have been some poison mixed in the cup, for when you entertained your friends on your birthday, I learned quite clearly that he had added poison for you all."

"And how, my child," he said, "did you come to know this?"

"Because, by Zeus, I saw you all making mistakes, both in your judgments and with your bodies, for in the first place, you yourselves were doing such things as you do not allow us boys to do, for you all shouted at the same time, and you did not comprehend each other at all. Then you sang very ridiculously, and even though you did not listen to the singer, you all swore that he sang most excellently. Then, after each spoke of his own strength, when you stood up to dance, far from dancing in time with the rhythm, you were not even able to stand up straight. You all forgot yourselves entirely, you that you were king, the others that you were their ruler. Then I learned for the first time that what you were practicing was that liberty of speech; at least you were never silent."

(11) And Astyages said, "My child, has not your father gotten drunk from drinking?"

"No, by Zeus," he said.

"But what does he do?"

"He quenches his thirst and suffers no harm, for a Sakas, grandfather, certainly does not pour his wine."

And his mother said, "But why ever, my child, do you make war on Sakas like this?"

"Because I hate him, by Zeus," said Cyrus, "for often when I desire to run up to my grandfather, this most wretched fellow[33] shuts me out. But I beg you, grandfather, give me three days to rule over him."

And Astyages said, "And how would you rule him?"

And it is said that Cyrus said, "Standing at the entrance, just as he does, whenever he wished to come in for lunch, I would say that it is not possible to have lunch yet, 'for he is busy with certain others.' Then, when he came for supper, I would say, 'He is washing.' If he were very much in earnest to eat, I would say, 'He is with his women.' I would detain him so long, just as he detains me, keeping me from you."

(12) Such amusement did he afford them at meals. At other times of the day, if he perceived either his grandfather or his mother's brother in need of anything, it was difficult for anyone else to take care of it before he did, for Cyrus was extremely delighted to gratify them in any way within his power.

(13) When Mandane was preparing to go back to her husband again, Astyages asked her to leave Cyrus behind. She answered that she wished to gratify her father in all things, but that she believed it to be difficult to leave the boy behind against his will. At this point Astyages said to Cyrus, (14) "My child, if you stay with me, in the first place, Sakas will not govern your access to me, but it will be up to you to come to me whenever you wish. And I will be more grateful to you to the extent that you come to me more often. Next, you will use my horses and as many others as you wish, and when you leave, you may take the ones you yourself want. Next, at meals, you may take whatever path you wish to what seems to you to be a measured [diet]. Next,

I give you the wild animals that are now in the park, and I will collect others of all kinds, which, as soon as you learn how to ride a horse, you may pursue and strike down with your bow and spear, just as the grown men do. I will also get you boys for playmates, and, if only you tell me, you will not fail to get whatever else you wish."

(15) After Astyages said this, his mother asked Cyrus whether he wished to stay or go. He did not hesitate but quickly said that he wished to stay. Again being asked by his mother as to why, it is said that he said,[34] "Because at home, mother, among those of my age, I both am and am thought to be the best at throwing spears and shooting the bow, but here I know quite well that I am inferior to those of my age at riding. Be well assured, mother, that this vexes me greatly. But if you leave me here and I learn how to ride a horse, when I am in Persia, I think that I will easily be victorious for you over those who are good on foot; but when I come to Media, I shall try for grandfather to be an ally to him by being the best horseman among these good horsemen."

His mother said, (16) "But, my child, how will you learn justice here when your teachers are there [in Persia]?"

And Cyrus said, "But mother, this, at least, I know accurately already."

"How do you know it?" Mandane asked.

"Because," he said, "the teacher appointed me to be judge for others, on the ground that I was already accurately versed in justice. And then, in one case, I was beaten because I did not judge correctly. (17) The case was like this: A big boy with a little tunic took off the big tunic of a little boy, and he dressed him in his own tunic, while he himself put on that of the other. Now I, in judging it for them, recognized that it was better for both that each have the fitting tunic. Upon this the teacher beat me, saying that whenever I should be appointed judge of the fitting, I must do as I did; but when one must judge to whom the tunic belongs, then one must examine, he said, what is just possession, whether it is to have what is taken away by force or to possess what [one has] made or purchased. Since, he said, the lawful is just, and the unlawful violent, he ordered that the judge always cast his vote in conformity with the law. So, mother, I am by all means already accurately versed for you at least in what justice is. If I need anything further in this, grandfather here will teach me."

(18) "But, my child," she said, "the same things are not agreed to be just here with your grandfather and in Persia, for among the Medes, he has made himself the master of everything, but in Persia to have what is equal is believed to be just. And your father is the first both to do what has been ordered by the city and to accept what has been ordered, and not his soul but the law is his measure.[35] How will you avoid being beaten to death when you come home if you arrive after having learned from him not the kingly [way] but the tyrannical, where the thought is that one ought to have more than all?"

"But mother," said Cyrus, "your father is more clever at teaching one to have less than to have more. Or do you not see that he has taught all the Medes to have less than himself? So take heart: Your father will not send any pupil onward, neither me nor anyone else, who will have learned how to be greedy."[36]

∽ CHAPTER 4 ∽

(1) So Cyrus often chattered like this. At last his mother went away, but Cyrus stayed and was raised there. He quickly became involved with his agemates so that he became on familiar terms with them, and he quickly attached their fathers to him, both by visiting and by making it plain that he was affectionate toward their sons. Consequently, if they needed anything from the king, they used to bid their sons to ask Cyrus to accomplish it for them, and Cyrus, because of his benevolence and his ambition, was very concerned to accomplish whatever the boys asked of him. (2) And Astyages was not able to refuse to gratify Cyrus in whatever he asked of him, for when his grandfather was sick, Cyrus never left him and never ceased weeping, but he made it plain to all that he was extremely afraid that he might die. Also at night, if Astyages needed anything, Cyrus used to perceive it first and would leap up with the greatest alacrity of all in order to serve him in whatever way he thought would gratify him. He thus won Astyages over to the highest degree.

(3) He was perhaps too ready with words, partly through his education (because he was compelled by his teacher both to give an account of what he was doing when he issued judgments and to obtain

an account from others). Moreover, because he loved to learn, he himself used to ask many questions of whomever was around about how things happened to be. Because he had such a sharp mind, he answered quickly whatever he himself was asked by others. As a result of all these things, his readiness with words developed. But just as in the case of the body, the youthfulness of those who grow large even while young nevertheless shines through and betrays their few years, so there appeared to be no boldness in Cyrus' talkativeness, but simplicity and affection, so that one would desire to hear still more from him rather than to be with him when he was silent.

(4) But as time, with an increase of stature, brought him into the season in which one becomes a young man, he then used fewer words and a gentler voice. He was so filled with shame that he blushed whenever he encountered his elders, and his puppyish running up to all alike was no longer so prominent in him. Thus, he was gentler but altogether charming in his associations, for even where those of the same age often compete against each other, he did not challenge his associates where he knew that he was superior, but he began right where he knew quite well that he himself was inferior, professing that he would perform more nobly than they. He would begin at once, leaping up on his horse, intending either to shoot his bow or throw his spear from horseback, even though he was not yet firmly mounted. When defeated, he would laugh at himself most vigorously.

(5) He did not run from being defeated into the refuge of not doing that in which he had been defeated; rather, he immersed himself in trying to do better the next time. He therefore quickly became the equal of his agemates in horsemanship, quickly surpassed them because he loved[37] the work, and quickly used up all the wild animals in the park, because he chased, threw at, and killed them. Consequently, Astyages was no longer able to collect wild animals for him. And Cyrus, perceiving that Astyages wished to provide him with many animals but was not able to, said to him, "Grandfather, why must you be bothered looking for wild animals? If you send me out on a hunt with my uncle, I will believe that you are raising for me whatever wild animals I see." (6) But even though he vehemently desired to go out on a hunt, he was no longer able to implore his grandfather as he had done when he was a boy, but he approached him with greater hesitation. And as for what he previously used to blame in

Sakas, that he did not admit him to his grandfather, he himself now became a Sakas to himself, for he did not approach without seeing whether it was opportune, and he begged Sakas by all means to indicate to him when it was allowable to approach and when it was opportune. Consequently, Sakas was now exceedingly friendly to him, as were all the others.

(7) Now when Astyages realized that he vehemently desired to go hunting outside the park, he sent him out with his uncle. He also sent along older guards on horseback, in order that they might protect him from dangerous places and in the event some fierce wild animal should appear. Therefore, Cyrus inquired enthusiastically of his attendants which wild animals one should not approach and which one should pursue boldly. They said that bears had already killed many of those who approached them, as had boars, lions, and leopards; but that deer, antelopes, wild pigs, and wild asses were harmless. They also said that one must guard against dangerous places no less than against wild animals, for many have been thrown from cliffs, horses and all. (8) So Cyrus was learning all these things with enthusiasm. But when he saw a deer leap out, he forgot everything he had heard and pursued it, seeing nothing but the way it went as it fled. His horse made a sort of leap, fell on his knees, and nearly threw Cyrus over his neck. Nevertheless, Cyrus somehow stayed mounted, though with difficulty, and the horse got back up. When he got to the open ground, he threw his spear and struck the deer down—a beautiful thing, and large. Now he, of course, was exceedingly delighted; but the guards, when they got near to him, reproached him and told him of the danger into which he had gone, and said that they would report him. So Cyrus stood there, dismounted, and was distressed by what he heard. But when he perceived a shout, he leaped up on his horse as would one possessed;[38] and when he saw a boar bearing down upon them, he rushed straight toward it, poised [his spear], and with a good aim struck the boar in the forehead and brought it down. (9) Now, however, after seeing his boldness, his uncle reproached him. Even though his uncle was reproaching him, he nevertheless begged him to allow him to carry off whatever he himself had taken and to give it to his grandfather.

They say that his uncle said, "But if he perceives that you were giving chase, he will reproach not only you but also me, because I allowed you."

"If he wishes," it is said that he said, "let him beat me, but after I give him the game. And you too, uncle, take vengeance in whatever way you wish, but gratify me in this."

And, of course, Cyaxares said at last, "Do what you wish, for it looks like you are now our king."

(10) Thus Cyrus, carrying off the wild animals, gave them to his grandfather and said that he himself had hunted them for him. He did not show him the spears, but he put them, still bloody, where he thought his grandfather would see them.

Astyages said, "My child, I accept with pleasure what you give me, but I certainly do not need any of this game so much that you should run such risks for it."

And Cyrus said, "Well, if you do not need it, grandfather, please give it to me, in order that I may distribute it to my agemates."

"Take it, my child," said Astyages, "and distribute to whomever you wish as much as you want of the rest as well."

(11) And Cyrus, taking it, carried it off and gave it to the boys, and at the same time said, "Boys, what triflers we were when we hunted the wild animals in the park! At least to me, that seems the same as hunting animals that are tied up. For, in the first place, they were in a small space. Secondly, they were skinny and mangy, and one was lame, another maimed. But with the wild animals in the mountains and in the meadows, how beautiful, how large, how sleek they appeared! The deer leaped toward heaven as if they had wings, and the boars came on at close quarters just as they say courageous men do. Nor, owing to their bulk, could one fail to hit them. At least to me, these seem to be more beautiful even when dead than do those pent-up animals when alive. But would your fathers let you come on a hunt too?"

"Readily," they said, "if Astyages should order it."

And Cyrus said, "Then who could mention it to Astyages for us?"

(12) "Who would be more capable of persuading him than you?" they said.

"But, by Hera,"[39] he said, "I do not know what sort of human being I have become! For neither am I up to speaking to my grandfather nor am I even capable of looking at him as I did before.[40] If I advance in this direction, I fear that I may become a dolt and simpleton. Yet when I was a little boy, I seemed to be quite clever at small talk."

"It is a bad problem," the boys said, "if you are unable to act on our behalf when it is needed; but, rather, it will be necessary for us to ask someone else for you."

(13) Cyrus was stung at hearing this, and going away in silence, he ordered himself to take the dare. After planning how he could speak to his grandfather with least pain and accomplish for himself and the boys what they wanted, he went in. He began, then, as follows: "Tell me, grandfather, if one of your servants runs away and you catch him, how do you treat him?"

"How else," he said, "than by chaining him and compelling him to work."

"And if he comes back again of his own accord," he said, "what do you do?"

"What else," he said, "except beat him, in order that he not do it again, and then treat him as before."

"It is high time, then," said Cyrus, "for you to get something ready to beat me with, since I am making plans about how to run away from you and take my agemates on a hunt."

And Astyages said, "You acted nobly in telling me in advance, for I forbid you to stir from within. How charming it would be if I should let my daughter's son stray off for a bit of meat!"

(14) On hearing this, Cyrus obeyed and stayed back, but he passed his time in silence, sulky and sullen-faced. When he realized that he was greatly distressed, Astyages of course wished to gratify him and led them out hunting. He assembled many infantry and cavalry troops along with the boys, chased the game onto the land suited for riding, and made a great hunt. He was himself present in kingly fashion[41] and forbade anyone to throw before Cyrus had his fill of hunting. But Cyrus would not allow him to hinder the others and said, "Grandfather, if you wish me to hunt with pleasure, let all those with me give chase and compete, that each may do as well as he is able."

(15) Of course, Astyages thereupon gave his permission, and, taking up a position, he watched them contending against the wild animals, striving for victory, giving chase, and throwing their spears. And he took pleasure in Cyrus, who, owing to his own pleasure, was not able to keep silent. Rather, like a well-bred puppy, crying out whenever he approached a wild animal, he called everyone on by name. And [Astyages] was delighted to see him laugh at one, while

he perceived him praising another, not being envious in any way whatsoever. At last Astyages went away with many animals. So pleased was he with this hunt that in the future, whenever it was possible, he always went out with Cyrus and took along both many others and the boys, for Cyrus' sake. So Cyrus spent most of his time like this, being for all a cause of pleasure and of some good, but of nothing bad.

(16) When [Cyrus] was about fifteen or sixteen years old, the son of the king of the Assyrians, who was about to get married, desired to have a hunt of his own at this time. So, hearing that there was a great deal of game in the borderlands between themselves and the Medians, and that it had not been hunted because of the war, he desired to go out to this spot. Now in order that he might hunt safely, he took along many cavalry and targeteers,[42] who were to drive the game out of the bushes into places that were cultivated and good for the chase. When he arrived where their forts and garrison were, he had his dinner, intending to go hunting early on the next day. (17) When evening came, a garrison of cavalry and infantry arrived from the city to relieve its predecessor, so it seemed to him that a great army was now on hand, for there were two garrisons of guards together, and he himself had come with many cavalry and infantry troops. He thus deliberated that it would be very good to take plunder from the Median territory, and he believed both that this deed would appear more brilliant than the hunt and that there would be a great abundance of victims for sacrifice. Getting up very early, therefore, he led his army out. He left the infantry collected on the borderlands, but he himself pressed on with his cavalry to the Median forts. And keeping the best and the greatest number with himself, he stayed there so that the Median guards would not try to help out against those who were overrunning the country. Such as were suited to the purpose he dispatched in groups, some to overrun one place and some another, and he ordered that they surround and seize whatever they chanced upon and bring it to him.[43] So this is what they were doing.

(18) But when it was reported to Astyages that there were enemies in the country, he went out in aid, both he himself toward the borders with his guard and his son similarly with such cavalry as happened to be at hand, and he signaled to all the others to come help. But when they saw the many Assyrians[44] drawn up in order, with their horses

standing still, the Medes also came to a halt. Cyrus, seeing others going in a rush to help, also went to help. And then he himself put on armor for the first time, though he had thought he never would, so much had he desired to be clad in it. His armor was very beautiful and fitted him, for his grandfather had had it made to suit his body. Having thus put on his armor, he set out on his horse. And when Astyages saw him, he wondered by whose order he came, but he nevertheless told him to remain near him.

(19) When he saw many knights[45] in front of him, Cyrus said, "Grandfather, are they enemies who are sitting quietly on their horses?"

"Of course they are enemies," he said.

"And those too who are riding in pursuit?"

"They also, of course," he said.

"By Zeus, then, Grandfather," he said, "though they seem to be worthless fellows mounted on worthless horses, they are plundering our things, so some of us must charge against them."

"But do you not see, my child," he said, "what a mass of cavalry. stands there in close order? If we charge against the others, they in turn will cut us off. Our full strength is not yet present."

"But," said Cyrus, "if you stay here and join with those who are coming up to help us, those [of the enemy who are in close order] will be afraid and will not move, while the plunderers will immediately drop their booty when they see others charging against them."

(20) When he said this, it seemed to Astyages that he had a point; and while wondering at how prudent and alert he was, he ordered his son to take a detachment of horses and charge those who were taking the booty. "I," he said, "will charge these [men in close order] if they move against you, so that they will be compelled to pay attention to us."

Accordingly, Cyaxares took some of the strongest horses and men, and attacked. And when Cyrus saw them starting out, he started out; and quickly becoming the first, it was he who led them at a rapid pace, and Cyaxares followed after, and the others did not fall behind. When the plunderers saw them approaching, they promptly dropped the booty and took flight. (21) Cyrus and his followers cut them off, and whomever they overtook they promptly struck down; and Cyrus was the first to do so. They also pursued those who had turned aside to elude them, and they did not slacken but took some of them. Just as a well-bred but inexperienced dog rushes without forethought against a boar, so also rushed Cyrus, seeing only that he struck whomever he caught, with forethought for nothing else. When the enemy saw their own troops in distress, they moved their main mass forward, expecting that the attackers would cease their pursuit as soon as they saw them move forward. (22) None the more did Cyrus slacken, but in his battle joy called out to his uncle and continued the pursuit; and pressing on, he made the enemies' rout complete. And Cyaxares followed, of course, perhaps also being ashamed before his father; and the others followed as well, being in such circumstances more than ordinarily enthusiastic to pursue, even those who may not have been very stout against the opposition.

When Astyages saw the one side pursuing without forethought, while the enemy, close together and in good order, marched to meet them, he was afraid that his son and Cyrus might suffer some harm from falling in disorder on others who were prepared to meet them. He thus immediately advanced against the enemy. (23) Now when the enemy saw the Medes move forward, they stood still, some with spears poised, others with bows drawn, in the expectation that [the Medes] would halt when they came within bowshot, as for the most part it was their habit to do, for they used to chase each other only to this point, even when they were at their closest, and they often skirmished at long range until evening. But when they saw their own troops coming toward them in flight, and Cyrus and his followers pressing close behind them, and Astyages with his cavalry being already within bowshot, they gave way and fled. Those pursuing at close range and with all vigor took many, and what they captured they struck, both horses and men, and what fell they killed. Nor did they stop until they came up with the Assyrian infantry. Here, however, fearing that an even greater force might lie in ambush, they halted. (24) Astyages then led his troops back, rejoicing greatly over the cavalry victory. As for Cyrus, Astyages did not know what to say about him, for he knew that he was the cause of the deed but also recognized that he was mad with daring. Even then when they were going home, in fact, he alone, apart from the others, did nothing but ride around and gaze at[46] the fallen, and it was with difficulty that those who were ordered to do so dragged him away and led him to Astyages. As he came he kept his escort very much in front, because he saw that his grandfather's face was angry at sight of him.

(25) So these things happened in Media. And not only did everyone else have Cyrus on his lips, both in speech and in song, but Astyages, who had honored[47] him even before, was then quite astonished by him. Cyrus' father, Cambyses, was pleased to learn these things; but when he heard that Cyrus was already performing a man's deeds, he recalled him in order that he might fulfill what was customary among the Persians. It is reported that Cyrus said on this occasion that he wished to return, in order that his father not be at all annoyed with him and that his city not blame him. It also seemed necessary to Astyages to send him away. So giving him the horses that he himself desired to take and furnishing him with many other things of all sorts, both because he loved him and at the same time because he had great hopes that he would be a man competent to help his friends and bring his enemies to grief, he sent him off. Everyone—children, his agemates, men, and elders—escorted Cyrus on horseback as he left, as did Astyages himself; and they said that there was no one who turned back without tears.

(26) It is said that Cyrus himself shed many tears when he departed. They also say that of the gifts that Asytages had given to him, he gave out many to his agemates, and that at last, taking off the Median robe he was wearing, he gave even this to someone, showing that he liked him especially. It is said that those who received and accepted the gifts carried them off to Astyages, that Astyages on receiving them sent them off to Cyrus, and that he again sent them back to the Medians saying, "If you wish, grandfather, for me to come back again to you with pleasure and without being ashamed, let everyone to whom I have given something keep it." When Astyages heard this, he is said to have done just as Cyrus had enjoined.

(27) If one must make mention also of an account about a boyfriend,[48] it is said[49] that when Cyrus was going away and they were taking leave of each other, his relatives sent him off with a Persian custom, kissing him on the mouth, for the Persians still do this even now. One of the Medes who was a very noble and good man[50] had been struck for quite a long time by Cyrus' beauty; and when he saw [Cyrus'] relatives kissing him, he stayed behind. After the others

went away, he came up to Cyrus and said, "Am I the only one of your relatives that you do not recognize, Cyrus?"

"What!" Cyrus said. "Are you a relative as well?"

"Certainly," he said.

"Then this is why," Cyrus said, "you used to stare at me, for I think that I often recognized you doing this."

"I always wished to approach you," he said, "but, by the gods, I was ashamed."

"But you ought not have been so," Cyrus said, "at least since you are a relative." He then went up to him and kissed him.

(28) Upon being kissed, the Mede asked, "So among the Persians is it a custom to kiss one's relatives?"

"Certainly," he said, "at least when they see each other after a length of time or when they are going away."

"It would be high time," said the Mede, "that you kiss me again, for, as you see, I am now going away."

Kissing him again, Cyrus dismissed him and went away. They had not yet gone far when the Mede arrived again with his horse in a sweat. On seeing him, Cyrus said, "Did you forget something you wished to say?"

"No, by Zeus," he said, "but I am returning after a length of time."

And Cyrus said, "Yes, by Zeus, cousin, a short one indeed."

"What do you mean, 'short'?" the Mede said. "Do you not know, Cyrus, that even so long as it takes me to blink seems to me to be an extremely long time, because I then do not see you, such as you are." Here it is said that Cyrus, in tears just before, laughed and told him to go away cheerfully because he would be with them again in a short time, so that it would be possible for him to look at him, if he wished, without blinking.

❖ CHAPTER 5 ❖

(1) Now after departing for Persia like this, Cyrus is said to have still been among the boys for another year. At first the boys used to mock him for having come back from Media after having learned there how to live for pleasure. But when they saw him eating and

drinking just as pleasantly as they themselves did; and when, whenever there was a feast or a holiday, they perceived him giving of his
own share rather than asking for more; and when in addition to these
things they saw him superior to themselves in other respects, of
course his agemates were once again intimidated by him. When he
passed through this education and entered among the youths, he
seemed also among them to be superior in caring for what he ought,
in being steadfast, in respecting his elders, and in obeying the rulers.

(2) In the progress of time, among the Medes, Astyages died, and
Cyaxares, the son of Astyages and brother of Cyrus' mother, came to
hold the kingship of the Medes. The king of Assyria, having subdued
all the Syrians, a very large nation, having made the king of Arabia
his subject, having the Hyrcanians as subjects already and besieging
the Bactrians as well, believed that if he should reduce the Medes, he
would easily come to rule over all those in the area, for their tribe
seemed to be the strongest of those nearby. (3) He thus sent messengers around to all those beneath him, and to Croesus the king of the
Lydians, to the king of the Cappadocians, to both Phrygias, to the Paphlagonians and Indians, to the Carians and Cilicians. In part, he slan-
dered the Medes and Persians, saying that these nations were great,
strong, and united toward the same end, that they had made mar-
riages with each other, and that they would be likely, unless someone
should reduce them first, to come to each of the other nations and subdue them in turn. Some, being persuaded even by these arguments,
made an alliance with him; others were persuaded by gifts and
money, for in these he abounded.

(4) When Astyages' son Cyaxares perceived this design and the
preparation of those uniting against him, he both immediately made
such counterpreparations as he could himself, and he sent messages
to the Persians, both to the common council[51] and to Cambyses, who
was married to his sister and was king of the Persians. He sent also
to Cyrus, asking that he try to come as the ruler of the men, if the common council of the Persians should send some soldiers, for Cyrus had
already completed his ten years among the youths and was among
the mature men. (5) So then, with Cyrus' acceptance, the elders in
council chose him as the ruler of the expedition to Media. They also
allowed him to choose two hundred of the Peers,[52] and in turn they
allowed each of the two hundred to choose four, with each of these

also to be from among the Peers. So this made one thousand. They ordered each of these one thousand to choose ten targeteers, ten slingers, and ten archers from among the Persian people. Thus there were ten thousand archers, ten thousand targeteers, and ten thousand slingers; and apart from these there was the first one thousand. So Cyrus was given an army of this size.

(6) Immediately on being chosen, he began with the gods. After sacrificing with good omen, he then chose the two hundred. When these also had each chosen their four, he assembled them, and then for the first time spoke to them as follows: (7) "Men, friends, I did not choose you testing you now for the first time, but from childhood on I have seen you work enthusiastically at what the city believes to be noble and seen you abstain altogether from what it holds to be shameful. I wish to make clear to you why I myself am not unwilling to be appointed to this command or to call you along as well. (8) I consider our ancestors to have been no worse than we. At least they too spent all their time practicing the very things that are held to be works of virtue. What good they acquired by being such, however, either for the community of the Persians or for themselves, I cannot see. (9) And yet I do not think that human beings practice any virtue in order that those who become good have no more than do the worthless. Rather, those who abstain from the pleasures at hand do so not in order that they may never have enjoyment, but through their present continence they prepare themselves to have much more enjoyment in the future. Those who are enthusiastic about becoming clever at speaking do not practice it so that they may never cease speaking well, but they expect by speaking well to persuade human beings and thereby to accomplish many and great goods. Those in turn who practice military affairs do not work at them in order that they never cease fighting, but these too do so believing that by becoming good in military affairs they shall secure much wealth, much happiness, and great honors both for themselves and for their city. (10) If any who have labored at these things see themselves become incapacitated by old age before they have reaped any fruit from them, they seem to me to suffer something similar to someone who, enthusiastic to become a good farmer, sows well and plants well, but when it is time for the harvest, lets his ungathered crop fall down to the earth again. And if an athlete, after undertaking many labors and becoming deserving of vic-

tory, should pass his life without a contest, it would not seem to me to be just that he not be blamed for folly.

(11) "But men, let us not suffer these things. Rather, since we ourselves are conscious of having practiced the good and noble deeds since our childhood, let us go against the enemy, for I know clearly (having myself seen that it is so) that as compared to us, they are too much like amateurs to contend against us, for those who know how to shoot, throw, and ride are not yet competent antagonists if they fall short when there is hard work to be done, but [our enemies] are amateurs in the face of hard work. Nor even are they competent who, when it is necessary to go without sleep, are overcome by it, but [our enemies] are amateurs in the face of sleeplessness. Nor even are they competent who are competent in these things but who are uneducated as to how to make use of allies and enemies, but it is clear that [our enemies] are inexperienced in the most important subjects of education. (12) But you, surely, would be able to make use of the night as others the day; you believe that labors are our guides to living pleasantly; you regularly use hunger as others use sauce; you endure the drinking of mere water more easily than do lions; and you have gathered into your souls the most noble and warlike possession of all, for you rejoice in being praised more than in all other things, and lovers of praise must of necessity take on with pleasure every labor and every risk.

(13) "If I should say these things about you while knowing them to be otherwise, I would deceive myself, for insofar as you do not turn out to be as I have said, your shortcoming would come right back to me. But I trust that my experience of you and of our enemies will not cheat me of these good hopes. Let us go forth with confidence, since the appearance of unjustly desiring what belongs to others is far from impeding us, for now our enemies are coming, beginning the unjust deeds, and our friends summon us to be auxiliaries. What is more just than defending ourselves or more noble than aiding friends? (14) But I think this also gives you a great deal of confidence, to make this expedition without my having neglected the gods, for since you have been together with me many times, you know that I always try to begin with the gods not only in great matters but even in small ones."

He said in conclusion, "What more must be said? Choose your men, gather them up, make your other preparations, and go to Media. After going back to my father again, I will go in advance. Thus, after learning about our enemies as quickly as possible, I may make whatever preparations I can so that we may contend as nobly as possible with god's [help]."[53]

So this is what they were doing.

ᴥ CHAPTER 6 ᴥ

(1) After returning home and praying to ancestral Hestia, ancestral Zeus, and the other gods, Cyrus set out on the expedition, and his father joined him in escort. There is said to have been auspicious lightning and thunder for him as soon as they were outside of the house. After these appearances, they traveled on without taking any further auguries, on the grounds that none could rescind the signs of the greatest god.

(2) As Cyrus went forward, his father began a discussion such as follows: "That the gods send you forth propitiously and favorably is clear, son,[54] both in the sacrifices and from the heavenly signs. You understand it yourself, for I purposely taught you this so that you would not learn the counsels of the gods through other interpreters. Both seeing what is to be seen and hearing what is to be heard, you would understand these things yourself and not be dependent on the prophets, in case they should wish to deceive you by telling you something different from the signals of the gods. Moreover, in case you should ever be without a prophet, you would not be at a loss as to which divine signs to use, but understanding through the art of divination the counsels that come from the gods, you would obey them."

(3) "And indeed, father," Cyrus said, "I take constant care, as much as I am able and in keeping with your advice, so that the gods may be propitious to us and be willing to give us counsel. I remember hearing you say once that he who did not flatter the gods when he was at a loss, but rather remembered them especially when he was faring very well, would probably be more effective in action with gods, just as also with human beings. And regarding friends, you said that it was useful to take care in this same way."

(4) "On account of this care, do you not now, son," he said, "come to the gods with more pleasure when you intend to make requests, and do you expect to obtain more of what you request because you seem to be conscious in yourself of having never neglected them?"

"Certainly, father," he said, "I am disposed to the gods as though they were my friends."

(5) "Why, son, do you then remember that we once decided that there are things in which the gods have granted to human beings who have learned to fare better than those who do not understand, and in which they have granted to workers to accomplish more than idlers, and in which they have granted to the careful to continue more safely than those off their guard, and that then we decided that it was necessary to ask for the good things from the gods only after rendering ourselves such as we ought to be?"

(6) "Yes, by Zeus," said Cyrus, "I certainly do remember hearing such remarks from you. It was also necessary for me to obey the argument, for I also know that you added that it would not even be right[55] for those who have not learned how to ride a horse to ask from the gods to be victorious in a cavalry battle, nor for those who do not know how to shoot to prevail with bows and arrows over those who know how to use them, nor for those who do not know how to be a pilot to pray to pilot ships safely, nor for those who do not plant grain to pray that a fine crop grow for them, nor for those who are not on guard in war to ask for safety, for all such things are contrary to what the gods have set down. You said that it is probable for those who pray for what is not right[56] to fail with the gods, just as it is probable for those who ask for what is unlawful to be ineffective with human beings."

(7) "But did you forget, son, those points by which you and I once calculated that it is a sufficient and noble work for a man, if he should be able to take care that he himself become truly[57] noble and good and that both he and the members of his household have sufficient provisions?[58] While this is already a great work, next, to know how to preside over other human beings so that they will have all provisions in abundance and so that they will all be as they must, this certainly appeared to us to be worthy of wonder."

(8) "Yes, by Zeus, father," he said, "I remember you saying this too. Ruling nobly used to seem to be a very great work to me also, and it

still does even now, when I calculate it by examining rule itself. But when I consider it by looking at human beings and seeing that they, even as they are, endure in their rule and that they, even as they are, will be our antagonists, it seems to me very shameful to be intimidated before such and not to be willing to go in contention against them, for I perceive that such people, beginning with these friends of ours, hold that the ruler must differ from the ruled by dining more sumptuously, by having more gold at home, by sleeping longer, and by spending his time freer from every labor than do those who are ruled. I think that the ruler ought to differ from the ruled not by his living easily but by taking forethought and by being enthusiastic in his love of labor."

(9) "But, son," he said, "there are some respects in which one must contend not against human beings but against matters themselves, and it is not very easy to overcome them readily; for instance, you certainly know that if the army does not have the provisions it needs, your rule will dissolve at once."

"Accordingly, father," he said, "Cyaxares says that he will provide for all who come hence, no matter how many they may be."

"So, son," he said, "you are going off trusting in these funds from Cyaxares?"

"I am," said Cyrus.

"Well," said he, "do you know how much he has?"

"No, by Zeus," said Cyrus, "I do not."

"And you nevertheless trust in these uncertainties? Do you not know that you will need many things and that he will now of necessity have many other expenses?"

"I know," said Cyrus.

"Then if his expenses outstrip him, or if he is willing to lie to you, what will the condition of your army be?"

"It is clear that it will not be a noble one. But, father," he said, "if you see any source [of resources], and one that I might make my own, tell me while we are still in friendly territory."

(10) "Are you asking, son," he said, "how you might provide a source [of resources] for yourself? From whom is it more probable that there arise such a source than from one who has power? You are going out with an infantry power in exchange for which I know that you would not accept another even many times as numerous, and the

Median cavalry, which is very strong, will be your ally. What sort of nation, then, of those around here, do you think will not serve you, both because they wish to gratify you and because they fear they might suffer something? These things you must consider in common with Cyaxares, so you do not lack anything you need to have, and, for the sake of habit, you must contrive a source of income. But above all else, remember for me never to delay providing provisions until need compels you; but when you are especially well off, then contrive [a source of income] before you are at a loss, for you will get more from whomever you ask if you do not seem to be in difficulty and, moreover, you will be blameless in the eyes of your soldiers. In this way you will get more respect also from others, and if you wish to do good to others with your power, or even harm, your soldiers will serve you more while they have what they need; be assured that you will be able to speak more persuasive words at just the moment when you are especially able to show that you are competent to do both good and harm."

(11) "What you are now saying, father," he said, "seems to me to be nobly said, both in general and because, as it is now, none of the soldiers will be grateful to me for what they have already been told they will receive, for they know the terms on which Cyaxares is bringing them in as allies. But as for whatever anyone receives in excess of these terms, they will believe it to be an honor, and it is probable that they will also be especially grateful to the one who gives it. If someone should have a power with which it is possible both, by doing good to his friends, to be helped in return and to try to acquire something from enemies (if he has any), and if he should then neglect to provide for his power—do you think that this would be any less shameful than if someone who had fields and workers with which to work them then left the land unworked and thus unprofitable? Be assured, then, that I shall never neglect to contrive provisions for my soldiers, whether in friendly or enemy territory."

(12) "What about the other things, son, that it once seemed to us necessary not to neglect? Do you remember?"

"I remember well," he said, "when I came to you for money with which to pay the man who professed to have educated me in how to be a general. As you gave it to me, you also asked something like this, 'Son, did the man to whom you are paying this wage make any mention of household management as being among the things that pertain to the general? Soldiers are certainly no less in need of provisions than are servants in a household.' When I told the truth and said that he made no mention of this whatsoever, you asked me again whether he spoke to me about health or strength, since the general needs to occupy himself with these things just as he also must with strategy.[59] (13) When I next denied that he did, you asked me in turn whether he taught any arts[60] that might become especially strong allies for the works of war. After I denied this as well, you next asked whether he educated me at all as to how I might be able to instill enthusiasm in an army, and you said that enthusiasm—as opposed to lack of enthusiasm—makes all the difference in every work. When I said no also to this, you cross-examined me again, asking whether in his teaching he made any argument about how one might especially contrive that his army be obedient.

(14) "And when it became apparent that this too had gone altogether unmentioned, of course you finally asked me whatever it was that he taught when he said that he taught me generalship. At this point, of course, I answered, 'Tactics.' You laughed and repeated each point for me, asking what was the benefit of tactics to an army without what it needs? What was it without health? What was it without knowing the arts that have been discovered for war? What was it without obedience? When you made it apparent to me that tactics was but a small part of generalship and I asked whether you were competent to teach me any of these other matters, you bade me go and converse with those believed to be skilled in generalship and inquire about them.

(15) "Then, of course, I frequented those whom I heard to be especially prudent in these matters. And concerning nourishment, I was persuaded that whatever Cyaxares was going to provide for us would be sufficient. Regarding health, since I heard and saw both that cities that desire to be healthy choose doctors and that generals take doctors with them for the sake of their soldiers, therefore, I too, when I received my present command, immediately concerned myself with this; and I think, father, that I shall have with me men who are very competent in the medical art."

To this his father said, (16) "But, son, just as there are menders of torn clothes, so also these doctors whom you mention treat people after they get sick. But your concern for health must be more magnificent than this, for you need to be concerned that the army not get sick in the first place."

"I?" he said. "And by taking what course shall I be competent to do this?"

"If you are going to stay a while in the same place, first of all you certainly ought not be unconcerned about having a healthy place to camp. To not err in this you must make it a concern, for human beings never cease talking about diseased and healthy places, and their bodies and complexions present clear witnesses of each sort of place. Secondly, it is not enough that you only examine places, but remember how you try to take care that you stay healthy yourself."

(17) And Cyrus said, "First, by Zeus, I try never to overeat, for it is oppressive. Secondly, I work off what I have eaten, for in this way it seems both that health stays to a greater degree and that strength is added."

"Then, of course, it is in this way, son," he said, "that you must take care of the others as well."

"And will there be leisure, father," he said, "for the soldiers to exercise their bodies?"

"Not only leisure, by Zeus," the father said, "but necessity as well, for surely if it is going to do what it must, an army must never cease preparing evils for its enemies and good things for itself. How difficult it is to maintain even one idle human being, and still more difficult, son, a whole household, but it is most difficult of all to maintain an idle army. For there are very many mouths in an army, it sets out with very few supplies, and it uses up most extravagantly whatever it takes, so that an army ought never be idle."

(18) "You mean, father, as it seems to me," he said, "that just as there is no benefit from an idle farmer, so also there is no benefit from an idle general."

"As regards at least the hardworking general," he said, "I accept that unless some god do him harm, he will both show that his soldiers have all they need and bring their bodies into excellent condition."[61]

"But as to their applying themselves to each of the works of war, father," he said, "it seems to me that if someone announces contests and proposes prizes, he would make them especially well exercised in each. Consequently, whenever he had need, he would be able to make use of troops who were already prepared."

"You speak most nobly, son," he said, "for if you do this, be assured that you will behold your formations always attending to what is fitting, just like choral dancers."

(19) "But," Cyrus said, "as for instilling soldiers with enthusiasm, it seems to me that nothing is more effective than being able to fill human beings with hopes."

"But son," he said, "this is the same sort of thing as in hunting, if one always calls the dogs with the same call he uses when he sees the game. At first, I am sure, he has them obeying enthusiastically. If he deceives them often, in the end they do not obey him even when he truly sees the game and calls. So it is also regarding hopes. If someone deceives often, instilling the expectation of good things, such a person ends up not being able to persuade even when he speaks of true sources of hope. One must avoid saying oneself what one does not know clearly, son, but sometimes others could produce the desired effect in their speeches. One must, as much as possible, preserve trust in one's own encouragement in the face of the greatest risks."

"But by Zeus, father," said Cyrus, "you seem to me to speak nobly, and I am more pleased with it like this. (20) As for making the soldiers obedient, father, I think that at least in this case, I am not without experience, for right from when I was a child you used to educate me in this, compelling me to obey. Later, you gave me over to teachers, and they in their turn did the very same thing. When we were among the youths, the ruler took rigorous care of this very thing. And the majority of the laws also seem to me to teach especially these two things, to rule and to be ruled. And reflecting about these things, I think I see in all of them that that which especially incites to obedience is the praising and honoring of the one who obeys and the dishonoring and punishment of the one who disobeys."

(21) "Yes, son, this is indeed the road to their obeying by compulsion, but to what is far superior to this, to their being willing to obey, there is another road that is shorter, for human beings obey with great pleasure whomever they think is more prudent about their own advantage than they are themselves. You might realize that this is so both from many other cases and surely from that of the sick, so enthusiastically do they call in others to give them orders as to what to

do; and at sea, so enthusiastically do the sailors obey their pilots; and whenever some believe others know the roads better than they themselves, so strongly do they want not to be left behind. Yet whenever people think that they will incur any harm by obeying, they are not very willing either to yield to punishments or to be seduced by gifts, for no one is willing to receive even gifts when they bring him harm."

(22) "You are saying, father, that for having obedient subjects, nothing is more effectual than to seem to be more prudent than they."

"I am," he said.

"And how, father, would someone be able to furnish himself with such a reputation as quickly as possible?"

"There is no shorter road, son," he said, "to seeming to be prudent about such things as you wish than becoming prudent about them. By examining each case individually you will realize that what I say is true, for if you wish, without being a good farmer, to seem to be a good one—or horseman, doctor, flute player, or anything else whatsoever—consider how many things you must contrive for the sake of seeming so. Even if you should persuade many to praise you, so as to gain a reputation, and should acquire beautiful accoutrements for each of these [arts], you would deceive but for the moment; a little later, when put to the test, you would be openly refuted and exposed as a boaster as well."

(23) "How could someone really become prudent about what is going to be advantageous?"

"Clearly, son," he said, "by learning whatever it is possible to know by learning, just as you learned tactics. As for whatever cannot be learned or be foreseen by human foresight, you would be more prudent than others by inquiring from the gods through prophecy. And whatever you know to be better when done, take care that it be done, for it belongs to the more prudent man to take care of what is necessary rather than to neglect it."

(24) "But as for being loved by one's subjects, which seems at least to me to be among the most important matters, it is clear that the road to it is the same as that one should take if he desires to be loved by his friends, for I think one must be evident doing good for them."[62]

"But son," he said, "it is difficult to be able at all times to do good for those for whom one would like to. But to be evident in rejoicing along with them if some good should befall them, in grieving along with them if some evil, in being enthusiastic to join in helping them in difficulties, in fearing lest they should fail in something, in trying to use forethought that they not fail—in these matters one must somehow keep them company very closely. (25) And in action, if it is summer, the ruler must be evident in being greedy for a greater share of the heat;[63] and if it is winter, of the cold; and if it is a time of toils, of labors, for all these things contribute to being loved by one's subjects."

"You mean, father," he said, "that the ruler must also have more endurance against everything than do his subjects."

"Yes, this is what I mean," he said. "Take heart, however, on this point, son: Be assured that the same labors do not affect similar bodies in the same way, when one of them belongs to a man who is ruling, the other to a common [man].[64] To the contrary, honor makes labors a bit lighter for the ruler, as does the very knowing that his acts do not go unnoticed."

(26) "When the soldiers have what they need, father, are healthy, are able to labor, are exercised in the arts of war, are ambitious to appear to be good, and when obeying is more pleasant for them than disobeying, would not one who wished to contend against his enemies as soon as possible seem to you to be moderate?"

"Yes, by Zeus," he said, "at least if one were going to get an advantage.[65] But if not, insofar as I thought that I were better and that I had better followers as well, I would to this extent be more on my guard, just as in other respects we also try to put in greatest security those things that we think are most valuable to us."

(27) "How, father, would one be especially able to get an advantage over his enemies?"

"By Zeus, son," he said, "this is no ordinary or simple[66] task you are asking about. But be assured that the one who is going to do this must be a plotter, a dissembler, wily, a cheat, a thief, rapacious, and the sort who takes advantage of his enemies in everything."

And Cyrus, laughing, said, "Heracles, father, what sort of man you say I must become!"

"Being such a sort, son," he said, "you would be a man both most just and most lawful."

(28) "Why, then," he said, "did you teach us the opposite of this when we were boys and youths?"

"By Zeus," he said, "we do so even now as regards friends and citizens. But in order that you might be able to do harm to enemies, do you not know that you learned many evil deeds?"

"Indeed, I, at least, do not, father," he said.

"Why did you learn to shoot a bow?" he said. "Why throw a spear? Why deceive wild boars with nets and trenches, and why deer with traps and snares? And with lions, bears, and leopards, why did you do battle without putting yourselves on an equal level with them, but instead you always tried to get the advantage when you contended against them? Or do you not realize that these are all evil deeds, ways of cheating, deceptions, and ways of getting the advantage?"

(29) "Yes, by Zeus, but against wild animals!" he said. "Yet with human beings, if I even seemed to wish to deceive anyone, I know that I used to get beaten."

"Nor, I think, did we allow you to shoot a human being with your bows or spears. Instead, we taught you to shoot at a target so that you might not now do harm to your friends, yet, if ever a war should arise, so that you might be able to take aim at human beings as well. And we educated you to deceive and take advantage not among human beings but with wild animals, so that you not harm your friends in these matters either; yet, if ever a war should arise, so that you might not be unpracticed in them."

(30) "Then, father," he said, "if it is useful to know how to do both good and harm to human beings, you ought to have taught both with human beings."

(31) "But it is said, son," he said, "that in the time of our ancestors there was once a man, a teacher of the boys, who taught the boys justice in the way you insist, both to lie and not to lie, to deceive and not to deceive, to slander and not to slander, to take advantage and not to do so. He defined which of these one must do to friends and which to enemies. And he taught moreover that it was just to deceive even one's friends, at least for a good [result], and to steal the belongings of friends for a good [result]. (32) Since this is what he taught, it was necessary that he also train the boys to do these things to each other, just as they say that the Greeks teach deception in wrestling and that they train the boys to be able to do this to each other. Some, then, having natural gifts for both deceiving and getting the advantage, and perhaps also not lacking in a natural gift for the

love of gain, did not abstain from trying to take advantage even of
their friends. (33) So, consequently, there arose a decree that we still
use even now, to teach the boys simply, just as we teach servants in
their conduct toward us, to tell the truth, not to deceive, not to steal,
and not to take advantage, and to punish whoever acts contrary to
this, so that being instilled with such a habit, they might become
tamer citizens. (34) When they reached the age that you now have, it
then seemed to be safe to teach also what was lawful toward enemies,
for it does not seem that you could still be carried away to become
wild citizens after having been raised together in mutual respect. Similarly, we do not converse about sexual matters with those who are
too young, lest, when license is added to strong desire, the young
might indulge this desire without measure."

(35) "Yes, by Zeus." he said. "Since I am a late learner of these ways
of getting the advantage, father, do not be sparing if you have anything to teach about how I can get the advantage over my enemies."

"Contrive, then, as far as is in your power," he said, "to catch your
enemies in disorder with your own troops in order; unarmed, with
yours armed; sleeping, with yours wide awake; visible to you, while
you are yourself invisible to them; and on bad ground, while you lie
in wait when you are yourself in a strong position."

(36) "And how, father," he said, "would someone be able to catch
the enemy when they are making such mistakes?"

"Because, son," he said, "necessity requires that both you and the
enemy suffer many of these [vulnerabilities], for it is necessary that
you both prepare meals, necessary also that you both go to sleep, and
at dawn that all must withdraw to attend to necessities at almost the
same time, and it is necessary to use such roads as there may be. Bearing all these things in mind, you must be on guard especially where
you know you are weakest, and you must set upon the enemy especially where you perceive that they are most easily overcome."

(37) "Then is it possible," Cyrus said, "to get the advantage only in
these ways, or in some others as well?"

"Much more in others, son," he said, "for in these, for the most
part, all take strong precautions, because they know they need them.
But those who deceive the enemy and make them overconfident are
able to catch them unguarded; and by offering themselves to be pursued, [they are able] to put them in disorder; and by leading them

onto bad ground by flight, [they are able] to set upon them there. (38) Although you are a lover of learning of all these matters, you must make use not only of what you learn; rather, you must yourself also be a poet of stratagems against the enemy, just as musicians not only use the tunes they learn but also try to compose other new ones. Even in music, fresh tunes are extremely well regarded; but in things military, new stratagems win still higher regard by far, for they are even more able to deceive opponents. (39) But son, if you should do nothing more than apply against human beings the stratagems that you used to use even against very small animals, do you not think that you would go a long way in getting the advantage over your enemies? You used to get up during the night in the severest winter and go out for birds; and before the birds moved, your snares had been composed, and the ground you moved had been likened to the unmoved. You educated birds to serve your advantage and to deceive birds of the same breed. You yourself would lie in ambush so as to see them, but not be seen by them. You would practice drawing in the snares before the winged creatures escaped. (40) Against the hare, because he grazes at night and runs away in the day, you used to raise dogs that would find him out by his scent. Because he used to flee quickly when found, you had other dogs that had been trained to take him in pursuit. If he should escape even these, you learned their paths and to what places hares go when they run away, and you would spread out nets that are hard to see; and since he was frantic to escape, he would fall in them and himself entangle himself. So that he not escape even from here, you would station scouts of what would happen; and they, from close at hand, would be ready to set upon him quickly. And you yourself from the rear—but with a cry that did not lag far behind the hare—would by your shouting so startle him that he was senseless when taken. Yet teaching those in front to be silent, you would make them escape detection as they lay in ambush. (41) So, as I said before, if you should be willing to contrive such things against human beings as well, I do not know whether you would come up short of any of your enemies.[67] If, after all, the necessity should ever arise to join battle on an even field, out in the open, and with both sides armed, in such a case, son, the ways of getting the advantage that have been prepared long in advance are very powerful. These that I mean are if the bodies of the soldiers have been well exercised, their souls well whetted, and the military arts well cared for.

(42) "This too you must know well, that all those whom you expect to obey you will expect in turn that you make plans on their own behalf. So never be unthinking, but at night consider in advance what your subjects will do for you when day comes, and in the day how things will be finest for the night.

(43) "As for how one ought to organize an army for battle; or how to lead it during day or night, or over narrow or broad roads, or mountainous or level ones; or how to pitch camp; or how to station guards by night or day; or how to advance against the enemy or retreat from the enemy; or how to lead past an enemy city; or how to advance against a fortress or retreat from one; or how to cross woods or rivers; or how to guard against cavalry, or against spearmen or archers; and if the enemy should appear while you are marching in column, how one ought to deploy against him; and if while you are marching in a phalanx the enemy should appear from somewhere else than from the front, how one ought to march against them; or how one might especially perceive the enemy's [affairs]; or how the enemy might least know yours, why should I say all this to you? What I know you have often heard; and when anyone else seemed to know any of these things, you have neither been negligent nor remain ignorant of any of it. So, then, I think, you must use in light of the circumstances whatever of these things seems to you to be advantageous.

(44) "But learn from me also these things, son, the most important,"[68] he said. "Never run a risk contrary to the sacrifices and auguries, either those for yourself or those for the army; and bear in mind that human beings choose their actions by conjecture and do not know from which the good things will become theirs. (45) You could come to know this from events themselves, for many—and those who seem wisest in these matters—have already persuaded cities to undertake wars against others by whom those persuaded to attack were then destroyed; many have elevated many private men and cities at whose hands, after they were elevated, they then suffered the greatest evils; and many, in the case of those they might have treated as friends, benefiting and being benefited, have wished to treat them as slaves rather than friends and have been punished by these same persons. To many it has not been acceptable to live pleasantly

with their share; yet because they desired to be lords over all, they lost even what they had. Many, on acquiring much-wished-for gold, have been destroyed because of it. (46) Thus human wisdom no more knows how to choose what is best than if someone, casting lots, should do whatever the lot determines. Yet the gods, son, being eternal, know all that has come to be, all that is, and what will result from each of these things. And, of the human beings who seek counsel, to whomever they may be propitious, they give signs as to what they ought to do and what they ought not. If they are not willing to give counsel to all, it is no matter for wonder, for there is no necessity for them to care for anyone or anything unless they want to."

BOOK II

∽ CHAPTER 1 ∽

(1) So engaged in a conversation like this, they arrived at the borders of Persia. When an eagle appeared to their right and went ahead of them, they prayed to the gods and heroes who occupy Persia to send them forth favorably and propitiously, and thus they crossed the borders.[1] After they crossed, they prayed again to the gods who occupy Media to receive them favorably and propitiously. After they did this and, as was to be expected, embraced each other, his father went back again into Persia, and Cyrus went into Media to Cyaxares.[2]

(2) When Cyrus reached Cyaxares in Media, first, as was to be expected, they embraced each other, and Cyaxares then asked Cyrus how large an army he was bringing. He said, "Twenty thousand of the sort who used to come to you even before as mercenaries, but others are coming from among the Peers, who have not ever come out [of Persia]."[3]

"How many?" asked Cyaxares.

(3) "It would not hearten you to hear the number," said Cyrus, "but keep in mind that, even though they are few, these so-called Peers easily rule the rest of the Persians, who are quite numerous. But is there any need of them, or was your fear unfounded? Is the enemy not coming?"

"By Zeus, they are," he said, "and in great numbers."

(4) "What makes this so clear?"

"Because," he said, "many people have arrived here from over there [in Assyria], and all say the same thing, though some in one way and some in another."

"Then we must contend against these men."

"Yes," he said, "of necessity we must."

"Then why do you not tell me," said Cyrus, "how great the advancing power is, if you know, and, next, how great ours is, so that, knowing both, we may deliberate accordingly about how best to contend?"

"Then listen," said Cyaxares. (5) "Croesus the Lydian is said to be bringing ten thousand knights, and more than forty thousand targeteers and archers. They say that Artacamas, the ruler of the greater Phrygia, is bringing about eight thousand knights and no fewer than forty thousand lancers and targeteers; Aribaeus, the king of the Cappadocians, six thousand knights and no fewer than thirty thousand archers and targeteers; the Arabian Aragdus about ten thousand knights, about one hundred chariots, and a vast mass of slingers. Nothing is yet said clearly, however, as to whether the Greeks who dwell in Asia will come. As for those from Phrygia by the Hellespont, they say that Gabaedus will assemble them on the Castrian plain and has six thousand knights and about ten thousand targeteers. They say the Carians, Cilicians, and Paphlagonians, however, have been summoned but are not coming. The Assyrian himself, who holds Babylon and the rest of Assyria, will bring, I think, no fewer than twenty thousand knights, chariots—I know well—no fewer than two thousand, and, I think, very many infantry soldiers. At least he is accustomed to, whenever he invades here."

(6) "You say," said Cyrus, "that the enemy knights are sixty thousand, their targeteers and archers more than two hundred thousand. Come, then, what do you say is the size of your power?"

"Among the Medes," said Cyaxares, "there are more than ten thousand knights, and perhaps sixty thousand targeteers and archers would come from our country. Of the Armenians who share our borders there will be four thousand knights and twenty thousand foot soldiers."

"You say," said Cyrus, "that our cavalry will be less than a third that of the enemies' cavalry, and our infantry around half."

(7) "Well then," said Cyaxares, "do you not believe the Persians you say you are bringing to be rather few?"

"We will deliberate later as to whether or not we need more men," said Cyrus. "Tell me what is the mode of battle of each."

"About the same for all," said Cyaxares, "for both their troops and ours are archers and spearmen."

"Then we must of necessity," said Cyrus, "skirmish at a distance, at least with weapons like this."

(8) "Yes, of necessity," said Cyaxares.

"In this case, therefore, the victory belongs to the more numerous, for the few would be much more quickly wounded and destroyed by the many than the many by the few."

"If this is so, Cyrus, then what plan could one find better than to send to Persia and teach them that if anything should happen to the Medes, the danger will extend to Persia, and at the same time ask for a larger army?"

"But be well assured of this," said Cyrus, "that even if all the Persians should come, we would not exceed our enemies in number."

(9) "What plan do you see that is better than this one?"

"If I were you," said Cyrus, "as quickly as possible and for all the Persians who are coming, I would make such arms as those with which our so-called Peers will come. These are a breastplate to cover the chest, a shield for the left hand, and a scimitar or small sword for the right. If you provide arms like this, you will make it safest for us to go to close quarters against our opponents, and preferable for the enemy to flee rather than to stand fast. We will deploy ourselves against those who do stand fast, but we assign to you and your horses whoever among them takes flight, so that they do not have the leisure either to stand fast or to turn back."

(10) So Cyrus spoke like this. It seemed to Cyaxares that he spoke well, and he no longer mentioned sending off for more troops but turned to providing the arms already discussed. They were nearly ready when the Persian Peers reported with the army from Persia.

(11) At this point Cyrus is said to have drawn them together and spoken as follows: "Men, friends, seeing you armed like this and prepared in your souls to join with the enemy in hand-to-hand fighting, but knowing that the Persians who follow you are armed in such a way as to fight when deployed farthest away, I was afraid that, being few and lacking in allies, you might suffer something when you fall upon our many enemies. But as it is, you have arrived with men

whose bodies cannot be faulted, and they will have arms similar to our own, so it is your work to whet their souls, for it belongs to the ruler not only to make himself good, but he must also take care that those he rules will be as good as possible."[4]

(12) So he spoke like this. They all were pleased, believing that they would enter the struggle with greater numbers, and one of them also spoke as follows: (13) "Perhaps I will seem to say something to be wondered at, if I advise that Cyrus speak on our behalf when those who are going to become our allies receive their arms. But I know that the arguments of those most competent to do good and evil especially sink into the souls of those who hear them. And if such people give gifts, even if they happen to be lesser than those from equals, the recipients nonetheless esteem them more. Now, then, our Persian comrades will be much more pleased at being called up by Cyrus than by us, and when they are placed in the ranks of the Peers, they will believe that they have attained this position more securely, when it is conferred by our king's son and our general, than if this same thing were conferred by us. Nor, however, ought our [efforts] be wanting, but in every way we must whet the men's spirit, for in whatever way they become better, it will be useful to us."

(14) Cyrus thus put the arms down in the middle and called all the Persian soldiers together and spoke as follows: (15) "Persian men, you were born and raised in the same land as we, and you have bodies no worse than ours, and it is not fitting for you to have souls that are any worse than ours.[5] Even though you are such as I say, you did not share equally with us in the fatherland, having been excluded not by us but by the necessity upon you to provide sustenance.[6] But it will be my care, with the gods' [help], that you will now have these; and it will be possible for you, if you wish, to take such weapons as we have, to enter upon the same risk as we, and, if anything noble and good should arise from it, to be held worthy of [rewards] similar to ours. (16) Now in the time up until now, both you and we were archers and spearmen, and if you were at all inferior to us in exercising these [skills], it is not at all to be wondered at, for there was no such leisure for you to practice them as there was for us. Yet in this armament we will have no advantage over you: There will be a breastplate for around the chest, fitted to each; a shield in the left hand, which we have all been accustomed to carry; and a dagger or small sword in

the right hand with which we must strike those opposed to us, not even needing to guard against missing as we strike. (17) Now how in these circumstances could one surpass another except by daring, which is no less fitting for you to nurture than for us?⁷ Why is it more fitting for us than for you to desire victory, which acquires and preserves all that is noble and good? Why is it appropriate that we more than you need strength, which bestows as gifts to the stronger what belongs to the weaker?"⁸

(18) He said in conclusion, "You have heard all; you see the arms. Let the one who wants take them and be enrolled with the captain into the same order as we. Let whoever is content with a mercenary's station remain in servile arms."⁹

(19) Thus he spoke. The Persians heard him and believed that if, upon being called up to obtain the same [rewards] by sharing in similar labors, they were not willing to do so, then justly would they live in want for all time. Accordingly, all enrolled, and all took the arms.

(20) During the time that the enemy was said to be approaching but had not yet arrived, Cyrus tried to exercise and bring strength to the bodies of his troops, to teach tactics, and to whet their souls for warlike [deeds]. (21) First, he obtained servants from Cyaxares and ordered them to furnish each of the soldiers with a sufficient quantity of all they needed, ready-prepared. Having made this provision, he left them nothing else than to practice what pertains to war, for he thought he had learned that they become best who, being freed from minding many matters, turn to one work. Even among the works of war themselves, he eliminated practice with both the bow and the spear and left them only this, that they fight with sword, shield, and breastplate. Consequently, he quickly equipped them with the judgment that they must go to close quarters or agree that they were worthless allies, for those who know that they are maintained for nothing other than to fight on behalf of those who maintain them, this is difficult to agree to. (22) In addition to these things, reflecting that human beings are much more willing to practice those things in which there are rivalries, he announced contests to them in whatever he knew to be good for soldiers to practice. This is what he announced: for the private soldier to render himself obedient to the rulers, willing to labor, eager for danger but in good order, knowledgeable in what pertains to soldiers, a lover of beauty regarding

weapons and a lover of honor in all such matters; for the corporal,[10] that he be just like the good private soldier and that, as far as possible, he so render his squad of five; for the sergeant, his squad of ten; for the lieutenant, his platoon; for the captain, that he, being blameless, take care that the rulers who are subordinate to him in turn render their subjects such as to do what they ought. (23) As prizes he announced that for the captains, those thought to render their companies best would become colonels; that those of the lieutenants thought to show that their platoons were best would go up into the places of the captains; that, in turn, the best of the sergeants would be seated in the places of the lieutenants; of the corporals in turn, similarly in those of the sergeants; of the private soldiers, of course, the best in those of the corporals.[11] The result for all these rulers was, first, that they were well served by their subjects; and next, other honors followed that were fitting for each. He held out even greater hopes for those who were worthy of praise, if a greater good should turn up in the fast-approaching future.[12] (24) He announced victory prizes also for those whole companies and whole platoons, and likewise for those squads of ten and of five, that showed themselves to be most obedient to their rulers and to practice most enthusiastically what was announced. The victory prizes in these contests were such as are appropriate for a multitude. This, then, is what was announced and what the army practiced. (25) He furnished them with tents as numerous as were the captains and large enough to suffice for each company, which was one hundred men. Thus they tented by companies. It seemed to him that in tenting closely together they would be benefited in the upcoming contest, for they would see each other similarly provided for and there would be no complaint of getting less.[13] Such complaints have the result that one will allow himself to be worse than another in the face of the enemy. They seemed to him to be greatly benefited also in getting to know each other from tenting together. It seems that shame also occurs more in all people when they know one another, and they who are not known seem somehow more inclined to easy living, just as if they were in the dark. (26) It seemed to him that troops were greatly benefited from tenting together also in keeping their formations precise, for the captains kept the companies under them just as well ordered as when their company went in single file; and similarly the lieutenants their platoons, the sergeants their squads of ten, the corporals their squads of five. (27) Keeping precise formations seemed to him to be exceedingly good both for their not falling into confusion and for their becoming quickly restored [to order] if they should become confused, just as is also the case of stones and pieces of wood that need to be fitted together: even if they happen to be cast down in any way whatsoever, if they have marks so that it is clear from which place each has come, it is possible to fit them together readily. (28) It seemed to him that they were benefited by being fed together also in that they would be less willing to desert each other, because he saw that even animals that are fed together have a terrible yearning if someone separates them from each other.

(29) Cyrus also took care that they would never come to lunch or dinner without sweating, for he made them sweat by taking them on a hunt; or he found out such games as would make them sweat; or if he happened to need to do something, he so conducted the action that they did not return without sweating, for he held this to be good for pleasant eating, for being healthy, and for being able to labor; and he held that these labors were good for their being more gentle to each other, because horses too, when they labor together, stand [in their stalls] more gently with each other. Certainly with regard to facing the enemy, those who are conscious of themselves as having exercised well become more high-minded.

(30) Cyrus provided himself with a tent that was sufficient to hold those he invited to dinner. He usually invited such of the captains as seemed to him opportune to invite, but there were times when he invited also some of the lieutenants, sergeants, or corporals. There were times when he invited even private soldiers, and times when he invited even a whole squad of five, a whole squad of ten, a whole platoon, or a whole company. He used to invite and honor any whom he saw doing the sort of thing he wished them all to do. What was set at table was always equal between himself and those he invited to dinner. (31) He always used to make even the servants of the army share equally in all things, for it seemed to him to be no less worthy to honor the servants in things military than to honor heralds or ambassadors, for he held it necessary that these be loyal, knowledgeable of things military, and intelligent, and, moreover, zealous, swift, unhesitating, and hard to confuse. In addition, Cyrus judged it necessary that

servants have the same [qualities] as those believed to be best, and that they practice not rejecting any work, for they should believe that it is fitting for them to do whatever the ruler commands.

(1) Now when he entertained in his tent, Cyrus always took care that discussions would be introduced that were both very charming and also motivating toward the good. He once settled on this discussion: "Now then, men, do our companions appear to be inferior to us because they have not been educated in the same way as we, or will they not differ from us either in social intercourse or when it will be necessary to contend against the enemy?"

(2) Hystaspas said in reply, "How they will be against the enemy, I at least do not yet know. However, in their social intercourse, by the gods, some of them appear hard to please. The day before yesterday, Cyaxares sent sacrificial victims to each company, and there were three or more pieces of meat passed around for each of us. And the cook began with me as he passed it around on its first circuit. When he came in to pass it a second time, I ordered him to begin from the person who had been last and to pass it the other way. (3) Then one of the soldiers reclining at mid-circle cried out, 'By Zeus, there is nothing equal about this, if, at least, no one ever begins with us in the middle.' On hearing this I was annoyed that he thought he had less,[14] and I called him directly to me. In this, at least, he obeyed with very good order. When the servings reached us—since, I suppose, we were the last to receive them—the smallest were left. He here clearly showed himself to be greatly troubled and said to himself, 'O fortune, that I happened to be called here now!'

(4) "And I said, 'Do not worry, for he will now begin with us, and you will be first and take the biggest piece.' And at this moment the cook was passing for the third time what was left of the meat to be circulated. So he took a piece, second after me. When the third person took a piece, and it seemed that he got a piece bigger than did he himself, he put back what he had taken in order to take another. Thinking that he did not want any more meat, the cook departed,

passing the tray onward before he took a different piece.[15] (5) He now
bore his suffering so heavily that he lost what meat he had taken. In
his vexation he overturned what he still had left of the gravy, from
being so startled and angry at his fortune. Now seeing this, the lieutenant who was nearest to us clapped his hands and enjoyed a laugh.
I, however, pretended to cough, for neither was I myself able to sup-
press a laugh. Thus, Cyrus, I show you of what sort one of our companions is." And at this, as was to be expected, they laughed.

(6) Another of the captains said, "As it seems, Cyrus, he happened
upon one hard to please indeed. Yet when you dismissed us after having taught us formations and ordered that each teach his own company what we learned from you, so I too, just as the others were
doing, went off and taught one platoon. And putting the lieutenant
first and positioning a young man right behind him and the others as
I thought I must, I then, standing at the front and looking at the platoon, ordered them to advance when I thought it time. (7) And that
young man of yours went in front of the lieutenant and took the lead.
And seeing him, I said, 'Human being, what are you doing?'

"And he said, 'I am going forward, just as you ordered.'

"And I said, 'But I ordered all to advance, not you alone.'

"And hearing this, he turned to his platoon mates and said, 'Do
you not hear his command that we all advance?' And all the men,
passing the lieutenant by, came to me.

(8) "When the lieutenant made them go back, they bore it ill and
said, 'Who must be obeyed? Now the one orders us to advance, but
the other does not allow it.' I, however, bearing it calmly, placed them
again as at first and said that no one of those in the back should move
before the one ahead leads, and that all should see to this alone, to
follow the one in front.

(9) "When someone going away to Persia came to me and bade me
give him the letter that I had written for home, I ordered the lieutenant to run and bring the letter, for he knew where it was. So he ran,
and that young man followed the lieutenant with his breastplate and
sword, and all the rest of the platoon saw him and ran along. And the
men came back with the letter. So accurately does my platoon, at least,
execute all your [instructions]," he said.

(10) Now the others, as was to be expected, laughed at a letter having an armed escort, and Cyrus said, "O Zeus and all the gods, we

have such men for companions as are so easily won by attention that it is possible to acquire very many of them as friends with even a little meat, and some are so obedient that they obey before knowing what is ordered. I do not know what sort of soldiers one should pray to have more than ones like these."

(11) So Cyrus at the same time laughed and praised the soldiers in this manner. But there happened to be among the captains in the tent a certain Aglaitadas by name, a man who in character was among the sourest of human beings. And he spoke somewhat as follows: "Do you think, Cyrus, that they are telling the truth in what they say?"

"But what can they wish for from telling lies?" asked Cyrus.

"What else," he said, "except that wanting to make a joke at another's expense,[16] they speak and boast as they do."

(12) Cyrus said, "Hush.[17] Do not say that they are boasters, for 'boaster' seems to me a name that sticks to those who pretend to be wealthier than they are, or braver [than they are], or to those who promise to do what they are not competent to do, or to those who in these matters are evidently acting for the sake of getting something and gaining. But those who contrive a laugh for their associates, not with a view to their own gain, or as a punishment of their listeners, or to any harm at all, why are these not more justly named urbane and charming rather than boasters?"

(13) Cyrus thus defended those who had furnished the laugh. The lieutenant[18] who had himself narrated the jest said, "Aglaitadas, if we were trying to make you weep, just as some who in their songs and discourses compose piteous things and try to move people to tears, you would certainly blame us vehemently, for now when you yourself know that we wish to delight you, not harm you, you nevertheless hold us in great dishonor."

(14) "Yes, by Zeus," said Aglaitadas, "and justly, for the one who contrives a laugh for his friends seems to me often to effect things less worthy than the very one who makes them weep. And if you calculate correctly, you too will discover that I speak the truth, for fathers contrive moderation for their sons by making them weep, and teachers good learning for their students,[19] and laws turn citizens to justice by making them weep. Would you be able to say that those who contrive a laugh benefit either bodies or souls, making them at all more suited for household or city?"

(15) Next Hystaspas spoke somewhat as follows: "If you obey me, Aglaitadas, you will be bold in expending this matter of such great worth on our enemies, and you will try to make them weep. But by all means lavish this matter of little worth, the laugh, on us your friends, for I know that you have a great one laid up in reserve, for you have not squandered it in using it yourself, nor do you voluntarily afford laughter to friends or strangers. There is consequently no excuse for you not to afford us a laugh."[20]

And Aglaitadas said, "Do you think, Hystaspas, that you will coax a laugh out of me?"

And the captain said, "By Zeus, he is certainly senseless if he does. Since one could more easily rub fire from a stone than drag a laugh out of you."

(16) At this the others laughed, since they knew his character, and Aglaitadas smiled. And seeing him brighten, Cyrus said, "You are unjust, captain, because you are corrupting our most serious man by persuading him to laugh, and doing so when he is such an enemy to laughter."

(17) These things ceased at this point. Next Chrysantas spoke as follows: (18) "But my reflection, Cyrus and all of you who are present, is that some have turned out better for us, while others are deserving of less. Yet if something good comes of this, they will all think they deserve equal shares. And yet I believe that there is nothing more unequal among human beings than thinking the bad and the good to deserve equal things."

And Cyrus said to this, "Then by the gods, men, is it best for us to announce a council to the army to decide whether, if the god grants something good from our labors, to make all share equally or, examining the deeds of each person, to assign honors to each in light of them?"

(19) "And why must you announce a discussion about this," said Chrysantas, "and not just proclaim that this is how you are doing it? Did you not proclaim both the contests and the prizes in this manner?"

"But by Zeus," said Cyrus, "the one is not like the other, for what they acquire while on campaign they will hold, I think, to belong to themselves in common. But the command of the army they still believe to be mine fairly, from home, so they do not believe, I think, that I am doing anything unjust when I appoint [contests and] overseers."[21]

(20) "And do you really think," asked Chrysantas, "that the assembled multitude would vote not for each person to obtain an equal share, but for the superior to get the advantage in both honors and gifts?"

"I do think so," said Cyrus, "partly because we advise it, and partly because it is shameful to deny that he who works hardest and especially benefits the community is deserving of the greatest things.[22] I think it will appear an advantage even to the worst that the good get more."

(21) It was also for the sake of the Peers themselves that Cyrus wished this vote to take place, for he held that they too would be better if they knew that they themselves, being judged by their deeds, would obtain what they deserved. It seemed to him to be opportune to put this issue to a vote now, when the Peers had misgivings about the mob sharing equally. Those in the tent thus decided to contribute speeches about this, and they said that whoever thought he was a man ought to advocate it.

(22) One of the captains laughed and said, "But I know a man even from among the people who will recommend that there not be this indiscriminate equal sharing."

Another asked in turn whom he meant. He answered, "He is, by Zeus, my tentmate, who craves to get more of everything."

Another asked him, "Even of labors?"

"Indeed not, by Zeus," he said. "But in this, at least, I have been caught lying, for of labors and other such things he gently allows whoever wishes to get more."[23]

(23) "But, men," said Cyrus, "I know that such human beings,[24] like this one whom you now mention, must be expunged from the military, if indeed we need to have an army that is active and obedient, for it seems to me that the bulk of the soldiers is such as to follow where anyone leads. I think that the noble and good endeavor to lead to what is noble and good, and the vile to what is vile. (24) And often, therefore, inferior [people] get more like-minded followers than do serious ones, for since vileness makes its way through the immediate pleasures, it has them as aides in persuading many to share its view. Yet virtue, since it leads uphill, is not very clever at drawing others along immediately, especially if there also are rivals who invite them to what is downhill and soft. (25) Therefore, when some are bad only

by doltishness and want of industry, I believe that they, like drones, punish their partners only by the expense [of their upkeep]. But they who are bad partners in labors, and are vehement and shameless in getting more, are also leaders to what is vile, for they are often able to show that vileness does get more. Consequently, we must completely expunge such persons [from the army]. (26) Do not, however, consider how you will again fill out your ranks with citizens, but just as you seek whatever horses may be best, not those from your fatherland,[25] so also take from all [sources] such human beings as you think will most contribute to your strength and good order. This too is also evidence for me toward the good:[26] Surely there could neither be a swift chariot with slow horses on it nor a just one with unjust [horses] in the yoke; nor is a household able to be well managed if it uses vile servants; in fact, it falters less even when it lacks servants than when it is confused by unjust ones. (27) Men, friends, know well," he said, "that expunging the bad offers not only the benefit that the bad will be gone but also that, of those who remain, they who have already been filled with evil will be again cleansed of it, while the good, after seeing the bad dishonored, will cling to virtue with much greater heart."

(28) Thus he spoke, and these things were so decided upon by all his friends, and they began to act accordingly.

After this Cyrus again began to jest, for having noted that one of the lieutenants had chosen as his guest and couchmate a man who was very hairy and very ugly, he called the lieutenant by name and spoke as follows: "Sambaulas, that youth who is reclining next to you, do you lead him around according to the Greek fashion, because he is handsome?"

"Yes, by Zeus," said Sambaulas, "I, at least, take pleasure being together with and gazing upon him."[27]

(29) When they heard this, those in the tent looked [at him]. When they saw that the man's face was surpassing in its ugliness, all laughed. And one said, "By the gods, Sambaulas, what sort of deed has he done to have so attached you?"

(30) He said, "By Zeus, men, I will tell you. As often as I called him, whether night or day, he never gave me the excuse that he was busy, nor ever did he obey at a walk, but always running. As many times as I ordered him to do something, I never saw him doing it without

sweating. He has also made all the squads of ten to be like this, not by speech, but showing them by deed how they must be."

(31) And someone said, "And, since he is such as he is, do you not kiss him as you do your relatives?"

And to this the ugly one said, "No, by Zeus, for he is not a lover of labor. And, if he were willing to kiss me, it would suffice to take the place of all his exercises."

⟡ CHAPTER 3 ⟡

(1) Such things, both laughable and serious, were said in the tent. Finally, after making the third libation and praying to the gods for the good things, they broke up the gathering to go to bed. On the next day Cyrus assembled all the soldiers and said the following: (2) "Men, friends, our contest is at hand, for our enemies are approaching. It is clear that the prizes of victory—if we conquer (and one must always say this and make it so)—are that the enemies and all their good things become ours. If, on the other hand, we are conquered, even so all the belongings of the conquered are always set before the conquerors as prizes. (3) You thus must know that human beings who are partners in war swiftly accomplish many noble things when each of them has in himself this thought: Unless each is himself zealous, nothing that must occur will occur. For [such partners], nothing that needs to be done is left undone. Yet when each has the thought that someone else will act and fight, even if he himself relaxes, be assured that every hardship will come upon them all with a rush. (4) And god made things something like this: To those who are not willing to command themselves to work for what is good, he provides that others be their commanders. Now, then, let anyone stand up here and speak to this very point, whether he thinks virtue will be more practiced among us if he who is willing both to labor and to risk the most will also obtain the most honor, or if we know that it makes no difference to be bad, for we all will similarly obtain equal shares."

(5) At this point Chrysantas stood up, one of the Peers and a man neither tall nor strong to look at, but distinguished by his prudence, and he said, "I do not think that you, Cyrus, propose this discussion

with the thought that the bad must have equal shares with the good, but rather to test whether there will be any man who will be willing to display himself with the thought of sharing equally in what others achieve by virtue, even though he does nothing noble and good. (6) I am neither swift of foot nor strong of arm, and I know that from what I will accomplish with my body, I would not be judged either first or second, or even, I think, one thousandth, or even, perhaps, ten thousandth. But I know clearly also that if those who are powerful take hold of affairs with vigor, I will get as big a share of something good as is just. If the bad do nothing, and the good and powerful are dispirited, I fear that I will get a bigger share than I want of something other than the good." (7) So Chrysantas spoke like this.

Pheraulas stood up after him. He was one of the Persian Commoners, a man who was somehow well acquainted with Cyrus even long ago and was agreeable to him. He was not without natural gifts in body, and in soul was not like a man lowborn. He spoke as follows: (8) "Cyrus and all Persians present, I hold that we all are now setting out on an equal footing in a contest of virtue, for I see that we all exercise our bodies in a similar regimen, that all are deemed deserving of like society, and that all the same [prizes] are set before us all, for to obey the rulers is required of all in common, and I see that whoever is evident doing so without excuse obtains honor from Cyrus. Being stout against the enemy is not something that is fitting for one but not another, but this too has been judged to be most noble for all. (9) Now the mode of battle that has been shown to us is one that I see all human beings understand by nature, just as also the various other animals each know a certain mode of battle that they learn not from another but from nature. For example, the ox strikes with his horn, the horse with his hoof, the dog with his mouth, the boar with his tusk. They all also understand how to defend against what they most need to, even though they have never gone to any teacher of these things. (10) I too understood, directly from my childhood, how to protect myself by fending off blows in front of whatever part I thought was to be struck. If I had nothing else, I used to block my attacker as well as I was able by thrusting out my hands. I did this not because I had been taught but even though I got beaten just for this, for fending off. Even when I was a boy, I used to seize a sword wherever I saw one, even though I did not learn how one must take hold of it from anywhere else, as I say, than from nature. I used to do this not because I was taught but even though I was opposed, just as there were also other things I was compelled to do by nature, though I was opposed by both my mother and father. And, yes, by Zeus, I used to strike with the sword everything I was able to without getting caught, for it was not only natural, like walking and running, but it also seemed to me to be pleasant in addition to being natural. (11) Now since the mode of battle granted is one in which the work is more a matter of enthusiasm than art, must we not contend with pleasure against these Peers, at least where the rewards for virtue are set before us equally? We enter upon the risk without staking equal things, for they [are staking] a life with honor, which is alone the most pleasant, while we [are staking] a laborious life and one without honor, which I think is most difficult. (12) It especially increases my enthusiasm for this contest against these [Peers], men, that Cyrus will be the judge, for he does not judge with envy; but I say, and even swear by the gods, that Cyrus seems to me to love all those he sees to be good no less than he loves himself.[28] At least I see him giving them whatever he has more than keeping it himself.[29] (13) And yet I know that they take pride in the fact that they have been educated, as they say, to endure against hunger, thirst, and cold, not knowing very well that we have been educated in just these things by a teacher superior to theirs, for there is no teacher of these things who is superior to necessity, which has taught them to us even too thoroughly. (14) These [Peers] used to practice hard labor by bearing arms, arms such as have been discovered by all human beings so as to be most easily borne, yet we used to be compelled both to walk and to run under great burdens, so that now the bearing of arms seems to me more like wings than a burden. (15) Consider me, then, Cyrus, as one who will both enter the contest and think I deserve to be honored in accord with my worth, no matter how I may be. And to you, men and fellow Commoners, I recommend that you enter into the fray of this battle against the educated, for they are men now caught in a democratic struggle."[30] So Pheraulas spoke like this.

(16) Many others rose and spoke in favor of each of the two speakers.[31] It was decided that each be honored in accord with his worth and that Cyrus be the judge. So these matters went forward like this.

(17) Cyrus once called to dinner even a whole company with its captain. He had seen him deploy the men of his company into halves on

two opposite sides for an attack. Both sides had breastplates and, on their left arms, shields; to one half he gave stout sticks for their right hands, and he told the others that they would have to pick up clods to throw. (18) When thus prepared they took their positions, and he signaled to them to do battle. At this point those with clods threw them, and some chanced to hit breastplates or shields, others a thigh or greave. But when they came to close quarters, the troops with the sticks struck them on their thighs, hands, or calves, and of those bending over for clods, they struck their necks and backs. The ones with sticks finally routed and chased them, striking them amid much laughter and sport. Then the others took up the sticks in turn and did again the same things to those who were throwing the clods. (19) Cyrus admired both the captain's plan and the troops' obedience, for they at one time got exercise and were inspirited, and victory went to those whose arms were like those of the Persians. Being pleased at this, he called them to dinner, and after seeing some of those in the tent who had bandages on their shins or hands, he asked them what had happened. They said that they had been hit with clods. (20) He asked next whether this happened when they were at close quarters or when they were far apart. They said it was when they were far apart. When they were at close quarters, the ones with sticks said that it was a most noble game. Those who had been beaten with the sticks cried out that being struck at close range did not seem to them to be a game at all. At the same time they showed the blows from the sticks on their hands, necks, and in some cases even on their faces. And then, as was to be expected, they laughed at each other. On the next day the plain was entirely full of troops imitating them, and if they had nothing more serious to do, they made use of this game.

(21) Once he saw another captain leading his company in single file away from the river, to the left, and when it seemed opportune to him he ordered the last platoon to come forward to the front, and so also with the third and the fourth. When the lieutenants were in the front, he gave the word for them to lead their platoons in two columns, so then, of course, the sergeants came forward to the front. When it next seemed opportune to him, he ordered each platoon to go forward in four columns. So also, in turn, the corporals came to the front of the four columns.[32]

When they were at the door of the tent, he next called for the first platoon to proceed in single file, and he directed it in. Then he ordered the second to follow at the rear of this one, and with similar announcements to the third and the fourth, he directed them in. After leading them in like this, he sat them down to dinner in the very way they entered. So admiring him for his gentle teaching and care, Cyrus called this company and its captain to dinner.

(22) Some other captain who was invited to the dinner and was present said, "Will you not invite my company to your tent, Cyrus? At least when it goes in to dinner, it does all these same things. And when our gathering is finished, the rear guard of the last platoon leads his platoon out, keeping in the rear those whose order in battle is first. Then the second rear guard leads out the next platoon right after these, and so too the third and the fourth, in order that, when we must retreat from enemies, we will understand how we must do so. When we have come to the track where we march, when we go to the east, I lead, and the first platoon is first, the second as it must be, and so the third and fourth, and so too the squads of ten and five within the platoons, until I give [another] order. When we go to the west, the rear guard and the last troops go first and lead us away. Nevertheless, they obey me, though I go last, in order that they may be accustomed to be similarly obedient both when following and when leading."

(23) And Cyrus said, "And do you always do this?"

"At least as often as we have dinner, by Zeus," he said.

"I invite you then," he said, "because you give practice to your ranks in both coming and going, and because you do so in both day and night, and because you exercise your bodies by marching and you benefit your souls by teaching. So since you do everything doubly, it is just to offer you a double feast as well."

(24) "No, by Zeus," said the captain, "at least not on one day, unless you will offer us double stomachs as well." And then they made an end to their gathering in this way. And on the next day Cyrus called that company, just as he had said, and on the following day as well. The others perceived this, and in the future they all imitated them.

∾ CHAPTER 4 ∾

(1) Once when Cyrus was making a muster and review of all his troops in arms, a messenger came from Cyaxares and said that an em-

bassy had arrived from India. "He orders you to come as quickly as possible. I am bringing you also this most beautiful robe from Cyaxares," said the messenger, "for he wishes that you come as brilliantly and splendidly as possible, since the Indians will see how you approach them."

(2) On hearing this, Cyrus told the captain who was deployed in the first position to take his stand facing forward at the head of his company in single file and to keep himself on the right; and he ordered the second captain to give this same command, and he ordered them to pass it along like this among all troops. Obeying, they quickly relayed the command, and quickly executed what was commanded. In a short time they were three hundred across in the front (for this is how many captains there were) and one hundred in depth. (3) When they stood in position, he ordered that they follow in whatever way he himself might lead, and he straightaway led at a brisk run. When he perceived that the street leading to the palace was too narrow for all to go through on a broad front, he ordered the first thousand to continue in its place, the second to follow after this one, behind it, and similarly for all. He himself led on without stopping, and the other groups of one thousand followed, each behind the one before. (4) He also sent two aides to the mouth of the street, in order that if anyone not know what must be done, they could indicate this to them.[33] When they arrived at Cyaxares' doors, he commanded his first captain to arrange his company to a depth of twelve, and to have the leaders of these squads of twelve stand facing front around the palace, and he ordered the second [captain] to command the same things, and similarly for all.[34]

(5) They then were doing these things, while Cyrus went in to Cyaxares in his Persian robe, which was in no way ostentatious.[35] Upon seeing him, Cyaxares was pleased at his promptness, but annoyed at the commonness of his robe, and he said, "Why this, Cyrus? What are you doing in appearing like this before the Indians? I wished that you appear as brilliant as possible, for it would have been an adornment to me as well that you appear as magnificent as possible, since you are the son of my sister."

(6) And to this Cyrus said, "Which would adorn you more, Cyaxares, if I heeded you by strolling in at my leisure, after dressing in purple garments, selecting bracelets, and putting a necklace around my neck; or now when, because I honor you, I have heeded you so

promptly with a power of such size and quality, and with myself adorned with sweat and zeal, and showing that the others are similarly obedient to you?" So this is what Cyrus said, and Cyaxares, believing that what he said was correct, called in the Indians.

(7) The Indians came in and said that their king had sent them and had commanded them to inquire into the source of the war between Medes and the Assyrian [king].[36] "After we hear you, he ordered us to go in turn to the Assyrian and ask him the same things. Finally, he ordered us to say to you both that the king of the Indians says that he, after examining justice,[37] will side with the one who has been unjustly treated."

(8) To this Cyaxares said, "Then hear from me that we are not at all unjust to the Assyrian. Now go to him, if you must, and ask what he says."

Cyrus, being present, asked Cyaxares, "May I also state my judgment?" Cyaxares bade him do so. "Then report back to the king of the Indians, unless Cyaxares decides otherwise, that if the Assyrian says he suffers some injustice at our hands, then we say we choose the Indian king himself as judge." After hearing this, they departed.

(9) After the Indians went out, Cyrus began a discussion like this: "Cyaxares, I came from home without much money of my own at all, and of what there was, I have very little left. I have used it up for the soldiers. And perhaps you wonder about how I have done so, since you are maintaining them. Be assured that I do nothing else, when I admire one of the soldiers, than honor and gratify [him], (10) for it seems to me that regarding all those whom one wishes to make into good co-workers, in any sort of matter whatsoever, it is more pleasant to incite them by speaking well and doing well than by causing them pain and compelling them. Regarding those whom one wishes to make into eager co-workers in the works of war, they especially, it seems to me, must be hunted with both good words and good deeds, for they must be friends, not enemies, who are going to be allies not given to excuses, nor inclined to envy when things go well for the ruler, nor to betrayal when they go badly. (11) Realizing in advance that this is the case, I think I need money. Now it seems to me to be strange to look to you for everything, when I perceive you spending a great deal. I think you and I in common should examine how to keep your money from running

out on you, for if you should have an abundance, I know that it would be [possible] for me to take from it whenever I might be in need, especially if what I should take, when spent, would make things better also for you. (12) I remember having heard you say once recently that the Armenian has contempt for you now that he hears that the enemy is coming against us, and he neither sends his army nor pays the tribute he owes."

"Yes, he is doing this, Cyrus," he said. "I am consequently at a loss as to whether it is better for me to mount a campaign and try to impose necessity upon him, or to let him be for the present, lest we add him too to our other enemies."

(13) And Cyrus asked further, "Are his residences in strong places or perhaps even in easily accessible ones?"

And Cyaxares said, "His residences are not in very strong places. I was not neglecting this point. However, there are mountains where he would be able to go away on the instant, and at least he himself would be protected against falling into our hands, as would as many of his things as he could have secretly conveyed there, unless one should sit down and besiege him, as my father once did."

(14) After this Cyrus said the following: "But if you are willing to send me, assigning to me what seems a measured number of cavalry troops, I think that, with the gods' [help], I could make him both send the army and pay you the tribute. Moreover, I expect that he will also become more a friend to us than he now is."

(15) And Cyaxares said, "I also expect that they would come to you more than to me, for I hear that some of their children used to go hunting with you, so perhaps they would come to you again. With them in our hands we could do everything as we wish."

"Does it not seem advantageous to you," said Cyrus, "that we plan about this in secret?"

"Yes," said Cyaxares, "for in this way one or another of them might even fall into our hands, and if one should attack them, they would be caught unprepared."

(16) "Then listen," said Cyrus, "[and decide] if I seem to you to say anything [worthwhile]. I have often taken all the Persians with me to go hunting around the borders of your land and that of the Armenians, and I have also previously taken along some knights from among my companions here."

"Then you would not be suspected if you did the same things again," said Cyaxares. "Yet if your power should appear much greater than that with which you were accustomed to hunt, this would then be suspected at once."

(17) "But it is possible, even in this case" said Cyrus, "to prepare a pretext that would not be distrusted, if someone should report it, namely, that I wish to make a great hunt, and I would ask you out in the open for cavalry troops."

"Beautiful!" said Cyaxares. "And I will not be willing to give you more than some moderate number, on the grounds that I wish to go to the guard posts facing Assyria, for I really do wish to go and fit them out as securely as possible. When you have gone ahead with the power that you have and have hunted for two days, I would send to you sufficient cavalry and infantry of those gathered around me. Taking these, you would advance right away, and I would myself try with the rest of my power to be not far from you, so that I could show myself if ever it should be opportune."

(18) So Cyaxares right away gathered knights and infantry for the guard posts, and he sent wagons of provisions in advance on the road to the guard posts. Cyrus offered sacrifices for the march, and at the same time he sent to Cyaxares and asked for the younger cavalry. Yet he did not send him many, even though very many wished to go. After Cyaxares with his infantry and cavalry power had already gone on in advance on the road to the guard posts, Cyrus' sacrifices for going against the Armenian were favorable. And thus he went out, prepared, of course, as if for a hunt.

(19) Right away in the first field as he was going along, a hare sprang up. An eagle of favorable omen was flying above, and seeing the hare in its flight, bore down upon it, struck it, seized it, and went off. Having taken it to a hill not far off, it treated its prey as it wanted. Cyrus was pleased on seeing the sign and bowed down to Zeus the king, and he said to those present: (20) "It will be a noble hunt, men" he said, "if the god is willing." When he came to the border, he proceeded right away to hunt just as he was accustomed to do. The multitude of the infantry and cavalry went forward for him in a line, in order to rouse the animals as they came upon them. The best infantry and knights dispersed, lay in wait for the roused game, and pursued them. And they took many boars, deer, antelope, and wild asses, for

there are many asses in these places even now. (21) When Cyrus ceased hunting, he approached the borders of Armenia and had dinner. On the next day he hunted again, going over toward the mountains that he was aiming at. When he ceased again, he had dinner. When he perceived the army from Cyaxares approaching, he sent in secret to them and told them to stay back about two parasangs and have their dinner, foreseeing that this would contribute toward their avoiding notice.[38] He told their ruler to come to him after they had dinner. He called the captains after dinner. When they were present, he spoke as follows: (22) "Men, friends, previously the Armenian was both ally and subject of Cyaxares. But now that he perceives our enemies approaching, he shows contempt and neither sends his army to us nor pays the tribute. Now, then, it is to hunt him, if we are able, that we have come. It seems [best] to do the following: Chrysantas, when you have rested a measured amount, take half of the Persians who are with us, go along the mountain road, and seize the mountains in which he is said to take refuge whenever he is at all afraid. I shall give you guides. (23) Now these mountains are said to be thickly wooded, so there is hope you will not be seen. Nevertheless, in front of your army send light-armed men who are likened in number and attire to bands of robbers. If they should happen upon any of the Armenians, they would silence the reports of the ones they capture; and as for the ones they are not able to capture, they would stop them from seeing your whole army by scaring them away, and this will lead them to make their plans as against a band of thieves. (24) So you do this, and I with half of the infantry and all of the knights will at daybreak go straight across the plain against the king's palaces. If he resists, it is clear that it will be necessary to fight. If instead he retreats across the plain, it is clear that it will be necessary to give chase. If he takes flight into the mountains, it will then be your task not to allow any of those who come to you to escape. (25) Believe that, just as in hunting, we will be the ones who seek from behind, and you the ones at the nets. Remember, then, that the paths must be secured before the game is roused. And those stationed at the mouths [of the paths] must not be noticed, if the game approaching is not to turn away. (26) Do not do as you sometimes do, Chrysantas, on account of your love of hunting, for you are often busy the whole night without sleep. But you now must allow the men to rest a measured amount so that they might be capable of fighting sleep. (27) Nor do this: Because you [usually] do not have human beings as guides, you wander up and down the mountains, and run wherever the animals lead you. And do not now go along the paths that are hard to walk, but order your guides to lead along the easiest road, unless it is much longer, for the easiest is quickest for an army. (28) And do not, because you are accustomed to run up and down mountains, lead at a run. Lead with measured haste, so that your army will be capable of following you. (29) It is good also that some of the most capable and eager troops sometimes stay back and offer encouragement. After the column goes by, it incites everyone to hurry when [these troops] are seen running past those who are walking."

(30) Chrysantas listened to this and exulted in the charge Cyrus gave him. Taking his guides, he went away and gave the necessary orders to those who were going to go along with him, and he rested. When they had been in bed what seemed a measured amount, he went toward the mountains. (31) But Cyrus, when day broke, sent ahead a messenger to the Armenian, and told him to tell him the following: "Armenian, Cyrus orders you to act in such a way that he may go away as soon as possible with the tribute and the army." "If he asks where I am, say the truth, that I am at the border. If he asks whether I am coming myself, say the truth in this case as well, that you do not know. If he inquires how many we are, bid him to send someone along and learn." (32) After so directing the messenger, he sent him off, believing that it was more friendly to go on like this than to say nothing in advance. After he himself formed up his troops in the way best both for completing the march and, if need be, for fighting, he advanced. He told his troops to be unjust to no one, and if anyone should chance upon an Armenian, to bid him be cheerful and say that whoever wanted to open a market might do so, wherever they might be, whether he wished to sell food or drink.

BOOK III

⟶ CHAPTER 1 ⟶

(1) Cyrus was involved in these things. When the Armenian heard from the messenger what Cyrus had said, he was stunned, as he reflected that he had been unjust in neglecting the tribute and in not sending the army. The greatest problem, which he especially feared, was that he was about to be discovered in the early stages of fortifying his palace so as to make it sufficient for armed resistance. (2) Hesitating because of all these things, he sent around to gather his own power, and at the same time he sent into the mountains his younger son Sabaris, his own wife, his son's wife, and their daughters. He sent along also the jewelry and property of greatest value, and he gave them an escort. He himself sent out scouts to see what Cyrus was doing, and at the same time he marshaled those of the Armenians who were nearby. And soon there were others present who said that he himself was already close at hand. (3) At this point the Armenian no longer dared to come to blows, so he withdrew. When the Armenians saw him do this, each ran immediately to what was his own, wishing to get his possessions out of the way.[1] When Cyrus saw the plain full of them running and hastening about, he sent out and said that he was not the enemy of anyone who stayed put, but if he caught anyone running away, he announced that he would treat him as an enemy. Consequently, many stayed, but there were some who withdrew with the king. (4) When those who were

going forward with the women fell in amidst the troops on the mountain, they immediately raised a cry and many of them were captured as they tried to escape. Finally, the sons, wives, and daughters were captured, along with as many valuables as they happened to be carrying with them. The king himself, when he perceived what was going on, was at a loss as to where to turn and fled to a hill. (5) Seeing this, Cyrus encircled the hill with the army that was with him, and sending to Chrysantas, he ordered him to leave a guard on the mountain and come back. So the army was gathered together for Cyrus, and he sent a herald to the Armenian and asked the following: "Tell me, Armenian, do you wish to remain there and do battle against hunger and thirst, or to come down onto a level field and do battle against us?"

The Armenian answered that he did not wish to do battle against either.

(6) Sending again, Cyrus asked, "Why then are you sitting there and not coming down?"

"I am at a loss as to what I ought to do," he said.

"But you ought not be at a loss," said Cyrus, "for it is possible for you to come down to a trial."

"Who will be the judge?" he asked.

"Clearly he to whom god granted to treat you as he wishes even without a trial."

At this point, recognizing necessity, the Armenian came down. And Cyrus took him and everything else into their midst, and encamped his army around them, having already brought his whole force close together.

(7) Meanwhile, the older son of the Armenian, Tigranes, came back from a journey; it was he who was once a hunting partner with Cyrus. And when he heard what had happened, he went directly—just as he was—to Cyrus. When he saw that his father, mother, siblings, and his own wife had become captives, he broke into tears, as was to be expected. (8) On seeing him, Cyrus showed him no sign of friendship but said, "You have arrived at an opportune time, for you may attend and listen to the trial concerning your father." And he directly called together the leaders of both the Persians and the Medes. And if any of the honored Armenians were present, he invited them too. He did

not send away the women who were present in their carriages, but he allowed them to listen as well.

(9) When all was well, he began the discussion. "Armenian," he said, "I advise you in the first place to tell the truth in your trial, so that you may avoid at least what is most hateful, for be assured that being detected in lying especially keeps people from obtaining sympathy. Besides, the children and wives here are aware of all you have done, as are all the Armenians who are present. If they perceive you saying things contrary to what has occurred, they will believe that even you yourself have condemned yourself to suffer all the most extreme things, if I learn the truth."

"Ask what you wish, Cyrus," he said, "on the assurance that I will speak the truth, and let come what may as a result."

(10) "Tell me, then," he said, "did you ever make war on Astyages, the father of my mother, and on the other Medes?"

"I did," he said.

"When you were conquered by him, did you agree that you would pay tribute and send an army wherever he directed, and that you would not have fortifications?"

"This is so."

"Then why were you neither paying the tribute nor sending an army, and why were you building fortifications?"

"I desired freedom, for it seemed to me to be noble both that I be free myself and that I leave freedom for my children."

(11) "Yes," said Cyrus, "it is noble to do battle never to become a slave. Yet if someone is conquered in war or enslaved in some other way, and is then detected trying to steal himself from his masters, do you, first of all, honor him as a good man and a doer of things noble, or do you punish him as unjust, if you catch him?"

"I punish him," he said, "for you do not allow lying."

(12) "Answer clearly on each of the following points," said Cyrus. "If there happens to be a ruler beneath you and he does wrong, do you allow him to rule or do you put another in his place?"[2]

"I put another there."

"But what further? If he has a lot of money, do you allow him to stay wealthy or do you make him poor?"

"I take away whatever he happens to have," he said.

"And if you know that he is also in revolt to the enemy, what do you do?"

"I kill him," he said. "For why should I die convicted of lying rather than tell the truth?"

(13) When his son heard this, he stripped off his tiara and rent his robes, and the women scratched their cheeks and cried out, as if their father were lost and they themselves already destroyed.[3]

Cyrus ordered them to be silent again and said, "So, this is your justice,[4] Armenian. What do you advise us to do on this basis?"

The Armenian, of course, fell silent, at a loss as to whether he should advise Cyrus to kill him or teach him to do the opposite of what he said was his own practice.

(14) His son Tigranes said to Cyrus, "Tell me, Cyrus, since my father seems like one at a loss, shall I advise what I think is best for you regarding him?"

And having noted when Tigranes hunted with him that a certain wise man used to accompany him and was revered by Tigranes, Cyrus very much desired to hear whatever he would say, and he bade him express his judgment with confidence.[5]

(15) "If you admire my father for what he has advised or what he has done," Tigranes said, "then I strongly advise you to imitate him. If, however, he seems to you to have done wrong in everything, I advise you not to imitate him."

"For in doing what is just, I would least imitate one who does wrong," said Cyrus.

"That is so," he said.

"Then your father must be punished, at least according to your argument, if it is indeed just to punish the unjust."

"Do you hold, Cyrus, that it is better to impose punishments that are in keeping with your good or those that are to your detriment?"

"I would then be punishing myself," he said.

(16) "But you would be greatly punished," said Tigranes, "if you should kill those who belong to you at the moment when they are most valuable to possess."

"How," said Cyrus, "would human beings be most valuable at the moment when they are caught being unjust?"

"Why, I think they would be, if they then become moderate, for it seems to me, Cyrus, to be like this: Without moderation, there is no benefit from any other virtue, for what use could anyone make of a strong or courageous person if he is not moderate, or of a knight, a wealthy person, or a master of a city? But with moderation, every friend becomes useful and every servant good."

(17) "Are you saying, then," he said, "that in this single day your father, who was immoderate, has become moderate?"[6]

"Certainly," he said.

"Then you are saying that moderation is something the soul experiences, like pain, not something it learns;[7] for certainly, if at least the one who is going to be moderate must become prudent, he could not become moderate immediately after having been immoderate."

(18) "But Cyrus," he said, "have you never perceived a man who, through his immoderation, undertook to do battle against someone superior to himself, and after he was defeated, ceased directly from his immoderation toward him? Again, have you never yet seen a city deployed against another city, which, after it is defeated, is immediately willing to obey it rather than doing battle?"

(19) "When you affirm so strongly that your father has been made moderate by a defeat, what defeat do you mean?" asked Cyrus.

"By Zeus," he said, "the one he is conscious of in himself, that he desired freedom, but became a slave as never before, and that he was not competent to accomplish any of the things he thought he had to, whether by staying hidden, by anticipation, or by compulsion. Where you wished to deceive him, he knows that you did deceive him just as one would deceive those who are blind, deaf, and altogether incapable of thinking. Where you thought you ought to stay hidden from him, he knows that you stayed so hidden that you got to the places he thought were waiting as his own strongholds, and you secretly turned them into jails. In speed you so far surpassed him that you came from far off with a large expedition before he could gather around himself a power that was already nearby."

(20) "Then does it seem to you," asked Cyrus, "that knowing others to be better than themselves is a sufficient defeat to make people moderate?"

"Much more," said Tigranes, "than when one is defeated in battle, for he who is conquered by strength sometimes thinks that by exercising his body, he will be ready to fight again, and captured cities think that by making additional alliances, they could fight again. Yet people are often willing to obey even without necessity those they hold to be better than they are themselves."

(21) "You are not likely to think, then," he said, "that the insolent know those who are more moderate than themselves, nor that thieves know those who do not steal, nor that liars know those who tell the truth, nor that the unjust know those who do what is just. Do you not know that your father just now lied and did not maintain his compact with us, although he knew that we were in no way violating the compact Astyages made?"

(22) "But I do not say that knowing one's betters moderates by itself, without also being punished by one's betters, as my father now is."

"But," said Cyrus, "your father has not yet suffered any evil whatsoever. Be assured that he fears, however, that he may suffer all the most extreme ones."

(23) "Do you think," said Tigranes, "that anything enslaves human beings more than intense fear? Do you not know that those who are beaten with iron, which is believed to be the most severe tool of punishment, are nevertheless willing to do battle again with the same people? But human beings are not even able to look at those of whom they are thoroughly afraid, even if they are encouraging them to do so."

"You say that fear punishes human beings more than does being harmed in deed," he said.

(24) "And you know that what I say is true," he said, "for you know that those who are afraid that they will be exiled from their fatherland, and those on the verge of battle who fear that they will be defeated, pass their time in despondency—as do sailors in fear of a shipwreck, and those who fear slavery or prison. Now these are not able to partake of either food or sleep because of their fear, but those who are already exiled, already defeated, or already enslaved are sometimes even more able to eat and sleep than are those who are happy. (25) It is still more evident what a burden fear is from the following, for some, fearing that they will be killed if caught, kill themselves in advance because of their fear—hurling themselves down, hanging themselves, or cutting their own throats. Thus, of all terrible things, fear especially subjugates souls. As for my father, how do you think his soul is now disposed, since he fears slavery not only for himself but also for me, his wife, and all his children?"

And Cyrus said, (26) "But I do not doubt that he is so disposed now. However, it seems to me to belong to the same man to turn insolent in good fortune and quickly to cower in fear if he blunders, and to think big again and cause trouble again, if he is again unconstrained."

(27) "But by Zeus, Cyrus," he said, "our wrongs offer excuses for you to distrust us. It is possible for you to fortify guard posts, to possess the strongholds, and to take whatever other precaution you wish. And you will nevertheless hold onto us without our feeling any great pain at these measures, for we shall remember that we are the causes of them. Yet if you give the reign to one who has done no wrong, and if you show that you do not trust them, beware that even as you benefit them, they will not believe that you are a friend. If, on the other hand, you protect yourself against being hated by not putting yokes on them against their turning insolent, beware that it not become necessary for you to moderate them still more than you just now needed to moderate us."

(28) "But by the gods," he said, "I think that I would be displeased to make use of such servants as I knew were serving out of necessity. Yet as for those of whom I should think I know that they contribute what they must out of goodwill and friendship for me, these I think I would endure more easily when they do wrong than those who hate me but labor greatly at all things out of necessity."

And Tigranes said to this, "From whom could you ever receive so much friendship as it is now possible for you to acquire from us?"

"From those, I think," he said, "who have never been enemies, if I should be willing to benefit them just as you now insist that I benefit you."

(29) "And would you now be able, Cyrus," he asked, "to find anyone else whom you could gratify in the present case as much as my father? For example, if you now allow someone to live who has never been unjust to you, what gratitude do you think he will feel to you for this? Further, if you do not take away his children and wife, who will befriend you for this more than one who believes that for him it is fitting that they be taken away? Do you know of anyone who, if he should not have the kingship over the Armenians, would feel more pain than we? Is it not then also clear that the one who feels most pain at not being king would also feel the greatest gratitude to you if he should obtain the reign? (30) If you care at all about leaving things as

little confused as possible when you depart, consider whether you think things here would be more tranquil with a new reign beginning or with the customary one remaining. If you care at all about leading out as large an army as possible, whom do you think could levy it more correctly than he who has done so many times? If you also need money, whom do you believe could provide it better than he who both knows and possesses all there is?[8] My good Cyrus, guard against punishing yourself more by throwing us away than by the harm my father was able to do to you." So such is what he said.

(31) Cyrus was deeply pleased as he listened, because regarding everything he had promised to Cyaxares to do, he believed it all was being accomplished for him, for he remembered saying that he thought he would make [the Armenian] even more a friend than he was before. And after this he asked the Armenian, "If I am persuaded by you in these matters, Armenian," he said, "tell me how large an army you will send with me, and how much money you will contribute toward the war."

To this the Armenian said, (32) "Cyrus, I have nothing simpler or more just to propose than for me to show all the power there is and for you, after seeing it, to lead away as large an army as seems [good] to you, and to leave the rest as a guard for the country. Likewise about money, it is just to show to you all there is and for you yourself to judge the matter and carry away as much as you wish and leave as much as you wish."

(33) And Cyrus said, "Come, tell me, how large is your power, and tell me also how much money you have."

Here the Armenian said, "There are about eight thousand Armenian cavalry troops, and about forty thousand infantry. Along with the treasuries my father left, there is in property more than three thousand talents when calculated in silver."

(34) And Cyrus did not hesitate but said, "Then since the Chaldaeans on your borders are making war, send along with me half of your army. As for the money, instead of the fifty talents that you paid as tribute, give double to Cyaxares, since you quit paying. Lend me another hundred. I promise you that, if god grants, in return for what you loan me, I will either benefit you in a way that is worth more or pay back the money, if I am able. If I am not able, I would come to light as incapable, I think, but I would not justly be judged to be unjust."

(35) And the Armenian said, "By the gods, Cyrus, do not even speak like this. Otherwise, you will find me despondent. Believe instead that what you leave behind is no less yours than what you go away with."

"Very well," said Cyrus. "How much money would you give me to get your wife back?"

"As much as was within my power," he said.

"How about for your children?"

"Also for them, as much as was within my power," he said.

"This, then, is already double what you have," said Cyrus. (36) "Now you, Tigranes, tell me what you would pay to get your wife back."

He happened to be newly married and very much in love with his wife.[9] "I would pay even with my life so that she never become a servant."[10]

(37) "Then take her back," he said, "for I do not believe that she was taken as a captive, since you, at least, never fled from us. You, Armenian, take back your wife and children without paying anything for them, that they may know that they return to you as free people. Now have dinner with us; after dinner go off where your spirit leads." So they stayed.

(38) While in the tent after dinner, Cyrus asked, "Tell me, Tigranes, where is that man who used to hunt with us and whom you seemed to me to regard with such wonder?"

"Indeed, this father of mine killed him," he said.

"After catching him in what injustice?"

"He said he was corrupting me. And yet, Cyrus, he was so noble and good that even when he was about to die he called me to him and said, 'Tigranes, do not be harsh toward your father because he kills me; he does this not out of malice toward you but out of ignorance. I, at least, believe that the wrongs human beings commit out of ignorance are all involuntary.' "

(39) To this Cyrus said, "Such a man!"[11]

The Armenian said, "Cyrus, those who catch other men consorting with their wives do not kill them on the grounds that they cause their wives to be less sensible;[12] but because they believe that they divert their affection toward themselves, they treat them as enemies. Similarly, I envied him, because he seemed to me to make my son wonder at himself more than at me."

(40) And Cyrus said, "But by the gods, Armenian, the wrongs you have committed seem to me to be human. Tigranes, have sympathy for your father." Having then discussed such things and shown such friendliness as was to be expected on account of the reconciliation, they went up on their chariots with their wives and rode away contented.

(41) When they went home, one spoke of Cyrus' wisdom, another of his steadfastness, another of his gentleness, and someone else of his beauty and height. Then Tigranes asked his wife, "Did Cyrus seem to be beautiful to you too, my Armenian [bride]?"

"But by Zeus," she said, "I did not even look at him."

"At whom, then?" asked Tigranes.

"At the one who said, by Zeus, that he would pay with his own life so that I not be a slave." Then, as was to be expected, after such [words and events], they went to rest with each other.

(42) On the next day, the Armenian sent presents to Cyrus and to his entire army, and he told those of his own troops who had to go on the campaign to report in three days. He counted out double the amount of money that Cyrus had stated, but Cyrus took just what he had stated and sent the rest back. He also asked whether he himself or his son would be the one who would lead the army. Speaking at the same time, the father said, "Whomever you command," and the son said, "I will not leave you, Cyrus, not even if I must tag along as a camp follower."

(43) And Cyrus said laughing, "And at what price would you be willing for your wife to hear that you are a camp follower?"

"But there is no need that she hear it," he said, "for I shall bring her, so it will be possible for her to see whatever I do."

"It is time, then, for you to get ready," he said.

"Believe, then," he said, "that after we make ready whatever my father gives us, we shall report."

Then, after receiving their presents, the soldiers went to rest.

∾ CHAPTER 2 ∾

(1) On the next day Cyrus took Tigranes, the best of the Median cavalry, and as many of his own friends as seemed to him to be op-

portune, and he rode around contemplating the country, considering where he should build a guard post. Coming to a certain high spot he asked Tigranes which were the mountains from which the Chaldaeans came down and plundered. And Tigranes showed him. He asked next, "Are these mountains now deserted?"

"No, by Zeus," he said, "but they always have scouts there who signal to others whatever they see."

"So what do the others do," he said, "when they perceive the signals?"

"They give help on the heights, each as he is able," he said.

(2) Now Cyrus listened to these things, and as he considered them, he noted that much of the Armenians' country was deserted and idle because of the war. And then they went away to the camp, and after dinner they went to bed. (3) On the next day Tigranes himself reported, having gotten things ready, and four thousand knights were assembled with him, as were ten thousand bowmen and this many targeteers as well. Cyrus was sacrificing while they assembled. When the auspices were favorable for him, he called together the leaders of the Persians and the Medes. (4) When they were together, he spoke like this: "Men, friends, these mountains that we see belong to the Chaldaeans. If we should take them and our guard post should be on the heights, it would be necessary for both the Armenians and the Chaldaeans to be moderate toward us. Now then, the auspices are favorable for us; and to join with human zeal that this be accomplished, there could be no other ally so great as speed, for if we anticipate them and get on top before they assemble, either we would take the heights without a fight at all or we would engage enemies who were both few and weak. (5) Thus no labor is easier or more free of risk than to be steadfast in hurrying. Come then, to arms!

"You, Medes, go along on our left. You, Armenians, lead on, half on our right and half in front of us. You, cavalry troops, follow in the rear, giving encouragement and pressing us on upward, and if anyone slackens, do not allow it." (6) After saying this and putting his platoons into columns, Cyrus led on. When the Chaldaeans perceived them rushing upward, they immediately began signaling to their own, shouting to each other, and assembling. Cyrus announced, "Persian men, they are signaling to us to hurry, for if we beat them to the top, our enemies' actions will be powerless."

(7) The Chaldaeans had shields and two spears. They are said to be the most warlike of those who come from around that area, and whenever anyone has need of them, they serve as mercenaries because of their being both warlike and poor. This is so because their country is mountainous, and little of it produces anything useful.

(8) When Cyrus' group was getting quite near the heights, Tigranes said as he went along with Cyrus, "Cyrus, do you know that we will ourselves need to fight very soon? The Armenians, at least, will not stand up to the enemy."

And saying that he knew this, Cyrus immediately announced to the Persians to get ready, for "it will soon be necessary to press onward, when the Armenians by pretended flight draw the enemy on into close range for us." (9) So the Armenians were leading in this way. While the Armenians were approaching, those of the Chaldaeans who were present gave war cries and swiftly rushed against them, as was their custom; and the Armenians, as was their custom, did not stand up to them. (10) Yet when the pursuing Chaldaeans saw swordsmen rushing up in opposition, some were quickly killed when they got near, and others fled. Of these, some were captured, and the heights were quickly taken. When Cyrus' group held the heights, they looked down on the households of the Chaldaeans and perceived people fleeing from the ones nearby. (11) When all the soldiers were together, Cyrus announced that they should have lunch. After lunch, Cyrus learned that the place where the Chaldaean spy posts were was strong and had water, and he immediately began to fortify a guard post there. He also bade Tigranes to send to his father and bade him to report with as many carpenters and stonemasons as there were. So a messenger departed for the Armenian, while Cyrus proceeded to build fortifications with those who were already present.

(12) At this time they brought to Cyrus the captives who had been bound and some others who were wounded. When he saw them, he immediately ordered that those in bonds be released, and he called doctors and ordered them to tend the wounded. Then he said to the Chaldaeans that he came neither desiring to destroy them nor needing to make war, but wishing to make peace between the Armenians and Chaldaeans. "I know that you did not need peace before the heights were taken, for your things were safe, while those of the Armenians you drove and carried off. But look at your situation now.

(13) I am sending your captives home, and I am allowing you to deliberate along with the other Chaldaeans as to whether you wish to
make war with us or be our friends. And if you choose war, you will
not come here again without weapons, if you are moderate. Yet if you
decide that you need peace, come without weapons. I will take care
that things go well for you, if you become friends." (14) Upon hearing this the Chaldaeans praised him greatly and offered many pledges
with their right hands, and then they departed homeward.

When the Armenian heard Cyrus' summons and what he had done,
he took his carpenters and as many other things as he thought he
needed, and he went to Cyrus as quickly as he was able. (15) When he
saw Cyrus, he said, "Cyrus, although we are able to foresee little about
the future, how many things we human beings undertake to do!
For even just now while undertaking to contrive freedom, I became
a slave as never before. And when we were captured and believed
that we were clearly done for, we now come to light as having been
saved as never before, for I now see that those who never ceased
doing us many evils are now as I used to pray they would be.
(16) And Cyrus, do understand that to have driven the Chaldaeans
from these heights I would have paid many times the amount of money
that you now have received from me. And as for the good things you
promised to do us when you took this money, you have already accomplished them, so that we have come to light as owing you other favors in addition. Unless we should be evil, we would be ashamed not
to pay them back to you." So this is what the Armenian said.

(17) The Chaldaeans arrived wanting Cyrus to make peace for
them. And Cyrus asked them, "Chaldaeans, do you not now desire
peace because you believe that you would be able to live more safely
if there is peace than by fighting, since we now hold these heights?"
The Chaldaeans said so.

(18) And he said, "What if still other good things came to you
through the peace?"

"We would be still more delighted," they said.

"Well then," he said, "do you not now believe that you are poor because you are lacking in good soil?" They said yes to this too.

"Well then," said Cyrus, "would you wish that it were possible for
you to work as much as you wanted of Armenian soil, while paying
the same rent as the Armenians do?"

The Chaldaeans said they would, "if we trusted that we would not suffer injustice."

(19) "What about you, Armenian?" he said. "Would you wish that your land that is now idle be worked, if those working it were going to pay what is customary among you?" The Armenian said that he would pay a great deal for this, for his income would be much augmented.

(20) "What about you, Chaldaeans?" he said. "Since you have mountains good for it, would you be willing to let the Armenians graze their flocks on them, if the herdsmen would pay you what is just?" The Chaldaeans said yes, and explained that they would be benefited greatly without laboring at all.

"And you, Armenian," he said, "would you be willing to use their pastures, if in benefiting the Chaldaeans a little you would be benefited much more?"

"Very much so," he said, "if I should think that we grazed our flocks in safety."

"Would you not graze them in safety if you possessed the heights, to be as allies?" he said. The Armenian said they would.

(21) "But by Zeus," said the Chaldaeans, "we could not work even our own land in safety, let alone work theirs, if they should hold the heights."

"What if, on the other hand," he said, "the heights were allied to you?"

"This would be fine by us," they said.

"But by Zeus," said the Armenian, "it would not be fine by us, if they should take the heights again, especially after they have been fortified."

(22) And Cyrus said, "Then I shall do the following: I shall surrender the heights to neither of you, but we shall guard them. And if either of you is unjust, we shall side with those suffering injustice."

(23) When they heard these things, both praised them and said that only in this way would the peace be secure. They also all gave and received pledges of trust on these terms, and they made accords that each be free from the other, that there be intermarriage, cross-cultivation, and cross-grazing, and that there be a defensive alliance in common if someone should be unjust to either. (24) So things were then done like this, and still even now they remain just so, the accords

that then arose between the Chaldaeans and him who held Armenia. After the accords were made, both began working together eagerly on a fort, for it was to be a guard post held in common, and they brought into it what was required. (25) When evening came, Cyrus brought both to himself, already friends, as his dinner guests. While they were dining, one of the Chaldaeans said that the new arrangements were very well received by all of them, except that there were some Chaldaeans who lived by plundering and neither understood how to work nor would be capable of it, since they were accustomed to live by war, for they always used to go plundering or serve as mercenaries—often for the king of the Indians (for they said he was a very rich man), and often also for Astyages.

And Cyrus said, (26) "Why then do not they serve as mercenaries for me even now? I will give as much as any other has ever given." They spoke in support and said that there would be many who would be willing.

(27) So these things were agreed to in this way. But when Cyrus heard that the Chaldaeans often went to the Indian [king], he remembered that [Indians] had come to Media in order to investigate their affairs and that they then departed to the enemy, in order to see also theirs, and he wished the Indian to learn what he had accomplished. (28) So he began a discussion like this: "Tell me, Armenian and you Chaldaeans, if I should now send one of my own troops to the Indian, would you send along for me some of yours who could guide him along the road and could collaborate so that we obtain what I wish from the Indian? I wish we had still more money, so that I could give wages abundantly to whomever I ought and could honor and give gifts to those on the campaign who are deserving. It is on this account that I wish to have money as abundantly as possible, believing that I need it; but it is pleasant for me to be sparing of yours, for I believe that you are already friends. I would, however, be pleased to take some from the Indian, if he would give it. (29) Now the messenger to whom I bade you to give guides and fellow workers will go there and say the following: 'Cyrus sent me to you, Indian. He says that he needs more money, since he expects another army from his home in Persia'—for I do expect one.'If you send him as much as is convenient for you, he says that if a god gives him a good result, he will try to act in such a way that you will believe you deliberated

nobly when you gratified him.' (30) This is what the one I send will
say. To those you send enjoin what seems to you to be suitable. If we
get money from him, we will use it bounteously. If we get nothing,
we will know that we owe him no favor, and it will be possible for us
as far as he is concerned to dispose everything with a view to our own
advantage." (31) This is what Cyrus said, and he believed that the Armenians and Chaldaeans who went would say such things about him
as he himself desired all human beings both to say and to hear about
him. And then, when it was fine to do so, they broke up the gathering and rested.

ᐩ Chapter 3 ᐩ

(1) On the next day Cyrus instructed his messenger in what he had
said, and sent him off, and the Armenian and the Chaldaeans sent
along those whom they believed to be most competent both to act as
fellow workers and to say what was appropriate about Cyrus. After
this Cyrus provided the guardhouse with competent guards and with
everything required; and after leaving them a ruler, a Median whom
he thought would be especially gratifying to Cyaxares, he assembled
his army—now consisting of the one he came with, together with the
one he added from the Armenians and the troops from the Chaldaeans, who numbered about four thousand and thought that they
were superior to all the others—and went away. (2) When he went
down into the inhabited country, none of the Armenians remained inside, neither man nor woman, but in their pleasure at the peace all
went out to meet him, and they carried or drove in herds whatever
they had that was of value. And the Armenian was not annoyed with
them, for he believed that Cyrus would be more pleased like this, with
an honor bestowed by all. Finally, the Armenian's wife with her
daughters and her younger son also went out to meet him, and along
with other gifts she brought the gold that Cyrus previously had not
been willing to take.

(3) On seeing it Cyrus said, "You will not make me go around and
do good deeds for a wage. But go, woman, and take with you the
valuables that you have carried here; and no longer let the Armenian

bury them, but use them to equip your son for the campaign and send him off as nobly as possible. From what is left, acquire for yourself, your husband, your daughters, and your sons those possessions with which you will both adorn yourselves more beautifully and live out your lives more pleasantly. But let it suffice to hide bodies in the earth, whenever each may meet his end." (4) Having said this, he rode past them, but the Armenian escorted him, as did all other people, repeatedly calling him "benefactor," "good man." This they did even until they had escorted him out of their country. And on the grounds that there was peace at home, the Armenian sent along with him an even greater army. (5) Thus Cyrus not only went back enriched with the valuables he took, but had also by his manner made ready much more than this for future use, so that he could take it when it might be needed.[13] He then camped upon the borders. On the next day he sent the army and the money to Cyaxares. He was nearby, as he had said he would be. He himself went hunting with Tigranes and the best of the Persians wherever they happened upon game, and they enjoyed themselves.

(6) When he arrived back in Media, he gave to each of his own captains as much of the money as seemed to be sufficient, in order that they too could bestow honors if they admired any of those beneath themselves, for he believed that if each could make his own part worthy of praise, the whole would be in fine condition for him. And he himself used to acquire whatever he saw that was beautiful for an army and use it for gifts to the most deserving, for he believed that he was himself adorned by whatever noble and good things the army had.

(7) When he gave them what he had taken, he spoke somewhat as follows into the midst of the captains, lieutenants, and all those he honored: "Men, friends, it seems that a certain satisfaction now attends us, both because an abundance has come to us and because we have the wherewithal by which we will be able to honor whomever we wish and be honored in whatever way each deserves. (8) But let us by all means remember what sort of deeds are the causes of these good things. You will find, on examination, that they are to go without sleep wherever one must, to work hard, to make haste, and not to yield to enemies. We must thus be good men also in the future, knowing that obedience, steadfastness, and, at the opportune

moment, hard work and facing dangers provide great pleasures and great goods."

(9) Now Cyrus was aware of how good for him his soldiers' bodies were at being able to bear up to military labors, and how good their souls were at holding the enemy in disdain; they each understood what was appropriate for their own sort of weaponry; and he saw that all were well prepared for obeying their rulers. From all this, then, he desired to take some action against the enemy now, knowing that rulers' noble preparations often are made otherwise by their hesitation. (10) He saw, moreover, that since they were ambitious in those things in which they competed, many of the soldiers were also envious of each other. He wished also for these [reasons] to lead them out into enemy territory as quickly as possible, knowing that common risks make allies friendly-minded toward each other, and in this situation they no longer envy either those who adorn themselves in their arms or those who desire reputation. Further, troops of this sort even praise and applaud those like themselves, believing them to be fellow workers for the common good. (11) Therefore, first he armed his army completely and arranged it as beautifully and as well as he was able; he next called together his brigadier generals, colonels, captains, and lieutenants. (These were exempted from being enrolled among the marshaled troops, and not even when they might have to attend their commander or pass along a command was anything left without rule, but everything left behind was kept in order by the sergeants and corporals.) (12) When these chief aides came together, he took them around, and he both showed them that things were in fine condition and taught them the strength of each of the allies.[14] After he had made also this group desirous of doing something right away, he told them to go back to their units, to teach each his own troops what he had himself taught them, and to try to implant into all a desire for beginning the campaign, so that they all might set out in highest spirits.[15] He also told them to report at Cyaxares' doors in early morning. (13) They then went away, and all acted accordingly.

At dawn of the next day, the chief aides were present at his doors. Along with them, then, Cyrus went in to Cyaxares and began a discussion like this: "I know, Cyaxares, that what I am about to say has been for a long time your thought no less than ours. But perhaps you are ashamed to speak of it, lest it be thought that you propose our marching out because you are annoyed at maintaining us. (14) Now since you are silent, I will speak on both your behalf and ours, for it seems [good] to us all, since we have made our preparations, neither to do battle at the time when the enemy thrusts into your country nor to sit and wait in friendly territory, but to go as quickly as possible into enemy territory, (15) for since we are now in your country, we involuntarily damage much of what is yours; if we go into enemy territory, we will with pleasure do harm to what is theirs. (16) Next, you now spend a great deal to maintain us; if we go out on campaign, we will maintain ourselves from the enemy's territory. (17) Further, if the risk were greater there than here, perhaps the safest course would have to be chosen. But as it is, their numbers will be the same whether we wait for them here or go out to meet them by going into their territory; our numbers will be the same when we fight whether we receive an attack of theirs here or join battle by moving against them. (18) However, we will avail ourselves of much better and more robust souls in our soldiers if we move against our foes and do not seem unwilling to look upon our enemy. And they will fear us much more when they hear that we are not sitting at home, cowering in fear of them; that, when we perceive them advancing, we go to meet them in order to join battle with them as quickly as possible; and that we do not wait around until our country is harmed, but we get a head start on them and are already ravaging their country. (19) And if we make them at all more frightened and we ourselves more confident, I believe this to be a very great advantage for us, and I thus calculate the risk to be smaller for us and greater for our enemy. And my father always said, and you also say, and all others agree, that battles are decided more by souls than by the robustness of bodies."

(20) Thus he spoke, and Cyaxares answered, "But Cyrus and the rest of you Persians, do not suspect that I am annoyed at maintaining you. However, as for going into enemy territory now, it seems to me too to be better than all alternatives."

"Then since we agree," said Cyrus, "let us prepare, and if the [signs] of the gods quickly favor us, let us go out as quickly as possible."

(21) After this they told the soldiers to get ready. Cyrus sacrificed first to Zeus the king, and then to other gods; he asked that they, being propitious and well disposed, be leaders for the army, as well as good assistants, allies, and advisers of what is good. He also invoked the

heroes of the Median soil, who were its inhabitants and protectors. (22) When he obtained favorable signs, and his army was collected at the borders, he then, after meeting with bird omens on the right, thrust into enemy territory. As soon as he had crossed the borders, he there again performed propitiatory rites both to Earth, with libations, and to gods, with sacrifices, and he also sought to propitiate the heroes of Assyria, who were its inhabitants. Having done these things, he again sacrificed to ancestral Zeus, and if any other of the gods came to his attention, he did not neglect it.[16]

(23) When things were fine in this regard, they at once led the infantry forward a short distance and made camp, and with the cavalry they made raids and captured vast and varied booty. And after this, while changing their camp, having what they required in abundance, and ravaging the country, they awaited the enemy. (24) Then, when in their approach they were said to be not ten days distant, Cyrus said, "Cyaxares, it is time to go to meet them, and not to seem either to the enemy or to our own troops to be afraid of going out in opposition. Let it be clear that we are not fighting unwillingly." (25) When this seemed [good] to Cyaxares as well, they therefore advanced in battle order as far each day as seemed to them to be fine. They always made dinner by daylight, and they did not burn fires at night in the camp. They burned them in front of the camp, however, in order that they might by the fire see whether anyone approached at night, while not being seen by those approaching. Often they also burned fires behind the camp in order to deceive the enemy. There were consequently times when scouts fell upon their advance guard, for because of the fires at the rear they thought that they were still far from the camp.

(26) Now when they were near each other, the Assyrians and those with them surrounded themselves with a trench, which the barbarian kings still do even now. Wherever they encamp, they easily surround themselves with a trench because they have many hands at work, for they know that at night a cavalry army is full of confusion and hard to use, especially a barbarian one, (27) for they keep their horses fettered at their mangers, and if anyone comes against them, it is a difficult task to free the horses, a difficult task to bridle the horses, a difficult task to saddle the horses, a difficult task to put on their breastplates, and altogether impossible to mount their horses and ride through the camp. On account of all these problems, both they and

the other barbarians surround themselves with defenses, and it also seems to them that being in a secure area grants them the liberty of fighting whenever they wish.

(28) So they were doing such things as they drew near to each other. When in their approach they were a parasang apart, the Assyrians made camp in the manner just said, in an entrenched spot, but one exposed to view.[17] Cyrus, however, by keeping villages and hills in front of him, camped in a spot as little visible as possible, for he believed that everything pertaining to war is more fearful to the opposition when seen suddenly. And after setting their advance guards for that night, as was fitting, each side went to rest.

(29) On the next day the Assyrian, Croesus, and the other leaders rested their armies inside the secure area, and Cyrus and Cyaxares waited in battle order, intending to fight if the enemy advanced. When it was clear that the enemy was not coming out of the fortification, and that they would not do battle that day, Cyaxares called Cyrus and the other chief aides and spoke as follows: (30) "It seems to me, men, that marshaled for battle just as we now happen to be, we should advance up to the fortification of these men and make it clear that we are willing to fight, for in this way, if they do not come out against us, our troops will go away more confident, and the enemy, having seen our daring, will be more afraid." So this is how it seemed to him.

(31) But Cyrus said, "No, by the gods, let us not do it at all like this, for if we march up while exposed to view, as you order, the enemy will gaze upon us as we approach but will not be afraid, knowing that they are safely protected against suffering any harm. Further, when we go away without having done anything and they see that our numbers fall much short of their own, they will hold us in contempt and will come out tomorrow much more robust in their judgments. (32) But now, knowing that we are present and yet not seeing us, do understand that they do not hold us in contempt, but they are wondering, 'Whatever is going on?'[18] and I am sure that they do not stop conversing about us. When they come out, then we must at once both show ourselves to them and go immediately to close quarters, having caught them where long ago we wished we would."

(33) After Cyrus had spoken like this, it was so resolved by Cyaxares and the others. And after they had dinner made, stationed guards, and

lit many fires in front of the guards, they went to bed. (34) Early on the next day Cyrus put on a wreath and sacrificed, and he passed the word also to the other Peers to put on wreaths and attend the sacrifices. When the sacrificing came to an end, he called them together and said, "Men, as the prophets say and as it seems to me as well, the gods fore-tell that there will be a battle, they grant victory, and they promise safety. This they do through the sacrifices.[19] (35) I would be ashamed to recite for you how you must act in a situation such as this, for I am sure that you understand this, that it has been a care of yours, and that you have heard and hear continually the same things as I, so it is likely you could teach others as well. Yet if you happen not to have consid-ered the following, listen. (36) In regard to those whom we have re-cently taken as allies and whom we are trying to make like unto our-selves, these we must remind of the terms on which we are maintained by Cyaxares, of what we practiced, of why we called them to our side, and of that for which they said they would gladly become our rivals. (37) Remind them also that this day will show what each is worth. Concerning those things in which human beings are late learners, it is not remarkable if some of them should require someone to give re-minders; rather, one should be content if they would be able to be good men even from mere prompts. (38) And at the same time as you do this, moreover, you will be taking a test also of yourselves, for who-ever is capable of making others better on such an occasion would properly be conscious in himself of being a completely good man; but he who keeps the admonition to these [good deeds] in himself alone, and is content with this, would properly believe himself to be only half complete. (39) Why I am not speaking to them, but am ordering you to do so, is so that they may try to gratify you, for you are near to them, each in his own part. Understand well that if you display yourselves to them as being confident, you will not by word but by deed teach them and many others to be confident as well." (40) In conclusion, he told them to withdraw, to put on wreaths and have breakfast, to make their libations, and to enter into their battle orders with their wreaths still on. After they went away, he next called the leaders of the rear guard, and he enjoined them like this: (41) "Persian men, you too are among the Peers and have been selected [for the rear guard] because you seem to be like the best in other respects, and you are also more prudent owing to your age. You therefore have a place no less hon-

ored than those in the front, for you who are in the back, by oversee-
ing and encouraging the good, could make them still better, and, if
anyone should be slack and you should see it, you would not allow it.
(42) Victory is advantageous for you, if for anyone, both because of
your age and because of the weight of your equipment. So if those in
front call upon you and command you to follow, heed them; and so
that you are not surpassed by them in this, do so while commanding
in return that they lead more swiftly against the enemy. Withdraw,
have breakfast, and enter with the others into your battle orders with
your wreaths on."

(43) Now Cyrus and his men were occupied like this, but the Assyrians had their breakfast, went out boldly, and were resolutely positioning themselves for battle. While driving around on his chariot,
the king himself was getting them into battle order and exhorting
them like this: (44) "Assyrian men, now you must be good men, for
now the contest is over your lives, over the land in which you were
born, over the houses in which you were raised, over your women
and children, and over all the good things that you possess, for if you
conquer, you will be lords over all these things just as before. If you
are defeated, surely you will surrender all this to the enemy. (45) So
inasmuch as you love victory, stand and fight: It is foolish if those who
wish to conquer run away and thereby assign the blind, unarmed,
and helpless parts of their bodies to face the enemy. If anyone who
wishes to live should undertake to run away, knowing that the victors save themselves, while those who run away are killed more often
than those who stand fast, he is a fool. If someone who desires money
embraces defeat, he is a fool. For who does not know that victors both
save what belongs to themselves and take in addition what belongs
to the defeated, while the defeated at the same time throw away themselves and everything that belongs to themselves?" So the Assyrian
was involved in things like this.

(46) But Cyaxares, sending to Cyrus, said that it was now opportune to lead on against the enemy. "For if those outside of the fortification are now still few," he said, "by the time we arrive, there will be
many of them. Let us not wait until they become more numerous than
we. Let us go while we still think we will overcome them easily."

(47) Cyrus answered, "Cyaxares, unless more than half of them are
defeated, they will surely say that we set upon a few out of fear of

their numbers. They will not believe themselves defeated, and you will still need to fight another battle, one in which they would perhaps deliberate better than they have deliberated now, since they are surrendering themselves to us to be counted out so that we may fight with as many of them as we wish." (48) After hearing this, the messengers departed.

Chrysantas the Persian then arrived along with some other Peers who were leading in captives. And Cyrus, as was to be expected, asked the captives about the enemy. They said that they were already going out with their weapons, that the king himself was outside getting them into order, and that he was exhorting them in many strong terms, as they had been told by those who had heard directly.

(49) Then Chrysantas asked, "Cyrus, what if you should call the troops together and exhort them while it is still possible, if perhaps you too could make the soldiers better?"

(50) And Cyrus said, "Chrysantas, do not be distressed by the Assyrian's exhortations, for there is no exhortation so noble that it will in a single day make good those who are not good when they hear it. It could not make good bowmen, unless they had previously practiced with care, nor spearmen, nor knights, nor even those competent to labor with their bodies, unless they had previously exercised."

(51) And Chrysantas said, "But Cyrus, it is sufficient if in your exhortation you make their souls better."

"And could a single spoken word on a single day," said Cyrus, "have the power to fill with respect the souls of those who hear it, or avert them from what is shameful; could it turn them to the view that they must embrace every labor and every risk for the sake of praise; could it bring it securely into their judgment that one must choose to die in battle rather than to be safe in flight? (52) If such thoughts are going to be inscribed in human beings and remain abiding, must not there first be such laws as will provide an honored and free life for the good and impose a lifetime wretched, grievous, and not worth living upon the bad? (53) Next, there must surely be teachers and rulers over them who will correctly show, teach, and habituate them to do these things until it is inbred in them to really believe that the good and famous are most happy, and to hold that the bad and infamous are most wretched of all, for those who are going to give evidence that their learning is stronger than the fear of enemies must be disposed like this. (54) If it should be in someone's power, as troops with their arms are going off into battle, on which occasion many people abandon even what they learned long ago, to make men warlike by some instant recitations, then it would be the easiest of all things both to learn and to teach the greatest virtue for human beings. (55) Regarding these whom we have now taken on and had exercise next to ourselves, I, at least, would not trust them to persevere if I did not also see that you are present, you who will be a model to them of how they ought to be and will be able to prompt them if they forget something. Regarding those completely uneducated in virtue, I would be amazed, Chrysantas, if a word nobly spoken would benefit them any more in the goodness of a man than a song beautifully sung would benefit in music those uneducated in music."

(56) So they were discussing such things. Cyaxares sent again and said that Cyrus was making a mistake in letting time pass and not marching against the enemy as soon as possible. Cyrus then responded to the messengers, "But be assured that there are not yet as many of them out as there ought to be. Report this to him in front of everyone. Nevertheless, since it seems [good] to him, I shall now march." (57) After saying this and praying to the gods, he led the army out. When he began to lead, he immediately led quite quickly, and they followed in good order, because they understood how and had carefully practiced marching in order; robustly, because they were competitive with each other, because they had done bodily labor, and because all their rulers were in the front ranks; with pleasure, because they were prudent, for they understood and had learned over a long time that going to close quarters with the enemy was safest and easiest, especially against archers, spearmen, and knights. (58) While they were still outside of the arrows' range, Cyrus passed the watchword, "Zeus, ally and leader." When the watchword was passed along and came back again, he began the customary paean to the Dioscuri; and they all devoutly joined the chant with a loud voice, for on such an occasion, those who fear divinities fear human beings less.[20] (59) After the paean, the Peers marched along radiantly, educated, looking at each other, calling by name those who were beside and behind them. Often saying, "Come on, men, friends! Come on, good men!" they called on each other to follow. Those in the rear, on hearing them, in turn exhorted the front ranks to lead robustly. Cyrus'

army was full of zeal, ambition, strength, confidence, mutual exhortation, moderation, obedience; this, I think, is most terrible for the opposition.

(60) Of the Assyrians, the charioteers who were supposed to fight in the forefront got back up onto their chariots and withdrew to their own multitude as soon as the Persian multitude came near. Their archers, spearmen, and slingers shot their missiles much before they could reach their targets.

(61) When in their advance the Persians were marching over the shot missiles, Cyrus cried out, "Best men, let someone now make himself conspicuous by going more quickly; pass it on." They passed it on, and out of zeal, strength, and haste to join with the enemy, some began to run, and the whole phalanx followed at a run. (62) Forgetting the walking pace, Cyrus himself led the run and at the same time cried out, "Who will follow? Who will be good? Who will be first to strike a man down?" On hearing him, they cried out these same things, and these words traveled through all the ranks in just the way Cyrus had urged, "Who will follow? Who will be good?"

(63) So this is how the Persians were as they brought themselves to close quarters; but the enemy was no longer able to stand fast, and they turned and began fleeing into their fortification. (64) The Persians, on the other hand, followed them to the gates where they were jostling with each other, and they slaughtered many. Those who fell into the trenches they leaped upon and killed, men and horses together—in their flight, some of the chariots were compelled to fall into the trenches. (65) When they saw all this, the Median cavalry attacked the enemy cavalry, and they too gave way. Then, of course, there was a great chase of horses as well as of men, and a slaughter of both. (66) There were those who stood upon the rampart of the trench inside the Assyrians' fortification, but as for shooting their arrows or throwing their spears at those who were doing the killing, they neither thought of it nor had the power because of the terrible sights and their fear. Learning that some of the Persians had cut through to the entrances of the fortification, they quickly began to turn away even from the inside ramparts. (67) When the women of the Assyrians and their allies saw that people were already in flight even inside the camp, they began to cry out and run in terror, some with children, others even younger; and they ripped their garments

and tore at their skin, begging whomever they happened upon not to flee and leave them but rather to defend them, their children, and themselves. (68) Then even the kings themselves stood with their most trusted troops at the entrances, and going up on the ramparts, they both did battle themselves and exhorted the others to do so. (69) When Cyrus recognized what was happening, he was afraid that, even if they should force their way inside, they might be overcome, since they were few against many, so he commanded them to obey and march backward in retreat until out of bowshot. (70) It was then indeed that one might have known that the Peers had been educated as they ought to have been, for they themselves obeyed quickly, and they quickly passed the word to others. When they were out of bowshot, they halted in their places, knowing much more accurately than a chorus where each of them had to be.

BOOK IV

～ CHAPTER 1 ～

(1) Cyrus remained there a measured amount of time with his army and showed that they were ready to do battle if anyone should come out. When no one came out in opposition, he withdrew as far as seemed noble and encamped. After posting guards and sending scouts forward, he took a central position, called together his own soldiers, and spoke as follows: (2) "Persian men, first I praise the gods as much as is in my power, as do you all, I am sure, for we have obtained both victory and safety. For these [blessings], then, thank offerings to the gods must be performed from what we have. Now I praise you all together, for the work that has been done has been nobly performed by you all together. After I inquire from the appropriate sources what each deserves to receive, I shall then try to assign to each his due in both speech and deed. (3) As for the captain nearest to me, Chrysantas, I do not need to inquire anything from others, but I myself know how he was, for he did the other things that I am sure you all did as well. Yet when I commanded you to retreat and called him by name, he obeyed, even though he had raised his sword to strike an enemy, and putting aside what he was about to do, he did what was ordered, for he both himself retreated and commanded it in all haste to others. He consequently got a head start on the enemy and withdrew his company outside of bowshot before they, realizing that we were retreating, bent their bows and threw their spears. He

is consequently unharmed himself, and because of obedience, he also has kept his own men unharmed. (4) I see others who have been wounded; I will disclose my judgment about them after I examine the time in which they were wounded. Yet now, as industrious in things military, as prudent, and as competent both to rule and to be ruled, I honor Chrysantas with a colonelcy. And whenever god may grant some other good, I shall not then forget him. (5) And I wish you all to remember: Do not ever cease taking to heart what you have just seen in this battle. You may then always judge for yourselves whether virtue saves lives more than does flight, whether those who are willing to fight escape more easily than do those who are not willing, and what sort of pleasure victory provides, for it is now that you could judge these things best, since you have experience of them and the event has just now occurred. (6) And if you always think these thoughts, you would be better. But now, as dear to the gods, good, and moderate men, have your dinner, pour your libations to the gods, begin the paean, and at the same time attend to what is announced."

(7) After saying these things, he mounted his horse and rode off. Coming to Cyaxares, he savored the pleasure in common with him, as was to be expected, and after seeing things there and asking if he needed anything, he rode back to his own army. And those with Cyrus, after having dinner and posting guards as needed, went to rest.

(8) As for the Assyrians, since both their ruler and with him nearly all the best troops were dead, all were despondent, and many of them had run away from the camp during the night. When Croesus and their other allies saw this, they became despondent, for everything was difficult, but what provided the greatest despondency for all was that the army's leading tribe was altogether corrupted in its judgment. Thus they left the camp and went away during the night. (9) When day came and the enemy camp appeared empty of men, Cyrus immediately had the Persians cross over first. Left behind by the enemy were many sheep, many cattle, and many carts filled with many good things. After this, Cyaxares then crossed over with all the Medes, and they made their breakfast there.

(10) After they had breakfast, Cyrus called his captains together and spoke as follows: "How great and numerous are the good things we seem to me to have thrown away, even though the gods gave them to us to take! For now you yourselves see that our enemies have run

away in fear of us. They were inside a fortification, left it, and are taking flight: How could anyone think that they would stand their ground if they should see us on a level field? They could not stand fast when inexperienced of us: How could they now stand fast after having been defeated and suffering many evils at our hands? The best of them have perished: How could the worse be willing to do battle with us?"

And someone said, (11) "Why do we not go in pursuit as quickly as possible, since these good things are so obvious?"

And he said, "Because we lack horses, for the best among our enemy, whom it would have been especially opportune to capture or kill, will be on horseback. Those whom, with the gods, we are competent to turn to flight we are not competent to take by pursuit."

(12) "Why, then," they said, "do you not go and say this to Cyaxares?"

And he said, "Then all of you follow me, so that he may see that this is how it seems to all of us." After this they all followed him and said the sort of things they thought required to get what they wanted.

(13) Now because they were the first to make the argument, Cyaxares was envious; perhaps it also seemed to him to be fine that they not run further risks, for he, as it happened, was busy enjoying himself, and he saw many of the other Medes doing the same thing. So he spoke as follows: (14) "Cyrus, that of all human beings you Persians take the noblest care not to be insatiably disposed toward any single pleasure I know both by seeing and by hearing. Yet it seems to me to be most especially advantageous to be continent in the greatest pleasure. And what provides human beings with a greater pleasure than the good fortune that has now come to us? (15) If then, when we enjoy good fortune, we guard it moderately, it would perhaps be within our power to grow old in happiness without risk. Yet if we are insatiable in this, and try to pursue first one and then another [instance of good fortune], watch out that we do not suffer what they say that many have suffered at sea, to be unwilling—on account of their good fortune—to cease sailing until they perish; and they say that many, chancing on one victory but desiring another, throw away the first, (16) for if our enemies fled because they were weaker than we, perhaps it would be safe also to pursue these weaker troops. But now bear in mind what a small

fraction of them we have conquered, though all of us fought. The others did not fight; if we do not compel them to fight us, they will go away in ignorance both of us and of themselves, because of their lack of learning and their softness. If they come to know that they will be running risks no less by going away than by standing fast, beware lest we compel them to become good, even if they do not want to, (17) for surely you do not desire to take their women and children more than they desire to save them.[1] Consider that sows flee with their offspring whenever they are seen, even if there are many of them; but whenever someone hunts one of their offspring, [the mother] no longer flees, not even if she happens to be alone, but she charges the one who is trying to make the capture. (18) And now they locked themselves up inside their fortifications and offered themselves to us to be counted out, so we fought with as many of them as we wished. If we go against them on the plain and they learn to oppose us in separate detachments—some right in our faces, as just now, but others from the sides and still others from behind—watch out that each of us not need many hands and eyes. Moreover, since I see the Medes enjoying themselves, I would not now wish to rouse them and compel them to go off in order to run risks."

(19) And Cyrus said in reply, "But do not compel anyone; rather, grant me those who are willing to follow along. And perhaps we would return bringing you and each of these friends of yours things with which you will all enjoy yourselves. We will not even pursue the main body of the enemy, for how would we catch them? But if we catch some part detached from the army, or left behind it, we will bring it back to you. (20) Consider that when you asked, we traveled a long way to gratify you. So it is just that you now gratify us in return, so that we may go home with something in our possession and that we not all look to your treasury."

(21) Then Cyaxares said, "But if someone should follow along willingly, I would even be grateful to you."

"Then send with me," he said, "one of these your trusted troops to announce what you command."

"Come and take," he said, "whomever of these you want."

(22) He who had once said that he was his relative, and had gotten kissed, happened now to be present, so Cyrus immediately said, "He is sufficient for me."[2]

"Then let him follow you. And you declare," he said, "that anyone willing is to go with Cyrus."

(23) Thus he took the man and went out. After they came out, Cyrus immediately said, "You will now show whether you spoke the truth when you said that you took pleasure in gazing on me."

"Then I will never leave you," said the Mede, "if this is what you mean."

And Cyrus said, "Then will you be enthusiastic in leading out others as well?"

He said with an oath, "Yes, by Zeus, to the extent that I shall make you also pleased to gaze on me."

(24) Then, having been sent out by Cyaxares, he reported with enthusiasm the other things to the Medes, and he added that he himself would not leave the noblest and best man, and most important, one descended from gods.

∽ CHAPTER 2 ∽

(1) While Cyrus was doing these things, messengers from the Hyrcanians arrived somehow divinely. The Hyrcanians are the Assyrians' neighbors, but they are not a great nation, so they were also the Assyrians' subjects. They were then reputed to be good riders and are still so reputed now, so the Assyrians used them just as the Lacedaemonians use the Sciritae, sparing them neither labors nor risks. And thus on this occasion they commanded them, being about a thousand cavalry, to guard the rear, so that if anything terrible should come from that direction, they would get it first. (2) Since the Hyrcanians were going to march in the back, they also had their own wagons and families in the back, for many of those who dwell in Asia take along the members of their households when they go on campaign, and this was how the Hyrcanians were then campaigning. (3) Reflecting that they suffered so at the hands of the Assyrians, that these had just been defeated and their ruler killed, that there was fear in their army, and that their allies were despondent and were deserting, it seemed to them, as they took these things to heart, that it was now a noble thing to revolt, if Cyrus and those with him should be

willing to join the attack. They sent messengers to Cyrus, for his name
had been greatly elevated because of the battle. (4) Those sent said to
Cyrus that it was just for them to hate the Assyrians and that now, if
he wished to attack them, they would be his allies and guides. At the
same time they also described the condition of the enemies' affairs,
wishing above all to incite him to go on campaign.

(5) And Cyrus asked them, "Do you think that we could still catch
them before they are in their forts? For we hold it to be a great misfortune that they got a head start on us in running away." He said this
wishing them to think as highly as possible of himself and his troops.

(6) They answered that if they started out at dawn without heavy
gear, they would catch them even on the next day. "Since they are a
mob with many wagons, they are scarcely marching. Further," they
said, "they have now made camp after only a short advance, for they
went without sleep on the previous night."

(7) And Cyrus said, "Do you have any assurance of what you say,
then, to teach us that you are telling the truth?"

"We are willing to ride at once and bring hostages during the
night," they said. "Only perform for us the assurances of the gods and
give us your right hand, so that we may take to the others the very
signs we ourselves receive from you."

(8) He then swore and gave them assurances that if they remained
firm in what they said, he would treat them as friends and trusted
troops, so that they would receive no less from him than either Persians or Medes. Even now it is still possible to see Hyrcanians who
are trusted and hold office, just as do those of the Persians and Medes
who seem to be deserving.

(9) After they had dinner, he led the army out while it was still light,
and he ordered the Hyrcanians to wait, in order that they might go
together. Now as was to be expected, all the Persians immediately
came out, as did Tigranes with his own army. (10) Of the Medes, some
came out because when they were boys, they had been friends with
Cyrus when he was a boy; others because when they had been with
him on hunts, they admired his manner; others because they felt
grateful to him, since he seemed to have warded off a major threat for
them; others also had hopes that because he appeared to be a good
and fortunate man, he would one day be exceedingly great; others, if
he did anything good for anyone when he was growing up among

the Medes, wished to gratify him in return (and because of his benevolence he had done through his grandfather many good things for many people).³ But when they saw the Hyrcanians, and the argument circulated that they would guide them to many good things, many came out also in order to get something. (11) Thus nearly all the Medes came out, except those who happened to be at Cyaxares' tent party; they and their subordinates stayed back. Yet all the others set out radiantly and enthusiastically, since they were going out not by necessity but willingly and for gratitude.⁴ (12) When they were outside, Cyrus went first to the Medes, and praised them and prayed especially that the gods be propitious in guiding them and the Persians, and next that he himself have the power to pay back the favor of their enthusiasm. He said in conclusion that the infantry would guide them, and he ordered them to follow with their horses. And wherever they rested or stopped their march, he commanded some of them to ride up to him, so they might know what the occasion demanded.

(13) After this he ordered the Hyrcanians to lead the way. And they asked, "What! Are you not waiting until we bring back the hostages, so that you may have guarantees from us as you march?"

And he is said to have answered, "No, for I consider that we have guarantees in all our souls and in all our hands. As it is, we think we have prepared ourselves, if you are telling the truth, to be competent to bestow benefits; but if you are deceiving us, we believe things to be such that we will not be in your hands, but rather, if the gods are willing, you will be in ours. And, Hyrcanians, since you say that your people are marching last, signal to us that they are yours as soon as you see them, in order that we may spare them." (14) After hearing this, the Hyrcanians led the way, as he had ordered, while they also wondered at the strength of his soul. They no longer feared either Assyrians or Lydians or their allies, but they were frightened entirely that Cyrus might think it of little moment whether they came or left.

(15) They were marching when night came on, and it is said that a light from heaven became plainly apparent to Cyrus and the army, so that there arose in all a shuddering toward the divine, but boldness toward the enemy. As they were marching without heavy gear and quickly, they are likely to have traveled a long way, and at dawn they were near the army of the Hyrcanians. (16) When the messengers recognized them, they said to Cyrus that these people were their own,

for they said they recognized them both by their being last and by the number of their fires. (17) After this he sent one of the Hyrcanians to them, enjoining him to tell them, if they were friends, to come to meet them as quickly as possible with their right hands raised. He sent along also one of his own group, and he ordered him to say to the Hyrcanians that Cyrus' troops would conduct themselves in whatever manner they saw them use in their approach. Thus one of the messengers remained with Cyrus, and the other rode to the Hyrcanians. (18) While he was examining the Hyrcanians to see what they would do, Cyrus brought his army to a halt. Tigranes and the foremost of the Medes rode to him and asked what was to be done. He said to them, "This nearby army is that of the Hyrcanians. The other of their messengers has gone to them, and with him one of ours, in order to ask that if they are friends, they all come to meet us with their right hands raised. Now if they do this, greet them with your right hands, each the person opposite him, and offer them encouragement at the same time. But if they raise their weapons or attempt to flee, we must try to be sure that not even a single one of them is left."

(19) So he gave commands of this sort. The Hyrcanians were pleased when they heard the messengers and, leaping upon their horses, they went up to them, stretching out their right hands as had been announced. The Medes and Persians held out their right hands to them in return and offered encouragement. (20) After this Cyrus said, "We plainly trust you already, Hyrcanians, and you too must be so disposed to us. First tell us how far away from here are the headquarters of our enemies and their main body." They answered that it was little more than a parasang.[5]

(21) Cyrus then said, "Come, men of Persia and Media, and you too, Hyrcanians, for I am already conversing with you too as with allies and partners. We must now know well that we are in a situation such that if we should go soft, we would obtain all the harshest things, since our enemies know what we have come for. If we go against our enemies with strength and spirit, and attack them steadfastly, you will at once see that, just like runaway slaves who have been discovered, some of them beg, others take flight, and others are not capable of thinking even of these things, for they will see us just after their defeat; and they will have been caught without expecting that we would arrive, without having put themselves in

order, and without having prepared themselves to fight. (22) So if it
is with pleasure that we wish to eat, to spend our nights, and to pass
our lives in the future, let us not grant them leisure either to deliberate or to prepare anything good for themselves, nor even to know
that we are human beings at all, but let them believe that shields,
swords, and scimitars have come against them and that beatings
have arrived. (23) And you, Hyrcanians, spread yourselves out and
march in front of us, in order that since your arms will be seen, we
may escape notice for the longest time possible. When I reach the
enemy's army, let each of you leave a cavalry unit with me so that
I, staying at the camp, may use them if there be any need. (24) Ride
massed together in close order, you rulers and elders, if you are
moderate, so that you not be harmed if you should chance upon another massed group, but release the younger troops to give chase.
And have them kill, since it is now safest to leave as few of the enemies as possible. (25) If we conquer, we must guard against turning
to plunder, which has overturned the fortune of many who have
conquered. He who does this is no longer a man but a camp follower, and whoever wishes to use him as a slave has license to do
so. (26) One must know that nothing leads to gain more than does
conquest, since he who conquers also plunders everything all at
once—men, women, valuables, and the entire country. Therefore,
look only to this, that we preserve our conquest, for if he is overcome, the plunderer is himself taken. Remember this too in your
pursuit: Come back to me while it is still light. We will no longer
admit anyone after it is dark."

(27) After saying these things, he dismissed each to his unit, and he
ordered each to signal these same instructions to his own sergeants
during the march (for the sergeants were in front so they could hear
instructions) and to command each of his sergeants to pass it along
to his squad of ten. After this the Hyrcanians began leading the advance, and he himself marched with the Persians at the center.

(28) As for their enemies, when it became light, some were wondering at what they saw, some already knew, some were spreading
the news, some were shouting, some were freeing horses, some were
packing up, some were throwing down arms from the pack animals,
some were arming themselves, some were leaping up on their horses,
some were putting bridles on, some were getting women up into

carts, some were taking the things of greatest value intending to save them, some were caught while trying to bury such things, but most were beginning to flee. One must suppose that they also did many and varied other things, except that no one was fighting, and they were perishing without a battle.

(29) Since it was summer, Croesus the king of the Lydians had sent the women forward in carriages during the night, so they might travel more easily when it was cool, and he himself followed with the cavalry. (30) They say that the Phrygian [king], the one who ruled the Phrygia by the Hellespont, did the same thing. When they perceived that they were being overtaken by people in flight, they inquired what had happened and themselves took flight at a breakneck pace. (31) But as for the kings of the Cappadocians and the Arabians, who were still nearby and offered resistance even unarmed, the Hyrcanians killed them. But most of those killed were Assyrians and Arabians, for since they were in their own land, they were least intent on flight.

(32) Now as the Medes and the Hyrcanians gave chase they did such things as it is likely that conquerors do. Cyrus ordered the cavalry that had been left with him to ride about the camp and, if they should see any coming out with weapons, to kill them. To those who submitted he announced that enemy soldiers, whether knights, targeteers, or archers, should tie their weapons together and carry them away, but leave their horses at the tents; and that whoever did not do this would at once be deprived of his head. Holding their swords stretched out, his troops stood round in order. (33) Now those with weapons brought them to the one place he ordered and threw them down, and those to whom he gave the command burned them.

(34) Cyrus reflected that they had come without food or drink, and without these it is impossible either to campaign or to do anything else. Considering how these things might be procured as nobly and as quickly as possible, he realized that for all those who go on a military campaign, there must of necessity be someone who takes care of their tent and sees to it that whatever is required has been prepared for the soldiers when they come in. (35) He realized moreover that of all those who were in the camp, it was especially likely that it was such servants who had just now been caught because they were busy with the baggage. He thus called for all the stewards to report, and if

there was a tent without a steward, for the oldest from that tent to report. He proclaimed all things harsh for whoever disobeyed. Seeing that even their masters were obeying, they obeyed quickly. (36) After they were present, he ordered all who had more than two months' provisions in their tents to sit down. After he saw them, he next ordered those who had a month's to sit down. Then nearly all were sitting. (37) After he learned this, he spoke to them as follows: "Come now, men, all of you who hate what is evil and would wish to obtain something good from us, take zealous care that there be prepared in each tent twice the food and drink you used to make each day for your masters and the members of their households.[6] Also make ready all the other things that will provide for a noble feast, for whichever side conquers will very soon be present, and they will think they deserve to have an abundance of all provisions. So be assured that it would be advantageous for you to receive the men in a way that cannot be faulted."

(38) So having heard these things, they were doing with great zeal what he ordered, while he called the captains together and spoke as follows: "Men, friends, we know that it is possible for us to have lunch now, sooner than our allies who are absent, and to put to good use this food and drink that has been so earnestly prepared. But it does not seem to me that this lunch would benefit us more than to be visibly concerned for our allies, or that this banquet would make us stronger by as much as if we should be able to make our allies enthusiastic. (39) If—while they are now giving chase, killing our enemies, and fighting if anyone offers opposition—we will seem to neglect them to the point that even before knowing how they are faring we openly have our lunch, beware that we not appear shameful and, at a loss for allies, become weak. To take care that those who are running risks and laboring will have what is required when they come back—this is a feast that would delight us more, as I say, than to gratify our stomachs immediately. (40) Bear in mind that even if there were no need for us to feel ashamed in their presence, neither satiety nor drink befits us now, for what we wish has not yet been accomplished, but these very things are now all in need of the utmost care, for we have enemies in the camp who are many times more numerous than are we ourselves, and they are on the loose. It is still fitting that we both be on guard against them and also guard over them, so

that they will do for us what is required. Moreover, our cavalry is absent, making us worry about where they are, and if they return, about whether they will stay with us. (41) Consequently, men, it now seems to me that we ought to take such food and drink as one would suppose to be especially advantageous for not being satiated with either sleep or immoderation.

(42) "Moreover, there is still a lot of money in the camp, and I am not ignorant of the fact that it is possible for us to appropriate as much as we wish, even though it belongs in common to those who joined in taking it. But it does not seem to me to be a greater gain to take it than, by appearing to be just to them, to try to make them delight in us still more than they do now.[7] (43) It seems to me that we should commit even the distribution of the money to the Medes, Hyrcanians, and Tigranes, when they come back. And if they allocate somewhat less to us, to hold it a gain, for because of these gains, they will be more pleased to stay with us, (44) for seizing the advantage now would provide us wealth that is short-lived, but letting this go and acquiring instead that from which wealth naturally springs, this, as it seems to me, would have the power of providing ageless riches to us and ours. (45) I think that even at home we practiced being superior to our stomachs and untimely gains so that we would be able to make advantageous use of this restraint if ever it should be needed. I do not see that we could display our education on an occasion greater than that now present." (46) Thus he spoke.

Hystaspas, a man who was one of the Persian Peers, spoke in support as follows: "It would be a terrible thing, Cyrus, if when we hunt we often persist without food in order to take some wild animal in hand, and perhaps one of very little worth; but if, in trying to hunt riches in their entirety, we should make an obstacle to ourselves of such [desires] as rule over bad human beings but obey the good, I think we would do what is not befitting us."

(47) Thus spoke Hystaspas, and all the others approved. Cyrus said, "Come; since we are of like minds on this, let each send five of the most serious troops from his platoon; let these go around and praise whomever they see preparing what is required; but let them punish more unsparingly than as masters whomever they see being negligent." So they set about doing this.

❧ CHAPTER 3 ❧

(1) As for the Medes, some had already caught wagons that had set out earlier; and having turned them around, they were driving them in, filled with what an army needs. Others had seized the covered carriages of the women of the highest rank,[8] some of them wedded wives, others concubines who were taken about because of their beauty; and they were bringing them in, (2) for all those who campaign in Asia still take along on the campaign what is most valuable, saying that they would fight more if what is dearest should be present, for they profess that necessity obliges one to defend them zealously. Perhaps this is so, but perhaps they also do this because they take delight in the pleasure.

(3) When he saw the deeds of the Medes and the Hyrcanians, it was as if Cyrus blamed both himself and those with him, since the others seemed at this time both to be flourishing more than they themselves and to be acquiring things, while [the Persians] themselves seemed to be waiting in a place of relative inactivity. For they would bring things in and show them to Cyrus, and then ride out again in pursuit of the others, as they said had been ordered to do by their rulers. Though of course annoyed at this, Cyrus nevertheless put these things in their places, but he also called the captains together again. Standing where all were going to hear the deliberations, he said the following: (4) "Men, friends, if we should secure the things now coming into view, I suppose we all know that great goods would belong to all Persians, and in all likelihood the greatest would be ours, through whom this is accomplished. But how we could become lords over them, when we are not self-sufficient in acquiring them, I do not see, unless the Persians will have a cavalry of their own. (5) Consider this: We Persians have arms with which we think we will turn our enemies by going to close quarters.[9] In turning them, what sort of fleeing knights, archers, or targeteers could we take or kill, since we are without horses? What archers, spearmen, or knights would be afraid to approach and harm us, being assured that there is no risk of their suffering any more harm from us than from trees, given their nature?[10] (6) If this is so, is it not clear that the knights now with us believe that everything in hand belongs no less to themselves than to us, and perhaps, by Zeus, even

more? (7) It is by necessity that this is now so. But if we should acquire a cavalry no worse than theirs, is it not obvious to us all that, in facing our enemies, we would be able to do even without our allies what we now can do only with them, and that we would also then have allies who thought about us in a more measured way? For if we ourselves should be sufficient unto ourselves without them, it would be less of a concern to us when they wished to be present or absent.

(8) "Well, then, I suppose no one would be of a contrary judgment to this, that it would be entirely different if the Persians had their own cavalry. But perhaps you are thinking about how it could come into being. Then let us examine, if we should wish to establish a cavalry, what we now have and what we need. (9) There are indeed many horses right here in the camp, ones that have been captured along with the bridles they obey and as many other things as horses must have to be used. We even have the things a man, a knight must use: breastplates as defenses for our bodies, spears that we could use either for throwing or by holding as lances. (10) What is left? It is clear that men are also needed. Now these we especially have, for nothing is so our own as we are to ourselves. But someone will perhaps say that we do not understand how [to ride]. No, we do not, by Zeus, but even of those who now understand, before they learned, no one understood. But someone could say that they learned when they were children. (11) Are children more prudent than men at learning what is said and demonstrated? Who is more competent to carry out with bodily labor what they have learned, boys or men? (12) And surely we have such leisure to learn as neither children nor other men have, for we need not learn how to shoot the bow, as do boys, for we already understand this, or how to throw spears, for we understand this as well. And unlike the situation of other men, farming does not occupy some of us, arts others, and domestic things others: For us, there is not only the leisure but even the necessity to continue campaigning. (13) And surely it is not like many other military matters, difficult but useful. Is not riding on a journey more pleasant than marching on one's own two feet? Is it not pleasant to be beside one's friend quickly, if it should be necessary in case of emergency, and if it should be necessary to give chase to a man or beast, is it not pleasant to catch him quickly? Is it not convenient that, whatever arms one carries, the horse joins in carrying them, for to hold onto and to carry

are not the same thing. (14) One might be afraid especially if it should be necessary for us to run risks on horseback before we are at our peak in this work, when we are no longer still foot soldiers and are not yet competent knights; but not even this problem is insoluble, for wherever we wish, it will be possible for us to fight as foot soldiers on the instant, for by learning how to ride we will not unlearn anything that belongs to the foot soldier." (15) So Cyrus spoke like this.

Speaking in support, Chrysantas spoke as follows: "But I so desire to learn how to ride that I believe that, if I become a knight, I will be a winged human being. (16) For if I set out to run on an equal basis with some human being, I am now content if I get in front only by a head; and if I see a beast running by, I am now content if I am able to take aim quickly enough so as to throw my spear or shoot my bow before it gets very far ahead. Yet if I become a knight, I will be able to bring down a man, even if he is as far away as I can see. Pursuing and catching beasts, I will be able to strike some at arm's reach and to spear others as if they were standing still, for even if both are moving quickly, when they are near to each other, it is nevertheless as if they were standing still.

(17) "That for which, of all animals, I think I have especially envied the centaur is this, that they were such—if indeed they were such—as to deliberate with the prudence of a human being and fashion what they needed with their hands, but also had the speed and strength of a horse, so that they caught what took flight and overthrew what stood fast. If I become a knight, do I too not provide all this for myself? (18) I will at least be able to take forethought for everything with my human judgment, I will carry my weapons with my hands, I will give chase with my horse, I will overthrow whoever opposes me with the impetus of my horse, but I will not be naturally joined together [with my horse] as were the centaurs. (19) Surely this is superior to being naturally joined, for I suppose that the centaurs were at a loss as to how they could use many of the good things that have been discovered for human beings, and also as to how they could enjoy many of the things naturally pleasant for horses. (20) Yet if I learn how to ride, surely I shall accomplish what the centaurs did, whenever I am on my horse; whenever I get down, I will eat, dress myself, and sleep like other human beings. What else do I become, then, than a centaur that can be divided and put together again? (21) Moreover, I will get an

advantage over the centaur also in this: For he sees with two eyes and hears with two ears, but I will take my bearings by four eyes and will perceive with four ears, since they say that a horse sees many things first with his own eyes and makes them visible to a human being, and that he hears many things first with his own ears and gives signs. Write me down, then, as one of those who very much desires to ride."

"Yes, by Zeus," said all the others, "us too."

(22) After this Cyrus said, "Since this is decided by us so vehemently, what if we should also make a law for ourselves that it be shameful for anyone to whom I provide a horse to be noticed going on foot, whether he must make a long trip or a short one, so that human beings may think that we really are centaurs?" (23) So he posed this question, and they all agreed. Consequently, the Persians since that time continue to use this [practice] today, and no one among the noble and good Persians is willing to be seen going anywhere on foot. So they were involved in these arguments.

∽ CHAPTER 4 ∽

(1) When it was past midday, the Median and Hyrcanian cavalry came in, bringing both the horses and the men they had captured, for they did not kill those who surrendered their arms. (2) When they came in, Cyrus asked them first whether all his troops were safe. When they said they were, he next asked what they had done. They narrated what they did, and gave great accounts of how courageous they were in doing it. (3) He listened with pleasure to everything they wished to say, and then he praised them like this: "But it is clear that you were good men, for you appear taller, more noble, and more terrible to look upon than before." (4) After this he asked them how far they rode and whether the land was inhabited. They said that they had ridden a long way, that it was all inhabited, and that it was full of sheep, goats, cattle, horses, grain, and everything good. (5) "We must be careful about two things," he said, "that we be superior to those who have these things and that they themselves stay put, for an inhabited land is a very valuable possession, but land bereft of human beings becomes bereft of the good things as well. (6) I know

that you killed those who put up a defense," he said, "and you acted
correctly, for this especially preserves a victory. You have led in as
captives those who surrendered; if we release them, we would effect
this advantage, as I say: (7) For first, we would not now need either
to guard against them or guard over them, or even to feed them (for
we will surely not kill them by starvation). Further, by releasing them,
we will have more captives to use, (8) for if we control the land, all
those who inhabit it will be our captives. When the others see that
these are alive and have been released, they will be more inclined to
stay put and to choose to obey rather than fight. I know that this is
so. If anyone sees anything better, let him speak." When they heard
these things, they agreed to do them.

(9) So Cyrus called in the captives and spoke as follows: (10) "Men,
because you obeyed, you just now saved your lives, and if you act
like this also in the future, there will be nothing new for you, other
than that the same person will not rule over you who did before. You
will inhabit the same houses, work the same land, dwell together with
the same wives, and rule over your own children, just as you do now.
You will not, however, fight with us, or with anyone else. (11) But
when someone is unjust to you, we will fight on your behalf. In order
that no one even call upon you to go on campaign, bring us your
weapons, for those who do bring them there will be peace, and we
will hold to what we say without deceit. As for those who do not turn
in their weapons of war, we will of course campaign against them.
(12) If any of you shows that he comes to us in a friendly way, and
that he does something for us or teaches us something, we will treat
him as a benefactor and a friend, not as a slave. Bear this in mind
yourselves, and report it to the others. (13) So if you wish to obey in
these matters but others do not, lead us to them, so that you may rule
over them, not they over you." He said these things, and they prostrated themselves and promised that they would act accordingly.

ᐧᐁᐧ CHAPTER 5 ᐧᐁᐧ

(1) After they departed, Cyrus said, "Medes and Armenians, it is
the hour for us all to have dinner. We have prepared what you need

in the best way we could. But go and send to us half of the bread that has been made, for it is sufficient for us both. Send neither relish nor anything to drink, for we have a sufficient amount prepared for ourselves. (2) Conduct them to the tents, Hyrcanians: the rulers to the largest, for you know them, and the others in whatever way seems finest. And you yourselves may also dine wherever is most pleasant for you, for your tents are safe and intact; preparations have been made for you here, as also for the others. (3) Let this too be known to you both: We will stand guard for you at night against what is outside, but you yourselves must see to what is inside your tents, and dispose your weapons well, for those in the tents are not yet our friends."

(4) Now the Medes and Tigranes' Armenians bathed and, since such preparations had been made, changed their clothes and had dinner; their horses also had what they required. They sent half their bread to the Persians, but they sent neither relish nor wine, for they thought that Cyrus and his troops had these things left in abundance. Yet Cyrus had meant that hunger was their relish and that their drink was from the river flowing by. (5) So after giving the Persians their dinner, Cyrus sent many of them out after dark in fives and tens, and he ordered them to hide in a circle around the camp. He believed that they would guard against anyone trying to enter from outside, and at the same time that they would capture anyone who might try to take money and run away from the inside. And so it was, for many sought to run away, and many were captured. (6) Cyrus allowed those who caught them to keep the money, but the human beings he ordered them to kill. In the future, consequently, you could not easily find anyone traveling at night, even if you wished to. (7) So the Persians conducted themselves like this, but the Medes were drinking, feasting, having flutes played, and sating themselves with every delight, for many such things had been captured, so those awake were not at a loss for something to do.[11]

(8) Cyaxares, the king of the Medes, on the night Cyrus left, both got drunk with those partying in his tent (on the occasion of their presumed good fortune) and also thought the other Medes were still present in the camp, except for a few, for he heard a great commotion. Since their masters had gone away, the Medes' servants were drinking without restraint and making a commotion, especially since they had taken

both wine and many other things from the Assyrian army. (9) When it was day, and no one but those who had dined with him came to his doors, and he heard that the camp was empty of Medes and knights, and he saw, when he went out, that it was so, then of course he fell into a rage at both Cyrus and the Medes for having departed and left him alone. And, as he is said to have been savage and without judgment, he immediately ordered one of those who were present to take his own knights and travel as quickly as possible to Cyrus and the army with him, and say the following: (10) "I did not think that you, Cyrus, would deliberate about me in a way so lacking in foresight,[12] or, if Cyrus is of this judgment, that you Medes would be willing to leave me so alone. Now, whether Cyrus wishes it or not, be here as quickly as possible." (11) So he commanded these things. The one assigned to go said, "And how, master, shall I find them?"

"How did Cyrus," he said, "and those with him get to those [they attacked]?"

"Because, by Zeus," he said, "I hear that some of the Hyrcanians revolted from the enemy and, after coming here, left again and guided him."

(12) After hearing this, Cyaxares became even much more angry at Cyrus for not having told him this, and he sent for the Medes with much more zeal, intending to strip [Cyrus of the Median cavalry]. Threatening still more strongly than before, he called the Medes back, and he threatened the envoy as well, if he should not report his message with severity.

(13) So the envoy went out with his own knights, about one hundred in number, distressed that he had not himself gone before with Cyrus. As they traveled on their journey they got separated at a certain path, and wandered around. They did not reach the friendly army until they chanced upon some retreating Assyrians and compelled them to be their guides. After thus coming to see the fires, they arrived somewhat around the middle of the night. (14) When they were at the camp, the guards, just as Cyrus had ordered, did not let them in before day. When day appeared, Cyrus first called the Magi and commanded that they select what was customary for the gods on the occasion of such successes.[13]

(15) So while they were busy with this, he called the Peers together and said, "Men, god is showing forth many good things, but we

Persians are presently too few to remain in control of them. If, on the one hand, we do not guard what our work is producing for us, it will again belong to others. If, on the other hand, we leave behind some of ourselves as guards over what has come to us, we will at once come to light as having no strength. (16) It thus seems to me that one of you should go to Persia as quickly as possible both to teach what I am saying and to urge that they send an army as quickly as possible, if at least the Persians desire that the rule of Asia and its fruits be theirs. (17) So come then, you who are the eldest, go and say these things, and say also that I will take care of the upkeep for the soldiers whom they send, after they have arrived. You see the very things we have; hide nothing of this from them. As for what I should send to Persia from what we have, in order that I perform nobly and lawfully what pertains to the gods, ask my father; regarding what pertains to the community,[14] ask the magistrates. Let them send overseers of what we are doing and others to respond to our questions. So get ready, and take your platoon as an escort."

(18) After this he called in the Medes as well, and at the same time the messenger sent from Cyaxares presented himself, and in front of everyone he reported both his anger against Cyrus and his threats against the Medes. He said in conclusion that he commanded the Medes to come back, even if Cyrus wished to remain. (19) Now the Medes fell silent when they heard the messenger, being at a loss as to how—since he called—they could disobey; and fearing as to how—since he was threatening—they could comply with him, especially since they knew his savagery.

(20) Cyrus said, "But I do not wonder at all, messenger and Medes, if Cyaxares, having then seen many enemies and not knowing how we are faring, has misgivings both about us and about himself. Yet when he perceives that many of the enemy have been destroyed, and that all have been driven away, he will first of all stop being afraid, and then he will recognize that now he is not alone, since his friends have been destroying his enemies. (21) But how do we deserve blame, we who are benefiting him and are not even doing this on our own initiative? For I then persuaded him to allow me to take you and go off, and you, unlike men who might have desired this expedition, did not ask to depart and come here. Rather, you—whoever among you was not annoyed to do so—came only after having been so ordered

by him. His anger, I know clearly, will have been assuaged by these successes and will vanish with the cessation of his fear.[15] (22) So get some rest now, messenger, since you too have labored; and, Persians, since we are expecting enemies to be present, either to do battle or to obey, let us deploy ourselves as nobly as possible, for it is more likely, if we are seen like this, that we will accomplish what we want. You, ruler of the Hyrcanians, order the leaders of your soldiers to arm their troops and then wait here."

(23) When he had done this, the Hyrcanian came back, and Cyrus said, "Hyrcanian, I am pleased when I perceive that you are here not only displaying your friendship, but you also seem to me to have acumen. And now it is clear that for us the very same things are advantageous, for the Assyrians are my enemies, and now they are even more hostile to you than to me. (24) Therefore, we must together make plans so that no one of the allies now with us leaves and, if we are able, so that we will take on others in addition. You heard the Mede recalling the cavalry. If they go away, we foot soldiers will be left alone. (25) You and I must therefore arrange things such that even the very one doing the recalling will wish to remain with us. So find and bestow upon him a tent where he will pass his time in the finest way with everything he needs, and I will in turn try to assign him some work that he will himself be more pleased to do than to depart. And converse with him about how many good things we hope will arise for all our friends, if things go well. After you do this, come back again to me."

(26) So the Hyrcanian departed and led the Mede away to a tent, while the [messenger] who was to go to Persia reported, completely prepared for the trip. Cyrus enjoined him to say to the Persians what had even before been made clear in their discussion, and to deliver what he had written to Cyaxares. "I wish to read to you what I am sending," he said, "so that knowing the contents you may speak in conformity with them if he asks you something in this regard."

In the letter was the following: (27) "Cyrus to Cyaxares: Greetings. We did not leave you all alone, for no one is bereft of friends just when he is conquering his enemies. And we certainly do not think that by going away we put you at risk; but to the extent that we are farther away, we believe that we are making your safety that much greater, (28) for those friends who sit nearby do not most of all provide safety for their friends, but those who drive the enemy farthest away do more to put their friends in a condition free from risk.

(29) "Examine how I have acted toward you, and how you have acted toward me, when you then go on and blame me. I brought you allies, not merely as many as you persuaded to come, but fully as many as I was able to get, while you gave to me only as many as I was able to persuade to come, and at a time when I was in a friendly place. Now when I am in a hostile place, you recall not only whoever is willing to go, but everyone. (30) Thus it is that previously I thought I owed gratitude to both of you, but now you compel me to forget you and to try to repay all my gratitude to those who followed me. (31) I, however, am not able to be like you, but even now, in sending to Persia for an army, I am commanding that, if you have any need of them before they come to us, all those coming to me be put at your disposal, to use in whatever way you wish, not only in whatever way they are willing to be used.

(32) "Even though I am younger, I advise you not to take back what you give, lest enmity be owed you instead of gratitude; when you wish someone to come to you quickly, do not send for him with threats; and when you declare you are alone, do not deliver threats to large numbers, lest you teach them to think nothing of you. (33) We will try to be back with you as soon as we accomplish what we believe would, when done, be goods in common for both you and us.[16] Farewell."

(34) "Give this to him, and whatever he may ask you about it, answer in conformity with what has been written, for my commands to you about the Persians are indeed as has been written." He spoke to him like this, and giving him the letter, dismissed him, enjoining him further to show the haste of one who knows that it is advantageous to be back quickly.

(35) After this he saw that the Medes, the Hyrcanians, and those with Tigranes were already all in arms; the Persians also were in arms. Some of [the locals] who were approaching were already leading in horses and carrying in weapons. (36) He ordered them to throw down the spears in the same place the others did earlier; they whose work it was were burning as many as they did not need themselves. As for the horses, he ordered those who brought them in to stay and guard them until some signal should be given to them.

Calling the rulers of the knights and the Hyrcanians, he spoke as follows: (37) "Men, [you who are] both friends and allies, do not be amazed that I call you together often, for since our present circumstances are new to us, many things are without order. Such things as are without order must of necessity provide constant problems until they take their places. (38) Now we have many valuables that have been captured, and men in addition to them. On account of our not knowing what among these things belongs to each of us, and their not knowing who is the master of each of them, one can readily see that not very many of them are doing what is necessary, and that nearly all are at a loss as to what they ought to do. (39) That this not be so, then, divide things up. And whoever receives a tent that has sufficient food, drink, people to do service, bedding, clothes, and the other things with which a soldier's tent is nobly furnished, then nothing else is needed further than that the recipient know that he needs to take care of these things as his own. Whoever gets a tent where something is needed, examine it and remedy the deficiency; I know that there will be many extra things, (40) for our enemies possessed more of everything than is required by our numbers. The treasurers came to me, both those of the king of the Assyrians and those of the other potentates, and referring to certain tributes, they said that they had coined gold. (41) Proclaim, then, that they carry it all in to you, wherever your make your seat, and put fear in whoever does not do what is announced. Take it and distribute a double share to each knight, a single share to each foot soldier, in order that if you need anything further, you may have something with which to buy it. (42) Let it be proclaimed that no one is to be unjust to the vendors in the market that is already in the camp, that the merchants are to sell what each has for sale, and that, as these things are dispensed, others are to be brought in, in order that our camp may be provided for." They proclaimed these things right away.

(43) The Medes and Hyrcanians said the following: "And how could we distribute these things without you and yours?"

(44) Cyrus in turn addressed this argument as follows: "Is it your judgment, men, that we all need to be present for everything that needs to be done, and that I will not suffice to act on your behalf when something is needed, nor will you on ours? How else could we have more problems and accomplish less than like this? (45) But look: We

guarded these things for you, and you trust us to have guarded them nobly. Distribute them in turn, and we will trust you to have distributed them nobly. (46) We will also try to do some other common good in turn. For you see first, of course, how many horses are now present for us, and others are being brought in. Now if we allow them to be without mounts, they will not benefit us, and they will provide us the problem of their care. If we put knights on them, we will at the same time ward off problems and attach further strength to ourselves. (47) So if you have others to whom you would give them, with whom you would be more pleased to run risks, if it should be needed, than with us, give them to them. If you especially wish to have us by your side, give them to us, (48) for when you just now were at risk after riding out without us, you gave us a great fright that you might suffer something, and you made us very ashamed that we were not on hand where you were. If we get these horses, we will follow you. (49) And if we seem to confer more benefits when we contend from them, we will in that case not be deficient in zeal. Yet if by becoming foot soldiers our presence should seem to present a greater opportunity, it is open to us to dismount and immediately stand by you as foot soldiers. As for the horses, we will manage to find some to whom we could hand them over."

(50) He spoke like this, and they answered, "But Cyrus, we neither have men whom we could mount upon these horses, nor if we had them would we choose anything else in place of what you wish. Now take them and do as seems to you to be best."

(51) "But I accept them," he said, "and may good fortune accompany our becoming knights and your distributing the common things. Now first choose out for the gods whatever the Magi direct. Then select also for Cyaxares whatever you think would especially gratify him." (52) And they laughed and said they had to choose women. "Then choose women," he said, "as well as whatever else may seem [good] to you. When you have chosen for him, Hyrcanians, make sure all these who have willingly followed me, as far as is in your power, have no cause to complain.[17] (53) Honor in turn, you Medes, these who were our first allies, so that they will hold that they deliberated well when they became our friends. Distribute a share of all things also to the envoy who came from Cyaxares, both to him himself and to those with him. Summon him to stay with us, as something de-

cided upon by me, in order that, after he learns about each particular, he may report how things are to Cyaxares.[18] (54) As for the Persians with me, whatever is left over after you have been nobly provided for will suffice, for we have not been raised with very much
delicacy but in rustic fashion, so that you would perhaps laugh at us,
if we were draped in anything elegant, just as we will surely afford
you a great laugh both when we are seated on our horses and, I think,
when we fall down on the ground."

(55) After this they proceeded to the distribution, laughing hard
over the matter of the horses. He called the captains and ordered that
they take the horses, the gear for the horses, and the grooms, and that
they count them, draw lots, and take them into the companies, an
equal amount for each. (56) Cyrus again ordered a proclamation, that
if there was any slave in the army of the Assyrians, Syrians, or Arabians who had been taken by force from the Medes, Persians, Bactrians, Carians, Cilicians, Greeks, or any other place, he should show
himself. (57) Many who heard the herald gladly showed themselves.
So he chose those who looked best and said that they were free but
would need to carry whatever weapons they gave them.[19] He said
that he would take care that they would have the provisions they required. (58) And leading them off right away, he assigned them to
their captains. He ordered that they give them their shields and their
light swords, so that they might follow with these behind the horses,
and that each take provisions for them just as for his own Persians.
He also ordered that they keep their breastplates and lances and that
they always ride their horses (and he began doing this himself), and
that each establish another ruler from the Peers, instead of himself,
over the Peers' infantry.

·✦· CHAPTER 6 ·✦·

(1) So they were involved in these things. Meanwhile, Gobryas,
an old Assyrian man with a mounted retinue, arrived on horseback,
and all had the weapons of cavalry troops. Now those assigned to
receive weapons ordered that they surrender their lances, so that
they might burn them like the others. But Gobryas said that he

wished to see Cyrus first. The aides detained the knights there and
led Gobryas to Cyrus. (2) When he saw Cyrus, he spoke as follows:
"Master, I am Assyrian by birth. I have a strong fort and rule over
much land. I have a cavalry of about one thousand, which I used to
furnish to the Assyrian king, and I was as friendly to him as I could
be. Yet since he, who was a good man, has died at the hands of your
troops, and since his son, who is most hateful to me, now has his rule,
I have come to you and fall at your feet as a suppliant, and I give myself to you as a slave and ally.²⁰ I ask you to become my avenger; and
as much as possible I make you my son, for I am without male children, (3) for he was my only son, and a noble and good one, master,
both loving me and honoring me in the very way a son's honoring
would make a father happy.²¹ He was summoned by the previous
king, the father of the present one, who intended to give his daughter to my son, and I sent him off with the high thought that I would
surely see my son as the husband of the king's daughter. Yet the present king called him to a hunt and allowed him to hunt with all his
might, believing that he [himself] was a horseman by far superior [to
my son]. So he went hunting as with a friend, and when a bear appeared and both gave chase, this present ruler threw his spear and
missed—would that he had not!—but my son threw—as he ought
not to have done!—and brought the bear down. (4) Though then [the
prince] was annoyed indeed, he held his envy down in darkness. Yet
when he missed again, after a lion chanced along, though to be sure
[such misses] were nothing to be wondered at, and when my son
again hit and brought the lion down, saying, "I have thrown two
times in succession and each time have struck down the prey!" then
the impious [prince] could no longer hold his envy down. Instead,
he seized a spear from one of his followers, struck my dear only son
in the chest, and took away his life. (5) Then I, wretched I, brought
home a corpse instead of a bridegroom, and I, old as I was, buried
with youthful down upon his cheeks the best son, the one I cherished. His murderer, as though he had destroyed an enemy, has
never shown that he repents, nor did he, to make amends for his evil
deed, deem worthy of any honor the one now beneath the earth. His
father, at least, pitied me, and clearly grieved with me in my misfortune. (6) Now if he were alive, I would never have come to you
to harm him, for I experienced many friendly [acts] at his hands, and

I served him. Since sovereignty has devolved upon my son's murderer, I would never be able to become well disposed to him, nor, surely, could he ever hold me to be a friend, for he knows how I am disposed toward him and how I, who lived radiantly before, stand now, isolated and living out my old age in sorrow. (7) Now if you accept me and I should get some hope of obtaining some vengeance for my dear son with you, I think that I would grow young again; in living I would no longer be ashamed, and I do not think that in dying it would annoy me to make my end."

(8) Now he spoke like this, and Cyrus answered, "Gobryas, if you show that your thinking corresponds to what you have said to us, I both accept you as a suppliant and promise, with the gods' [help], to avenge the murder of your son. Tell me, if we do this for you, and allow you to have the fortifications, land, weapons, and power that you had before, what service will you do for us in return for these things?"

(9) He said, "My fortifications I will provide you as a house whenever you come; the tribute from the land which I used to pay to him I will bring to you; and wherever you go on campaign, I will go along with the power that comes from my land. There is also my daughter, whom I cherish, a maiden already ripe for marriage, whom previously I thought I was rearing as a wife for the present king. Now my daughter has herself, lamenting often, begged me not to give her to her brother's murderer, and I am similarly resolved. I now grant to you to deliberate also about her in whatever way I show that I deliberate about you."

(10) Cyrus spoke like this: "I give you my right hand, and take yours, on the condition that these things are true. Let the gods be our witnesses." When these things were done, he ordered Gobryas to go, keeping his weapons, and he asked how far it was to his [fort], as if he intended to go. He said, "If you go tomorrow morning, you could spend the night of the next day with us."

(11) So Gobryas left a guide and departed. The Medes came up, having delivered to the Magi what the Magi declared that they choose for the gods. The Medes also chose for Cyrus the most beautiful tent and the Susan woman, who is said to have been certainly the most beautiful woman in Asia, and the two best music girls. Secondly, they chose the second-best for Cyaxares, and they supplied themselves

fully with such other things as they needed, that they might lack nothing as they campaigned, for there was much of everything.

(12) The Hyrcanians also took what they needed. They had the messenger from Cyaxares share equally. They gave the extra tents, as many as there were, to Cyrus, that the Persians might have them. They said that they would distribute the coined money when it all was collected. And they did distribute it.

BOOK V

ᴥ CHAPTER 1 ᴥ

(1) This, then, is what they said and did, but Cyrus bade those he knew to be Cyaxares' closest associates to receive and guard his things. "I accept with pleasure what you are giving me," he said. "Whoever among you is especially in want of them may use them."

One of the Medes who was a lover of music said, "Indeed, Cyrus, at night I listened to the music girls who are now yours, and I did so with pleasure. If you give me one of them, I think I would enjoy more pleasure when I am on campaign than when I stay at home."

Cyrus said, "I give her to you, and I think I owe you more gratitude for having asked than you owe me for getting her, so thirsty am I to do favors for you all."

So he who asked received her.

(2) Cyrus summoned Araspas the Mede, who was his companion when he was a boy and to whom he had given his Median robe, the one he was wearing when he was going away from Astyages to Persia.[1] He summoned him to guard a woman and her tent for him. This woman was the wife of Abradatas the Susan. (3) Her husband happened not to be in the Assyrians' camp when it was captured, for he had gone as an ambassador to the king of the Bactrians.[2] The Assyrian had sent him to discuss an alliance, for he happened to have ties of hospitality with the king of the Bactrians.[3] So Cyrus bade Araspas guard her until such time as he should take her for himself.

(4) Upon being so bidden, Araspas asked, "Cyrus, have you seen the woman whom you bid me guard?"

"No, by Zeus," said Cyrus, "I have not."

"But I did," he said, "when we selected her for you. And indeed, when we went into her tent, at first we did not recognize her, for she was sitting on the ground and all her attendants were around her, and she wore clothes similar to those of her slave girls. Since we wished to know which was the mistress, we looked around at all of them, and she immediately became manifest in her superiority to all the others, even though she was sitting, in veils, looking down at the ground. (5) When we bade her stand up, all those encircling her stood up with her. She at this point surpassed them first in height, then also in both virtue and grace, even though she stood with a posture of dejection. Her tears were also evident, some falling on her robes, others even on her feet. (6) Then the oldest of us said, 'Take heart, woman: We hear that your husband is noble and good; now, however, we are selecting you for a man who, be well assured, is no worse than he in looks, in judgment, or in the power he has.[4] We believe that Cyrus deserves to be regarded with wonder if any other man does, and you will henceforth be his.' When the woman heard this, she tore at her upper robe and began wailing, and her servant girls also cried out with her. (7) At this point most of her face became visible, as did her neck and hands. And be sure of it, Cyrus," he said, "as it seemed to me and to all the others who saw her, such a woman has never yet been begotten nor born of mortal parents in all Asia. But by all means, you too must see her."[5]

(8) And Cyrus said, "No, by Zeus, much less so if she is such as you say."[6]

"Why so?" said the youth.

"Because," he said, "if hearing from you that she is beautiful persuades me to go to see her now, even though I do not have much leisure, I fear that she in turn will much more quickly persuade me to come to see her again. Consequently I would perhaps sit gazing at her, neglecting what I need to do.'"[7]

(9) The youth laughed and said, "Do you think, Cyrus, that the beauty of a human being is sufficient to compel one who does not wish to, to act contrary to what is best? Yet if this were naturally so, it would compel all in a similar way. (10) Do you see how fire burns

all in a similar way? For it is naturally like this. But concerning beautiful things, they love some, but not others, and one loves one, another loves another. For it is voluntary, and each loves whatever he wishes. For example, a brother does not love his sister, but another loves her; nor a father his daughter, but another loves her, for fear and law are sufficient to prevent love. (11) If a law were set down that those who do not eat must not be hungry and that those who do not drink must not be thirsty, and that one must not be cold in the winter or hot in the summer, no law would have the power to bring human beings to obey these things, for they are naturally overcome by them. But loving is voluntary. At any rate, each loves what suits him, just as with clothes and shoes."

(12) "How then," said Cyrus, "if falling in love is voluntary, is it not possible to stop when one wishes? But I have even seen people in tears from the pain of love; and people enslaved to those they love, even though before they fell in love they believed that it was bad to be enslaved; and people giving away many things of which it was better that they not be deprived; and people praying that they get free from it, just as they would from a disease, and yet not being able to get free, but being bound by some necessity stronger than if they had been bound in iron. At any rate, they surrender themselves to serve the many whims of those they love. They nevertheless do not even try to run away, even though they suffer these evils, but they even stand guard so that those they love do not run off."

(13) And the youth said to this, "People do do these things. Such people, however, are wretched weaklings. Therefore I think they also pray constantly that they may die, because they are in misery, and even though there are thousands of contrivances for getting free of life, they do not employ them. These same people also try stealing and do not refrain from others' belongings. But whenever they rob or steal something, do you see that you are the first to blame the thief or robber, on the grounds that stealing is not compulsory, and you are not sympathetic but you punish him? (14) So too, people who are beautiful do not compel human beings to love them or to desire what they should not. Wretched little human weaklings, however, do lack control over all their desires, and then they blame love. Yet the noble and good, although they do desire gold, good horses, and beautiful women, are nevertheless easily able to refrain from all these things

so as not to touch them contrary to what is just. (15) Although I have seen her and she seemed to me to be very beautiful, I, at least, am still by your side, I ride my horse, and I perform the rest of what is proper to me."

(16) "Yes, by Zeus," said Cyrus, "for perhaps you came away more quickly than the time it takes for love, in its nature, to prepare a human being [for its use], for it is possible to touch fire and not be burned immediately, and wood does not immediately flame up.[8] Nevertheless, I, at least, do not willingly either touch fire or look at beautiful people. And I advise you, Araspas, not to allow your sight to linger upon beautiful people. Because fire burns those who touch it, but beautiful people ignite even those who gaze from afar, so that they are inflamed by love."

(17) "Be confident, Cyrus!" he said. "Not even if I never stop gazing, I will not be overcome so as to do anything I ought not to."

"You speak most nobly," he said. "Then stand guard as I bid you, and take care of her, for perhaps this woman could become something quite opportune for us."

(18) After having said these things, they parted.

The youth saw that the woman was beautiful; perceived her nobility and goodness; was attentive to her and thought he thereby gratified her; perceived that she was not without gratitude and that she took care through her own servants that he have what he needed when he came, and that he would need nothing if ever he fell sick. From all this, he was captured by love, and in this he quite possibly experienced nothing to wonder at. So this is how this episode was unfolding.

(19) Wishing that the Medes and the allies stay with him willingly, Cyrus summoned all his chief aides. When they assembled, he said the following: (20) "Median men and all who are present, I know clearly that you have come along with me neither because you are in need of money nor because you believe that in so doing you are serving Cyaxares. Rather, wishing to gratify me in this, and honoring me, you were willing to march all night and to run risks with me. (21) I am grateful to you for this and would be unjust not to be, but I think that I do not yet have the power to pay you back properly.[9] Now I am not ashamed to say this, but be assured that I would be ashamed to say, 'If you stay with me, I will pay you back.' I believe it would be

as though I said this in order to get you to be more willing to stay with me. Instead of this, I say the following: 'Even if in obedience to Cyaxares you go away now, I will nevertheless try, if I accomplish anything good, to act in such a way that even you who leave will praise me.' (22) For I myself will not go back, but I will be firm in the oaths and pledges that I gave to the Hyrcanians and will never be caught betraying them. As for Gobryas, who is giving us a fortress, land, and his forces, I will try to act so that he not regret his journey to me. (23) Most important, however, since gods are giving good things so openly, I would both fear them and be ashamed to go away heedlessly, abandoning these [gifts from the gods]. This, therefore, is how I will act; you act in keeping with your judgment, and tell me what you decide." (24) Thus he spoke.

First the one who once said that he was Cyrus' relative spoke.[10] "But I, king," he said, "for you seem to me to have been born a king by nature, no less than is the naturally born leader of the bees in the hive, for the bees obey him voluntarily. If he stays in a place, not one leaves it; and if he goes out somewhere, not one abandons him, so remarkably ardent is their innate love of being ruled by him. (25) And human beings seem to me to be somewhat similarly disposed toward you, for even when you were going away from us to Persia, who among the Medes, whether young or old, failed to follow you, until Astyages turned us back?[11] And when you set out from Persia to help us, we again saw nearly all your friends willingly following along. Further, when you desired this expedition, all Medes followed you here voluntarily. (26) Now too we are so disposed that we are confident when with you, even though in enemy territory, but without you we are even afraid to go home. The others will say for themselves what they will do, but I, Cyrus, and those I control, will stay beside you: We will put up with seeing you and remain steadfast in the face of your benefactions."[12]

(27) Thereupon Tigranes spoke as follows: "Never be surprised, Cyrus, if I am silent, for my soul has been made ready not to deliberate but to do whatever you order."

(28) The Hyrcanian said, "If you should go away now, Medes, I would say that it must be the plot of a divinity to keep you from becoming especially happy, for who by human judgment would turn back from enemies who are in flight, or not receive their arms as they

surrender them, or not accept them as they give up both themselves and their possessions, especially since we have a leader who seems to me—and I so swear to you by all the gods—to be such as to take more pleasure in doing good to us than in enriching himself?"

(29) Thereupon all the Medes spoke as follows: "You, Cyrus, led us out; when it seems to you to be opportune, also lead us back home with you."

When he heard this Cyrus prayed, "O greatest Zeus, I ask you to grant that I surpass in doing good the honor they now show me."

(30) He then bade the others to post their guards and attend to themselves, and the Persians to distribute the tents—to the knights those fitting for them, and to the infantry those suited to them. He also bade them arrange it so that the stewards prepare all things necessary and bring them to the Persians' formations, and furnish them their horses fully cared for, so that there be no other thing for the Persians to do than to labor at the works of war.[13] So they spent this day like this.

ᐁ· CHAPTER 2 ·ᐁ·

(1) After rising at dawn, they marched toward Gobryas. Cyrus went on horseback, as did the Persian knights, who had become about two thousand strong. Those who carried their shields and scimitars followed after them, and they were equal in number. The rest of the army marched in order. He bade all say to their new servants that if any of them appeared behind the rear guard, or went in front of the forward troops, or was captured outside of those proceeding in formation along the flanks, they would be punished. (2) In the afternoon of the second day they came to Gobryas' property. They saw that the fortress was exceedingly strong and that on its walls everything had been prepared so that one could fight from them with the greatest strength. They saw many cattle and very many sheep that had been led up under the fortifications. (3) Gobryas sent to Cyrus and bade him to ride around and see where the approach was easiest and to send to him some of his trusted troops, so these could see what was inside and report back to Cyrus. (4) So since Cyrus himself in fact

wished to see if there was any place the wall could be taken, should Gobryas show himself to be false, he rode around everywhere, and he saw that everything was too strong to approach. Those sent in to Gobryas reported to Cyrus that, as it seemed to them, there were so many goods inside that the people inside could not consume them in a generation of human life.[14]

(5) Now Cyrus was in thought about what all this meant,[15] when Gobryas himself came out to him and led out all those who were inside. They carried out wine, barley meal, and flour, while others drove out cattle, goats, sheep, pigs, and if there was anything else to eat, they brought it all in a quantity sufficient to feed the entire army with Cyrus. (6) Then those assigned to do so divided the food and made the dinner. When all his men were outside, Gobryas bade Cyrus enter in whatever way he believed to be safest. So after sending in scouts and an advance force, Cyrus himself also went in. After he went in, and while keeping the gates open wide, he called to him all of his friends and commanders of the troops with him. (7) When they were inside, Gobryas brought out golden cups, pitchers, vases, every sort of adornment, Darics without measure, and many other things, which were all beautiful.[16] Finally he brought out his daughter, a marvel in beauty and stature, though she was in mourning for her dead brother. Then he spoke as follows, "Cyrus, I give you all these things as gifts, and I turn my daughter over to you to dispose of as you wish. Yet we both ask in supplication, I, even as before, that you avenge my son, she, now, that you avenge her brother."

(8) Cyrus said to this, "But even then I promised you that if you did not play false, I would avenge you to the limit of my power.[17] Now, when I see that you are speaking the truth, I owe already the repayment of my promise. I also promise to her that, with the gods' [help], I will do just as I have promised to you. I accept these valuables, but I give them to this child of yours and to whoever may marry her. Yet I will go away with one gift from you, a gift in exchange for which I would not be more pleased even with the treasures of Babylon, which are the greatest, nor even with all those of everywhere else."

(9) And Gobryas, wondering whatever this was and suspecting that he meant his daughter, asked him, "And what is this, Cyrus?"

And Cyrus answered, "Gobryas, I think there are many human beings who would not willingly be either impious or unjust, nor would they voluntarily play false, but because no one is willing to bestow upon them vast valuables, tyranny, fortified walls, or children who are worthy of love, they die before it becomes clear what sort of people they were. (10) But you have now put in my hands fortified walls, every sort of wealth, your forces, and your daughter, worthy to be acquired. You have made it clear to all human beings that I would not be willingly impious where hospitality is required, unjust for the sake of valuables, or voluntarily false in agreements. (11) Be assured that as long as I am just and am praised by human beings because I seem to be so, I shall never forget this but will try to honor you in return with all things noble. (12) And do not fear that you will be at a loss for a husband for your daughter, one worthy of her, for I have many good friends, and one of them will marry her. Whether, however, he will have as many valuables as you are now giving away, or even many times as many, I would not be able to say. Be assured, however, that there are some of [my friends here] who do not regard you with any more wonder because you are giving away these valuables. Rather, they are now jealous of me and pray to all the gods that it may sometime happen for them to show that they are not less faithful to their friends than I am, and that they would never, so long as they live, give in to their enemies, unless some god should cross them; and that in exchange for virtue and good reputation, they would not even choose all the possessions of the Syrians and Assyrians if they were added to yours. Be assured that such men are seated here."

(13) Gobryas laughed and said, "By the gods, Cyrus, show me where they are, so I may ask one of them to become my son."

And Cyrus said, "Do not worry; you will not have to inquire of me: If you follow along with us, you'll even be able to point out each of them to someone else."

(14) Having said such things, he took Gobryas' right hand, got up, and led out all those with him. Although Gobryas asked him many times, he was not willing to have dinner inside, but he dined in his camp and took Gobryas along as his tablemate. (15) Reclining on a mat, he asked him the following: "Tell me, Gobryas, do you think that you have more blankets than each of us?"

And he said, "By Zeus, I know well that you have both more blankets and more couches, and your house is much larger than mine: You use the earth and heaven as your house, and you have as many couches as there are places to sleep on the earth. You do not believe blankets to be the wool that sheep naturally grow but whatever twigs and leaves the mountains and plains yield up."

(16) Now dining with them for the first time and seeing the coarseness of the food that was set beside them, Gobryas believed his people to be much freer than they. (17) But then he noted the restraint of his tablemates, for none of the educated Persian men became visibly distracted by any food or drink, neither in their eyes nor by grabbing nor in their minds, so as to fail to consider just what they would have even if they were not at table. Just as skilled horsemen, who are not rattled by being on horseback, are able to see, hear, and say what they must even while riding, so too when at table [the educated Persians] think it necessary to appear to be prudent and restrained. It seems to them that being excited by food and drink is very piggish and bestial. (18) So he took note of them and of how they asked each other such things as are more pleasing to be asked than not, and made such jests as are more pleasing to be made than not, and he noted how the jokes they made stayed very far from insolence, very far from anything shameful, and very far from irritating each other. (19) Yet what seemed to him of greatest importance was their thinking, when on campaign, that one must not be served more than the others who enter upon the same risk and, similarly, their believing that it is a most pleasant feast to render as good as possible those who are going to fight together as allies. (20) When Gobryas got up to go home, he is said to have said, "I no longer marvel, Cyrus, if we have acquired more cups, clothes, and gold than you, even though we ourselves are worth less than you, for we take care that we will have as much as possible of these possessions, while you seem to me to take care that you yourselves will be as good as possible."

So this is what he said. (21) Cyrus replied, "See to it that you are here at dawn with your cavalry in their armor so we may see your force. You will also lead us through your country so we may know which parts we need to believe to be friendly and which parts hostile." (22) After having said these things they went away, each to what was fitting for him.

When it became day, Gobryas reported with his cavalry, and he began to lead the way. Cyrus, as was fitting for a man who ruled, not only paid attention to marching along the road, but as he went forward he also considered whether it was at all possible to make his enemies weaker and his own troops stronger. (23) So summoning the Hyrcanian and Gobryas, for he believed that they especially knew what he thought he himself needed to learn, he said, "Men, friends, I do not think that it would be a mistake to deliberate about this war with you as with men I trust, for I see that you must examine even more than I how to keep the Assyrian from overcoming us. If I fail here, perhaps I have another refuge. But if he overcomes you, I see that all of what is yours will fall to others. (24) He is hostile to me, not because he hates me but because he thinks it to his disadvantage that we are great, and this is why he marches against us. But you he also hates, believing that he has suffered injustice at your hands." They both responded to this in the same vein, that he should complete what he had to say and regard them as quite aware of their situation and as being most concerned about how events would unfold.

At this point he began as follows: (25) "Tell me, does the Assyrian believe that you alone are hostile toward him, or do you know of anyone else who is also hostile?"

"Yes, by Zeus," said the Hyrcanian, "the Cadusians are extremely hostile to him, and they are a numerous and strong people. So are our neighbors the Sacians, who have suffered many evils at the hands of the Assyrian, for he tried to subdue them just as he did us."

(26) "Then do you think," he said, "that they would both be pleased to go with us against the Assyrian?"

"Exceedingly so," they said, "if at least they were in some way able to join up with us."

"What," he said, "is in the way of our joining up?"

"Assyrians are," they said, "the same nation through whose territory you are now marching."

(27) When Cyrus heard this he said, "Gobryas, did you not accuse this young man who has now come into the kingship of being unusually arrogant in character?"

"Yes," said Gobryas, "for I think I have suffered acts of this sort at his hands."

"Then was he such only to you," said Cyrus, "or also to others?"

(28) "Yes, by Zeus," said Gobryas, "also to many others. Yet why even mention his insolence toward the weak? On one occasion, however, he was drinking with one of his companions (my son having been another

such), the son of a man much more powerful than I. He had him seized and castrated, only because, as some say, his mistress had praised his companion saying that he was handsome and that the woman who was going to be his wife would be happy. But as he himself now says, it was because his companion had made an attempt on his mistress. So now he is a eunuch, but he is a ruler, for his father died."

(29) "Do you think that he too would be pleased to see us, if he thought that we would help him?"

"I am quite sure of it," said Gobryas, "but it is difficult to see him, Cyrus."

"Why?" asked Cyrus.

"Because if someone is going to join with him, he must pass by Babylon itself."

(30) "So why is this difficult?" he asked.

"Because, by Zeus," said Gobryas, "I know that a force many times greater than the one you now have would attack from it. Be assured that the Assyrians now tend less than before to bring you their weapons and drive in their horses, and this is because your force seems small to those of them who saw it. This account of it has already circulated widely, so it seems better to me to proceed with caution."

(31) And hearing the preceding from Gobryas, Cyrus said the following to him: "You seem to me to speak nobly, Gobryas, in ordering that we make our journey as safely as possible. Upon consideration I am unable to conceive that there is any journey safer for us than marching right up to Babylon itself, if the strongest part of our enemies is there. Yes, they are numerous, as you say; what I say is that if they become confident, they will also be terrible for us. (32) Now if they do not see us and think that we are out of sight because we are afraid of them, be quite assured that they will lose the fear that arose in them, and in its place will naturally arise a confidence that becomes ever greater as the time that they do not see us increases. But if we go against them now, we will find many of them still weeping over those who died at our hands, many who are still wearing bandages on the wounds they received from our troops, and all of them still mindful of the daring of this army and, on the other hand, of their own flight and disaster. (33) Be assured, Gobryas, that you may know this too: Large masses of human beings, when they are confident, offer an irresistible spirit. Yet whenever they grow

afraid, to the extent that they are more numerous, so much the greater is their terror and its impact, (34) for the fear that accompanies them has grown great by many reports of evil suffered, by the pale complexions of many wretched [victims],[18] and by many despondent and distraught faces. The result is that because of its greatness, it is not very easy to quench this fear with words, or to put strength into them by driving against the enemy, or to renew their spirit by retreating, but they will hold they are in greater danger to the extent that one exhorts them to be more confident.

(35) "By Zeus, let us, however, consider exactly how this matter stands, for if victories in military deeds will in the future belong to those with the vaster mob, you are correct to be afraid for us, and we really are in danger. If, however, battles are still determined now as they were before, by those who fight well, you would not err in being confident, for—as you will discover—those who fight willingly will, with the gods' [help], be much more numerous on our side than on theirs. (36) That you may be still more confident, think this over: Our enemies are much fewer now than they were before they were defeated by us, and much fewer than they were when they ran away from us. We are both more numerous now, since we have conquered, and stronger, since you have joined us. Do not continue to dishonor your troops, since they are with us. Be assured, Gobryas, that even camp attendants are confident when they follow conquerors. (37) Nor let it escape your consideration that it is possible even now for our enemies to see us. Be assured that there is no way we could appear more terrible to them than by marching against them. As this is how I judge the matter, lead us to the route to Babylon."

❧ CHAPTER 3 ❧

(1) Marching in this way, they reached the boundaries of Gobryas' land on the fourth day. When he entered enemy territory, [Cyrus] stopped and brought into his own order the infantry and as many of the cavalry as he thought fine. He sent out the rest of the cavalry to make raids. He bade them kill all those in arms but bring to himself whatever other people and cattle they might capture. He bade also

the Persians to join in the raids, and while many of them returned after having been thrown from their horses, many also brought back a great deal of booty. (2) When the booty was present, he summoned both the Peers and the rulers of the Medes and Hyrcanians, and he spoke as follows: "Men, friends, Gobryas has regaled us all with many good things. If, then, after selecting out what is customary for the gods and what is sufficient for the army, we should give the rest of the booty to him, would we not do something noble? Then it would be immediately evident that we try to be victorious also in doing good to those who do good."

(3) When they heard this, all praised the proposal, all applauded it. One also spoke as follows: "Let us certainly do this, Cyrus, for it seems to me that Gobryas believes us to be beggars because we were not loaded with Darics when we came, and we do not drink from golden cups. If we do what you say, he would know that it is possible to be free even without gold."[19]

(4) "Come then," he said, "give to the Magi what belongs to the gods, select as much as is sufficient for the army, and summon Gobryas and give him the rest." So after taking what was needed, they gave the rest to Gobryas.

(5) After this he went to Babylon, keeping the same order as when the battle was fought. When the Assyrians did not come out in opposition, Cyrus bade Gobryas to ride up and say that if the king wished to come out and fight for his country, even he himself would fight on his side, but that if he did not defend his country, necessity required obedience to its masters. (6) So Gobryas rode up where it was safe and said this, and the other sent out to him one who answered as follows: "Gobryas, your master says, 'I do not regret that I killed your son, only that I did not kill you as well. But if you wish to do battle, come back in a month.[20] We do not have the leisure now, for we are still preparing.'"

(7) Gobryas said, "May you never stop having this regret! For it is clear that I have been causing you some pain since the time this regret took hold of you."

(8) So Gobryas reported the remarks of the Assyrian, and on hearing them Cyrus had the army draw back. He summoned Gobryas and asked, "Tell me, did you not say that you thought the one who was castrated by the Assyrian would join us?"

"I think I know it well," he said, "for he and I said many things
openly to one another."

(9) "Then when it seems fine to you, go to him. And arrange it first
so that [only] you yourselves know what you say. When you are with
him, if you know that he wishes to be a friend, you must contrive that
it not be noticed that he is our friend, for one could not do more good
things for friends in war in any other way than by seeming to be an
enemy, nor could anyone harm enemies more in any other way than
by seeming to be a friend."

(10) "Indeed," said Gobryas, "I know that Gadatas would even pay
for the opportunity to do some great evil to the present king of the
Assyrians. But we need to consider what he would be able to do."

(11) "Tell me," said Cyrus, "as regards the fort on the frontier of this
country, the one you say was fortified to be a bulwark for it in the war
against the Hyrcanians and the Sacians, do you think, if the eunuch
came to it with a force, that he would be admitted into it by its
commander?"

"Clearly," said Gobryas, "if he arrived there unsuspected, as he
now is."

(12) "Would he be unsuspected if I should attack his lands as if I
wished to take them, and if he should fight back vigorously? And if
I should capture something from him and he in turn should capture
from us some troops or even some messengers sent from me to the
others you said were hostile to the Assyrian? And if when they were
captured they would say that they were going for troops and ladders, in order to bring them to the fort? And if the eunuch would pretend that on hearing this he went [to the fort] because he wished to
report it?"

(13) Gobryas said, "If things were like this, he would clearly admit
him. He even would beg him to stay until you went away."

"Then," said Cyrus, "if he but once gets in, would he be able to
bring the fortress over into our hands?"

(14) "It is quite likely at least," said Gobryas, "if he takes care of the
inside, and you make a strong assault from without."

"Come, then," he said, "try to explain and settle the matter, and
then come back.[21] Nor could you mention or show him greater signs
of trust than what you yourself happen to have received from us."

(15) After this Gobryas departed. The eunuch was glad to see him; he agreed to everything and settled what was necessary. After Gobryas reported back that the eunuch had strongly approved all the proposals, on the next day Cyrus attacked and Gadatas fought back. There was also a fortress that Cyrus took, one that Gadatas had indicated. (16) Cyrus sent messengers and indicated in advance which route they were to travel by. Gadatas let some of these escape, that they might bring troops and provide ladders,[22] but he caught others. These he interrogated in the presence of many, and when he heard them say where they were going, he swiftly made preparations as if he were going to convey this message and marched off during the night. (17) In the end, he was trusted and entered the fortress as if he had come in aid. In the meantime he made what preparations he could with the fort's commander, but when Cyrus came, he made collaborators of Cyrus' captured messengers and took the fort. (18) When this happened and as soon as Gadatas the eunuch settled things inside, he went out to Cyrus, and prostrating himself in keeping with the custom, he said, "Joy to you, Cyrus."

(19) "But I am already joyful," he said, "for you, with [the help of] the gods, not only bid me to be joyful, but even compel me to be so. Rest assured that I place a high value on leaving this fortress friendly to my allies here. From you, Gadatas, the Assyrian has taken away the fathering of children, as it seems; however, he has not deprived you of being able to acquire friends. Be assured that you have made us friends by this deed and that we, if we are able, will try to stand by you in aid no worse than would children of your own, if you possessed them." Thus he spoke.

(20) Having just perceived what had happened, the Hyrcanian then ran up to Cyrus, and taking his right hand said, "Cyrus, you who are so great a good to your friends, how much gratitude you make me owe to the gods because they led me to you!"

(21) "Come now," said Cyrus, "take the fortress on account of which you greet me so joyfully, and dispose of it in such a way that it will be worth the most to your tribe, to the other allies, and especially to Gadatas here, who took it and gives it to us."

(22) "Well then," said the Hyrcanian, "when the Cadusians, Sacians, and my fellow citizens come, shall we invite him as well,[23] so that all

of us for whom it is fitting may deliberate in common about how we might use the fortress in the most advantageous way?"

(23) Cyrus applauded this suggestion. And when those concerned about the fortress got together, they determined that they would guard it in common, all those to whom it was good for it to be friendly. Thus, it would be a bulwark for them in war and be fortified against the Assyrians.

(24) After this event, the Cadusians, Sacians, and Hyrcanians campaigned with much more enthusiasm and in greater numbers. Hence an army of Cadusians was collected that numbered up to twenty thousand targeteers and four thousand cavalry, of Sacians up to ten thousand archers and two thousand mounted archers.[24] The Hyrcanians sent along as many infantry troops as was in their power, and they filled up the ranks of their cavalry to two thousand. Previously, large numbers of their cavalry had been left at home, because both the Cadusians and the Sacians were enemies of the Assyrians. (25) For as long a time as Cyrus was occupied with the disposition of the fortress, many of the Assyrians in the country nearby brought in their horses, and many turned in their weapons, for they were already fearful of their neighbors all around.[25]

(26) Gadatas then came to Cyrus and said that his messengers heard that when the Assyrian learned about the fortress, he took it hard and was preparing to invade his land. "If you will allow me, Cyrus, I will try to save my forts; the rest is of less account."

(27) And Cyrus said, "If you go now, when will you be home?"

And Gadatas said, "On the third day I will dine in our land."

"But do you not think you will find the Assyrian already there?" he asked.

"I am sure of it," he said, "for he will make haste while you still seem to be far away."

(28) "On what day could I get there with my army?" asked Cyrus.

Gadatas said to this, "You have a large army, master, and you would not be able to arrive at my residence in less than six or seven days."

"Then you go as quickly as possible," said Cyrus, "and I will march as best I can."

(29) So Gadatas left, and Cyrus summoned all the allies' rulers. And it seemed that there were already many noble and good rulers on hand. Cyrus said this to them: (30) "Men, allies, Gadatas did things

that seem to us all to be worth a great deal, and he did so before having experienced any good at our hands. It is now reported that the
Assyrian will invade his land. Clearly he wishes to take vengeance
on him, because he thinks he has been greatly harmed by him. Perhaps he also has in mind that if those who revolt to us suffer nothing
bad from him, while those by his side perish at our hands, it is likely
that soon no one will wish to be on his side. (31) Now then, men, we
would seem to me to be doing something noble if we should enthusiastically give aid to Gadatas, a man who is our benefactor. And we
would also be doing what is just by paying back his favor. But it seems
to me that we would also be doing what is advantageous for ourselves. (32) If it should be plain to everyone that we try to win victory
over those who do evil by doing more evil to them, and plain as well
that we surpass our benefactors in good deeds, it is likely that thanks
to such actions many will wish to be our friends and no one will desire to be our enemy. (33) But if we should seem to neglect Gadatas,
then by the gods, with what arguments would we persuade anyone
else to gratify us in anything? How could we dare to approve of ourselves? How would any of us be able to return Gadatas' stare if we
who are so many should be outdone in doing good by him, who is
only one man and is in such a condition?" (34) Thus he spoke, and all
together they strongly approved the proposed course of action.

"Come, then," he said, "since it has been so decided by you too, let
us each leave in the rear those most suited to march with the oxen
and wagons. (35) Let Gobryas rule and guide them for us, for he has
experience with the road and is competent also in other respects. We
will march with the most capable horses and men, taking provisions
for three days. To the extent that what we prepare is lighter and simpler, on the coming days we will have breakfast, have dinner, and
sleep with greater pleasure. Now let us march in the following way:
(36) You go first, Chrysantas, leading the troops in breastplates, and
since the road is level and broad, keep all the captains in the front.[26]
Let each company march in single file. We will march in both the
quickest and safest way if we are collected together. (37) I bid those
in breastplates to take the lead because this is the heaviest part of the
army. When the heaviest part leads, it is necessary that all the swifter
parts follow with ease. Whenever the quickest part leads at night, it
is not surprising that armies are pulled apart, for the part put in front

races off. (38) Behind these, let Artabazus lead the Persians' targeteers and archers;[27] behind these, Andamyas the Mede with the Medes' infantry; behind these, Embas with the Armenians' infantry; behind these, Artouchas with the Hyrcanians; behind these, Thambradas with the Sacians' infantry; behind these, Datamas with the Cadusians. (39) Let all these also march with their captains in the front, their targeteers on the right, and their archers on the left of their own rectangular formation, for they are easiest to use when they march like this. (40) Behind these, let the baggage carriers follow everyone. Let their rulers be careful that they have prepared everything before they go to sleep, that they report with their gear to their assigned places at daybreak, and that they follow in good order. (41) Behind the baggage carriers, let Madatas the Persian lead the Persian cavalry, keeping the captains of the cavalry in the front. Let each cavalry captain lead his company in single file, like the infantry captains. (42) Behind these, let Rambacas the Mede likewise lead his cavalry. Behind these, you, Tigranes, lead your cavalry. And let each of the other cavalry captains lead those with whom he came to us. You Sacians march behind these. Let the Cadusians go last, just as they came. Alceuna, at least for the time being, lead and take care of all those in the back, and do not let anyone behind your cavalry. (43) Take care to march in silence, you rulers and all who are moderate, for in the night it is necessary to perceive things and get them done relying more on our ears than on our eyes. And being confused in the night is a matter of much greater consequence and is more difficult to compose than in the day. Silence must therefore be practiced and order guarded. (44) When you are going to get the troops up to march before dawn, you must make the night watches as numerous and as short as possible, so that loss of sleep does not become excessive and harm anyone on the march. When it is time to march, the signal must be given with the horn. (45) Each of you report on the road to Babylon with what you need, and as each starts his advance, let him pass the word to the one behind to follow."

(46) They then set off for their tents, and as they were going they remarked to each other with what a good memory Cyrus called them by name as he gave commands to all those he was putting into order. (47) Now Cyrus was careful to do this, for it seemed to him to be amazing if each mere mechanic knows the names of the tools of his

art, and a doctor knows the names of all the tools and drugs he uses, but a general should be so foolish as not to know the names of the leaders beneath him, and yet necessity compels him to use them as tools when he wishes to take something, guard something, inspire confidence, or cause fear. And if ever he should wish to honor someone, it seemed to him fitting to call him by name. (48) Those who think they are known by their ruler seemed to him both to have a greater yearning to be seen doing something noble and to be more inclined to refrain from doing anything shameful. (49) It also seemed to him to be foolish, when he wished something to get done, to give orders in the way that some masters do on their estates: "Someone go for water," "Someone split wood." (50) When orders are given like this, all seem to him to look at one another and no one to carry out the order, and all seem to be at fault and yet no one at fault (and so too ashamed and afraid), for each is at fault equally with many others. He himself therefore called by name everyone to whom he gave an order. (51) So this is how Cyrus judged these things.

The soldiers, however, after having dinner, posting guards, and preparing everything they needed, then went to bed. (52) At midnight, the signal was given with the horn. After saying to Chrysantas that he would wait on the road up ahead of the army, Cyrus departed with his personal aides. Chrysantas reported a short time later leading the troops with breastplates. (53) Giving him guides to show the way, Cyrus bade him march calmly, for all were not yet on the road. He positioned himself on the road, and as each soldier approached, he sent him ahead in order. Whoever was late he sent for. (54) When all were on the road, he sent some cavalry to Chrysantas to say, "All are already on the road, so now lead on more quickly." (55) He himself calmly rode his horse to the front and contemplated the ranks. He rode to those whom he saw advancing in good order and in silence and asked them who they were, and when he was informed, he praised them. If he perceived any making a commotion, he looked into the cause and tried to quench the confusion.

(56) Only one thing has so far been left out about his precautions for the night, that he sent out in front of the entire army a small number of light-armed foot soldiers. These were in sight of Chrysantas and kept him in their sight. They listened, and also if they were in any other way able to perceive something, they signaled to Chrysantas

whatever seemed opportune. There was a commander over these troops as well, and he kept them in order; and he signaled what was worthy of mention, but because he did not say what was not, he avoided being a burden. (57) So they marched in this way during the night. When it was day, because the Cadusians' infantry was marching last, he left their cavalry at their side, in order that they not march without a cavalry escort. The rest of the cavalry he bade ride up to the front, because the enemy was also in front. This way, if anything should confront him, he might meet it and do battle with his strength in order, and if anything should be seen fleeing, he might pursue it with the utmost readiness. (58) There were always troops in order with him, some of whom were to go in pursuit and others who were to remain beside him, but he never allowed the general order to be broken.

(59) So this is how Cyrus led the army. He himself, however, did not stay in one place, but riding around from one place to another, he looked things over and he took care of anything needed. So this is how Cyrus' troops marched.

᭡ CHAPTER 4 ᭡

(1) When one of the powerful men in Gadatas' cavalry saw that he had revolted from the Assyrian, he believed that he himself would receive from the Assyrian all that belonged to Gadatas, if the latter should suffer some mishap. So he sent to the Assyrian one of his trusted troops. He bade him—if he overtook the Assyrian army already in Gadatas' land—to tell the Assyrian that if he wished to lay an ambush, he would capture Gadatas and his followers. (2) He commanded him to make plain both the limited extent of Gadatas' power and that Cyrus was not accompanying him. He also showed him the road on which [Gadatas] was going to arrive. In order to be trusted further, he also commanded the members of his own household to surrender to the Assyrian the fortress, along with what was in it, which he himself happened to have in Gadatas' territory. He declared that he himself would come there, if he were able, only after he killed Gadatas, and that if he could not, he would at least be on

the Assyrian's side in the future. (3) So the one assigned to this mission rode as swiftly as possible, reached the Assyrian, and made plain why he had come. After [the Assyrian] heard it, he took the fortress right away, and with a large number of cavalry and chariots he prepared an ambush in a group of villages.

(4) When Gadatas was near these villages, he sent some troops forward to investigate. When the Assyrian knew that the scouts were approaching, he ordered two or three chariots and some cavalry to rise up and take flight, as if they were frightened and few in number. When the scouts saw this, they went in pursuit themselves and also signaled to Gadatas, and he, since he was deceived, pursued with all his might. When it seemed that Gadatas was all but captured, the Assyrians rose up from their ambush. (5) When Gadatas and his followers saw them, as one would expect, they fled, and those on the other side, as one would expect, pursued them. Then he who had plotted against Gadatas struck him. Although he missed a vital spot, he did strike him on the shoulder and wounded him. Having done this, he took off and joined with the others in pursuit. When it was known who he was, he pressed his horse eagerly alongside the Assyrians and rode in pursuit along with the king. (6) At this point, clearly, those with the slowest horses were captured by the fastest. Already having been very hard pressed from the rigors of their march homeward, Gadatas' cavalry saw Cyrus approaching with his army. One must suppose that they went up to them with delight, as to a harbor out of a storm.

(7) Cyrus was at first amazed. But when he recognized what was happening,[28] he himself continued—even as the enemy were all riding forward in opposition—to lead his army in good order, opposed to the enemy. When the enemy recognized how things were,[29] they turned to flight. To those troops who had been put in order just for this, Cyrus gave the command to pursue, while he himself followed with the rest of the army in the way he thought advantageous. (8) Now chariots were captured, some whose drivers had fallen out (some from turning over and others fell out in other ways) and also others that had been cut off by the cavalry. They killed the one who had struck Gadatas and many others. (9) As for the Assyrian infantry, which happened to have been besieging Gadatas' fortress, some took refuge in the fortress, which had revolted from Gadatas, others got

away to a large city of the Assyrian, where even the Assyrian himself took refuge with his cavalry and chariots.

(10) Having accomplished these things, Cyrus retreated into Gadatas' territory. After having arranged for those who ought to attend to the spoils to do so, he went right away to see how Gadatas was as a result of his wound. With his wound already bandaged, Gadatas went to meet him as he approached. Cyrus was pleased upon seeing him and said, "I was coming to you to see how you are."

(11) "But I, by the gods," said Gadatas, "was coming in order to contemplate you again, how you appear in sight, you who have such a soul. You need from me now I know not what, nor did you promise me that you would do these things, nor have you experienced at my hands anything good, at least for yourself personally. But because I seemed to you to benefit your friends a bit,[30] you helped me so enthusiastically that—although on my own I would be done for—I have been saved, thanks to you. (12) By the gods, Cyrus, if I were now as I naturally was from the beginning and if I had begotten children, I do not know whether I would have secured for myself a child such as you, for I know both other children and this present king of the Assyrians, who brought much more pain to his own father than he is now able to bring to you."

(13) To this Cyrus responded as follows: "Gadatas, you omit a much greater wonder in mentioning your wonder at me."

"And what is this?" asked Gadatas.

"That so many Persians are so earnestly concerned about you," he said, "and so many Medes, so many Hyrcanians, and all the Armenians, Sacians, and Cadusians who are present."

(14) And Gadatas prayed, "Zeus, may all the gods give many blessings to these people, and the most to the cause of their being the way they are. However, so that we may entertain nobly these whom you praise, Cyrus, accept these gifts of hospitality; they are such as I am able to give." At the same time he brought out a vast abundance of things. Consequently, whoever wished to offer sacrifice could do so, and the whole army was entertained in a manner worthy of their noble deeds and noble success.

(15) The Cadusian [leader] was guarding the rear and did not share in the pursuit. Wishing to do something splendid himself, he plundered the land toward Babylon without having made common plans

with Cyrus or having said anything to him. Now the Assyrian was returning from the city in which he had taken refuge, and he happened to have his own army in very close order, while the cavalry of the other was spread out. (16) When he realized that the Cadusians were alone, he attacked them, and he killed both their ruler and many others. He took some of the Cadusians' horses and took away whatever booty they happened to be leading off. The Assyrian pursued as far as he thought to be safe and then turned back. The first Cadusians got safely to the camp toward evening.

(17) When Cyrus perceived what had happened, he went to meet the Cadusians. Whenever he saw anyone who had been wounded, he received him, and sent him to Gadatas to be cared for. He also helped others into tents and took care that they had the provisions they needed. He took along some of the Persian Peers to help in giving care, for in such circumstances, the good are willing to persevere in their labor. (18) It seemed that he was severely distressed indeed, since when it was time and the others were having dinner, Cyrus— still with the doctors and their servants—was not willing to leave anyone without care: He either watched over them with his own eyes or, if he could not manage this, was conspicuous in sending others who would care for them.

(19) So thus they went to bed that night. But as soon as it was day, he had heralds call together the rulers of the others, but all of the Cadusians. He spoke as follows: "Men, allies, what has happened is human, for I do not think it is at all amazing that human beings make mistakes. It is worth our while, however, to enjoy something good from what has happened, namely, to learn never to separate from the whole a force weaker than the force of our enemies. (20) I am not saying that it is never necessary to go out with a part that is even smaller, where there really is need, than that with which the Cadusian now departed. But consider the case when someone sets out only after making common plans with someone else who is competent to bring help. It is still possible that he be deceived, but it is also then possible that [his ally], who has stayed behind, may deceive the enemy and draw them aside from the advance force, and it is also possible to provide safety to friends by distracting enemies with other problems. In this way, not even he who is apart is fully absent, for he remains attached to the main strength. Yet whoever goes away without having made common

plans, wherever he may be, is in the same condition as he who makes war alone. (21) In return for what has happened, if god is willing, we will before long punish our enemies. As soon as you have had your breakfast, I will lead you where the event occurred. We will at once bury the dead and show our enemies that on the very spot where they believe they conquered, others are stronger than they, if god is willing. If they do not come out in opposition, we will burn their villages and ravage their land, in order that they not take delight in seeing what they did to us, but to the contrary feel pain in gazing on their own evils. We will see to it that it is no pleasure for them to see the land where they killed our allies. (22) The rest of you, therefore, go and have breakfast. But you, Cadusians, first go and in your customary way choose yourselves a ruler who, with the gods' [help] and ours, if you are in need, will take care of you. When you have made your choice and have had your breakfast, send me the one chosen."

(23) They then did as he said. When he led out the army, Cyrus put the Cadusians' newly chosen [leader] in position and bade him keep his company close by, "in order," he said, "that we may restore the confidence of the men, if we are able." So they marched like this. And when they arrived, they buried the Cadusians, and ravaged the land. After so doing, they went back again into Gadatas' land with provisions taken from that of the enemy.

(24) [Cyrus] realized that those who had revolted to his side but lived near Babylon would suffer severely unless he himself were always present. He thus ordered the enemy troops he released to tell the Assyrian that he was ready to allow those who worked the earth to do so and not to harm them, if [the king] also were willing to allow the workers who had revolted to [Cyrus] to do likewise. [Cyrus] himself also sent a herald to him to say the same things.[31] (25) "And yet," he said, "if indeed you are able to hinder [workers in the land I control], you will hinder but a few, for the land of those who have revolted to me is only a little, but I would allow a lot of land to be worked for you. As for the gathering of the crops, I suppose that if there is war, the victor will do it; if peace, clearly, you will. If, however, any of mine take up weapons against you, or any of yours against me, each of us will punish them as we are able."

(26) After so directing the herald, he sent him off. When the Assyrians heard the proposals, they did everything to persuade the king to

consent to them and to limit the war as much as possible. (27) And whether he was persuaded by those of his own tribe or whether he himself also wished that it be so, the Assyrian gave his approval. Thus there arose compacts that there be peace for those working, but war for those in arms.

(28) So Cyrus accomplished these things concerning the workers. As for the grazing of the flocks, however, he bade his friends do it in security, if they wished, on land under their own control. As for plunder from their enemies, they brought it in from wherever they were able, in order that the campaign might be more pleasant for the allies, for the risks were the same even without taking these provisions, and feeding off the enemies seemed to lighten the burdens of the campaign.

(29) Just when Cyrus was preparing to go away, Gadatas arrived bringing and leading in many and varied gifts, such as one would expect from a great estate, and he also led in many horses that he had taken away from those of his own knights he distrusted because of the plot. (30) When he came near, he said such things as follow: "Cyrus, I give you these things now so that you may use them if, in the present situation, you have any need of them at all, but believe that all my other things are also yours, for neither is there nor shall there ever be a natural descendant of my own to whom I may leave my estate. But our entire line and name must of necessity be extinguished with my death. (31) And I swear to you, Cyrus, by the gods who both see all and hear all, that I have so suffered even though I have neither said nor done anything unjust or shameful." And as he said this he broke into tears at his fortune and was no longer able to speak.

(32) And on hearing this, Cyrus did pity him for what he had suffered, but he spoke as follows: "I accept the horses, for I will benefit you by giving them to troops better disposed toward you than were those troops of yours who just had them, as it seems, and for my part, I will more quickly increase the Persian cavalry up to ten thousand knights, something I have long desired to do. As for the other valuables, take them away and guard them until you see me having enough that I not be outdone in reciprocating with gifts to you. If you go away after giving to me more than you receive from me, by the gods I do not know how I could possibly avoid being ashamed."

(33) To this Gadatas said, "I certainly trust you in this, for I see your character. However, see whether I am fit to guard them. (34) As long as we were friends with the Assyrian, my father's property seemed the finest, for in being near the greatest city, Babylon, we used to enjoy as many benefits as are possible from a great city. As for the burdens, we avoided them by coming back to our home here. Yet now, since we are enemies, it is clear that when you leave, we ourselves and our whole estate will be the target of plots, and I think we will pass our lives in pain, having our enemies nearby and seeing that they are stronger than we are. (35) Now perhaps someone might say, 'Why, then, did you not consider this before you revolted?' Because of suffering insolence and being angry, Cyrus, my soul did not lead by considering what was safest but was always pregnant with this [thought]: Will it ever be possible to take vengeance on him who is hateful to both gods and human beings, who passes his time in hatred not when someone does him an injustice but if he suspects that someone else is better than he is? (36) Therefore, I think, being worthless himself, he makes use of allies who are all even more worthless than he is. If, then, any one of them should come to light as better than he, be confident, Cyrus, that there will be no need for you to do battle with this good man, for the [Assyrian] will be sufficient for this, always contriving until he captures the one who is better than he is. As for causing me pain, however, I think he will easily be strong enough even with worthless allies."

(37) On hearing this, Cyrus thought that what was said deserved attention. He said directly, "Why do we not make your fortifications strong with guards, that they may be safe for you to use in security whenever you enter them, and why do you not campaign with us in order that if the gods are with us, as they just were, he may fear you and not you him? Bring whatsoever of yours is pleasant for you to see or with whom you enjoy associating, and march! At least as it seems to me, you would be very useful to me, and I will try to be so to you as far as I am able."

(38) On hearing this Gadatas breathed anew and said, "If I pack up, would I be able to be ready before you depart? I wish to bring my mother with me too."

"Yes, by Zeus," he said, "you will surely be ready, for I will wait until you say it is fine to go."

(39) Thus Gadatas went away, and with Cyrus' help he strengthened his fortifications with guards. He packed up all the things with which a large estate is nobly supplied. He led his own troops, both the trusted ones in whom he took pleasure and many he did not trust, compelling some to bring their wives and others their sisters, that he might control them when they were bound by these ties. (40) Cyrus promptly got started, keeping also Gadatas in his circle, as an adviser about roads, water, fodder, and food, that they might camp in the places with the greatest abundance.

(41) When in his march he saw the city of the Babylonians, and the road that he was taking seemed to him to run right beside the wall itself, he summoned Gobryas and Gadatas and asked whether there was any other road that did not lead so near to the wall. (42) And Gobryas said, "There are indeed many roads, master. But I thought you would wish to march now as near as possible to the city so you could show him that your army is already large and noble. Even when you had a smaller one, you went right up to the wall itself, and he gazed on us when we were not numerous. Now even if he is somewhat prepared (and he said to you that he would be making preparations to do battle with you), I know that when he sees your power, his own will again seem most unprepared."

(43) And Cyrus said to this, "You seem to me, Gobryas, to be amazed that when I came with a lesser army I marched up to the wall itself, but now, when I have a greater power, I am not willing to march under the walls themselves. (44) But do not be amazed, for to march up to and to march by are not the same: All march up in the order they think best for fighting, and those who are moderate retreat in the safest way, not in the quickest way. (45) But one must of necessity march by with the wagons extended and the rest of the baggage train kept back in a long narrow file. Yet all these things need to be covered by armed troops, and the baggage train must not appear to the enemy to be anywhere bare of weapons. (46) The fighting part of those who march like this must of necessity be in a thin and weak order. So if they wished to attack in a mass from the wall, at whatever point they engaged at close quarters, they would be much stronger than those who were marching by. (47) Moreover, for those who march in a long line, help is a long way off, while for those who charge out from a wall against others nearby, there is but a short way both to charge out

and to retreat again. (48) If we march by their walls while staying at least as far from them as is the distance over which we now extend in our march, they will see our multitude, and behind weapons that frame a formation, every mob seems terrible. (49) So if even in this case they come out and attack, we would see them from far away and so would not be taken unprepared. But rather, men, they will not even try it, when it is necessary for them to go out far from the wall, unless they suppose that they are stronger with their whole [force] than we with ours, for retreat would be fearful."

(50) When he said this, he seemed to those present to speak correctly, and Gobryas led just as he had ordered. As the army passed by the city, he always, as he moved away, increased the strength of the part in the rear.

(51) After marching like this on the following days, he arrived at the borderlands of the Syrians and Medes, from which he had set out. There being here three forts of the Syrians, he himself took the weakest one by attacking it with violence. As for the other two, Cyrus by terror and Gadatas by persuasion induced their guards to surrender.

ᕦ CHAPTER 5 ᕤ

(1) After this was completed, he sent to Cyaxares and directed him to come to the camp so that they might deliberate about how to make use of the forts they had taken and also so that after seeing the army he might join in deliberating more generally about what they should do next. "But if he orders that I come to him," he said, "tell him that I will do so in order to camp together with him." (2) So the messenger departed in order to report these things. Cyrus meanwhile gave orders to prepare the tent of the Assyrian [king], which the Medes had selected for Cyaxares, and to do so in the best possible way, not only stocking it with all the other provisions they had but also installing into the woman's quarters of the tent a woman, and with her the music girls who had been selected for Cyaxares.[32] (3) So this is what they were doing.

The one sent to Cyaxares said what had been commanded. After hearing him, Cyaxares knew that it was better for the army to remain

in the borderlands, for the Persians that Cyrus sent for had also ar-
rived.³³ There were forty thousand archers and targeteers. (4) Seeing
that even these were damaging Median territory in many ways, it
seemed more pleasant to be rid of them than to receive another mob.
He who had led the army out of Persia asked Cyaxares, in accord with
Cyrus' letter, whether he had need of the army.³⁴ When he said that
he did not need it, he went on that same day with the army to Cyrus,
since he heard that he was nearby.

(5) On the next day Cyaxares marched out with those of the Median knights who had remained with him.³⁵ When Cyrus perceived
that he was approaching, he went to meet him and brought along
with him the Persian cavalry, which was already numerous, all the
Medes, Armenians, Hyrcanians, and, of the other allies, those with
the best horses and weapons, thus showing his power to Cyaxares.

(6) When Cyaxares saw many noble and good troops following
Cyrus, yet with himself a retinue both small and of little worth, it
seemed to him to be something dishonorable, and he was seized by
grief. When Cyrus got down from his horse and approached in order
to kiss him according to custom, Cyaxares got down from his horse
but turned away. He did not kiss him but was crying visibly. (7) Cyrus
next bade all the others stand apart and be at ease, and he himself
took Cyaxares' right hand and led him away off the road and under
some palm trees. He ordered some Median rugs to be put down for
him, and he sat him down; then sitting down beside him, he said the
following: (8) "Tell me, by the gods, uncle," he said, "why are you
angry at me, and what harsh sight do you see that you are so harshly
disposed?"

Then Cyaxares answered, "Because, Cyrus, I think that I am a natural descendant of a father who was a king and of ancestors [who were
kings] for as far back as the memory of human beings reaches, and I
believe that I myself am a king. Nevertheless, I see myself riding here
in this humiliating and unworthy fashion, and I see you present here,
great and magnificent, accompanied by my own retinue along with
additional power. (9) I think that it is harsh to suffer these things even
at the hands of enemies, and much more harsh, by Zeus, at the hands
of those from whom I ought least to have suffered them: I think that
it would be more pleasant to sink into the earth ten times than to be
seen so humiliated and to see my own troops neglecting me and

laughing at me. I am not ignorant of this, that not only are you greater than I, but even my slaves are stronger than I in this present encounter, and they have been so prepared that they have the power to do me more harm than they can suffer at my hands." (10) And as he was saying this, he was still more overcome by tears, so that he also led Cyrus' eyes to be filled with tears.

After pausing a little, Cyrus said such things as follow: "But in this, Cyaxares, you neither speak the truth nor judge correctly, if you think that Medes have been so prepared by my presence that they are capable of harming you. (11) I do not wonder, however, that your spirit is roused and that you are afraid. As for whether you are justly or unjustly severe with them, however, I shall let this go, for I know that you would not take it well if you should hear me making a defense on their behalf. It seems to me to be a great error, however, for a man who is a ruler to be severe with all his subjects at the same time: He must of necessity, by frightening many, make many enemies, and by being severe with them all at the same time, he must of necessity instill the same attitude in them all. (12) This is why, I assure you, I did not send these troops back without me, for I was afraid that your anger might provoke something painful for all of us. Since I am now present with the gods' [help], this is now no danger for you. That you believe you have been unjustly treated by me, however, I take ill—if working as much as is within my power to do as many good things for my friends as is possible, I then seem to have accomplished the opposite of this. (13) But let us not blame ourselves so pointlessly. Rather, if it is possible, let us see most clearly what sort of unjust act I have committed. I put forward the proposition most just for among friends: If I shall come to light as having done you some harm, I agree that I am unjust. If, however, I come to light as having done no harm, and as having wished none, will you agree in turn that you have not been unjustly treated by me?"

(14) "I must," he said, "of necessity."

"If I plainly appear to have done good things for you and to have been enthusiastic to do as many as I was able, would I not be even more deserving of your praise than of blame?"

"It would be but just," he said.

(15) "Come then," said Cyrus, "let us examine one by one all the things I have done. In this way both what is good and what is bad

will be especially clear. (16) Let us begin with this command of mine, if this seems sufficient also to you.[36] Doubtless when you perceived that many enemies had assembled, and that these had set out against you and your country, you sent directly to the Persians' common council asking for allies and to me personally asking that, if any Persians were to come, I try to come myself as their leader.[37] Was I not in this persuaded by you, and did I not report to you, leading as many men, and as good, as I was able?"

"Yes, you came," he said.

(17) "In this, then, first of all," he asked, "tell me whether you discerned any injustice of mine toward you, or rather a good deed?"

"A good deed, clearly," said Cyaxares, "at least in this."

(18) "What about when the enemies came," he asked, "and it was necessary to contend against them, did you detect somewhere in this that I either withdrew from labor or avoided risks?"[38]

(19) "No, by Zeus," he said, "certainly not."

"What about then, after victory became ours, with the gods' [help], and the enemies retreated? When I proposed to you that we pursue them in common, that we take vengeance in common, that, if any noble and good thing should result, we harvest it in common,[39] are you able to accuse me of seizing the advantage in this?"

(20) Now Cyaxares fell silent at this.

Cyrus spoke again, as follows: "But since in this case it is more pleasing for you to be silent than to answer, tell me whether you believed you were at all unjustly treated because, when going in pursuit did not seem to you to be safe, I excused you from sharing in this risk yourself but asked you to send some of your knights with me. If I was unjust in asking this, even though I had stood by you before as an ally, show it."

(21) When Cyaxares fell silent at this too, he said, "But if you do not wish to answer this either, speak to the next point and say whether I was unjust here: When you saw the Medes enjoying themselves, you answered me by saying you did not wish to make them stop and compel them to go out to risk their lives. Do I here seem to you to have done something harsh because I avoided getting angry at you for your response, and I asked you for what I knew to be the most minor thing for you to give and the easiest thing to be commanded to the Medes: I asked that you grant me anyone who wished to follow along.

(22) Obtaining this from you would accomplish nothing, if I did not persuade them. I went, therefore, and tried to persuade them, and with those whom I persuaded, I marched, since you had allowed it. If you believe that this deserves blame, then, as it appears, it is not even blameless to accept from you what you give. (23) So this is how we started. But after we departed, what did we do that is not obvious? Was the enemies' camp not captured? Were not many of those who came against you killed? And of the enemies who are still living, have not many been deprived of their weapons, and many of their horses? Now you see your friends possessing and leading away the valuables of those who before used to carry and lead your valuables away, and they bring them partly to you, partly to those under your rule. (24) The greatest and most noble thing of all is that you see your country being enlarged and your enemies' being diminished; you see your enemies' forts occupied; those of yours that previously ended up under the power of the Syrians you now see, in opposite fashion, have come over to you. If there is in these events some evil for you, or something that is not good for you, I do not know how I could say that I wish to learn it; nothing prevents me from listening, however. (25) So tell me what your judgment is in this regard."

Having spoken like this, Cyrus stopped. Cyaxares said the following in response: "But Cyrus, I do not know how one could say that the things you have done are bad. Be well assured, however, that they are good in such a way that the more numerous they appear, the more they oppress me, (26) for I would wish to make your country greater by my power rather than to see mine so enlarged by you, for your deeds are noble to you who do them, but somehow the same deeds bring dishonor to me. (27) And as for valuables and the way you are now giving them to me, I think it would be more pleasant to bestow them upon you than to receive them from you like this, for being enriched in them by you, I perceive even more those things in which I am becoming ever more impoverished. And I think that if I should see my subordinates unjustly treated by you, at least in small things, it would cause me less pain than seeing now that they have experienced great goods at your hands.

(28) "If I seem to you to lack judgment in the way I take these things to heart, put yourself in my situation, and then see how they appear to you. If you were raising dogs to guard yourself and what belongs

to you, and if someone were attentive to them and thereby made them more familiar to himself than to you, would he delight you by this attention? (29) If this seems to you to be a small matter, consider this: If someone should so dispose your attendants, whom you maintain for the sake of your protection and military expeditions, such that they wish to be his rather than yours, would you owe him gratitude in return for this good deed? (30) What about this, which human beings long for most of all and attend to most dearly:[40] If someone is so attentive to your wife that he makes her love himself rather than you, would he delight you by this good deed?[41] Far from it, I think, and I know well that in acting like this, he would be unjust to you to the highest degree. (31) In order to mention also what pertains especially to my experience, if someone should be so attentive to the Persians whom you led here that they followed him with more pleasure than they followed you, would you believe him to be a friend? I think not, but more of an enemy than if he had killed many of them. (32) What about this, if you—in a friendly way—bid one of your friends to take what he wants, and on hearing this he then takes as much as he is able to get and leaves, and if he then becomes rich with what is yours, while you do not have the use of even a moderate amount, would you be able to believe such a person to be a blameless friend? (33) Now, however, if I have not suffered this at your hands, Cyrus, I think I have suffered something similar. Admit the truth: When I said to lead those who were willing to go, you took my entire power and left, leaving me deserted. And what you took with my power, now, of course, you bring to me, and my country you enlarge with my power. Since I am in no way responsible for these blessings, I seem to offer myself up to be treated well, like a woman, and both to other human beings and to these my subordinates you appear a man and I unworthy of rule. (34) Do these seem to you to be good deeds, Cyrus? Be assured that if you cared for me at all, you would guard against depriving me of nothing so much as my dignity and honor. What do I gain if my land is extended but I am myself dishonored? For I was not ruler of the Medes because I was stronger than all of them but rather because they esteemed us to be better than they in everything."

(35) Interrupting him as he was still talking, Cyrus said, "By the gods, uncle, if I ever gratified you before in anything, gratify me now in what I ask: For the time being, stop blaming me. When you get

more evidence of how we are disposed toward you, then, if what I have done comes to light as having been done for your good, greet me in turn when I greet you and believe me to be a benefactor, but if the reverse, blame me then."

(36) "Perhaps," said Cyaxares, "you speak nobly. I will do so."

"Well then," said Cyrus, "shall I kiss you?"

"If you wish," he said.

"And you will not turn from me as you did just now?"

"I will not turn from you," he said.

So he kissed him.

(37) When the Medes, Persians, and the many others saw this (for the result was a matter of concern for all of them), they took immediate pleasure and beamed with joy. Cyrus and Cyaxares mounted their horses and both rode in the lead. The Medes followed Cyaxares (for Cyrus gave them a nod to do so), the Persians followed Cyrus, and the others followed after them. (38) When they arrived at the camp and settled Cyaxares into the tent that had been prepared for him, those so assigned got busy preparing provisions for Cyaxares. (39) For as long as Cyaxares was at leisure before dinner, the Medes came to him, some by themselves and of their own accord, but most having been so ordered by Cyrus; and they brought gifts: someone a beautiful cupbearer, another a good cook, another a baker, another a musician, another cups, another beautiful clothes. Nearly everyone brought him at least some gift from what he himself had received. (40) Cyaxares consequently changed to the opinion that Cyrus was not leading them to revolt from him and that the Medes were not paying him any less attention than before.

(41) When it was time for dinner, Cyaxares called Cyrus, expecting to dine with him, since it was some time since he had seen him. But Cyrus said, "Do not order it, Cyaxares. Do you not see that the troops who are here are all here because they have been made expectant by us? I would not be acting nobly if, neglecting them, I should seem to attend to my own pleasure. When they think they are neglected, good soldiers become much more despondent, while the worthless ones become much more insolent. (42) But especially since you have come a long way, have your dinner now. If some come and honor you, greet them in turn, and entertain them so that they may have confidence in you. I shall leave and turn to what I mentioned. (43) Early tomorrow

morning the chief aides will report here at your doors in order that we may all deliberate with you about what ought to be done in the future. Come and put forward for us the question as to whether it still seems that we should campaign or whether now is the moment to dissolve the army."

(44) After this, Cyaxares was busy about his dinner, but Cyrus assembled those of his friends who were the most competent at both thinking and, if needed, acting in concert, and he spoke as follows: "Men, friends, the things we prayed for at first are now, with the gods' [help], ours. Wherever we march, we control the land. We see our enemies being diminished, and we ourselves becoming more numerous and stronger. (45) If our newly added allies should be willing to remain by our side, we would be able to accomplish much more, both by force, if it should be the moment for that, and by persuasion, if that should be needed. To contrive that as many of our allies as possible decide to remain is no more my work than yours. (46) But just as when it is necessary to do battle, the one who subdues the most will be regarded as the strongest, so also when it is necessary to persuade, the one who makes the most people share our opinion would justly be judged to be most skilled in speech and action. (47) Do not be concerned, however, about how you will display to us what sort of speech you would say to each of them. Rather, make your preparations bearing in mind that those you persuade will become evident by what they do. (48) Let this, then, be your concern. I will try to make it my concern that when the soldiers deliberate about campaigning further, they have all that they require, to the extent I am able to provide it."

BOOK VI

✧ CHAPTER 1 ✧

(1) So they spent the day like this, and after dinner they went to rest. All the allies arrived early on the next day at Cyaxares' door. For as long as Cyaxares continued to adorn himself, he could hear that there was a great mob at his door. During this same time some of Cyrus' friends presented Cadusians who begged him to remain, others Hyrcanians, another Sacians, and another Gobryas as well. Hystaspas led in Gadatas the eunuch, who also begged Cyrus to remain. (2) Here, then, knowing that Gadatas had long ago all but perished in fear that the army would be disbanded, Cyrus laughed and said, "Gadatas, it is clear that you express this judgment just because you have been persuaded by Hystaspas to do so."

(3) And Gadatas stretched his hands toward heaven and swore an oath that it was not because he had been persuaded by Hystaspas that he judged things as he did. "But I know," he said, "that if you all go away, it is all over for me. This is why I approached him, on my own, and asked whether he knew what you had in mind to do about the disbanding of the army."

(4) And Cyrus said, "Then I am unjustly blaming Hystaspas."

"Unjustly indeed, by Zeus, Cyrus," said Hystaspas, "since I only said to Gadatas here that it was impossible for you to keep on campaigning; I told him that your father sent for you."

(5) And Cyrus said, "What are you saying? Did you dare to bring this up also, whether I wished it or not?"

"Yes, by Zeus," he said, "for I see you are a bit too desirous of being looked on admiringly as you circulate among the Persians and of showing your father how you have accomplished each particular."

Cyrus said, "Do you not desire to go back home?"

"No, by Zeus," said Hystaspas, "nor will I be going back. I will be general and stay until I make Gadatas here the master of the Assyrian."

(6) So they said such things joking with each other, yet in earnest. At this point Cyaxares came out augustly adorned and sat down on the Median throne. When all who needed to had assembled and silence prevailed, Cyaxares spoke as follows: "Men, allies, since I happen to be present and am older than Cyrus, perhaps it is proper that I begin the discussion. It now seems to me to be opportune to converse first about whether it seems to be opportune to continue with this campaign or to disband the army now. So let anyone state his judgment about this very issue."

(7) After this, first the Hyrcanian said, "Men, allies, I do not know whether speeches are at all needed where deeds themselves show what is superior, for we all know that when we stay together we do the enemy more evil than we suffer. Yet when we were apart from each other, they treated us in the way that was most pleasant for themselves, but for us was surely most severe."

(8) Next the Cadusian said, "What should we say about being separated, each going back home, when, as it seems, it is not advantageous even for men on campaign to be separated? At least when we went on campaign apart from your multitude, and not even for long, we paid the price, as you also know."

(9) Next Artabazus, the one who once said that he was a relative of Cyrus,[1] said such things as follow: "Cyaxares, I differ with the first speakers to this extent: They say that it is still necessary to stay and campaign, but I say that when I was at home, I used to be on campaign. (10) There, I often had to go to the rescue when our things were led off, and I was often bothered with fear and worry about our forts, which were ever the objects of plots. Further, I had to do all this at my own expense. Now I possess their forts, and I fear them not: I feast on their things and drink what belongs to the enemy. Since what is at

home is a campaign, but this is a holiday, I do not think we should disband this festive gathering."

(11) Next Gobryas said, "Men, allies, I praise Cyrus' fidelity up to this point, for he has not been false in what he promised.[2] But if he leaves the country, it is clear that the Assyrian will be refreshed, even though he has not paid retribution for the injustices he tried to do to you and did do to me. I, for my part, will pay to him the price of having become your friend."

(12) After all these Cyrus said, "Men, it does not escape me that if we disband the army, our situation would become weaker, and that of the enemy would wax again. As many as have had their weapons taken away will swiftly again have others made. As many as have been deprived of their horses will swiftly again acquire others. In place of those who have been killed, others will reach their prime and others will be born. It would consequently not be amazing if they should very quickly be able to bother us again.

(13) "Why then did I bid Cyaxares introduce a discussion about dissolving the army? Be well assured that it was because I fear the future, for I see advancing upon us rivals against whom, if we will campaign like this, we will not be able to fight. (14) Winter is certainly approaching, and even if there are shelters for ourselves, then, by Zeus, there are not for the horses, the attendants, or the bulk of the soldiers, and without all these things, we would not be able to campaign.[3] As for provisions, we have exhausted them wherever we have gone. Wherever we have not gone, they, because they fear us, have carried them up into their forts so that they may have them themselves and we not be able to take them. (15) Who, then, is so good or so strong that he would be able to campaign while also fighting hunger and cold? Now if we are going to campaign like this, I say we ought to disband the army voluntarily rather than be driven out involuntarily by our lack of means. But if we wish to keep campaigning, I say we ought to do this, to try as quickly as possible to take from them as many secure places as possible and to construct as many secure places as possible for ourselves. If this happens, whichever side is able to take and lay up more will have more provisions, and whichever side is stronger will be besieged.[4] (16) We do not differ now from those who sail the sea, for they sail constantly, yet they leave what has been sailed over no more their own than what has not been

sailed over. If we have forts, these will deprive our enemies of the land, and everything will go more smoothly for us.

(17) "Some of you might perhaps fear that you will need to stand guard far from your own country. Do not balk at this. Since we are far from home even as it is, we will take it upon ourselves to guard the posts nearest to our enemies; you possess and cultivate the parts of Assyria that are on your borders. (18) If by standing guard we are able to keep safe the places that are near to them, you who possess those that are farther from them will live in great peace, since I do not think they will be able to neglect those who are near to themselves and plot against you who are far away."

(19) After this was said, all the rest stood up and said that they were enthusiastic to join in promoting these measures, and Cyaxares did so also. Gadatas and Gobryas each said that they would build a fort, if the allies consented, so that these too would be friendly to the allies. (20) Now when Cyrus saw that all were enthusiastic to do everything he said, he said in conclusion, "If we wish to carry out as much as we say we ought to do, it would be necessary to procure as quickly as possible siege engines for taking down the enemies' forts, and builders for raising up fortresses for ourselves."

(21) After this Cyaxares promised that he would himself make and provide a siege engine, as did Gobryas and Gadatas, and Tigranes as well. Cyrus himself said that he would try to make two. (22) After these things were decided, they began bringing in engine makers, and each furnished what was needed for the engines. They appointed men who seemed to be most suited to be involved in these matters.

(23) Since Cyrus realized that these things would take time, he sat the army down where he thought it was healthiest and of easiest access for whatever needed to be brought in. He attended to whatever points were in need of secure fortification, so that, if ever he camped farther off with his main strength, whoever stayed back would remain in safety. (24) In addition, of those he thought would know most about the land, he asked from which places the army would be benefited as much as possible, and he constantly led out foraging parties. He did this that he might take as many provisions as possible for the army, that they might become healthier and stronger from laboring on their marches, and that they might remember their positions on expeditions. (25) So Cyrus was involved in these matters.

The deserters and captives from Babylon were saying the same thing, that the Assyrian had departed for Lydia, taking many talents of gold and silver, and other possessions and all sorts of jewelry. (26) Now the mob of the soldiers said that he had already gone off in fear to secure his valuables. Yet Cyrus knew that he had departed in order, if it should be at all possible, to put together a [force] to rival his own, so he vigorously made counterpreparations in the belief that fighting would still be necessary. He consequently filled out the Persian cavalry, taking some horses from captives and some others from friends, for these he accepted from all, and he never refused if someone gave him a beautiful weapon or a horse. (27) He also prepared chariots both from the chariots of captives and from anywhere else he was able. He abolished the Trojans' way of using chariots, which existed before, and the Cyrenaeans' way, which exists even now, and previously those in Media, Syria, Arabia, and all those in Asia used their chariots just as the Cyrenaeans do now. (28) It seemed to him that what was probably the superior part of the power, since the best troops were on the chariots, formed a part of those who only skirmished at long range and contributed no great weight to conquering, for three hundred chariots take three hundred fighters, and these use twelve hundred horses. Their drivers, as was to be expected, are these whom they especially trust, the best.[5] So this is another three hundred who harm the enemy in no way whatsoever. (29) So he did away with this way of using chariots. In its place he provided war chariots, chariots with strong wheels so that they do not shatter easily, and with long axles, for everything broad is less often overturned. The box for the drivers he made like a turret out of strong timbers. Its height reached to their elbows, so that the horses could be guided from above the box. He clad the drivers in armor all over, all except for their eyes. (30) He also attached iron scythes of about three cubits to the axles on both sides of the wheels, and others that looked downward from the chariot box toward the earth, in order that the chariots might thrust directly into the midst of their opponents.[6] Those in the land of the king even now make use of their chariots in the way that Cyrus then equipped them.[7] He also had many camels, of which some were collected from friends and others were captured, and they were all collected together. (31) So this is how these things were concluded.

[Cyrus] wished to send someone as a scout to Lydia to learn what the Assyrian was doing, and Araspas, the one who was watching over the beautiful woman, seemed to him to be suited for this. Things had turned out in the following way for Araspas: Having been seized by love for the woman, he was compelled to address her with proposals of a union. (32) She denied him, however, and was faithful to her husband even though he was absent, for she loved him intensely.[8] She did not accuse Araspas to Cyrus, however, for she was hesitant to set at odds these men who were friends. (33) Thinking that it would help him to get what he wished, Araspas then threatened that if the woman did not wish to voluntarily, she would do so involuntarily. Because she now feared his violence, the woman no longer hid it, but she sent her eunuch to Cyrus and bade him tell all. (34) When he heard, he laughed at the one who had professed to be stronger than love. He sent Artabazus back with the woman's eunuch and bade him to tell him not to use violence with such a woman, but he said that if he were able to persuade her, he would not prevent it. (35) Artabazus went to Araspas and reviled him, calling the woman a sacred trust and telling him of his impiety, injustice, and incontinence.[9] Araspas consequently cried many painful tears, was downcast with shame, and had all but perished from the fear that he would suffer at Cyrus' hands.

(36) Now when Cyrus learned this he summoned him and spoke with him in private. "I see, Araspas," he said, "that you are afraid of me and are terribly ashamed: Cease being so. I hear that gods are overcome by love, and I know that human beings, even those seeming to be very prudent, have suffered similarly from love. It was I myself who knew that I would not be able to be so steadfast as to neglect the beautiful when in their company. And I am the cause of this problem for you, for I shut you up with this unconquerable problem."

(37) And Araspas interrupted and said, "But you, Cyrus, are similar in this matter as also in others, gentle and forgiving of human failings. Other human beings make me sink with grief. Since the rumor of my misfortune has circulated, my enemies take pleasure at my expense, and my friends come and advise me to get myself out of here, so that I not suffer at your hands, for they hold that I have been very unjust."

(38) And Cyrus said, "Then be well assured, Araspas, that with this reputation you are able to gratify me greatly and to bestow great benefits on our allies."

"Would that some occasion might arise," said Araspas, "in which I might again be useful to you in an opportune moment!"

(39) "Then if you pretended to run away from me and were willing to go over to our enemies, I think you would be trusted by our enemies."

"I do too, by Zeus," said Araspas, "and also by our friends, for I know I could spread the word that I had fled from you."

(40) "Then you could come back to us," he said, "when you know all the enemies' affairs. They would even make you a partner in their conversations and deliberations, I think, since they would trust you, so that not even one iota of what we wish to know would escape your notice."

"Consider me as already on the move this instant," he said, "for perhaps it will help bring trust if I seem to have fled when on the brink of suffering at your hands."

(41) "And will you be able to leave the beautiful Panthea?" he said.

"Yes," he said, "for I clearly have two souls. I have now concluded this while philosophizing with the unjust sophist, Love. If indeed the soul is one, it is not at the same time both good and bad, nor does it love both noble and shameful deeds at the same time and at the same time both wish and not wish to do the same things. But it is clear that there are two souls, and whenever the good one conquers, it does what is noble, but whenever the vile one, it undertakes what is shameful. Now, since it took you as an ally, the good soul conquers, and very much so."

(42) "If, then, you have decided to go," said Cyrus, "you must do so as follows, in order that you may be trusted more also by them. Report our affairs to them, and report them in such a way that what you say would especially be a hindrance to what they wish to do. They would be a hindrance if you should say that we are preparing to invade somewhere in their country, for hearing this, with each one afraid about what he has at home, they would to a lesser degree assemble with all their strength. (43) Stay with them as long as possible, for it will be especially opportune for us to know what they are doing when they are nearest to us. Advise them to order themselves in

whatever way may seem to be superior. They will hesitate to change their order, and even if they do change it on the spur of the moment, they will become confused."

(44) Thus Araspas went out, and taking along his most trusted attendants and saying to some what he thought advantageous for the affair, he departed.

(45) When Panthea perceived that Araspas was departing, she sent to Cyrus and said, "Feel no pain, Cyrus, over Araspas' departure for the enemy, for if you allow me to send to my husband, I promise you that a friend much more trustworthy than Araspas will arrive. As for power, I know that he will report to you with as much of it as he is able to bring. The father of him who is now king was his friend, but this present king once even undertook to separate my husband and me from each other. So since he believes him to be insolent, be well assured that he would gladly escape to a man such as you are."

(46) When Cyrus heard this, he bade her send to her husband, and she did so. When Abradatas recognized the tokens from his wife and perceived how things stood, he gladly marched to Cyrus with about a thousand horse. When he reached the Persian lookouts, he sent to Cyrus saying who he was. Cyrus ordered that they lead him directly to his wife.

(47) When the woman and Abradatas saw each other, they embraced, as was to be expected after so hopeless a period. After this, Panthea spoke of Cyrus, of his piety, moderation, and pity toward herself. When Abradatas heard her he said, "Then what could I do, Panthea, on your behalf and my own to repay the favor to Cyrus?"

"How else," said Panthea, "than by trying to be for him as he was for you."

(48) After this Abradatas went to Cyrus. When he saw him, he took his right hand and said, "In return for the good you have done for us, Cyrus, I have nothing better to say than that I give myself to you as a friend, as an attendant, and as an ally. And in whatever I see that you are serious, I will try to become as strong a helper as is in my power."

(49) And Cyrus said, "I accept. Now I dismiss you to dine with your wife, but some other time you will need to be with me in my tent, with both your friends and mine."

(50) After this, when Abradatas saw that Cyrus was serious about the scythe-bearing chariots and covering both horses and knights in armor, he tried to contribute to him up to one hundred similar chariots from out of his own cavalry, and he prepared to lead them on chariot himself. (51) He harnessed his own chariot with four poles and eight horses. [From her own valuables, his wife Panthea made a golden breastplate and a golden helmet for him, and similarly also his armpieces.][10] He equipped the horses of his chariot entirely with armor of bronze.

(52) So this is what Abradatas was doing. When Cyrus saw his four-poled chariot, he conceived that it was possible to make one also with eight poles, so eight yokes of oxen could pull the lowest story of the siege engines.[11] This was about three fathoms from the ground, including the wheels.[12] (53) It seemed to him that such towers following with each division would be a great aid to its own phalanx and a great harm to their enemy's divisions. On their stories he made galleries and battlements, and he sent up twenty men on each tower. (54) Once everything concerning the towers was organized, he experimented with the pulling of one. The team of eight yokes drew the tower and the men on it much more easily than each team drew its usual weight of baggage, for the weight of baggage for a yoked team was about twenty-five talents.[13] The load for each team on the tower, with timbers in thickness like those of a tragic stage, along with twenty men and weapons, was less than fifteen talents. (55) When he knew that the pulling was easy, he made preparations with the intention of pulling the towers along with the army, believing that seizing the advantage in war was safety, justice, and happiness all at the same time.

∾ CHAPTER 2 ∾

(1) At this time a delegation arrived from the Indian [king] bringing money, and they reported to him that the Indian sent the following message: "Cyrus, I am pleased that you reported to me what you needed, and I both wish to have ties of hospitality with you and am

sending you money. If you need more, send for it. The messengers I have sent have been commanded to do whatever you bid them do."

(2) After hearing this, Cyrus said, "Then I bid the rest of your delegation to remain here where you have pitched your tents, to guard the money, and to live in the way that is most pleasant to you. But I bid three of you to go to the enemy as though you had been sent by the Indian to discuss an alliance. After learning about matters there, both what they are saying and what they are doing, report back as quickly as possible both to me and to the Indian. If you serve me well also in this, I will owe you still more gratitude for this service than because you have come and brought me money. Spies disguised as slaves are able to know and report back only as much as everyone knows, but men like you often learn even what is planned."

(3) The Indians listened with pleasure and then were treated with hospitality by Cyrus. After making their preparations, they left on the next day, promising that after learning as much from the enemy as they possibly could, they would return as quickly as possible.

(4) As a man who was intending to do nothing minor, Cyrus prepared for the war in a magnificent manner. He did so both in other respects and in that he did not limit his care to what was decided upon by the allies. He also stirred up mutual strife among his friends in order that they would each show themselves most well armed, best at riding, best with the spear, best in archery, and most eager for labor. (5) He worked at this by leading them out on hunts and honoring those who were superior in each [skill]. When he saw rulers taking care that their own soldiers would be superior, he spurred them on by praising them and gratifying them in whatever way he was able. (6) If ever he made a sacrifice or conducted a festival, even on this occasion he made contests in all things human beings care about for the sake of war, and he gave prizes in a magnificent way to the winners. And there was great delight in the army.[14]

(7) Nearly as many things as Cyrus wished to have when he went on campaign had now been completed for him, except the siege engines, for the Persian cavalry was already filled out at ten thousand troops. As for the scythe-bearing chariots, the ones he himself was preparing were already filled out at one hundred, and the ones Abradatas the Susan undertook to prepare like Cyrus' were also filled out at another one hundred. (8) And the Median chariots as well, which

Cyrus had persuaded Cyaxares to transform from the Trojan and Libyan mode into the same as his own, were filled out at another one hundred. And mounted on the camels were assigned two men each, as archers. The greatest part of the army thus reached the opinion that it had already conquered completely and that the enemy was insignificant.

(9) When they were of such a disposition, the Indians whom Cyrus had sent as spies came back from the enemy. They said that Croesus had been chosen as the leader and general over all of the assembled enemies; that it had been decided by all the allied kings that each should report with his entire power, that they contribute a vast sum of money, and that they spend it both by hiring what mercenaries they could and by giving gifts to whom they ought. (10) They said also that many Thracian swordsmen had already been hired and that Egyptians were sailing in. These, they said, were as many as one hundred and twenty thousand in number, with shields reaching to their feet and large spears, such as they still have now, and swords. They said moreover that an army of Cyprians was coming; and that all the Cilicians, the Phrygians from both Phrygias, the Lycaonians, the Paphlagonians, the Cappadocians, the Arabians, the Phoenicians, and the Assyrians (along with the ruler of Babylon) had already reported; and that Ionians, Aeolians, and nearly all the Greeks dwelling in Asia had been compelled to follow along with Croesus; and that Croesus had sent to Lacedaemonia about making an alliance. (11) They said that the army was assembling by the Pactolus River; that they were about to go forward into Thymbrara, where even now they hold the assembly of the barbarians of Lower Syria who are subject to the king; and that orders had been given to all to prepare a marketplace there.

The captives too said nearly the same things as these, for Cyrus also took care to capture those from whom they were likely to learn anything. He also sent out spies disguised as though they were runaway slaves.

(12) Now when Cyrus' army heard these reports, they got worried, as was to be expected. They went about more subdued than was their habit, they did not appear so radiant, they formed groups, and every place was full of people asking questions of one another and talking about these reports.

(13) When Cyrus perceived that fear was spreading through his army, he called together both the rulers of the armies and all those whose despondency would, he thought, do some harm, and whose enthusiasm would bring some benefit. He told his aides not to hinder it if any others who bore arms wished to stand by in order to hear the speeches. When they assembled, he spoke such things as follow: (14) "Men, allies, I called you together because I saw some of you, when the reports came from the enemy, who looked very much like human beings who were afraid. It seems to me to be amazing if any of you is afraid because the enemy is assembling, while you are yet not confident even though you see that we have now assembled in much greater numbers than when we were victorious over them, and that we have with the gods' [help] prepared much better now than we did before. (15) By the gods, what would you have done, you who are now afraid, if some people reported that our rival was advancing equipped as we are, and if you heard, first of all, that those who conquered us previously were coming against us again, possessing in their souls the victory they gained before? And, next, that those who then made short work of the skirmishing of archers and spearmen were coming again now and with very many others similar to them? (16) Next, what if you heard that just as they conquered before by arming their infantry with heavy weapons, now their cavalry was coming against our cavalry after itself having been prepared in the same way, that is, that they had rejected both bows and spears, and that each had taken up a strong lance and formed the intention of coming up close in order to make the battle hand-to-hand? (17) Further, chariots are coming, but not those that stand still, as they used to do, turned backward as if for flight. The horses on these chariots have been clad in armor; the drivers stand in wooden turrets, covered over on all their upper parts with breastplates and helmets; and iron scythes have been fitted about the axles, since these too intend to drive directly into the ranks of those who oppose them. (18) Further still, they will attack also on camels, and one hundred horses could not endure the sight of even one of these. Further, they are coming with towers from which they will give aid to those on their side, and by shooting down from above they will prevent us from fighting against them on a level field. (19) Now if someone had reported to you that these were your enemies' preparations, what would you have done, you

who are now afraid because it has been reported that Croesus has been chosen as the enemies' general! He was so much worse than the Syrians that while the Syrians ran away when they were defeated, Croesus ran away when he saw them defeated, instead of assisting his allies. (20) Next, as has indeed been announced, our enemies themselves do not hold that they are competent to do battle with us, and they are hiring others, in the belief that these will fight better on their behalf than would they themselves. Nevertheless, if, even though their circumstances are like this, they seem terrifying to some, while ours seem contemptible, I say, men, that we ought to send them off to the opposition, for they would help us much more by being over there than by being present here."

(21) After Cyrus said this, Chrysantas the Persian stood up and spoke as follows: "Cyrus, do not be amazed if some of the troops get sullen-faced when they hear what is being reported, for they are so disposed not because they are afraid but because they are annoyed. Similarly, if some people wished to have lunch and thought they were going to right away, and then some task were announced that had of necessity to be finished before lunch, no one, I think, would be pleased on hearing it. In the same way, then, while thinking that we were going to be rich right away, when we heard that there is still a task remaining that needs to be done, we too became sullen-faced, not out of fear but because we would wish that it had been done already. (22) However, since we will contend not only over Syria, where there is grain in quantity, sheep, and date-bearing palms, but also over Lydia, where there is much wine, many figs, and much olive oil, and whose shore is washed by the sea, over which more good things come than anyone has ever seen—when we bear all this in mind, we are no longer annoyed. Rather, our confidence returns immediately, that we may enjoy more quickly these Lydian goods as well." Thus he spoke, and the allies all were pleased at his speech and praised it.

(23) "It seems to me, men," said Cyrus, "that we should go against them as quickly as possible, in order that, in the first place, we may beat them in arriving, if we are able, where their provisions are collected. Secondly, the faster we go, the less we will find them to have, and the more we will find them to lack. (24) This is what I say, but if anyone judges it to be safer or easier for us in some other way, let him teach us."

After many concurred that it was expedient to march against their enemies as quickly as possible, and no one spoke in opposition, Cyrus then began a speech such as follows: (25) "Men, allies, the souls, bodies, and weapons that we will need to use have, with god's [help], already been prepared for a long time. But now for the journey we need to prepare provisions for no less than twenty days both for ourselves and for as many four-footed [creatures] as we use. Upon calculation I find that the journey on which we will find no provisions will last more than fifteen days, for we have removed some of them, and our enemies have removed as much as they were able. (26) So we must prepare sufficient food, for without this we would not be able either to do battle or to live. Each must have as much wine as will suffice for us to habituate ourselves to drink water, for the part of the journey when we are without wine will be long, and even if we prepared a very great quantity of wine, it would not suffice. (27) That we may not fall into disease from suddenly going without wine, we must do the following: Let us begin directly to drink water with our food, for since we already do this, it will not be a big change. (28) Whoever eats barley bread eats a barley cake that has already been kneaded with water, and whoever eats wheat bread eats bread that has been mixed with water, and all things boiled have been prepared with water in the greatest quantity. If we only drink wine after our food, our soul, having no less [than it needs], will be refreshed. (29) Next, we must take away also our after-dinner wine until we become water drinkers without noticing it, for adjusting little by little makes every nature bear up under changes. God also teaches in this way, leading us little by little from the winter's cold to endure intense summer heat and from the summer's heat to the intense winter's cold. Imitating him, we must proceed toward the point we need to reach by habituating ourselves beforehand.

(30) "Trade the burdensome weight of your blankets for provisions, for extra provisions will not be useless. Do not be afraid that you will not sleep with pleasure because you are in need of blankets. If you do not, blame me. Whoever has clothes in greater abundance, however, will be aided by them greatly in both sickness and health.

(31) "We must prepare meats and side dishes that are spicy, pungent, and salty, for these lead us to eat bread and last longest.[15] When we go out into the areas not yet plundered, where it is likely that we

will get grain right away, we must provide on the spot hand mills with which to make the bread, for these are the lightest of bread-making tools. (32) We must also provide the things human beings need when they are sick. Their bulk is quite small, but if such a fortune befalls us, they will be most necessary. We must also have straps, for most things, for both human beings and horses, are attached with straps. When they wear out and break, one is of necessity reduced to idleness, unless one has some extras. It is good that whoever has been taught how to smooth a lance not forget a rasp, (33) and good also to bring a file, for he who whets his spear whets in some measure his soul as well, for it is shameful to be bad after having sharpened one's spear. We must also have extra wood for chariots and wagons, for when there are many motions, there must of necessity also be many things that fail. (34) We need to have also the most indispensable tools for all these things. Although artisans will not be present everywhere, almost everyone is competent to make what will suffice as a temporary repair. We must also have a shovel and a mattock for each wagon, and an ax and a scythe for each pack animal. These things are both useful for each in private and often beneficial for the sake of the common [enterprise].

(35) "Now as for what is needed for provisioning, you leaders of those bearing arms examine those subordinate to you. We must not neglect anything that one of them might need, for their need will become ours. As for what I order us to bring with the beasts of burden, you rulers of the baggage carriers examine them and compel whoever does not have what has been ordered to procure it. (36) Next, you rulers of the road builders have on lists from me those who have been dismissed, whether from the spearmen, the archers, or the slingers. Of these, you must compel those dismissed from the spearmen to march with a wood-cutting ax, those from the archers with a mattock, and those from the slingers with a shovel. They must march in squads with their tools in front of the wagons so that if there is any need of roadmaking, you may get to work directly, and so that if I need them at all, I may know where I may find and use them.

(37) "I will also bring smiths, carpenters, and leather cutters, all with their tools and of an age for military service. Thus, if the army has any need of such arts, nothing may be left undone. These will have been released from the formation of those who carry arms, but

they will be in an assigned place. They will serve whoever wishes to pay them a wage for what they understand.

(38) "If any merchant wishes to follow along because he wishes to sell something, he may. If he is caught selling anything on the days it has been announced that we must have our own provisions, he will be deprived of everything.[16] When these days have gone by, he may sell as he wishes. Whatever merchant comes to light as providing the largest market will obtain gifts and honor from both the allies and me. (39) If any of the merchants believes that he needs money for purchases, if he brings me references and sureties as a pledge that he will indeed go along with the army, let him take what money we have.

"So these are my declarations. If anyone else sees anything else needful, let him indicate it to me. (40) You go away and make preparations; I will offer sacrifices for our departure. Whenever the omens are favorable, we will indicate it.[17] All must report to their leaders in the place that has been ordered and must have the things that have been specified. (41) Each of you leaders get your own order ready and then all come to me, so that you may each learn your various places."

❧ CHAPTER 3 ❧

(1) When they heard this, they began their preparations, and Cyrus sacrificed. When the sacred victims brought noble results, he departed with the army. On the first day he camped as nearby as possible so that if someone forgot something, he might go after it, and if someone should realize that he needed something, he could provide himself with it. (2) Now Cyaxares stayed back with one-third of the Medes so that matters at home not be left abandoned. Cyrus marched as quickly as he was able. He kept the cavalry first, but he continually sent scouts and lookouts in front of them up onto the best points for forward observation. He led the baggage train behind the cavalry. Where it was flat, he formed many chains of wagons and pack animals. Since the phalanx followed in the rear, if any of the baggage train lagged behind, the rulers who chanced to come by would take care that nothing hinder them from marching forward. (3) Where the road was narrower, those bearing arms put the baggage train in the

middle and marched on both sides. If anything impeded their march, those of the soldiers who were nearby took care of it. The companies usually used to march keeping their baggage beside themselves, for all baggage carriers had been ordered to proceed beside their own respective companies unless some necessity should prevent it. (4) The captain's baggage carrier led holding an insignia recognized by those in his own company. They consequently marched close together, and they each took great care that their own things not be left behind. Since they formed up like this, it was not necessary to go searching for each other, all things were at the same time both ready at hand and more safe, and the soldiers quickly got what they needed.

(5) When the scouts who went forward thought they saw human beings on the plain getting both fodder and wood, and when they saw pack animals carrying other such things away, and other pack animals grazing, and moreover when looking off in a forward direction they thought they detected either smoke or dust up in midair, from all this they pretty nearly knew that the army of their enemies was nearby. (6) So the commander of the scouts directly sent someone to report this to Cyrus. When he heard this, he ordered them to stay at their lookout posts and to keep reporting whatever new things they saw. He sent a cavalry company forward and ordered them to try to capture some of the people on the plain, in order that they might learn more clearly how things were.[18] (7) They who were so ordered did so. He himself brought the rest of the army to a halt right there, in order that they might prepare what he thought useful before they got too close. He passed the word for them to eat lunch first and then to stay in their companies and be attentive to announcements. (8) After they had lunch, he summoned leaders of the cavalry, infantry, and chariots, and also the rulers of the divisions of the siege engines, baggage train, and wagons, and these assembled. (9) But those who had raced down onto the plain captured people and brought them back. Upon being questioned by Cyrus, those who were captured said that they had gone forward from the army camp for fodder (and others for wood) and that they had gone past their advance guard posts, for everything was scarce because of the size of the army.

(10) On hearing this Cyrus asked, "How far distant is the army from here?"

They said, "About two parasangs."[19]

At this Cyrus asked, "Was there any talk of us among them?"

"Yes, by Zeus," they said, "a great deal, to the effect that you were approaching and were already nearby."

"Well, then," said Cyrus, "and were they delighted on hearing that we were coming?" This he asked for the sake of those present.

"No, by Zeus," they said, "they were not delighted but were even greatly distressed."

(11) "What are they doing now?" said Cyrus.

"Getting in order," they said. "And yesterday and the day before they were doing this same thing."

"Who is doing the ordering?" said Cyrus.

They said, "Croesus himself and, with him, both some Greek man and someone else, a Mede. It is said, in fact, that he is a fugitive from you."

And Cyrus said, "But O greatest Zeus, would that it should come to pass for me to seize him as I wish!"

(12) Next he ordered them to lead the captives away, and turned as if to say something to those who were present. At this moment someone else reported from the commander of the scouts and said that a large order of cavalry was visible on the plain. "And we expect," he said, "that they are riding forward because they wish to see our army, for about thirty other cavalry troops are riding a considerable distance in front of this larger order and, in fact, are coming against us, perhaps because they wish to take our lookout post if they are able. We at this post are one squad of ten."

(13) Cyrus ordered some of the knights who were always with him to ride up beneath the post and keep still, out of the enemy's sight. "When our squad of ten leaves the post, get up out of your cover and attack those who are going up against the post. In order that those from the large order do not cause you problems, Hystaspas, advance with your thousand knights and show yourself in opposition to the enemy's formation. Do not pursue anywhere into the unseen, but advance only after having taken care that the lookout posts remain yours. If any men ride toward you raising their right hands, receive them in a friendly way."

(14) So Hystaspas went away and put on his armor, but the aides rode off directly, as [Cyrus] had ordered.[20] Just within the line of lookout posts the one who had been sent long ago as a spy, the guard of

the Susan woman, met them. (15) Now Cyrus, when he heard, leaped from his seat, went to meet him, and shook his right hand, but the others, as was to be expected since they knew nothing, were stunned by his action. Then Cyrus said, "Men, friends, an excellent man has returned to us, and now all human beings must know his deeds right away. He did not go away because he was overcome by shame or because he was afraid of me. Rather, he went because I sent him in order to learn clearly how things were for the enemy and to report back to us.[21] (16) Now I remember what I promised to you, Araspas, and I will fulfill it in conjunction with all who are here.[22] Men, it is just that you all honor him as a good man, for it was for our good that he both ran risks and endured such oppressive blame."

(17) After this they all embraced Araspas and shook his right hand. Cyrus then said that there had been enough of that and said, "Tell us, Araspas, what it is opportune for us to know. Neither lessen nor reduce the enemy's size from the truth, for it is superior to see them fewer after having thought them greater than to discover them stronger after having heard them fewer."

(18) "Indeed," said Araspas, "I acted so that I might know most certainly the size of their army, for I myself was present and helped to put it in order."

"Then you know," said Cyrus, "not only their number but also their order."

"I do indeed, by Zeus," said Araspas, "and how they intend to conduct the battle."

"But tell us first," said Cyrus, "their general number."

(19) "They are all ordered, then," he said, "to a depth of thirty, both infantry and cavalry (except for the Egyptians), and they extend about forty stadia, for I took great care to know how much land they occupied."[23]

(20) "And how," asked Cyrus, "are the Egyptians ordered? You said, 'except for the Egyptians.'"

"The brigadier generals were ordering each brigade of ten thousand into a square of one hundred on every side, for they said that this was their customary formation also at home. It was only most unwillingly that Croesus gave his consent to them to be so ordered, for he wished to outflank your army by as much as possible."

"And why," said Cyrus, "did he desire this?"

"So that, by Zeus," he said, "he would encircle you with his longer line."

And Cyrus said, "But they would not know whether the encirclers might themselves be encircled. (21) What it was opportune for us to learn from you we have heard. Men, you must act like this: As soon as you leave here, examine the armor of both your horses and yourselves, for often a man, a horse, and a chariot become useless because of some little deficiency. Early tomorrow morning, while I am sacrificing, it is necessary first that both men and horses have their morning meal in order that we not need it whenever it may be opportune to act. Then you, [Arsamas, the left, and you, Chrysantas] take the right wing, since you have it [now],[24] and you other brigadier generals the ones that you have now, for when the contest is close at hand, it is not opportune for any chariot to change horses. Give orders to the captains and lieutenants to form up with each platoon in a phalanx two deep." Each platoon was twenty-four troops.

(22) And one of the brigadier generals said, "And if we are in an order so shallow, Cyrus, does it seem to you that we will be sufficient against so deep a phalanx?"

And Cyrus said, "Does it seem to you that phalanxes too deep to reach the enemy with their weapons either harm their enemies or help their allies at all? (23) I would wish that these hoplites who are one hundred deep be ordered instead to a depth of ten thousand, for in this way we would fight against very few [at any one time].[25] From the depth at which I will set our phalanx, however, I think I will make the whole of it active and itself everywhere an ally to itself. (24) Behind those with breastplates I will order spearmen, and bowmen behind the spearmen, for why would anyone put first in order those who even agree themselves that they would not persevere in a hand-to-hand battle? When they are covered by troops with breastplates, both the spearmen and the bowmen will stand their ground and will cause the enemy pain over the heads of all those in front. In whatever one harms one's opponents, in all this one clearly lightens the load for his allies. (25) However, behind all I will station those who are called 'ultimates.'[26] Just as there is no benefit from a house without either a firm foundation or those things that make a roof, so not even from a phalanx is there any benefit if the first and the last will not be good.

(26) "Put yourselves in order as I direct. You who rule over the targeteers, position your platoons in a similar fashion behind these, and you who rule over the bowmen position them in a similar fashion behind the targeteers. (27) You who rule over those who are behind all the others, keep your men last and direct each to oversee those in front of them.[27] Direct them to encourage further those who are doing what is needful and to threaten severely those who are soft, and if anyone turns around, willing to desert, to punish them with death. It is the work of those who are first to encourage by both word and deed those who follow. But you who are put in order behind all others need to provide more fear to the bad than does the enemy. So carry out these orders.

(28) "You, Euphratas, who rule over those who are on the siege engines, act in such a way that the yoked teams that pull the towers will follow the phalanx as closely as possible. (29) You, Dauchas, who rule over the baggage train, lead the entire army of this sort behind the towers. Have your aides punish severely those who advance ahead of time or lag behind. (30) You, Carduchas, who rule over the carriages that carry the women, place them last, behind the baggage train, for having all these things follow will both provide the appearance of numbers and be an opportunity for us to set an ambush, and if the enemy tries to encircle us, it will compel him to make his circumference greater. Insofar as they need to surround a greater area, they must of necessity become weaker to this same extent. (31) So carry out these orders.

"You, Artaozus and Artagerses, each keep a regiment of one thousand of your infantry behind these. (32) And, Pharnuchus and Asiadatas, you each rule a regiment of one thousand cavalry. Do not put them in order in the phalanx, rather put them in arms behind the wagons, off by yourselves. Then come to me with the other leaders. You need to prepare yourselves in the expectation that you will have to be the first to enter the contest. (33) And you, ruler of the men on the camels, put them in order behind the carriages, and do what Artagerses directs. (34) You leaders of the chariots cast lots, and let the one of you whose lot it is take his one hundred chariots and put them in position in front of the phalanx. Of the other groups of one hundred chariots, let one follow in a column along with the phalanx on the right side of the army, and let the other do so on the left." So Cyrus was putting them in order like this.

(35) Abradatas the king of Susa said, "For you, Cyrus, I am a willing volunteer for the position immediately in front of the rival phalanx, unless something else seems better to you."

(36) Both admiring him and taking his right hand, Cyrus asked the Persians on the other chariots, "Do you consent to this?" When they answered that it was not noble to yield in this, he had them cast lots. Abradatas received by lot the position for which he had volunteered, and he was opposite the Egyptians.

(37) Then, after going away and taking care of the things I mentioned above, they had their dinner, and after stationing guards, they went to rest.

✧ CHAPTER 4 ✧

(1) Early on the next day, Cyrus was offering sacrifices, and the rest of the army, after having a meal and pouring libations, were putting on their armor, donning many beautiful tunics and many beautiful breastplates and helmets. They also put armor on the horses, both pieces for their foreheads and others for their chests. On the single horses they put thigh pieces; on those that pulled the chariots, side pieces.[28] Consequently, the entire army flashed with bronze and was brilliant with purple.

(2) Abradatas' chariot with four poles and eight horses had been very beautifully adorned. When he was about to put on the linen breastplate that was worn in his country,[29] Panthea brought him a golden helmet, armlets, broad bracelets for his wrists, a purple tunic that reached down to his feet and whose lower parts had deep folds, and a plume dyed dark red. Having measured his armor, she had had these things made in secret from her husband. (3) He was amazed when he saw them, and he asked Panthea, "Surely, my wife, you did not have this armor made for me by breaking up your own jewels, did you?"[30]

"No, by Zeus," Panthea said, "at least not my most precious one, for you will be my greatest jewel, if you appear also to others as you do to me." As she said this, she put his armor on him, and although she tried to avoid being noticed, her tears poured down her cheeks.

(4) Since Abradatas was a sight worth looking at even before he was clad in this armor, he appeared most handsome and most free, since his nature was already such. Taking the reins from the groom, he was already prepared to go up onto the chariot. (5) Then Panthea bade all those present withdraw and said, "Abradatas, if any other woman ever honored her husband more than her own life, I think you know that I too am one of these. Now why should I need to state each point one by one, since I think I have provided you with deeds more persuasive than the words I say now? (6) Being disposed to you as you know me to be, I nevertheless swear to you on my friendship and yours that I would wish to be put under the earth in common with you, when you have been a good man, rather than live on, a woman in shame with a man in shame, so worthy of what is most noble have I deemed both you and myself. (7) And I think we owe Cyrus a great favor, because when I was a captive and had been selected for him, he did not think it worthy to possess me either as a slave or as a free woman under a dishonorable name, but he guarded me for you as if he had taken his brother's wife. (8) In addition, when Araspas, the one who was watching over me, defected, I promised him that if he would allow me to send to you, a man much more loyal and better than Araspas would come to him."

(9) So she said this; and Abradatas, admiring her words and laying his hand on her head, looked up to heaven and swore this oath: "Greatest Zeus, grant that I may come to light as a husband worthy of Panthea, and a friend worthy of Cyrus, who has honored us." Having said this at the doors of the chariot box, he went on up into the chariot. (10) When he had gone up and the groom closed up the chariot box, Panthea, having no other way to take her leave of him, kissed the chariot. His chariot was already advancing, but she followed along behind, unnoticed, until, turning and seeing her, Abradatas said, "Take heart, Panthea, farewell, and now go back." (11) After this her eunuchs and servant women took her and led her back to the carriage, and laying her down, they concealed her behind the carriage cover. Although the sight of Abradatas and his chariot was a beautiful one, people were not able to look at him until Panthea went away.

(12) When the omens from Cyrus' sacrifices were favorable and the army had been drawn up in order for him just as he directed, and while he was taking possession of one lookout post after another, he called his leaders together and said the following: (13) "Men, friends, allies: As for our sacrifices, the gods show us signs of the same sort as when they granted the previous victory. As for you, I wish to remind you of such things as I think, if you bear them in mind, would enable you to enter the contest in much better spirits. (14) You have practiced what pertains to war much more than have our enemies, you have taken your meals together and have been formed into order together in the same place and for a much longer time than have our enemies, and you have been victorious together with each other. Of our enemies, the majority have been defeated together with each other. Of those on each side who have not yet been in battle, our enemies' [new allies] know that they have traitors for partners, while you who are with us know that you will fight alongside troops who are willing to give aid to their allies. (15) It is to be expected that those who trust each other will stand their ground and fight with one mind, while it is necessary that those who distrust each other will each deliberate about how most quickly to get out of harm's way. (16) So let us go, men, against our enemy—with armed chariots against the enemy's unarmed, just as also with armed cavalry and horses against their unarmed—to do battle at close quarters. (17) You will fight against infantry troops, most of whom you have fought before, and the others, the Egyptians, are as poorly armed as they are deployed, for they have shields too big for them to do or see anything, and since they are deployed to a depth of one hundred, it is clear that they will prevent each other from fighting, except for a very few. (18) If they trust that they will drive us out by pushing, it will first be necessary that they hold out against horses and iron made even stronger by [charging] horses; and even if some one of them does persevere, how will he at the same time be able to fight a cavalry battle, to fight an infantry phalanx, and to fight against our towers? Those on the towers will aid us further, and striking our enemies from above they will lead them not to fight but put them in an insoluble position. (19) If you think you are still in need of anything, talk to me. For with the gods' [help], we will not be at a loss for anything. And if any one wishes to say anything, let him speak. If not,

after you have gone to the sacrifices and prayed to the gods to whom we sacrificed, then go to your companies. (20) And let each of you remind his troops of what I reminded you, and let one show himself to the ruled to be worthy of rule, showing himself fearless in bearing, countenance, and words."

BOOK VII

ᐁ CHAPTER 1 ᐁ

(1) After praying to the gods, they rejoined their companies,[1] and attendants brought in things to eat and drink to Cyrus and his followers while they were still at their sacrifices. Cyrus, standing just as he was, offered up the first fruits, had his dinner, and continued to share with whoever was in want. After both pouring a libation and praying, he drank, and the others who were around him did likewise. After this, he besought ancestral Zeus to be their leader and ally, and he got up on his horse and so ordered those around him. (2) All those around Cyrus had been armed in the same arms as Cyrus—with purple tunics, brass breastplates, brass helmets, white crests, swords, and one spear of cornel wood for each. Their horses had been armed with bronze pieces for their foreheads, chests, and shoulders, and these very shoulder pieces also served as thigh pieces for the rider.[2] Cyrus' arms were different only in that whereas the others had been painted with a golden color, Cyrus' arms shone like a mirror. (3) When he mounted and kept still, looking off in the direction in which he was going to march, thunder sounded on the right, and he said, "We will follow you, greatest Zeus." He set forth with the cavalry commander Chrysantas and the cavalry on the right, and with Arsamas and the infantry on the left. (4) He passed the word to look toward the standard and to follow in an even line. His standard was a golden eagle with its wings spread open, mounted on a long spear. Even now

this still remains the standard for the king of the Persians. Before seeing the enemy, he made the army halt as many as three times.

(5) When they had advanced about twenty stadia,[3] they already began to see their enemies' army coming on in opposition. When all were visible to each other and the enemy recognized that their phalanx extended far beyond on both sides, they halted their own phalanx— for otherwise there is no way to encircle—and began bending their line forward for the encirclement, making their own formation like a gamma on both sides, so that they might engage everywhere at the same time.[4] (6) Cyrus, on seeing this, did not draw back but led on just as before. Noting how far out on each side they made the hinge around which they turned and stretched out their wings, he said, "Have you noted, Chrysàntas, where they have made their hinges?"

"Certainly," said Chrysantas, "and I am amazed, for they certainly seem to me to be drawing off the wings far from their own phalanx."

"Yes, by Zeus," said Cyrus, "and from ours."

(7) "Why is this?"

"It is clear that they are afraid that if their wings come near to us when their phalanx is still far away, we will attack them."

"Then," said Chrysantas, "how will the one group be able to help the other when they are so distant from each other?"

"But it is clear," said Cyrus, "that when the wings are extended and are opposite the sides of our army, turning into a phalanx, they will come at us with the intention of fighting on all sides at once."

(8) "Then do they seem to you," said Chrysantas, "to plan well?"

"For what they see, at least. For what they do not see, they are coming at us in still worse a way than in column. But you, Arsamas," he said, "lead on calmly with the infantry as you see me doing. You, Chrysantas, follow along with your cavalry at a pace equal to his. I will go off to that place from which I think it opportune to begin the battle, and as I go along I shall examine how things stand for us. (9) When I am there, and when we are already close to each other and still approaching, I will begin the paean, and you press onward more quickly. At the moment we make contact with the enemy—and you will perceive it, for I think there will be no little uproar—Abradatas will then drive with his chariots into those who oppose him, for he will have been told to do so. You need to follow staying as close as possible to the chariots, for it is especially in this way that we will fall on our enemies while they are in confusion. I will be there too, as quickly as I am able, in pursuit of the men, if the gods are willing." (10) Having said this and having begun the passing of the watchword, "Zeus, savior and leader," he went on. As he passed between the chariots and troops in breastplates, when he looked at some in their formations, he would then say, "Men, how pleasant it is to see your faces!" Again, later, he would say among others, "Do you realize, men, that the contest at hand is not only about today's victory, but also about the one that you won before and about every happiness?" (11) Going up among others he would say, "Men, in the future, one must no longer blame gods, for they are allowing us to acquire many good things. But let us be good men." (12) Again, alongside others, as follows: "To what more noble club could we ever invite each other than to this one?⁵ For now it is possible by being good men to contribute many good things to each other." (13) Again, alongside others, "You know, men, I think, that the prizes now set before the victorious are to pursue, to strike, to kill, to have good things, to hear noble things, to be free, to rule. But to the bad, clearly the opposite of these. So whoever loves himself, let him fight along with me, for I will never voluntarily bring myself to do anything evil or shameful."

(14) When he was alongside any of those who had fought along with him before, he would say, "What must I say to you, men? You know what sort of day the good have in battle, and what sort the bad."

(15) When, as he was going around, he came alongside Abradatas, he stopped, and Abradatas gave over his reins to the groom and went to him. Others of the infantry and charioteers who were in order nearby also ran up. Cyrus said among those who had come up beside him, "God, Abradatas, just as you did, thought you and those with you to be deserving of being positioned first among the allies.⁶ Remember that when you must enter the contest, there will be Persians who will look upon you, who will follow you, and who will not allow you to contend without support."

(16) And Abradatas said, "What is set against us seems fine to me, Cyrus, but the flanks trouble me. There I see the wings of our enemies stretched out in strength with both chariots and arms of all sorts, but on our side there is nothing ordered against them but chariots. Consequently, had I not obtained this position by lot, I would be ashamed to be here, so much do I think I am in the safest position."

(17) And Cyrus said, "But if your own situation is fine, be confident also about those on the flanks. With gods' [help], I will soon show these same flanks to be devoid of enemies. And do not, I beg of you, hurl yourself upon the Egyptians, your adversaries, until you see that those whom you now fear are running away." Thus did he boast when the battle was about to occur; otherwise, he was not much of a boaster. "When, however, you see them in flight, believe that I am already at hand and charge into the men, for you then would find your adversaries at their worst and your own troops at their best. (18) But while you still have leisure, Abradatas, by all means drive among your chariots and summon your troops to the attack, encouraging them with your looks and buoying them up with hopes. Implant in them the love of victory, that you may appear the best of those on chariots;[7] and be assured, if this turns out well, all will say in the future that nothing is more profitable than virtue." So after going up on his chariot, Abradatas drove around and did this.

(19) When, as Cyrus continued his rounds, he was on the left, where Hystaspas was with half of the Persian cavalry, he called him by name and said, "Hystaspas, now do you see? Your swiftness has work to do, for if we now get a head start in killing our enemies, none of us will die."

(20) And Hystaspas laughed and said, "But we will take care of the troops opposite to us, but assign to others the enemies on our flank so that they may not be at leisure."

And Cyrus said, "But I am myself going against them. But remember this, Hystaspas: To whichever of us god grants victory, if anything is left of the enemy anywhere, let us keep on joining in against whatever part continues to fight." Having said this, he went on.

(21) As he went along the flank, when he came to the ruler of the chariots there, he said to him, "I come to bring you aid. When you perceive us attacking the tip of their wing, then you too must try to drive through the enemy, for you will be in a much safer spot getting through to the outside than being taken on the inside."

(22) When, as he continued his rounds, he was behind the carriages, he ordered Artagerses and Pharnuchus to remain there with their regiments of infantry and cavalry. "When you perceive me attacking those on the right wing, then you too must attack those against you. You will fight against a wing, where an army is weakest, and you will

have a phalanx, the way in which you would be strongest. As you see, the enemy's cavalry is at the extreme end of the wing; be sure to send the company of camels against them, and be assured that you will see the enemy become ridiculous even before you fight them."

(23) Having accomplished these things, Cyrus went over to the right side. Croesus believed that the phalanx with which he himself was marching was already nearer to the enemy than were the out-stretched wings, so he raised a signal to the wings not to keep marching forward but to turn there in their places. When they stood opposite, looking toward Cyrus' army, he signaled to them to march against the enemy. (24) And thus did three phalanxes advance against Cyrus' army, one against the front, then two others, one against the right and one against the left. Great fear consequently spread throughout all of Cyrus' army, for like a little tile that has been put inside a big one, Cyrus' army was surrounded on all sides except the rear by the enemy with cavalry, heavy infantry, targeteers, archers, and chariots.[8] (25) Nevertheless, when Cyrus directed, they all turned to face against the enemy, and there was everywhere a great silence owing to their hesitancy about what was coming. When it seemed to Cyrus to be opportune, he began the paean, and all the army chanted along. (26) After this they raised the war cry to Enyalius,[9] and at the same time, Cyrus shot forward. Directly taking the enemy on their flank with his cavalry, he engaged them at close range in the quickest way. The infantry assigned to him followed quickly, and they began to envelop them from two sides, so that he was clearly getting the advantage, for he attacked with a phalanx against their flank.[10] Consequently, the enemy was soon in vigorous flight.

(27) When Artagerses perceived Cyrus at work, he himself attacked the left and sent the camels forward, just as Cyrus had ordered. The horses, even from very far off, did not await their attack, but some became senseless and fled, others began rearing, and others crashed into each other, for such is the effect of camels upon horses. (28) With his own troops in order, Artagerses set upon them in their confusion. The chariots charged against both right and left at the same time, and many who were fleeing the chariots were killed by the troops following up the attack on the flank, and many who were fleeing these troops were caught by the chariots.

(29) Abradatas waited no longer. Shouting, "Men, friends, follow me," he plunged in and did not spare his horses but severely bloodied them with his whip, and the other charioteers joined his attack. The enemy chariots promptly began to flee from them, some after picking up their dismounted fighters, others even abandoning them.[11] (30) But Abradatas dashed right through and charged into the Egyptian phalanx. Those nearest to him in the order also charged with him. Now it is clear also from many other times and places that there is no phalanx stronger than one assembled from allies who are friends, and it was also shown here too: His companions and tablemates charged in with him, but when the other drivers saw the Egyptians waiting in a great mass, they veered off after the chariots in flight and followed them. (31) Where Abradatas and those with him made their charge, since the Egyptians were not able to withdraw because others on their sides stood fast, they struck and knocked down those who stood upright with the impetus of the horses, and they crushed the fallen, both the [men] and their weapons, with their horses and wheels. Wherever the scythes reached, they cut up everything with their violence, both arms and bodies. (32) In this indescribable confusion, because of heaps of all sorts of things, Abradatas and others of those who joined in the charge fell out of their chariots when their wheels bounced off, and so these men who had been good were here cut down and killed.[12] The Persians followed up, and where Abradatas and his cohorts had charged, they fell on and killed the enemy in their confusion. Yet those Egyptians who had suffered nothing, and there were many of them, advanced in opposition to the Persians.

(33) Here, then, there was a terrible battle with spears, lances, and swords. Nevertheless, with their numbers and weapons, the Egyptians were getting the advantage, for their spears were strong and long, and they continue to use them even today; and their large shields cover their bodies much more than breastplates and normal shields, and since they extend to the shoulder, they are helpful in pushing.[13] So locking their shields together, they pushed and advanced. (34) Since they held out their smaller shields with their arms extended, the Persians were not able to hold out against them, but striking and being struck, they withdrew backward foot by foot until they were under the [protection of the] siege engines. When they came here, however, the Egyptians were struck again, this time from

the towers. And the rear guard did not allow either the archers or the spearmen to flee, but they extended their swords and compelled them to shoot and throw. (35) There was thus a great slaughter of men, a great crash of weapons and arrows, and much shouting by those who were calling out to each other for help, by others who were yelling encouragements, and by others who were invoking gods.

(36) At this time Cyrus arrived in pursuit of those who had been arrayed against him. When he saw that the Persians had been pushed from their positions, he was grieved, and realizing that he could in no way stop the enemy from their advance more quickly than if he should ride around to their rear, he directed his cohorts to follow and rode around to their rear. And they fell upon and struck them as they looked the other way, and they killed many. (37) When the Egyptians perceived it, they shouted that the enemy was in their rear, and they faced about even while getting hit. And here, then, infantry and cavalry were jumbled together in battle. Someone who had fallen beneath Cyrus' horse and was being trampled stabbed his horse in the belly with his sword. Once stabbed, the horse lurched and threw Cyrus. (38) Here, then, one could have come to know how worthwhile it is for a ruler to be loved by his cohorts, for all immediately shouted out and fought their way toward him: They pushed and were pushed, they struck and were struck. And some one of Cyrus' aides leaped down from his own horse and threw him up onto it.

(39) After Cyrus was mounted, he saw that the Egyptians were already being hit from all sides, for Hystaspas was already on hand with the Persian cavalry, and Chrysantas was also present. He no longer allowed these to charge into the Egyptian phalanx, but he ordered them to shoot their arrows and throw their spears from the outside. He then rode around, and when he was next to the siege engines, he decided to go up on one of the towers and investigate whether any other part of the enemy anywhere was standing their ground and fighting. (40) After he had gone up, he saw the plain full of horses, human beings, chariots—fleeing, pursuing, conquering, being conquered. But he was not able to detect that any part was still standing its ground anywhere, except for the Egyptians. Since they were at a loss, they made a circle all around and sat down beneath their shields so that only their weapons could be seen. Thus they no longer did anything, but they suffered much that was terrible.

(41) Admiring and pitying them because they were good men and were being destroyed, Cyrus had all the encircling troops back off and allowed no one to continue to do battle. He sent them a herald and asked whether they all wished to be destroyed by those who had betrayed them or to save themselves and their reputation of being good men.[14]

They answered, "How could we save ourselves and our reputation of being good men?"

(42) Cyrus again said, "Because we see that you alone are standing your ground and are willing to fight."

"Yes, but after this," said the Egyptians, "what could we do that is noble to save ourselves?"

And Cyrus next said to this, "If you should save yourselves without having betrayed any of your allies, and if without surrendering your weapons you become friends to those who choose to save you, even though it is possible for them to destroy you."[15]

(43) On hearing this they asked further, "If we become your friends, how will you see fit to treat us?"

Cyrus answered, "By exchanging benefits."

The Egyptians again asked, "What benefits?"

To this Cyrus said, "For as long as the war lasts, I would give you a wage greater than you now receive. When there is peace, I will give land, cities, women, and servants to any of you who wish to stay with me."

(44) When the Egyptians heard this, they asked that he exempt them from campaigning against Croesus, for they said that they were known to him alone. Agreeing on the other points, they gave and received pledges. (45) The Egyptians who remained at that time continue to be trusted by the king even now, and Cyrus gave them cities, some in the interior, which are even now called Egyptian cities, as well as Larisa and Cyllene by Cume, near the sea, which their descendants possess even now. Having accomplished such things and it being already dark, Cyrus led the army back and camped in Thymbrara.

(46) Of the enemy it was only the Egyptians who distinguished themselves in the battle, and of Cyrus' troops the Persian cavalry seemed best. Consequently, the armament that Cyrus then established for his cavalry continues even now. (47) The scythe-bearing chariots also distinguished themselves impressively. Consequently this war chariot too continues in use even now by whoever is king. (48) The

camels only frightened the horses, however, and the knights mounted
on them certainly did not kill and neither were they killed by [the
enemy] knights, for no horse came close. (49) They seemed to be useful, and yet no noble and good man is willing either to raise a camel
for riding or to practice with one for fighting. Thus they took their old
position again and remain among the pack animals.

ᓇ CHAPTER 2 ᓇ

(1) And after having their dinner and posting their guards, as was
necessary, Cyrus and his cohorts went to bed. Croesus, however, immediately fled with his army toward Sardis, and the other tribes withdrew as far as they were able during the night, each on the road toward its home. (2) When it was day, Cyrus led directly toward Sardis.
When he was at the wall around Sardis, he raised up the siege engines
as if he intended to attack the wall, and he prepared his ladders.
(3) Although he did this, during the coming night he had Chaldaeans
and Persians go up what was thought to be the most precipitous part
of the fortifications of Sardis. A Persian man directed them, one who
had been a slave of one of the guards on the acropolis and had learned
a descent to the river and an ascent back by the same way. (4) When
it became clear that the heights had been taken, all the Lydians fled
from the walls, each to whatever part of the city he could. Cyrus entered the city with the coming of daylight, and he commanded that
no one stir from his post. (5) Having locked himself in the king's quarters, Croesus called out for Cyrus. Cyrus left guards around Croesus,
but he himself led off to the occupied heights. When he saw that the
Persians were guarding the heights as was necessary but that the arms
of the Chaldaeans had been abandoned (for they had run off to sack
the possessions of the houses), he immediately called the Chaldaean
rulers together and told them to leave his army as soon as possible.
(6) "I could not endure," he said, "to see troops in disorder getting
the advantage. You know well that I was prepared to make you
who were campaigning with me blessedly happy in the eyes of all
Chaldaeans. But now do not be amazed if someone stronger happens
upon you as you are going away."

(7) When they heard this, the Chaldaeans became afraid and begged him to cease from his anger and said that they would give back all valuables. But he said that he had no need of them. "But if you wish me to stop being annoyed," he said, "give all you took to those who guarded the heights. For if the other soldiers perceive that those who are in good order get the advantage, all will be fine by me."

(8) So the Chaldaeans did as Cyrus bade them, and the obedient received many and varied valuables. Encamping his own troops in what seemed the most suitable part of the city, Cyrus directed them to remain by their arms and have their lunch.

(9) Having accomplished these things, he bade that Croesus be brought to him. When Croesus saw Cyrus, he said, "Greetings, master, for fortune grants that henceforth you should have this title and I should address you with it."

(10) "And [greetings to] you too, Croesus," he said, "since we are both human beings, at least. But Croesus, would you be willing to give me some advice?"

"Yes, Cyrus," he said, "and I would wish that I might find something good for you, for I think this would be good for me too."

(11) "Then listen, Croesus," he said. "For since I see that the soldiers have performed many labors, run many risks, and now believe that they possess the wealthiest city in Asia after Babylon, I think the soldiers ought to enjoy some benefit. I know that unless they receive some fruit from their labors, I will not be able to keep them obedient for long. Yet I certainly do not want to permit them to plunder the city. I believe that the city would be destroyed, and I know very well that the most worthless troops would get the advantage in the looting."

(12) When he heard this Croesus said, "But allow me to go to some of the Lydians and say that I have obtained from you the policy that looting will not be permitted and that children and wives will not be carried off. Let me say that in return for this I promised you would obtain everything beautiful and good that there is in Sardis and do so from Lydians who are quite willing to give it. (13) If they hear this, I know that every beautiful possession here, whether a man's or a woman's, will be brought to you. Further, in the same way next year, the city will again be full of many beautiful things for you. Yet if you loot it, even the arts will be destroyed, and they say these are foun-

tains of the beautiful things. (14) It will still be possible for you, even after you have seen what is brought in, to deliberate about looting [the city]. First send to my treasuries, and let your guards take them over from my guards." So Cyrus consented to do everything as Croesus had said.

(15) "But by all means, Croesus, tell me how the responses of the Delphic oracle turned out for you," he said, "for it is said that you served Apollo very much and that you obeyed him in everything you did."

(16) "I would wish, Cyrus, that this were so," he said. "As it is, I have approached Apollo with just the opposite behavior, right from the beginning."

"How?" asked Cyrus. "Teach me, for what you say is quite contrary to what one would expect."

(17) "Because, in the first place," he said, "neglecting to ask the god if I needed something, I instead tested whether he was able to tell the truth. Even when noble and good human beings, not to mention gods, realize that they are distrusted, they are not friendly toward those who distrust them. (18) When, however, he realized what I was doing, even though it was very odd and even though I was far from Delphi, of course I sent and inquired about children.[16] (19) At first he did not even answer me. But when, as I thought, I propitiated him by sending many offerings of gold and many of silver, and by sacrificing many victims, then when I asked what I could do to have children, he answered me. He said that there would be children. (20) And born they were, for not even in this did he lie. Yet though they were born, they brought no benefit, for one passes his life a mute, and the best one perished in the prime of his life. Being weighed down by the misfortunes concerning my children, I sent again, and I asked the god what I could do to live out the rest of my life in the happiest way. And he answered me, 'Knowing yourself, Croesus, you will pass through it happily.' (21) I was pleased on hearing the oracle, for I believed that he was granting me happiness, having assigned me the easiest thing. Regarding other people, I believed it was possible to know some but not others, but I believed that every human being knows himself, who he is. (22) And in the period after this, while I kept at peace, I had no complaints about my fortunes after the death of my son. But when I was persuaded by the Assyrian king to campaign against you, I entered upon every risk. I got off

safely, however, and sustained nothing evil, nor do I blame the god in this regard, for when I came to know myself not to be competent to do battle with you, I went away safely with the god's [help], both I myself and those with me. (23) Then again recently, having been softened up by my present wealth and by those who asked me to become their leader, and by the gifts that they gave me and by the human beings who flattered me (for they said that if I were willing to rule, all would obey me and I would be the greatest of human beings)—being puffed up by such words, when all the kings around chose me to be their leader in the war, I undertook the generalship as if I were competent to become greatest, (24) not knowing myself, as we now see, because I thought I was competent to make war against you—you who in the first place have sprung from gods have in the second place descended through a line of kings, and thirdly have been practicing virtue since your childhood.[17] But of my ancestors I hear that the first to rule as a king became both king and freeman at the same time.[18] So not having known these things," he said, "I am justly punished. (25) But now, Cyrus," he said, "I know myself. But does it seem to you that Apollo's word will still be true, that knowing myself I will be happy? I ask you because it seems to me that at the present you could best surmise it, for you would even be able to fulfill it."

(26) And Cyrus said, "Allow me to deliberate about this, Croesus. When I consider your previous happiness, I pity you and I grant already that you may have again the wife you had, as well as the daughters (for I hear you have some), the friends, the servants, and meals with which you used to live. But battles and wars I forbid you."

(27) "By Zeus," said Croesus, "then deliberate no longer to answer about my happiness. I will tell you now that if you do for me what you say, I now have and shall lead the very life that others have believed to be most blessedly happy, and on which I agreed with them."

(28) And Cyrus said, "Who is it that has this blessedly happy life?"

"My wife, Cyrus," he said. "She shared equally in all of my good, refined, and delightful things, but of my cares about how to secure these things, and of war and battle, she did not partake. You seem to be putting me in just the same condition in which I put her whom I loved more than any other human being.[19] Consequently, I think I shall owe other tokens of gratitude to Apollo."

(29) On hearing his arguments, Cyrus was amazed at his good spirits, and in the future he took Croesus wherever he himself went, either because he believed that he was somehow useful or because he held it to be safer in this way.

✬ CHAPTER 3 ✬

(1) Thus they then went to bed. On the next day, Cyrus summoned his friends and the leaders of the army. He assigned some of them to take over the treasuries; he ordered others, with regard to all the valuables Croesus handed over, first to select for the gods whatever the Magi prescribed, then to receive the rest of the valuables, to put them in boxes, to pack them up on wagons, to divide up the wagons by lot, and to take them wherever they themselves went, in order that whenever it was opportune, each could receive what he deserved. (2) They then were doing this.

Cyrus summoned some of the aides who were present and said, "Tell me, has any one of you seen Abradatas? I wonder why, since he previously came often to us, now he is nowhere apparent."

(3) One of his aides answered, "Because, master, he is not alive: He died in the battle charging his chariot into the Egyptians. Except for his companions, the others veered off, they say, when they saw the mass of the Egyptians. (4) And now it is said that his wife took up his corpse, put it into the carriage in which she herself was riding, and brought it somewhere here by the Pactolus River. (5) His eunuchs and attendants, they say, are digging a grave on a certain hill for him who has died. But as for his wife, they say that having adorned her husband with [the jewelry] she had, she is seated on the ground, holding his head on her knees."

(6) On hearing this Cyrus struck his thigh and, leaping up on his horse at the same time, immediately rode with one thousand knights to the scene of the sorrowful event.[20] (7) He bade Gadatas and Gobryas follow with whatever beautiful adornment they were able to get for a dear and good man who had died. He told the person who had charge of the herds that followed [the army] to drive cattle, horses, and many sheep as well to whatever place they

learned him to be, that they might be slaughtered in sacrifice for Abradatas.

(8) When he saw the woman seated on the ground and the corpse lying there, he wept at the sorrowful event and said, "Alas! You good and faithful soul, are you going away and leaving us?" And at the same time he grasped Abradatas' right hand, but the hand of the corpse stayed with his, for it had been cut off with a sword by the Egyptians. (9) On seeing this, he was still more grieved by far. And the woman wailed, and taking the hand back from Cyrus, kissed it and attached it again as best she could, and said, (10) "The rest is also like this, Cyrus. But why must you see? I know that he suffered this not least because of me, and perhaps also no less because of you, Cyrus. For I, foolish I, frequently encouraged him to act in such a way that he might show himself to be a noteworthy friend for you. I myself know that he did not have in mind what he would suffer but what he could do in gratitude to you. Accordingly, he himself died a blameless death, but I who exhorted him sit beside him alive."

(11) Cyrus wept for some time in silence, and then raised his voice, "But woman, surely he has obtained the noblest end, for he has died victorious. Take these things from me and adorn him with them." For Gobryas and Gadatas had arrived bringing many beautiful adornments. "Besides, be assured that he will not be without honor in other respects either, for many will also heap up a memorial mound worthy of us, and as much as is appropriate for a good man will be slaughtered in sacrifice for him. (12) And you," he said, "will not be left isolated, but on account of your moderation and your every virtue, I will honor you also in other respects and will assign someone to you who will escort you wherever you yourself wish. Do but indicate to me to whom you desire to be taken."

(13) And Panthea said, "Take heart, Cyrus: I shall not hide from you to whom it is that I wish to go."

(14) Having so spoken, he went away pitying both the woman for the sort of man she was deprived of and the man for the sort of woman he had left and would no longer see. The woman ordered her eunuchs to go away, as she said, "until I mourn for my husband as I wish." She told her nurse to remain, and she enjoined her, when she was dead, to cover her and her husband with one cloak. The nurse begged her many times not to do it; when she accomplished nothing

and saw her getting angry, she sat down crying. Having long ago secured a short sword, [Panthea] drew it and stabbed herself.[21] Putting
her own head on her husband's chest, she lay dying. The nurse began
to wail aloud and covered them both as Panthea had directed.

(15) When Cyrus perceived the woman's deed, he was stunned and
hurried in the event that he would be able to help out. As for the eunuchs, who were three in number, when they saw what had happened, they also drew their short swords and stabbed themselves,
after standing where she had ordered. It is said even now that the memorial mound of the eunuchs is still standing, piled high even into
the present. They say that on the top of the marker the names of the
man and the woman have been inscribed in Syrian letters, and down
below they say that there are three markers and that "Mace-bearers"
has been inscribed on them. (16) Cyrus, after he approached the scene
of the sorrow, both admiring the woman and mourning, went away.
As was appropriate, he took care that they obtained all things noble,
and a huge memorial mound was heaped up, as they say.

ᘓ· CHAPTER 4 ·ᘓ

(1) After this the Carians fell into faction and were at war with each
other, and since the dwellings of each side were in fortified positions,
they each appealed to Cyrus. Cyrus himself remained at Sardis while
making siege engines and battering rams to knock down the walls of
the disobedient, and he gave Adousius an army and sent him to Caria.
He was a Persian man, who neither was without good sense in other
respects nor was unwarlike, and in particular he was quite charming.
Both Cilicians and Cyprians went on the campaign with him very enthusiastically. (2) This is why [Cyrus] never sent a Persian satrap over
either Cilicians or Cyprians, but the kings from their own regions always sufficed for him.[22] He did take a tribute from them, however;
and whenever an expedition was needed, he summoned them.

(3) So Adousius led an army to Caria, and Carians from both sides
came to him and were ready to receive him into their fortresses to
harm the rival faction. Adousius acted the same way toward both. To
whichever side he was conversing, he said their statements were more

just, and he said it had to be kept a secret from their opponents that they had become friends, as he could in this way better fall upon these opponents unprepared. He declared it right that they offer pledges [of good faith], and that on the one hand the Carians swear to receive them without deceit into their fortresses for the good of Cyrus and the Persians, and that on the other hand he himself be willing to swear that he would enter their fortresses without deceit for the good of those receiving him. (4) Having done these things, he made compacts with both on the same night and in secret from the other, and during this night he marched into the fortresses and took over the strong points of both. When day came, he sat with his army in the middle between the two and summoned the chiefs of both sides. They became angry when they saw each other, for both believed that they had been deceived.

(5) Adousius, however, said the following: "I swore to you that I would without deceit enter into your fortresses for the good of those receiving me. Now if I destroy either of your factions, I believe that I will have come for the harm of the Carians. But if I make peace for you and make it safe for you both to work your land, I believe that I will have been here for your good. Now starting today it is therefore necessary that you have friendly dealings with each other, that you work your land without fear, and that you give and receive children [in marriage] with each other. If, contrary to these [rules], anyone attempts to be unjust, we and Cyrus will be enemies to them."

(6) After this the gates of the fortresses were opened, the roads were filled with people traveling to visit each other, and the fields were filled with people working. They held festivals in common, and everything was full of peace and good cheer. (7) At this time messengers from Cyrus arrived and asked whether he needed siege engines or a larger army. Adousius answered that it was already possible to make use of his army elsewhere. As he said this, he led his army away, leaving garrisons on the heights. The Carians begged him to remain. Since he was not willing, they sent to Cyrus and asked him to send Adousius as their satrap.

(8) Cyrus had meanwhile sent Hystaspas leading an army to the Phrygia on the Hellespont.[23] When Adousius returned, he ordered him to march anew in the direction Hystaspas had gone in order that

[the Phrygians] might more readily obey Hystaspas when they heard that another army was coming.

(9) Now the Greeks who live on the sea gave many gifts and thereby arranged not to have to receive barbarians within their fortresses but to pay tribute and campaign wherever Cyrus directed. (10) The king of the Phrygians, however, was making preparations to withhold the strong points and not submit, and such were his orders. When his subordinate officers revolted from him and he became isolated, he finally surrendered to Hystaspas on condition of receiving a judgment from Cyrus. Leaving strong garrisons of Persians on the heights, Hystaspas went away leading many Phrygian cavalry and targeteers along with his own troops. (11) Cyrus directed Adousius to join Hystaspas and lead the Phrygians who had chosen their own side, leaving them their weapons, but to take away the horses and the weapons from those who had desired to make war and to order them all to follow with nothing but slings.

(12) So this is what they were doing. Cyrus set out from Sardis, leaving behind in Sardis a large infantry garrison, taking Croesus, and leading off many wagons with abundant and varied valuables. Croesus came with accurate written descriptions of what was in each wagon. Giving the writings to Cyrus, he said, "With these, Cyrus, you will know who correctly returns to you what he is transporting and who does not."

(13) And Cyrus said, "You do well taking forethought, Croesus. However, those who are transporting the riches for me are the very ones who also deserve to have them. Consequently, if they should steal anything, they will steal from what belongs to themselves." As he said this, he gave the writings to his friends and officers that they might know who among their overseers returned things safely and who did not.[24]

(14) Regarding the Lydians whom he saw making noble displays with weapons, horses, and chariots and trying in all things to do what they thought would gratify him, these he led with their weapons. Regarding those whom he saw following along ungraciously, he gave their horses to the Persians who joined the campaign first, and he burned their weapons. These too he compelled to follow with slings. (15) Of those who became his subjects, he compelled the ones without weapons to practice being slingers, believing that this was the

most servile weapon.[25] When present along with the rest of one's power, there are times when slingers are exceedingly beneficial, but they themselves, in and of themselves, could not withstand a very few who came to close quarters with weapons for fighting up close— not even if there were all the slingers in the world.

(16) While going on to Babylon he overturned the Phrygians of Greater Phrygia, he overturned Cappadocia, and he made Arabians subjects.[26] From all these he armed no fewer than forty thousand Persian knights,[27] and he distributed many horses from the captives to all his allies. He arrived at Babylon with a vast number of knights, a vast number of archers and spearmen, and innumerable slingers.

᭟ CHAPTER 5 ᭟

(1)When Cyrus reached Babylon, he surrounded the city with his entire army. Then he himself rode around the city with his friends and chiefs of the allies. (2) After he contemplated the walls, he prepared to withdraw the army from the city. A certain deserter came out and said that they were going to set upon him when he was withdrawing his army: "For your phalanx seemed to them to be weak as they contemplated it from the wall." And it is no wonder that it was so. For since they encircled a long wall, it was necessary that their phalanx came to a depth of but a few. (3) On hearing this, then, Cyrus stood with his personal troops in the middle of his army and ordered that the heavy-armed troops fold back the phalanx from the extremity on each wing and withdraw to the stationary part of the army, until the extremity from each side was beside him and the middle.[28] (4) By doing this, then, those who remained stationary immediately became more confident because they were doubled in depth, and those who withdrew likewise became more confident, for the troops that remained stationary immediately became the ones who were adjacent to the enemy. (5) With the phalanx folding back like this, it was necessary that the first and the last be the best, and that the worst be arranged in the middle. An order like this seemed well prepared both for doing battle and for avoiding flight. And, to the extent that the phalanx became shorter by being doubled up, the cavalry and the light-armed troops from the wings came ever closer to the ruler. (6) When they were thus coiled together in close order, they withdrew. As long as arrows reached them from the wall, they did so backward, but when they were beyond arrow shot, they turned around, and going forward at first but a few steps, they turned quickly to the shield side and stood looking toward the wall. As they got farther away, they turned less often. When they seemed to be in safety, they withdrew without stopping until they reached their tents.

(7) When they had encamped, Cyrus summoned his chief aides together and said, "Men and allies, we have seen the city all around. How someone might take such strong high walls by assault I do not think I see, but to the extent that there are more human beings in the city, to this extent I hold that they could be the sooner captured by hunger, since they are not coming out to fight. So unless you have another way to suggest, I say that the men must be besieged like this."

(8) Chrysantas said, "Does not this river, with a breadth of more than two stadia, flow through the middle of the city?"[29]

"Yes, by Zeus," said Gobryas, "and with a depth such that not even two men, with one standing on the other, would reach above the water's surface. Consequently, the city is even stronger by means of the river than by means of the walls."

(9) And Cyrus said, "Chrysantas, let us drop such things as are beyond our power. As quickly as possible, after measuring out sections for each of us, we dig a trench as broad and deep as possible, in order that we need as few guards as possible."

(10) So after measuring out a circle around the wall, but leaving enough room by the river for large towers, he began digging a huge trench at different places along the wall, and they cast the earth up on the side toward themselves.

(11) He began to build towers first by the river, laying their foundations with date palms no less than a plethron in length (for there are some that have grown even greater).[30] For of course when compressed by a load, the date palms bend upward, like the backs of pack asses. (12) He put these down in order that he might seem especially like one preparing to begin a siege, [and] so that if the river should escape into the trench, it would not carry his towers off. In order that

there be as many guard posts as possible, he also raised many other towers on the earth that had been cast up.

(13) This, then, is what they were doing. Those in the fortress were laughing at the siege on the grounds that they had provisions for more than twenty years. On hearing this, Cyrus divided his army into twelve parts, that each part might stand guard for one month a year. (14) When the Babylonians heard this, they laughed much more by far at the thought that Phrygians, Lydians, Arabians, and Cappadocians, whom they believed to be better disposed to themselves than to the Persians, would stand guard.

(15) The trenches had already been dug. Since Cyrus heard that there was a festival in Babylon in which all the Babylonians drank and reveled the entire night, on this night, as soon as it was dark, he took many people and opened the mouths of the trenches toward the river. (16) When this was done, the water traveled down through the trenches during the night, and the path of the river through the city became passable for human beings. (17) When the problem of the river had been taken care of in this way, Cyrus directed his Persian colonels of both infantry and cavalry to report to him with their regiments two abreast, and he directed the other allies to follow behind ordered as they had been previously. (18) So they reported. He sent aides, both infantry and cavalry, down into the dry part of the river, and he bade them consider whether the riverbed was passable.

(19) When they reported that it was passable, he then called together the leaders of the infantry and cavalry and said the following: (20) "Men, friends, the river has yielded us the road to the city. Let us enter with confidence, fearing nothing within, bearing in mind that the troops against whom we are now marching are the very ones we conquered when they had allies in addition to themselves, were all wide awake, sober, armed, and organized.[31] (21) Now we are going against them at a time when many of them are asleep, many are drunk, and all are disorganized. When they perceive us inside, they will be even much more useless than they are now, for they will be thoroughly startled. (22) It is said to frighten those who enter a city that [the city dwellers] go up onto the roofs and throw things down from this side and that. If someone has this in mind, the following will especially bring confidence: If some go up on the houses, we have

an ally in the god Hephaestus. Their porches burn well, for their doors have been made of date palm and are covered over with bitumen, a fuel. (23) We, in turn, have a lot of wood, which will quickly give birth to much fire, and we have pitch and tow, which will quickly excite great flames, so it is necessary that they either flee the houses quickly or quickly be burned up. (24) But come, take up your weapons. I shall lead with the gods' [help]. You, Gadatas and Gobryas, show the way, for you know it. When we are inside, lead in the quickest way to the king's palace."

(25) "Indeed," said Gobryas and those with him, "it would not be amazing if the gates of the king's palace were even unlocked, for the entire city is reveling tonight. We will, however, encounter guards in front of the gates, for some are always posted there."

"We must not delay," said Cyrus, "but advance in order to catch the men as unprepared as possible."

(26) When these things had been said, they went on. Of those who came out in opposition, some were struck and killed, others fled back inside, and others shouted out. But Gobryas and those with him shouted along with them, as if they themselves were also revelers. Going as quickly as they were able, they arrived at the king's palace.

(27) The troops assigned to Gobryas and Gadatas found the gates of the king's palace locked. Those who had been assigned to attack the guards fell upon them drinking beside a great fire, and they promptly treated them as enemies. (28) Since there was shouting and crashing, those inside perceived the uproar, and when the king ordered them to investigate what the matter was, some opened the gates and ran out. (29) When Gadatas and those with him saw the open gates, they rushed in, and after falling upon and striking those who were fleeing back inside, they reached the king. They found him already standing and having drawn the short sword that he had. (30) Gobryas, Gadatas, and those with them subdued him; those who were with him were killed, one as he sought to shield himself, another as he took flight, another attempting a defense with whatever he could. (31) Cyrus sent companies of cavalry through the streets. He told them to kill whomever they found outdoors; he told those who knew Assyrian to declare that those in their houses were to remain inside and that if anyone were caught outside, he would be put to death.

(32) So this is what they were doing, and Gadatas and Gobryas arrived. They first lay prostrate before the gods, because they had avenged themselves upon the impious king; then they kissed Cyrus' hands and feet, shedding many joyous tears and taking delight. (33) When it was day and those who held the heights saw that the city had been captured and the king killed, they surrendered the heights as well. (34) As for the heights, Cyrus immediately took them over and sent up both guards and guard officers; as for the dead, he allowed their relatives to bury them.[32] He ordered the heralds to declare that all Babylonians were to give up their arms. Wherever arms might be taken in a house, he commanded that all those inside would be killed. So they gave up their weapons, and Cyrus deposited them in the citadels so that they would be ready if there were ever any need to use them. (35) After these things had been done, he in the first place summoned the Magi, and because the city had been captured by force of arms, he bade them select first fruits of the booty and sanctuaries for the gods.[33] After this he distributed both houses and government buildings to the very ones he believed were partners in what had been accomplished. He allocated them just as had been decided, the best to the best.[34] If someone thought that he got too little, he bade them come forward and explain.[35] (36) He told the Babylonians to work the land, pay the tribute, and serve those to whom they each were given. He commanded the Persians who were his partners and as many of the allies as chose to remain with him to converse as masters with [the Babylonian subjects] they received.

(37) After this Cyrus was already desirous of establishing himself in the way he held to be fitting for a king. He decided to do this with the concurring judgment of his friends, so that he could appear seldom and with dignity, while provoking as little envy as possible. So he contrived this as follows: When day came, he positioned himself with his army where it seemed suitable, received whoever wished to say something, and, after giving an answer, sent him away. (38) When people knew that he would receive them, countless numbers arrived, and there was much contriving and fighting by those pushing to get in. (39) The aides admitted them, judging as best they could. Whenever any of his friends became visible breaking though the mob, Cyrus extended his hand, led them to him, and spoke as follows: "Men, friends, wait around until we get safe from the mob, then we

shall be together in peace." So his friends would wait around, but the mob would stream in more and more. Consequently, it was evening before he was at leisure to be together with his friends. (40) So Cyrus then said, "Men, it is now the opportune time to part; come early tomorrow, for I wish to converse with you about something." After hearing this his friends departed gladly and ran off, for they had been punished by [neglecting] necessities of all sorts. Thus they then went to bed.

(41) Cyrus reported to the same place on the next day, and a much greater multitude of people who wished to approach him was standing there, and they reported there much earlier than did his friends. So Cyrus stationed a large circle of Persian lancers and told them no one was to enter except his friends and officers of both the Persians and the allies.

(42) After they came together, Cyrus said such things as follow to them: "Men, friends and allies, we cannot possibly blame the gods with the charge that, up to this point, not all we prayed for has been accomplished. If, however, to have great success entails the result that it is not possible to have leisure either for oneself or to enjoy oneself with friends, I bid farewell to this happiness. (43) For surely you took note just yesterday that we began at dawn, and not before evening did we stop listening to those who came here. And now you see these others, more numerous than those yesterday, who are here to give us trouble. (44) Now if one surrenders oneself to them, I calculate that you will have but a small part of me, and I but a small part of you. Of myself I know clearly that I will not have any part whatsoever. (45) I see another ridiculous matter besides. For I am doubtless disposed to you as is to be expected, but of these standing all around here I probably know few or none, yet they all have so prepared themselves [as to think] that if they are victorious in pushing you aside, they will sooner accomplish what they wish from me than you will. I thought it right, if one of them needs something from me, that they serve you my friends and ask for access. (46) Now perhaps someone could ask why I did not arrange it to be so from the beginning, for instead I put myself in the center [of everyone]. It is because I knew the things of the war to be such that the ruler must not be late either in knowing what he must know or in doing what it is opportune to do, and I believed that generals who are seldom seen neglect many of the things

that need to be done. (47) Now, since labor-loving war has gone to rest, it seems to me that my soul also thinks it right to obtain some rest. So then, since I am at a loss as to what I might do to put our [affairs] in a noble condition, and likewise with the [affairs] of the others we need to take care of, let anyone offer counsel about what he sees as being most advantageous."

(48) So Cyrus spoke like this. After him rose Artabazus, who once professed that he was his relative,[36] and he said, "You acted nobly in beginning the discussion, for beginning when you were still young, I very much desired to become your friend, but seeing that you were not in need of me, I was hesitant to approach you. (49) When once you happened to need me to be enthusiastic in reporting Cyaxares' [message] to the Medes, I calculated that if I should embrace these affairs for you with enthusiasm, I would become a familiar of yours, and it would be possible for me to converse with you as long as I wished.[37] And those [services] were done in such a way that you praised me. (50) After this, first the Hyrcanians became our friends when we were very hungry for allies, so we all but carried them around in our arms, cherishing them. After this, when the enemy camp was captured, I did not think there was leisure for you to be around me, and I forgave you. (51) After this, Gobryas became our friend, and I rejoiced. And next Gadatas, and it was already a task to get hold of you. When, however, the Sacians and Cadusians became our allies, it was in all likelihood necessary to court them as well, for they too were courting you.[38] (52) When we came back again to the point from which we set out,[39] and I saw you busy with your horses, chariots, and siege engines, I held that when you were at leisure from these things, then you would have leisure for me. When, however, the terrible message came that all the world was assembling against us, I knew that this was most important.[40] If this went nobly, I thought I knew well that there would be abundant opportunities for you and me to associate.[41] (53) And now we have been victorious in the great battle, we have Sardis and Croesus in hand, we have taken Babylon, and we have subdued everyone, and yet yesterday, by Mithras,[42] if I had not fought through many others, I would not have been able to get close to you. When, however, you greeted me with your right hand and bade me remain beside you, I immediately caught everyone's attention—because I got to spend the

day with you without eating or drinking. (54) Now then, if there will be any way that we who have been most deserving will obtain the greatest part of you, [fine]; if not, I am willing once again to proclaim in your name that everyone is to go away from you except us, your friends from the beginning."

(55) Cyrus and many others laughed at this. Chrysantas the Persian rose and spoke as follows: "But before, Cyrus, you properly presented yourself out in the open both because of what you said yourself and because we were not the ones you especially had to court.[43] We were present for our own sakes, but the multitude had to be acquired in every way, in order that they might be willing to join in our labors with as much pleasure as possible and risk their lives with us. (56) But now, when you not only have these[44] but also have the power to acquire others whom it is opportune to acquire, it is a worthy thing for you now to obtain a house. What would you enjoy from your rule, if you alone did not receive a hearth as part of your share? No place on earth is more holy, more pleasant, or more one's own.[45] Besides, do you not think that we would be ashamed if we should see you enduring hardships out of doors, while we ourselves were in houses and seemed to be taking advantage of you?"[46]

(57) After Chrysantas said this, many spoke along the same lines as he. After this, of course, [Cyrus] moved into the palace of the king, and those who conveyed the riches from Sardis returned them here. When Cyrus moved in, he sacrificed first to Hestia, then to Zeus the king and to any other god indicated by the Magi.

(58) After doing this, he began to manage all the other things right away. He kept his own problem in mind, that he was undertaking to rule many human beings, that he was preparing to dwell in the biggest of all cities in evidence, and that it was as hostile to him as a city could be to any man. So of course in light of these calculations, he held that he needed bodyguards. (59) Recognizing that human beings are nowhere more easily overcome than when eating, drinking, washing, in bed, or asleep, he considered who would be most trustworthy to have about him at these times. He believed that there could never be a trustworthy human being who was more friendly to someone else than to the one in need of the guard. (60) So he recognized that those who had children, or wives well suited to them,

or boyfriends, were compelled by nature to love especially these. Seeing that eunuchs were deprived of all these ties, he held that they would most value those who were especially able to enrich them; to help them, if they should be treated unjustly; and to bedeck them with honors. He held that no one would be able to surpass him in doing good to eunuchs. (61) Besides these points, since eunuchs are deemed disreputable by other human beings, they therefore need a master as a protector, for there is no man who would not think he deserved to have more than a eunuch in everything, unless something stronger should prevent it. But if he is trustworthy to a master, there is nothing to prevent even a eunuch from having the first position. (62) One might especially think that eunuchs would lose their strength, but this did not appear to him to be so. From other animals he took it as evidence that unruly horses when castrated cease biting and being unruly, but they become no less warlike;[47] and bulls when castrated give up their big thoughts and disobedience, but they are not deprived of their strength and energy; and dogs, similarly, cease to abandon their masters when they are castrated, but they become no worse at guarding and for the hunt. (63) And human beings become similarly more gentle when deprived of this desire, but they do not, however, become more neglectful of what is assigned them, nor at all less skilled as riders, nor at all less skilled as spearmen, nor less ambitious. (64) It showed quite clearly in wars and on the hunt that they safely retained the love of victory in their souls. It is especially on the ruin of their masters that they have given evidence of their being faithful, for none have shown more faithful deeds amidst the misfortunes of their masters than have eunuchs. (65) If, then, they seem to be diminished somewhat in bodily strength, iron makes the weak equal to the strong in war. So realizing these things, he made all those who served near his own person, beginning with the doormen, eunuchs.[48]

(66) Because he held that this guard was not sufficient against the multitude of those who harbored ill will, he considered whom he should take from among the others as the most faithful guards around the king's palace. (67) So knowing that Persians at home had the hardest lives because of their poverty, and that they lived most laboriously because of the ruggedness of the country and because they did their own work, he believed that it was especially they who would cher-

ish the way of life they would lead with him. (68) So he took from among them ten thousand spearmen who, when he was resting inside, stood guard night and day in a circle around the king's palace, but when he went out somewhere, they marched in order on each side. (69) Believing that there also had to be sufficient guards for Babylon as a whole, whether he himself happened to be residing there or traveling abroad, he established sufficient garrisons in Babylon as well. He ordered that the Babylonians also pay them their wages, for he wished that they be as deprived of resources as possible, in order that they be most submissive and easily restrained. (70) So, then, this guard that was then established, both around him in particular and in Babylon, still endures today, just as it was.

Considering both how his whole empire might be continued and how still more might be added to it, he held that these mercenaries were not so much better than their subjects as they were less numerous.[49] He realized that the good men, the very ones who with the gods' [help] provided for his conquest, must be kept together and that one must take care that they not slacken in their practice of virtue.[50] (71) In order that he might not seem to be giving commands to them, but that they might abide in and care for virtue because they themselves realized this to be best, he called together both the Peers and all those who were chief aides and seemed to him to be most worthy partners in both hard work and its rewards.[51]

(72) When they had come together, he said such things as follow: "Men, friends, and allies, let there be the greatest gratitude to the gods because they granted that we obtain what we believed we deserved, for we now have both a great deal of good land and people who will work it and support us. We also have houses and furniture in them. (73) And let no one of you believe that in having these things we have what belongs to others: It is an eternal law among all human beings that when a city is captured by those at war, both the bodies of those in the city and their valuables belong to those who take it. It will not be by injustice, then, that you will have whatever you may have, but it will be by benevolence that you refrain from taking something away, if you allow them to have anything.

(74) "As for the future, however, I know that if we turn toward easygoingness and the pleasure seeking of bad human beings, who believe that laboring is misery and living without labor happiness, I

say that we will quickly be of but little worth to ourselves and quickly be deprived of all good things, (75) for that men have been good does not suffice for them to continue being good, unless one cares about it to the end. Just as also the other arts become worth less when neglected, and bodies, or at least those in good condition, are again worse when one abandons them in favor of easygoingness,[52] so also moderation, continence, and strength turn again to worthlessness whenever one abandons their practice. (76) One ought therefore not be negligent or abandon oneself in favor of the immediate pleasure, for I think it is a great work to gain an empire, but it is an even much greater work to keep one safe after taking it. One who has shown only daring has often succeeded in taking, but as for holding on after one has taken, this does not occur without moderation, without continence, or without great care. (77) Realizing this, we must now practice virtue much more than before we acquired these good things; being well aware that when someone has the most, then most people envy him, plot against him, and become his enemies, especially if he also has his possessions and service from unwilling [subjects], just as we do. Now the gods, we must think, will be with us, for we do not have [what we have] unjustly, having plotted against others, but after having been plotted against, we took vengeance.

(78) "What is next best, however, we must prepare by ourselves. This is that we deem it right to rule by being better than our subjects. We must of necessity share with our slaves heat and cold, food and drink, and labor and sleep. In this sharing, however, we need first to try to appear better than they in regard to such. (79) Military science and practice, on the other hand, we must by all means not share with those whom we wish to establish as our workers and tributaries. Rather, realizing that the gods have revealed these to be the tools of freedom and happiness for human beings, we need to get the advantage of [our subjects] in these exercises. And just as we took away their weapons, so we ourselves must never become separated from our weapons, being well aware that they who stay closest to their weapons are most the masters of their wishes.[53]

(80) "If someone has in mind a question like this, 'What indeed is the benefit for us to have achieved what we desired if we will still need to endure hunger, thirst, labor, and care?' he needs to learn that one enjoys the good things more to the extent that one goes to them

after having labored in advance, for labors are a sauce for good things:[54] Unless one happens to be in need of something, nothing could be prepared in so costly a fashion as to be pleasant [to him]. (81) If the divinity has provided for us these things that human beings especially desire and if someone will [then] prepare them for himself in the way that they would appear most pleasant, such a man will get the advantage over those more needy in the means of life [only] in that he will obtain the most pleasant foods when hungry, he will enjoy the most pleasant drinks when thirsty, and he will go to rest in the most pleasant way when in need of rest. (82) This is why I say that we must now accept being commanded toward manly goodness,[55] both in order that we may enjoy the good things in the way that is best and most pleasant and in order that we may be without experience in the harshest of all things, for not to have taken the good things is not so harsh as it is painful to be deprived of them after having taken them. (83) Also bear this in mind: With what excuse would we allow ourselves to become worse than before? Is it because we are ruling? But it is surely not fitting that the ruler be more worthless than his subjects. But is it because we think that we are happier now than before? Then will someone say that vice befits happiness? But is it because, since we have acquired slaves, we will punish them if they are worthless? (84) And why is it fitting for one who is himself worthless to punish others on account of their worthlessness or laxity?

"Also bear in mind that we have made preparations to support many troops as guards of both our houses and our bodies. How would it not be shameful if we should think we ought to obtain safety using others to wield our spears, while we ourselves will not wield the spear for ourselves? Moreover, one must know well that there is no other such protection as that one be noble and good himself. This [conviction] must accompany us, for it is not fitting that anything else be noble for one who is lacking in virtue. (85) What, then, do I say that we must do? Wherein must we practice virtue? Wherein exercise care? It is nothing new, men, that I shall say. Just as in Persia the Peers pass their time at the government buildings, so also I say that all of us who are Peers[56] here must practice the very things we did there; and that on seeing me when you are here, you must consider whether I pass my time caring for what I ought, and I will consider and watch you, and I shall honor those whom I see practicing what is noble and good. (86) And as for the children who may be born of us, let us educate them here. We ourselves will be better by wishing to provide ourselves as the best possible patterns for our children, and our children could not easily become worthless, even if they wished to, spending their day in noble and good practices, not even seeing or hearing anything shameful."

BOOK VIII

~ CHAPTER 1 ~

(1) So Cyrus spoke like this. Chrysantas stood up after him and spoke as follows: "But even on other occasions, men, I have often reflected that a good ruler is no different from a good father. For fathers take forethought for their children so that they never lack the good things, and Cyrus seems to me now to be giving us the sort of advice from which we could especially pass our lives in happiness. Yet there is something he seems to me to have clarified less than should be the case, and I will try to teach those of you who may not know it. (2) Consider what enemy city could be captured by troops who are not obedient? What friendly one could be protected by troops who are not obedient? What sort of army of disobedient troops could obtain victory? How could human beings be defeated in battle more than when they begin to deliberate in private, each about his own safety? What other good could be brought to fulfillment by those who do not obey their superiors? What sort of cities could be lawfully managed, or what sort of households could be preserved? How could ships arrive where they must? (3) As for the good things we now have, by what else did we attain them more than by obeying the ruler? By this we quickly got where we needed to be in both night and day, following our ruler in close formation we were irresistible, and we left nothing half-finished of what was commanded. If, then, obeying the ruler appears to be a very great good for attaining the good things,

be assured that this same thing is a very great good also for preserving what must be preserved. (4) Before, of course, many of us did not rule over anyone but were ruled. Now all of you who are present are prepared to rule over others, some over more, others over fewer. Then just as you yourselves think it right to rule over those beneath you, let us similarly obey those whom it is seemly to obey. We need to be different from slaves in this: Whereas slaves serve their masters involuntarily, if in fact we think it right to be free, we need to do voluntarily what appears to be most worthwhile. You will find that even where a city is managed without monarchy, the one that is especially willing to obey its rulers is least compelled to submit to its enemies. (5) Let us report to the official buildings, therefore, just as Cyrus orders, let us exercise in the things by which we will especially be able to hold fast to what must be held, and let us offer ourselves to Cyrus to use in whatever way might be needed. We must also be well assured that Cyrus will not be able to find any way to use us for his own good that will not be good for us as well, since the same things are advantageous for us, and our enemies are the same."

(6) After Chrysantas said these things, thus did many others stand up to speak in support, both of the Persians and of the allies.[1] And it was decided that those in honor always report at the gates and offer themselves to Cyrus to use in whatever way he wished, until he should dismiss them.[2] As it was then decided, so even now do those who are subjects of the king in Asia still act: they serve at the gates of the rulers.

(7) As Cyrus has been shown in this account to have established his empire with a view to protecting it both for himself and for Persians, so the kings after him even to this day spend their time observing the same lawful things.[3] (8) As it is with the other things, so it is with these: When the person in control is better, the lawful things are observed with greater purity. When he is worse, they are observed in an inferior way.

So those in honor used to come to Cyrus' gates with their horses and spears, since it was so decided by all the best of those who joined in subduing the empire. (9) Cyrus appointed different people to be responsible for different matters. He had those who collected revenues, those who paid expenses, those who were in control of works, those who guarded possessions, those who were responsible for the provisions for daily life. To be responsible for horses and dogs he appointed those who he believed would render also these beasts in the best condition for his use. (10) As for those whom he thought he must have as fellow guardians of his happiness, he did not similarly assign to others the responsibility of seeing that they be as good as possible, but he believed this had to be his own work. He knew that if ever there were any need of battle, he would have to select from these [fellow guardians] those who would stand beside and behind him, with whom the greatest risks would be run. He realized also that he had to appoint the captains of both the infantry and the cavalry from among them. (11) If also generals should be needed somewhere in his absence, he knew that he had to send them from among these [fellow guardians]. He knew that he had to use some of these as guards and satraps of both cities and whole peoples, and that he had to send some from this group as ambassadors, which he held to be among the most important ways of obtaining what he needed without war.⁴ (12) He held that his own affairs would go badly if those [fellow guardians] through whom the greatest and most numerous actions were going to be performed were not as they ought to be. Yet if they were as they ought to be, he believed all would be fine. So, judging things in this way, he assumed this responsibility. He believed that the same exercise of virtue had to be his as well, for if he were not himself such as he needed to be, he did not think it would be possible to incite others to noble and good works.

(13) Since he was of such a mind about these things, he held that there was need of leisure first, if he was going to be able to be responsible for the most important affairs.⁵ Now he believed that it was not possible to neglect revenues, for he foresaw that it would be necessary to spend a great deal on a great empire. Yet on the other hand, since there were many possessions, he knew that his being always busy with them would allow him no leisure for taking care of the safety of the whole. (14) Considering, therefore, how administrative matters might be nobly handled and how he might yet have leisure, he somehow began reflecting on military organization.⁶ In general, the sergeants are responsible for their ten squad members, the lieutenants are responsible for their sergeants, the colonels are responsible for their lieutenants, the brigadier generals are responsible for their colonels, and thus no one is without responsible supervision,

not even if there are very many brigades of ten thousand human beings each; and whenever the general wishes to use the army in some respect, it is sufficient if he gives his orders to the brigadier generals.[7] (15) So Cyrus centralized his administrative affairs in just this way. Consequently, it turned out also for Cyrus that even though he spoke to few, nothing of what belonged to him was without responsible supervision.[8] And accordingly he now had more leisure than someone responsible for but a single house or a single ship. Having in this way arranged his own [administration], he taught also those about him to use this approach.

(16) In this way, then, he provided leisure both for himself and for his circle, and he began to take charge of having his partners be as they should. In the first place, for those who were sufficient [in rank] to be maintained by the work of others, he made inquiries if they did not report at his gates, for he believed that those who reported were not willing to do anything either evil or shameful, both because of their being in the ruler's presence and because of their knowing that they would be seen by the best in whatever they should do. Those who did not report he held to be absent because of some incontinence, injustice, or neglect. (17) So first we will describe how he compelled such to report. He bade one of his closest friends to take what belonged to the person who did not show up, and to profess that he was taking what belonged to himself. Now as soon as this would be done, those who had been dispossessed would come immediately with the charge that they had suffered injustice. (18) Cyrus would not find leisure to listen to such people for a long time. When he did hear them, he would postpone his judgment for a long time. In doing this he held that he habituated them to serve, and did so in a less hateful way than if he himself used punishments to compel them to report. (19) This was one of his ways of teaching attendance. Another was assigning the easiest and most profitable assignments to those who were present. Another was never sharing anything with those who were absent. (20) Surely his greatest way of compulsion, if someone did not heed any of these, was taking away from him what he had, and giving it to another who he thought would be able to report when needed. And in this way he came to have a useful friend in return for a useless one. The present king also inquires after anyone absent who ought to be present.

(21) So this is how he conducted himself toward those who did not report. As for those who did present themselves, he believed that he would especially induce them toward what was noble and good if he himself, since he was their ruler, tried to display himself to his subjects as having been most of all adorned with virtue. (22) He thought he perceived human beings becoming better even through written laws, but he believed that the good ruler was a seeing law for human beings, because he is sufficient to put into order, to see who is out of order, and to punish. (23) So being of such judgment, he first of all displayed himself laboring more over things concerning the gods at this very time, when he was happiest.[9] And then the Magi were first charged with singing hymns to all the gods with the coming of every day, and he sacrificed every day to the gods the Magi named. (24) Thus what was established then still endures even now in the court of whoever may be king.

The other Persians, therefore, first imitated him in this, believing both that they themselves would be more happy if they served the gods just as did he who was both happiest and their ruler, and they held that in doing these things they would please Cyrus. (25) Cyrus believed that the piety of those with him was also good for himself, calculating just as do those who choose to sail with the pious rather than with those who seem to have been impious in something. In addition to this, he calculated that if all his partners were pious, they would be less willing to do anything impious both concerning each other and concerning himself, for he believed that he was a benefactor of his partners. (26) He also thought that, if he should show that it was very important to him not to be unjust to any friend or ally, and if he should watch justice intensely, others would abstain from shameful gains and be willing to make their way by the just course. (27) He held that he would also fill all with more respect if he himself were visible with such respect for everyone as not to say or do anything shameful. (28) His evidence for this being so was from what follows: Human beings show respect for those who show respect more than for those who do not, not only in regard to a ruler but even in regard to those they do not fear. And even in the case of women, people are more willing, when they see them, to return the respect of those women whom they perceive to be respectful.[10] (29) Next, as for obedience, he thus thought it would be especially abiding in his circle if he openly honored those who obeyed without excuses more than those who thought they contributed the greatest and most arduous virtues. Judging things like this, he acted accordingly.

(30) And displaying even more his own moderation, he made all exercise in this as well, for whenever people see that he is moderate for whom it is especially possible to be insolent, then the weaker are more unwilling to do anything insolent in the open. (31) He distinguished respect and moderation like this: Those who show respect flee what is shameful where it is in the open, but the moderate do so even where it is invisible. (32) And continence he thought would be exercised especially if he himself should display himself not being dragged away from the good things by the pleasures of the moment but being willing to labor first, in accord with what is noble, for what is delightful. (33) Being such, he therefore produced at his gates a great deal of good order among the inferior troops, who deferred to their betters, and much respect and decorous conduct toward each other. You would not have perceived anyone there shouting in anger, or taking delight in insolent laughter, but on seeing them you would have held that they really lived nobly. (34) So they passed their time at his gates doing and seeing such things.

For the sake of military exercise, he took hunting those whom he thought needed this exercise, for he held that it was altogether the best exercise of military [skills] and of horsemanship the truest. (35) This especially makes for riders who can stay seated in all sorts of places, because they follow after fleeing animals, and this especially turns out troops who are active from their horses because of their ambition and desire of catching [the game]. (36) Here especially he habituated his partners in continence and in being able to bear labor, cold, heat, hunger, and thirst. The king and the rest of his circle still even now pass their time doing these things.

(37) He did not think it was fitting for anyone to rule who was not better than his subjects, and this is made clear by everything that has been said above; [it is also clear] that in exercising his circle so much he himself especially worked at continence and the military arts and cares, (38) for he took others hunting whenever there was not any necessity to stay back. Even when there was such a necessity, he hunted the wild animals raised in the parks at home. Neither did he himself ever take his dinner before working up a sweat, nor did he distribute

food to horses that had not been exercised. He also called his circle of
mace bearers along for these hunts. (39) Therefore, he himself greatly
excelled in all noble deeds, and his circle also greatly excelled, because
of this constant care. So, then, he offered himself as a pattern of this
sort. In addition to this, any of the others he especially saw pursuing
what is noble he used to reward with gifts, offices, positions, and all
honors. Consequently, he injected much ambition in everyone to appear to Cyrus as excellent as possible.

(40) We think we learned of Cyrus that he did not believe that rulers
must differ from their subjects by this alone, by being better, but he
also thought they must bewitch them. At least he himself both chose
to wear a Median robe and persuaded his partners to dress in one as
well, for this robe seemed to him to hide it if anyone should have
some bodily defect, and they displayed their wearers as especially
beautiful and tall, (41) for they have shoes in which it is especially
possible to avoid detection when inserting something underneath, so
those who wear them seem to be taller than they are. And he allowed
them to use color beneath their eyes, so that their eyes might appear
nicer than they were, and to rub on colors so that they might be seen
as having better complexions than they did by nature. (42) He took
care also that they not spit or wipe their noses in the open, and not
turn at the sight of anything, as if they wondered at nothing. He
thought that all of this contributed somewhat toward their appearing to their subjects as harder to hold in contempt.

(43) So thus, by himself,[11] he prepared those whom he thought must
rule, both by their training and by presiding over them with dignity.
On the other hand, regarding those whom he was preparing for slavery, he neither urged them to train in any of the labors of freemen nor
permitted them to possess weapons. He did take care that they would
never go without food or drink for the sake of the training undertaken
by freemen, (44) for when they drove game onto the plains for the
knights, he allowed them—but none of the freemen—to bring food
for the hunt. And when there was an expedition, he led them to water
like beasts of burden. And when it was time for dinner, he waited
until they might eat something, so that they might not be so terribly
hungry. Consequently, even these called him "father," as did the best,
because he took care that they might pass their time as slaves forever
and without dispute.

(45) So thus he provided safety for the entire Persian empire. As for himself, he was exceedingly confident that there was no risk of suffering anything at the hands of those who had been subdued, for he held that they were without strength, and he saw that they were without order, and in addition to this, none of them approached him either night or day. (46) Regarding those whom he held to be strongest, however, these he also saw both armed and gathered together, and he knew that some of them were leaders of cavalry and others were of infantry. He perceived many of them also having the high thought that they were competent to rule. It was especially these who approached his guards, and many of them often mingled with Cyrus himself. (For they did so of necessity, if he was going to make use of them.) Thus, it was especially at their hands that there was a risk that he himself might suffer something in any one of many ways.

(47) Considering, then, how they too might pose no risk to him, he resolved not to take their weapons from them and make them unwarlike, both holding it to be unjust and believing this to be the dissolution of his rule. Next, as for not letting them come close and being openly distrustful, he held this to be the beginning of war. (48) Instead of all these policies he judged one to be both best for his own safety and most noble, if he should be able to make the strongest become more friendly to himself than to each other. How, then, he seemed to us to set out to become loved we will try to narrate.[12]

❧ CHAPTER 2 ❧

(1)In the first place, he continually made his benevolence of soul every bit as visible as he could, for he believed that just as it is not easy to love those who seem to hate you, or to be well disposed toward those who are ill disposed toward you, so also those known as loving and as being well disposed could not be hated by those who held that they were loved. (2) Now for as long as he was relatively unable to confer benefits with money, he used to try to hunt the friendship of his associates by taking forethought on their behalf, by laboring for them, and by being both visibly pleased along with them on good occasions and visibly grief-stricken along with them on bad occasions. When it happened that he had money with which to confer benefits, it seems to us that he judged there to be, in the first place, no such charming benefaction for human beings to give to one another as the sharing of food and drink, at least not at an equal cost. (3) Believing this to be so, he ordered at his own table, in the first place, that they always put beside him foods similar to those on which he himself was dining, but sufficient for very many people. He used to distribute all that was put beside him, except for what he and his fellow diners were consuming, to whichever of his friends he wished to show his remembrance or friendliness. He sent food around also to those in whom he was pleased either in how they stood guard, in how they served at court, or in any sort of action, indicating that he did not fail to notice those who wished to gratify him. (4) He even used to honor his servants with food from his table, whenever he praised one of them. He also had all the servants' food placed on his own table, thinking that even in this way he would engender a certain goodwill, just as it does with dogs. If he wished that any of his friends be courted by large numbers, he sent from his table to them as well. And still even now, all court more those to whom they see things sent from the table of the king, believing that they are the ones in honor and competent, if they need anything, to get it done. Moreover, what is sent from the king does not bring delight only because of what has been said, but what comes from the king's table really differs greatly also in the pleasure it affords.[13] (5) That this is so, however, is nothing amazing, for just as also the other arts have been developed to an exceptional degree in great cities, in the same way the food of a king has been labored over to a very exceptional degree. In small cities, the same person makes a bed, a door, a plow, a table, and this same person is frequently a house builder too, and he is content if he gets enough customers to support him even in this way. It is impossible, then, for a human being who does many things by art to do them all nobly. In great cities, because many people are in need of each kind of artisan, even one art suffices for supporting each—and frequently not even one whole art, but one person makes men's shoes, another women's. There are places also where one is supported merely by sewing shoes, and another by cutting them out, and another by cutting only the uppers, and another who does none of these things but puts them together. It is by necessity, then, that he who passes his time engaged in a narrower work certainly be compelled to do it best.

(6) The same thing holds for what pertains to one's dwelling, for it is by necessity, I think, that whoever has the same person make his bed, adorn his table, knead, and make different sauces at different times must be content with each thing in just whatever way it may turn out. But where it is a sufficient work for one person to boil meats, for another to roast them, for another to boil fish, for another to roast them, for another to make loaves of bread—and not even loaves of all kinds, but it is sufficient if he provides some one form that is well regarded—it is by necessity, I think, that each develops in quite an exceptional way such things as are done like this.

(7) So by doing such things, he went far beyond everyone in courting with food. How he used to win great victories courting also in all other ways I shall now narrate. For although he far surpassed human beings in receiving the greatest income, he surpassed human beings still much more in giving the most gifts. Cyrus began it, and giving on a large scale still continues with the kings even now. (8) Whose friends are visibly richer than those of the king of the Persians? Who visibly adorns his associates with robes more beautifully than does the king? Whose gifts are recognized so readily as some of those from the king are—bracelets, necklaces, and horses with golden bridles? For it is not possible there, of course, for anyone to have these things except him to whom the king gives them. (9) Who else, by the magnitude of his gifts, is said to make people prefer himself to their brothers, to their fathers, and to their children? Who else was able to take vengeance on enemies who were a journey of many months in distance as was the king of the Persians? Who else besides Cyrus, after overturning an empire, was called "father" when he died? This is the name, clearly, of one who confers benefits rather than of one who takes things away.

(10) We learned that he also acquired the so-called Eyes of the king and Ears of the king in no other way than by giving gifts and honors. For by richly benefiting those who reported what it was opportune for him to learn, he made many human beings keep their ears and eyes open for things to report that would benefit the king. (11) Consequently, of course, it came to be believed that there were many Eyes of the king, and many Ears. But if someone thinks that one is chosen

to be an Eye for the king, he does not think correctly, for one person would see little, and little would one hear. And it would be as if others were ordered to neglect it, if this [task] were assigned to one person only. Moreover, people would know that they needed to be on their guard against whomever they recognized as an Eye. So it is not like this, but the king listens to everyone who professes that he has heard or seen something worthy of care. (12) Thus there are believed to be many Ears of the king, and many Eyes; and people are everywhere afraid to say what is not advantageous to the king, just as if he were listening, and afraid to do what is not advantageous, just as if he were present. There is no way, therefore, anyone would have dared to mention anything disparaging about Cyrus to anyone else, but each was disposed to whoever was present as if they all were Eyes and Ears of the king. As for human beings being disposed to him like this, I do not know how one could explain it more than to say he was willing to do great benefactions in return for small.

(13) It is not to be wondered at, of course, that he, who was wealthiest, exceeded in the greatness of his gifts. That he was superior in attending to and caring for his friends, even though he was king, is more worthy of mention. It is said, then, to have been apparent that there was nothing at which he would have been so ashamed at being defeated as in the service of his friends. (14) And an argument of his is remembered that says the functions of a good shepherd and a good king are similar, for he said that just as the shepherd ought to make use of his flocks while making them happy (in the happiness of sheep, of course), so a king similarly ought to make use of cities and human beings while making them happy. So it is not to be wondered at, if in fact he was of this judgment, that he competed to be superior to all human beings in service.

(15) Cyrus is said to have made also the following beautiful display to Croesus, when the latter warned him that he would become poor because he was giving many things away, when it was possible for him to put more treasuries of gold in his house than did any other one man.

(16) And Cyrus is said to have asked, "And how much money do you think that I would have now if I had been gathering gold together in the way you bid for as long as I have been ruling?"

And Croesus mentioned a very big number.[14]

And Cyrus said to this, "Come, Croesus, send a man whom you trust in the highest along with Hystaspas here. Hystaspas, go around to my friends and tell them that I need gold for a certain action, for I really do need some more. Order them each to write down how much money they are able to provide me, to put their seal on their letter, and to give it to Croesus' servant to carry here."

(17) After writing down what he had said, and sealing it, he gave it to Hystaspas to carry to his friends. He also wrote that all should receive Hystaspas as a friend of his. After he had come back and Croesus' servant had brought back the letters, Hystapas said, "King Cyrus, you must now treat me as a wealthy man, for I am here with many gifts because of what you wrote."

(18) And Cyrus said, "He is already one treasury for us, Croesus. Examine the others and calculate how much money is ready if I need to use any."

It is said, of course, that on calculation Croesus found that there was many times as much as he had told Cyrus he would now have in his treasuries if he gathered it together. (19) When this was clear, it is said that Cyrus said, "Do you see, Croesus, that I too have treasuries? But you bid me to gather them together beside me and hence to become envied and hated because of them, and, further, after appointing mercenaries to guard them, you bid me trust them. I, on the other hand, make these friends of mine wealthy and believe that they are treasuries and, at the same time, that they are more trustworthy guards both of myself and of our good things than if I appointed garrisons of mercenaries. (20) And I will tell you another thing. Not even I myself, Croesus, am capable of becoming superior to that by which the gods, when they put it into the souls of human beings, made us all poor: I too am insatiable for money, just as others are. (21) I think that I differ from most people by this, however. Whenever they acquire an abundance in excess of what suffices, they bury some of it, they let some of it spoil, and because of their counting, measuring, weighing, cleaning, and guarding, the rest of it gives them trouble. And even though they have so much inside their houses, they neither eat more than they are able to bear, for they would burst, nor do they wear more clothes than they are able to bear, for they would suffocate, but with their superabundant valuables they get only trouble. (22) I serve the gods, and I desire always more. Yet when I acquire, I minister to the needs of my friends with what I see to be an abundance in excess of what suffices for me. By enriching and benefiting human beings, I acquire goodwill and friendship, and from these I harvest safety and glory. These neither spoil nor harm us by over-abundance, but glory, to the extent there is more of it, becomes that much greater, more noble, and lighter to bear, and it frequently makes lighter even those who bear it. (23) Know this too, Croesus: I do not hold those to be happiest who possess the most and guard the most. If this were so, those who guard the walls would be the happiest, for they guard everything in cities. But he who is able to acquire the most while keeping to what is just and to use the most while keeping to what is noble, him do I believe to be happiest."[15] And of course Cyrus openly acted in just the way he spoke.

(24) In addition to these things, he reflected that if they pass their time in good health, the majority of human beings make preparations so that they will have required provisions, and they put money aside with a view to the life led by people in good health. He saw on the other hand that they did not care much about seeing that they have what is advantageous, in the event they become sick. So he decided to work at this. By his willingness to pay for them, he secured the best doctors for himself. As for as many tools, drugs, foods, or potions as any one of them said would be useful, there was none of these that he did not provide and treasure up for himself. (25) And whenever anyone fell sick whom it was opportune to court, he investigated and provided everything needed. And Cyrus acknowledged his gratitude to the doctors when one of them cured anyone using something taken [from him].

(26) These and many such others, then, were the things he contrived with a view toward being in first place for those by whom he wished to be loved.

From the instances in which he announced contests and set out prizes, wishing to implant a competitiveness over noble and good works, Cyrus received praise for taking care that virtue be practiced. For the best, however, these contests against each other injected strife as well as competitiveness. (27) In addition to these things, Cyrus established it as a law that whenever a judgment should be required, whether in a civil suit or over a disputed contest, those who required the judgment must concur on the judges. Now it is clear that both antagonists would aim at having the best [men] and those who were especially their friends as judges. The one who was not victorious would envy those who were, and he would hate those who had cast their judgments against him. The one who was victorious, on the other hand, would lay claim to have been victorious because of his justice, and he would consequently hold that he did not owe gratitude to anyone. (28) And like others who inhabit cities, those who wished to be first in Cyrus' friendship would also be envious of one another, and consequently most of them wished one another to be simply out of the way rather than do anything for their mutual good. So this makes it clear how he contrived that all those who were superior would love him more than each other.

∾· CHAPTER 3 ·∾

(1) Now we will narrate how Cyrus for the first time marched in procession out of his palace, for it seems to us that the majesty of the procession itself was one of the arts contrived so that his rule not be easy to hold in contempt. So first, before the procession, he called to himself those of the Persians and of the allies who held offices, and he gave them Median robes. Then for the first time did the Persians put on the Median robe. As he distributed them he told them he wished to march to the sanctuaries that had been chosen for the gods and to sacrifice with them. (2) "So after you adorn yourselves with these robes in the morning," he said, "report at the gates before the sun rises, and station yourselves in whatever way Pheraulas the Persian declares to you in my name. And when I lead, follow in your stated place. If it seems to any of you that it would be more noble to march in any way other than as we now will, teach me when we get back, for everything needs to be established in whatever way seems noblest and best to you." (3) After he distributed the most beautiful robes to those who were superior, he brought out still other Median robes, for he had prepared very many, sparing cloaks of neither purple, nor sable, nor scarlet, nor dark red. After distributing a share of these to each of the leaders, he bade them adorn their own friends with them, "just as," he said, "I am adorning you."

(4) And one of those present asked him, "What about you, Cyrus? When will you adorn yourself?"

He answered, "Why, do I not seem to you to be adorning myself even now by adorning you? Do not worry; if I am able to benefit you who are my friends, I will appear noble in whatever robe I happen to have."

(5) Thus they went away, and sending for their friends, they adorned them with the robes.

Cyrus believed that Pheraulas, who was from the class of Commoners, was intelligent, a lover of beauty, good at putting things in order, and not unconcerned with gratifying him (he was the one who once supported his plan that each be honored in accord with his merit).[16] So he called him in and deliberated with him about how he could make his procession most noble for those of goodwill to see, and most frightening for those who harbored ill will. (6) After the two of them considered it and reached the same conclusions, he bade Pheraulas take care that the procession on the next day turn out in just the way they decided would be noble. "I have told everyone to obey you concerning the order of the procession," he said. "But that they may hear your commands with greater pleasure, take these tunics and bring them to the leaders of the spearmen, give these cavalry cloaks to the leaders of the knights, and these other tunics to the leaders of the chariots." (7) So he took them and carried them. When the various leaders saw him, they each said, "Are you not great, Pheraulas, since you will put even us in order and tell us what we must do!"

"No, by Zeus," said Pheraulas, "not only [am I not great], but I will even be a baggage carrier. At least I am now carrying two cloaks, one for you and one for someone else. You, however, may take whichever of them you wish."

(8) As a consequence, of course, the one receiving the cloak forgot his envy, and he immediately consulted him about which he should take. And he, after giving advice about which was better, also said, "If you accuse me for having given the choice to you, when I serve you in the future, you will find me to be a different sort of servant."

So Pheraulas, after making the distribution in the way he had been ordered, immediately began taking care that each particular for the procession would be as noble as possible.

(9) When the next day came, everything was clean before sunrise. Rows of troops stood on each side of the road, just as they still stand even now wherever the king is going to march, and between these rows it is not possible for anyone who has not been honored to enter. Troops with whips were stationed there, who struck anyone who became an annoyance. First of all, in front of the gates there stood about four thousand of the spearmen, four deep, two thousand on each side of the gates. (10) And all the knights were present, having dismounted from their horses and passed their hands through their robes, just as they pass them through even now, whenever the king sees them.[17] The Persians stood on the right, the other allies on the left side of the road, and the chariots were similarly half on each side.

(11) When the gates of the king's palace opened, first some very beautiful bulls were led out, four abreast, for Zeus and for whichever of the other gods the Magi prescribed, for the Persians think that they must rely on experts in what concerns the gods much more than in other things. (12) After the cattle, horses were led as a sacrifice for the Sun. After these, a chariot was led out, drawn by white horses, wreathed and with yokes of gold, consecrated to Zeus. After this, a chariot drawn by white horses [consecrated to] the Sun, and these too were wreathed like the ones before. After this, another chariot was led out, the third, its horses covered with scarlet, and men followed behind it carrying fire on a great altar.

(13) After these, Cyrus himself then appeared from the gates. He was on a chariot, with an upright tiara and a purple tunic mixed with white (it is not possible for anyone else to have one mixed with white), with red pants about his legs, and with a robe entirely purple. He also had a band around his tiara, and his relatives also had this same sign, and even now they have this same sign. (14) He had his hands outside of his sleeves. A tall driver rode beside him, yet shorter than he (either really or in some other way), and Cyrus appeared much taller.[18] On seeing him, all prostrated themselves, either because some had been ordered to initiate it or because they were stunned by the display and by Cyrus' seeming to appear tall and beautiful. Previously, no one of the Persians used to prostrate himself before Cyrus. (15) When Cyrus' chariot advanced, the four thousand spearmen took the lead, with two thousand following along on either side of the chariot. Then followed his personal mace bearers with their spears,

about three hundred of them, adorned and on horses. (16) Next horses that had been raised for Cyrus came by, with golden bridles and covered with embroidered blankets, about two hundred. After these, two thousand lancers. After these, the first ten thousand who became knights, ordered to a depth of one hundred on all sides. Chrysantas led them. (17) After these another ten thousand Persian knights similarly ordered, and Hystaspas led them. After these, another ten thousand similarly ordered, and Datamas led them. After these, another [ten thousand], and Gadatas led them. (18) After these, Median knights; after these, Armenian; after these, Hyrcanian; after these, Cadusian; and after these, Sacian. After the knights, chariots ordered four abreast, and Artabatas the Persian led them.

(19) After he passed by, vast numbers of people followed along outside of the markers, each begging Cyrus for a different action. He thus sent some of the mace bearers to them, for three of these followed next to him on each side of his chariot to do this reporting. He ordered them to say that if someone needed anything from him, they should inform one of the cavalry commanders of what they wished, and he said that they in turn would tell it to him. So immediately going away from him, of course, they went to the knights, each deliberating about whom he should approach. (20) Cyrus sent someone to those of his friends whom he wished to be most courted by the human beings, and calling them to him one by one, he spoke to them like this, "If any of those following along informs you of something, pay no attention to anyone who seems to you to say nothing important, but whenever someone seems to ask for what is just, report it to me so that we may deliberate in common and accomplish it for them."

(21) When he called, the others certainly responded by riding hard, thus strengthening Cyrus' rule and showing that they were exceedingly obedient. Yet there was a certain Daiphernes, a human being whose manner was rather clumsy, who thought that he would appear to be more free if he did not respond quickly. (22) When Cyrus noticed this, before this fellow came to him and conversed with him, he sent one of his mace bearers and ordered him to tell him that he was no longer needed; nor did he call him ever after. (23) When one who was called later than Daiphernes arrived sooner, Cyrus gave him one of the horses that were following along and ordered one of the mace bearers to lead it away for him, wherever he should direct. This

seemed to those who saw it to be an honor, and accordingly many more human beings paid him court.

(24) When they arrived at the sanctuaries, they sacrificed to Zeus and made a holocaust of the bulls; then they sacrificed to the Sun, making a holocaust of the horses. Then slaughtering victims to the Earth, they did as the Magi directed; then [they slaughtered victims] to the heroes that inhabit Syria.

(25) After this, since it was beautiful country, he pointed out a goal about five stadia distant,[19] and told each tribe to race its horses there with all their might. He himself rode with the Persians, and he was victorious by far, for horsemanship had been a special care of his. Of the Medes, Artabazus was victorious, for Cyrus had given him his horse; of the Syrians who had revolted, Gadatas; of the Armenians, Tigranes; of the Hyrcanians, the son of the cavalry commander. Of the Sacians, a private man with his horse left the other horses nearly half a racecourse behind. (26) Then Cyrus is said to have asked the youth whether he would accept a kingdom in return for his horse. He answered, it is said, "I would not accept a kingdom for it, but I would accept a good man's gratitude."

(27) And Cyrus said, "And I am certainly willing to show you where, even if you throw with your eyes shut, you could not fail to hit a good man."

"By all means, then, show me, and I will throw with this clod," the Sacian said, picking one up.

(28) And Cyrus showed him where most of his friends were, and he shut his eyes, threw the clod, and hit Pheraulas as he rode by, for Pheraulas happened to be conveying an order from Cyrus. Even though he had been struck, he did not turn around, but he went off where he had been ordered. (29) On looking up, the Sacian asked whom he had hit.

"By Zeus," he said, "none of those who are present."

"But certainly not any of those who are absent," said the youth.

"Yes, by Zeus," said Cyrus, "you hit that one who is riding his horse so fast beside the chariots."

"And why," he asked, "did he not even turn around?"

(30) And Cyrus said, "Because he is a madman, as it seems."

Hearing this, the youth went off to investigate who he was, and he found Pheraulas with his chin quite covered with earth and blood, for having been hit, his nose was bleeding. (31) When he approached him, he asked whether he had been hit.

He answered, "As you see."

"Then I am giving you this horse," he said.

He asked, "In return for what?"

Then the Sacian narrated the matter, and said in conclusion, "And I think that I have not failed to hit a good man."

(32) And Pheraulas said, "But if you were moderate, you would give it to someone wealthier than I; yet, as it is, I will accept it. I pray to the gods, who brought it about that I was hit by you, to grant that I bring it about that you not regret your gift to me. And now mount my horse and ride off. I will come to you another time." So thus they made their exchange.

Of the Cadusians, Rhathines was victorious.

(33) He also raced the chariots by individual tribes. To all the victors he gave cattle, so that they might sacrifice and feast, and cups. He himself also took the ox as his prize for victory, but his share of the cups he gave to Pheraulas, because he thought he had beautifully organized the procession from the king's palace. (34) Thus the procession from the king's palace as then established by Cyrus still endures even now, except that the sacred victims are absent when [the king] does not sacrifice. When these things came to an end, they came back again into the city and went to their lodgings. Those who had been given houses went to them; those who had not went with their companies.

(35) When he invited over the Sacian who had given him the horse, Pheraulas entertained him and provided him with things in abundance. When they had dinner, he filled up the cups he had received from Cyrus, drank to him, and gave them to him as a gift. (36) On seeing many beautiful couch and bed spreads, much beautiful furniture, and many servants, the Sacian said, "Tell me, Pheraulas, were you among the wealthy even at home?"

(37) And Pheraulas said, "What do you mean, wealthy? I was unmistakably one of those who lived by the work of his own hands, for it was with difficulty that my father educated me in the education of the boys, while he himself worked to support me. When I became a youth, he was not able to support me in idleness, so he led me off into the country and bade me work. (38) Then, of course, I supported him

in return, while he lived, I myself digging and sowing a very small bit of earth, yet not a worthless one, but the most just of all, and from what seed it received, it nobly and justly gave back a return of both the seed itself and some interest, but not much at all. Once, owing to its gentility, it gave back a return of twice what it received.[20] So this is how I used to live at home. Everything you see now Cyrus gave me."

(39) And the Sacian said, "You blessedly happy person, both in other respects and in this very thing, that you have become rich after having been poor. I think that it is much more pleasant for you to be rich because you have become rich after having been hungry for money."

(40) And Pheraulas said, "Do you suppose, Sacian, that I now live with an increase of pleasure in keeping with the increase in my possessions? Do you not know that I now eat, drink, sleep in no way more pleasantly than then when I was poor? As to there being more, here is what I gain: I need to guard more, to distribute more to others, and to have the trouble of having more to take care of. (41) For now, of course, many servants demand food of me, many demand drink, and many demand clothes. Others need doctors, and another comes in carrying either sheep that have been mangled by wolves, or cattle that have fallen off cliffs, or professing that a disease has come upon the flocks. Consequently, I think," said Pheraulas, "that I am in more pain now because I have many things than I was before because I had few."

(42) And the Sacian said, "But by Zeus, when they are safe and sound, to see your many things brings you many times as much delight as I have."

And Pheraulas said, "Having money is not so pleasant as losing it is painful. You will know that I speak the truth. For of the wealthy, no one is compelled by his pleasure to lose sleep, but of those who lose something, you will see that no one is able to sleep, for they experience such pain."

(43) "No, by Zeus," said the Sacian. "Nor would you see any one of those who get something nodding off, for they experience such pleasure."

(44) "What you say is true," he said, "for if having were just as pleasant as getting, then the wealthy would by far exceed the poor in happiness. And doubtless there is a necessity, Sacian, that he who has

a lot also spend a lot on gods, on friends, and on guests. Be assured that whoever is intensely pleased by money also feels intense pain on spending it."

(45) "By Zeus," said the Sacian, "but I am not one of these, but I believe that this is happiness, to have a lot and spend a lot."

(46) "Why then, by the gods," said Pheraulas, "do you not become very happy at once and make me happy? Take all these things and possess them, and use them however you wish. Support me in no other way than as a guest, or even more cheaply than a guest, for it will suffice for me to share in whatever you have."

(47) "You are joking," said the Sacian.

And Pheraulas swore and said that he was speaking seriously. "I will attain even other things for you from Cyrus, that you not pay court at Cyrus' gates or go on campaign. But you just stay at home and be wealthy, and I will do these things both on your behalf and on mine, and if I get anything good from service at Cyrus' court, or from some campaign, I will bring it to you, in order that you may rule over still more. Only free me from this care, for if I have leisure from this, I think that you will be useful in many respects to both Cyrus and me."

(48) With things having been said like this, they agreed to these terms and acted on them. And the one held that he had become happy, because he ruled over much money; the other, on the other hand, believed that he was most blessedly happy, because he had a steward who provided him leisure to do whatever was pleasant to him.

(49) Pheraulas' character was companion-loving, and nothing seemed so pleasant or beneficial to him as to serve human beings, for he held human beings to be the best of all the animals and the most grateful. He saw that those who are praised by someone praise them eagerly in return; that they try to gratify in return those who have gratified them; that those whom they regard as being well disposed to them they are well disposed to in return; that those whom they know love them, these they are not able to hate; and that they are more willing than all other animals to return their parents' services, both when they are alive and after they are dead. He judged the other animals to be more ungrateful and more unfeeling than human beings. (50) Thus, of course, Pheraulas was exceedingly pleased that it would be possible for him, having been set free of the care of the rest

of his possessions, to be busy over his friends, and the Sacian because, having many things, he also had much to make use of. The Sacian loved Pheraulas because he always brought in something further, and he loved the Sacian, because he was willing to take everything in and, even though he always had more to take care of, gave him no less leisure. So these, then, passed their time like this.

ᐁ· CHAPTER 4 ·ᐁ

(1) After he had sacrificed, when Cyrus was giving a victory feast, he invited those of his friends who had been especially evident both in their wish to elevate him and in their honoring of him with the greatest goodwill. With them he invited also Artabazus the Mede, Tigranes the Armenian, the Hyrcanian cavalry commander, and Gobryas. (2) Gadatas ruled the mace bearers for him, and the whole way of life inside was arranged in the order he selected. Whenever any guests dined together with Cyrus, Gadatas did not even sit down; rather, he took care of things. But whenever it was they themselves, he dined together with Cyrus, for he²¹ took pleasure in being with him. In return, he was honored with many great things both by Cyrus and, because of Cyrus, also by others.

(3) When guests came to dinner, he did not seat each of them at random, but whomever he honored most he sat by his left hand, on the grounds that this side was more vulnerable to treachery than the right. He sat the second by his right hand, the third back again on the left, the fourth by the right, and so forth, if there were more. (4) It seemed to him to be good to make clear the way he honored each because of this: Wherever human beings think that the one who is best will neither be heralded nor receive prizes, here it is clear that they are not competitively disposed toward each other. Yet wherever the best person is especially evident in getting the advantage, here all are also evident contending with the greatest enthusiasm. (5) Cyrus thus made it clear who the superiors were in his company, beginning immediately from one's sitting and standing position. He did not establish one's assigned seat in perpetuity, however, but he made it customary to advance by good works into a more honored

seat, and if one slacked off, to retreat into a seat of diminished honor. He used to be ashamed if the one seated first were not evident in having the most good things from him. And things having come to be like this in Cyrus' time, thus do we perceive them enduring still even now.

(6) When they were dining, it seemed to Gobryas that it was not at all amazing for a man who ruled many people to have many things. Yet it did seem amazing that Cyrus, who was faring so very well, should not be alone in consuming whatever it might seem pleasant to him to take, but he took on the work of asking those present to share in it. He often saw him sending things in which he happened to be pleased even to some of his absent friends. (7) Consequently, when they had dined and Cyrus passed around all the many things there were from his table, Gobryas then said, "Cyrus, I held before that you most surpassed human beings in being the most skilled general. Now I swear by the gods that you seem to me to surpass them more by your benevolence than by your generalship."

(8) "Yes, by Zeus," said Cyrus. "And I display the works of benevolence with much more pleasure than those of generalship."

"Why?" said Gobryas.

"Because one must display the one by harming human beings, the other by benefiting them."

(9) After this, when they were drinking, Hystaspas asked Cyrus, "Cyrus, would you be annoyed with me if I should ask you what I wish to learn from you?"

"But by the gods," he said, "I would be annoyed with you in the opposite case, if I should perceive you being silent on those points that you wished to ask."

"Tell me, then," he said, "have I ever not come when you have called?"

"Do not say such a thing!" said Cyrus.

"But if I obeyed, did I obey in a leisurely fashion?"

"No, not like this."

"Once something was ordered, did I not do it for you?"

"I do not accuse you in this regard," he said.

"Has it ever happened that you have detected me doing what I do without enthusiasm or pleasure?"

"Least of all," said Cyrus.

(10) "Then why, by the gods," he said, "did you write that Chrysantas is to be seated in a more honored place than I?"

"And shall I tell you?" said Cyrus.

"By all means," said Hystaspas.

"And you in turn will not be annoyed with me when you hear the truth?"

(11) "I shall be pleased," he said, "if I know that I am not treated unjustly."

"Then in the first place, Chrysantas here did not wait for our call; he instead reported before he was called, for the sake of our affairs. Secondly, not only did he do what was ordered; he also did what he himself knew would be better for us if it were done. Whenever it was necessary to say something to the allies, he counseled me on what he thought it fitting for me to say. Whatever points he perceived that I wished the allies to know, but was ashamed to say about myself, he said himself, declaring them as his own judgment. Consequently, in these matters at least, what prevents him from being even better for me than I am myself? And as for himself, he always says that his present possessions suffice, but for me it is always evident that he considers what possible further acquisition would be beneficial; and he rejoices and takes pleasure in what is noble for me much more than I do."

(12) To this Hystaspas said, "By Hera, Cyrus, I am pleased I asked you this."

"Why in particular?" said Cyrus.

"Because I shall try to do this. Of one thing only am I ignorant," he said. "How should I make clear my delight in what is good for you? Must I clap my hands? Must I laugh? What must I do?"

And Artabazus said, "You must dance the Persian dance."

At this, of course, a laugh arose.

(13) As the drinking party advanced, Cyrus asked Gobryas, "Tell me, Gobryas, do you think it would be more pleasant for you to give your daughter to one of these now than when you first came together with us?"

"Shall I too tell the truth?" said Gobryas.

"Yes, by Zeus," said Cyrus, "since no question requires a lie."

"Then be assured," he said, "that I would do so with much more pleasure now."

"And would you be able," said Cyrus, "to say why?"

"I would."

"Then speak."

(14) "Because then I saw them bearing labors and risks with enthusiasm, but now I see them bearing good things moderately. It seems to me, Cyrus, to be more difficult to find a man who bears good things nobly than one who bears evil things nobly, for the former infuse insolence in the many, but the latter infuse moderation in all."

(15) And Cyrus said, "Did you hear, Hystaspas, Gobryas' saying?"

"Yes, by Zeus," he said. "And if he says many more such things, he will get me as a suitor for his daughter much more than if he shows me many cups."

(16) "Indeed I have many such writings, which I shall not refuse you if you take my daughter as your wife. But as for my cups, since it appears to me you cannot stand them, I do not know whether I may not just give them to Chrysantas here, since he has usurped also your seat."

(17) "And certainly," said Cyrus, "Hystaspas and you others here, if you speak to me when one of you is getting ready to marry, you will know what sort of colleague I shall be for you."

(18) And Gobryas said, "And if someone wishes to give his daughter away, to whom must he speak?"

"To me," said Cyrus, "also about this, for I am very clever in this art."

"Which?" said Chrysantas.

(19) "Knowing what sort of marriage would be harmonious for each."

And Chrysantas said, "Tell me, by the gods, what sort of wife you think would be harmonious for me in the most noble way."

(20) "First," he said, "a short one, for you yourself are also short. And if you marry a tall one, if you ever wish to kiss her when she is standing up, you will need to jump up, like a puppy."

"In this," he said, "you are taking forethought correctly, for I am not at all a jumper."

(21) "Next," he said, "a snub-nosed wife would be of great advantage to you."

"Why is this so?"

"Because you are hook-nosed. Be assured, then, that snub-nosedness would harmonize best with hook-nosedness."

"You are also saying," he said, "that a dinnerless person would harmonize with one who had dined well, just as I now have."

"Yes, by Zeus," said Cyrus, "for the stomach of those who are full hooks out, but that of the dinnerless is snubbed."

(22) And Chrysantas said, "By the gods, would you be able to say what sort of wife would be advantageous for a cold king?"

Here, of course, Cyrus burst out laughing and the others did likewise. (23) While they were laughing, Hystaspas said, "I am very jealous of you in your kingship, Cyrus, especially for this."

"For what?" said Cyrus.

"Because you are able to provide a laugh even though you are cold."

And Cyrus said, "Then would you not pay a great deal to have been the one who had said these things, and to have it reported to the woman with whom you wish to enjoy the reputation of being urbane?"

It was in this way, then, that these things were said in jest.

(24) After this he brought out some feminine adornment and told Tigranes to give it to his wife, because she had courageously campaigned along with her husband; and for Artabazus, a golden cup; and for the Hycarnian, a horse; and he gave also many other beautiful gifts.

"To you, Gobryas," he said, "I shall give a husband for your daughter."

(25) "Then you will please give me," said Hystaspas, "in order that I may receive the writings."[22]

"And do you have substance worthy of what the girl has?"[23]

"Yes, by Zeus," he said, "in valuables worth many times as much as hers."

"And where," said Cyrus, "is this substance of yours?"

"Here," he said, "where you are sitting, since you are my friend."

"This suffices for me," said Gobryas. And immediately stretching out his right hand, he said, "Give him, Cyrus, for I accept him."

(26) Taking the right hand of Hystaspas, Cyrus gave it to Gobryas, and he accepted it. After this he gave many beautiful gifts to Hystaspas, in order that he might send them to the girl. Drawing Chrysantas over, he kissed him.

(27) Artabazus said, "By Zeus, Cyrus, the cup you gave to me and your gift to Chrysantas are not of similar gold."

"But I will give one to you too," he said.

He next asked, "When?"

"After thirty years," he said.

"Be prepared, then, for I will be waiting and will not die."

So then the tent party ceased in this way. When they stood up, Cyrus also stood up and escorted them to the door.

(28) On the next day, he dismissed to go home each of those who willingly became his allies, except as many of them as wished to dwell with him. To these he gave land and houses, and even now the descendants of those who then remained still have them. Most of them are Medes and Hyrcanians. After giving many gifts to those who were going away, and giving them no reason to complain, he dismissed both the rulers and the soldiers. (29) After this he distributed to the soldiers in his circle as much money as he took from Sardis. To the brigadier generals and to his personal aides he gave things selected with a view to the worth of each, and he divided the rest. Giving a share to each of the brigadier generals, he allowed them to distribute it just as he himself had distributed it to them. (30) They gave out the rest of the money, each ruler assessing those who ruled beneath himself. Finally, the rulers of six assessed the privates beneath themselves and gave out the last things in accord with the worth of each. Thus all received their just share.

(31) When they received what was then given, some said things like this about Cyrus: "He himself has a lot, I suppose, since he has given so much to each of us." Others of them said, "What do you mean 'a lot'? Cyrus' character is not such as to make money; rather, he takes pleasure in giving more than in acquiring."

(32) On perceiving these arguments and opinions about himself, Cyrus gathered together his friends and chief aides, all of them, and he spoke as follows: "Men, friends, I have seen human beings who wish to seem to possess more than they have, thinking that in this way they would appear to be more free.[24] These people seem to me to bring on the opposite of what they wish. For when one who seems to have a great deal does not manifestly benefit his friends in accord with the worth of his substance, it seems to me to smack of illiberality. (33) On the other hand, there are those who wish that what they have not be noticed. Now these too seem to me to be worthless to their friends, for when their friends are in need, because these friends do not know what their companions' possessions are, they frequently do not report their neediness to them; instead, they are overcome.[25] (34) This seems to me to belong to one who is most straightforward,

that he make his power manifest and contend on this basis over nobility and goodness. And I wish to show you all my possessions it is
possible to see, and to describe all those it is not possible to see."

(35) Having said this, he showed them many beautiful possessions,
and what had been deposited so as not to be easy to see he described.
In conclusion he spoke as follows: (36) "Men, you must hold all these
things to be no more mine than yours, for I am gathering them neither to spend them myself nor to use them up myself (for I would not
be able). I do so rather so that I am able to give gifts whenever one of
you does something noble and, if any of you believes he needs something, so that he may come to me and take whatever he happens to
need." These things were said like this.

ᴄᴏ· CHAPTER 5 ·ᴄᴏ

(1) As soon as the situation in Babylon seemed fine to him, so that
he might travel out, he began preparing for an expedition to Persia,
and he directed the others to do likewise. When he believed he had
enough of what he thought he needed, then, of course, he moved out.
(2) We will describe this too, how—even though it was a great expedition—he made camp and broke camp in good order and how he
quickly took a position where it was required, for wherever the king
camps, all those in the king's circle take the field with their tents, both
summer and winter. (3) Cyrus immediately adopted the custom of
pitching his tent facing the east. Next he determined, first of all, how
far distant from the king's tent his bodyguards should pitch their
tents; then he showed a place on the right for the breadmakers, and
one on the left for the saucemakers, and another on the right for the
horses, and another on the left for the rest of the pack animals. He
also arranged the other things so that each knew his own place, in
both size and location. (4) When they break camp, each gathers together the equipment he has been assigned to use, and others in their
turn put it up on the pack animals. Consequently, all the baggage carriers come at the same time to the pack animals assigned to carry
things, and all at the same time load these animals, each his own.
Thus, of course, the same time suffices to load up and carry off all

tents as it does for one. (5) So it is also in regard to making camp. And regarding the preparation of all provisions at the right time, what must be done is similarly assigned in shares to each. And because of this, the same time suffices for everything to be done as for one part. (6) Just as each servant involved with provisions had a fitting place, so also those who bore arms for him both had a place in the camp suited to each sort of armament and knew which it was, and all took positions about which there could be no doubt. (7) Cyrus held orderliness to be a noble practice also in a household, for whenever anyone needs anything, it is clear where he needs to go to get it. But he believed the orderliness of the divisions of an army to be still more noble by far, insofar as the opportunities for using things in war are more sudden and the errors from being late more costly. He saw possessions[26] of the greatest worth arising in wars when things are on hand in opportune moments. He therefore was especially careful about such orderliness.

(8) And he himself, in the first place, established himself in the middle of the army camp, on the grounds that this was the strongest place. Next, he had his most trusted troops around himself, as was his custom; and in a circle around these he kept both knights and charioteers. (9) He believed that these too needed a strong place, because they encamp without having any of the weapons with which they fight ready at hand, but they need a lot of time for arming, if they are going to be useful. (10) On the right and the left of both him and the knights was a place for targeteers; and next there was a place for archers both in front of and behind himself and the knights. (11) Hoplites and those with the great shields he had in a circle around everything, like a wall, in order that if it should be at all necessary to get the knights ready, having those most able to stand fast in the front would provide them safety for arming. (12) As he had the hoplites sleep in order, so also with the targeteers and the archers. Thus, if there should be some need even at night, just as the hoplites are prepared to strike whoever comes within reach, so also the archers and the spearmen, if any approach, might promptly throw their spears and shoot their arrows over the hoplites. (13) All the officers also had insignias over their tents.[27] Just as also in cities moderate servants know the houses of most people, and especially of the chiefs, so also—of the troops in his camps—Cyrus' aides both

knew the places of the leaders and also recognized the insignias that each had. Consequently, they did not go searching for whomever Cyrus needed, but they ran along the shortest route to each. (14) And because the several divisions were not mixed, it was also much more clear when someone was in good order and if someone was not doing what was commanded. When things were like this, he held that if someone were to attack during night or day, the attackers would fall upon his camp as into an ambush. (15) And as for being a tactician, he held it not enough if someone should be able to stretch a phalanx out easily; or to deepen one; or to change a formation from a column into a phalanx; or to countermarch correctly with an enemy appearing from the right, from the left, or from behind; but he held that separating when necessary was part of tactics, and putting each part where it would be especially beneficial, and speeding up where it should be necessary to get the jump on the enemy—all these and such things he believed to belong to the man skilled in tactics, and he took similar care on all of these points. (16) On his marches, he always marched with a view to the circumstances, but in his army's camp, he positioned things, for the most part, as has been said.

(17) When in their march they were beside Media, Cyrus turned his course toward Cyaxares. When they greeted each other, first, of course, Cyrus told Cyaxares that a house had been selected for him in Babylon, as had official buildings, in order that he might be able to lodge in places of his own whenever he went there. Then he gave him many other beautiful gifts. (18) Cyaxares accepted them, and sent him his daughter bearing a golden crown, bracelets, a necklace, and a Median robe as beautiful as possible. (19) The girl crowned Cyrus, and Cyaxares said, "I give you, Cyrus, this woman, who is my daughter. Your father married the daughter of my father, from whom you were born. This is she whom you, when you were a boy, often tended when you stayed with us.[28] And whenever anyone should ask her whom she would marry, she used to say, 'Cyrus.' Along with her I also give all of Media as a dowry, for I have no legitimate male children."

(20) Thus he spoke, and Cyrus answered, "Cyaxares, I praise your family, your daughter, and your gifts, but I wish to concur with you on these things in conformity with the judgment of my father and mother." So Cyrus spoke like this. Nevertheless, he gave the girl all

gifts that he thought would gratify Cyaxares as well. Having done these things, he marched to Persia.

(21) When in his march he was at the borders of Persia, he left the rest of the army there, and he himself marched into the city with his friends, bringing sufficient sacred victims for all Persians to offer in sacrifice and feast on. He brought in such gifts as were fitting for his father, his mother, and other friends; and such as were fitting for magistrates, elders, and all the Peers. He gave [gifts] also to all the Persian men and Persian women, as many as the king still now gives whenever he arrives in Persia. (22) After this, Cambyses called the Persian elders and magistrates together, those who presided over the greatest matters. He also summoned Cyrus, and he spoke as follows: "Persian men and you, Cyrus, I am of goodwill toward you both, as is to be expected, for of you I am king, and you, Cyrus, are my son. It is just, then, that I say openly as many things as I think I know to be good for both of you. (23) Regarding past events, you [Persians] elevated Cyrus, giving him an army and establishing him as its ruler, and Cyrus, leading it with the [help of the] gods, made you, Persians, famous among all human beings, and honored in all Asia. Of those who campaigned with him, he both enriched the best and provided a wage and support for the many. By establishing a cavalry of Persians, he has made for the Persians a tie to the plains. (24) Now if in the future you will judge things in this manner, you will be the causes of many good things for each other. But if either you, Cyrus, being raised up by your present fortunes, undertake to rule Persians as you do others, with a view to your own special advantage, or you, citizens, envying him for his power, try to depose him from his rule, be assured that you will hinder each other from many good things. (25) In order that these things not occur, but good ones instead, it seems to me," he said, "that, sacrificing in common and invoking gods as witnesses, you should make a compact: You, Cyrus, that if anyone marches against Persian land or tries to tear up Persia's laws, you will give aid with all your strength; and you, Persians, that if someone either undertakes to depose Cyrus from his rule or if any of his subjects undertakes to revolt, you will give aid both to yourselves and to Cyrus, in whatever way he demands. (26) And as long as I am alive, the kingship in Persia is mine. When I die, it is clear that it belongs to Cyrus, if he is alive. Whenever he returns to Persia, it

would be pious for you to have him offer in sacrifice on your behalf those sacred victims that I now offer. Whenever he is away, I think it would be noble for you if whoever from our family seems best to you would be the one to perform the [rites] of the gods."

(27) Cambyses having said these things, they were so decided by Cyrus and the Persian authorities. Having made this compact at that time and having invoked gods as witnesses, even now the Persians and the king continue to act in this manner toward each other. When these things were done, Cyrus went away.

(28) When he was in Media on his return, since it seemed good to his father and mother, he married Cyaxares' daughter, of whom there is still even now talk of her as having been very beautiful. Some writers say that he married his mother's sister. But this girl would by all means have been an old woman. Having married, he immediately set out with [her].

ᴄᴠ· CHAPTER 6 ·ᴄᴠ

(1) When he was in Babylon, he decided to send satraps to the subdued nations. Nevertheless, he wished that the commanders in the citadels and the colonels of the guards in the country listen to no one but himself. Thinking ahead, he foresaw that if any of the satraps became insolent because of their wealth and the number of their subjects and undertook to disobey him, he would immediately have rivals in the country.[29] (2) So wishing to achieve this [force independent of the satraps], he resolved first to call his chief aides together and speak to them in advance, so that those who were going [out as satraps] might know the terms on which they were going. He believed that in this way they would bear these terms more easily. Otherwise, if he should establish someone as ruler and he should perceive these terms later, he thought they would bear it ill, believing that these terms stemmed from distrust of themselves. (3) So gathering them together, he spoke as follows: "Men, friends, in the cities that have been subdued, we have garrisons and their commanders, whom we left there at the time. Before I went away, I ordered them to busy themselves with nothing but keeping the fortresses safe. So

since they have nobly guarded what has been assigned to them, I shall not deprive them of their rule, yet I have decided to send others as satraps, who will rule over the inhabitants and who, receiving the tribute, will both pay the garrisons their wage and pay for whatever else may be needed. (4) It also seems to me that whomever I trouble from among those of you who remain here by sending you out to these nations to do something, you should have lands and houses there, both so that a tribute may be brought to you here and so that you may be able to lodge in residences of your own whenever you go there."

(5) This is what he said, and to many of his friends he gave houses and subjects throughout all the cities that had been subdued. Even now lands still remain for the descendants of those who received them then, different ones in different countries, but they themselves dwell beside the king.

(6) "It is necessary," he said, "that we look for those going out as satraps to the various countries to be such as will remember to send also here whatever may be noble or good in each land, so that we who are here may share in the goods that arise from all places, for if something terrible arises anywhere, it will also be up to us to defend against it."

(7) Having said these things, he then stopped the argument. Next, from those of his friends he knew desired to go on the stated terms, he selected those who seemed to be most suitable and sent them as satraps—Megabyzus to Arabia, Artabatas to Cappadocia, Artacamas to the Greater Phyrygia, Chrysantas to Lydia and Ionia, Adousius to Caria (just as they had asked), and Pharnuchus to the Phrygia on the Hellespont and Aeolia. (8) He did not send Persians as satraps over Cilicia, Cyprus, and the Paphlagonians, because they seemed to join the campaign against Babylon voluntarily. He did, however, order even these to pay tribute. (9) As Cyrus then established it, so even now the king still has guard posts in the citadels, and the guards' colonels are appointed by the king and registered with the king. (10) He told all those being sent out as satraps to imitate all the things they saw him doing: First, that they establish a cavalry from the allies and Persians who were sent along with them, and charioteers as well; that they compel those who receive land and offices to come to court and, practicing moderation, to offer themselves up for the use of the

satrap, if anything should be needed; that they educate at court also
the children who are born, just as also was done with him; that the
satrap take those in his court out hunting, and exercise both himself
and his circle in military matters.

(11) "Whoever," he said, "in proportion to his power, displays the
most chariots, and the most and best knights, I shall honor as a good
ally and as a good fellow guardian of the empire for both Persians
and me. Let it be with you as it is with me, that the best are honored
even by where they sit, and that you have a table like mine, which
supports the members of the household in the first place but which
then is adorned sufficiently for your friends to share in and to honor
whoever does anything noble each day. (12) Acquire parks too, and
raise wild animals, and neither yourselves ever sit down to your food
without exercise nor throw fodder to unexercised horses. Since I am
but one [person], I would not be able to preserve with human virtue
all your good things. Rather, I must, being good and having good
[men] with me, be a protector for you; and you, similarly, being yourselves good and having good [men] with you, must be allies to me.
(13) I would wish that you also consider that I am not commanding
slaves in any of the things that I prescribe to you. What things I say
you need to do, I too try to do myself, all of them. Just as I order you
to imitate me, so you too must teach those who have offices beneath
you to imitate you."

(14) So Cyrus then arranged these things like this. Still even now
in the same way all the safeguards beneath the king are similarly
maintained; all the rulers' courts receive similar service; all the households, both great and small, are similarly managed; all the best of
those on hand are honored by where they sit; all the expeditions are
put in order in the same way; and all political actions are concentrated
in a few who are in control.

(15) Having said how they each had to do these things, and having
given a force to each, he sent them out. And he told all to make preparations in the expectation that there would be an expedition in the
next year and a display of men, weapons, horses, and chariots.

(16) We considered also this practice that Cyrus began, as they say,
and that still endures even now: Each and every year a man with an
army goes on patrol in order that, if one of the satraps needs assis-
tance, he may render it; and if anyone has become insolent, he may

make him moderate; and if one neglects either the paying of the tribute or the guarding of the inhabitants, or if he disregards that the land
is to be worked or anything else that has been ordered, he may
straighten out all these things. If he is not able to, he reports back to
the king; and when he hears about it, he deliberates about the one
who is out of order. And these of whom it is often said that a son of
the king is coming, or a brother of the king, or the Eye of the king, are
those who go on patrol; and sometimes they do not appear, for each
of them turns aside in the direction the king orders.

(17) We also learned still another contrivance of his for the greatness of his empire, one from which he quickly perceived how things
were even at a very great distance. Having considered how long a
distance a horse could complete in a day if it was ridden so as not to
deplete its strength, he made stations for the horses at just this distance. In them he put horses and people to take care of them, and he
ordered that the appropriate man at each post receive the letters
brought in, and pass them on, and that he take in the tired horses and
human beings and send on other fresh ones. (18) There are times, they
say, when this travel is not halted even at night; instead, the nighttime messenger relieves the daytime one. These things being like this,
some say that they complete this travel more swiftly than do cranes.
But if they say this falsely, it is quite clear that this is nevertheless the
quickest human travel on land. It is good to perceive everything as
quickly as possible and to take care of it as quickly as possible.

(19) When the year was out, he assembled his army at Babylon, and
he is said to have had up to one hundred and twenty thousand
knights, up to two thousand scythed chariots, and up to six hundred
thousand infantry. (20) When these were ready for him, he started the
expedition on which it is said that he subdued all the nations that inhabit the land as one goes out of Syria as far as the Indian Ocean.[30]
After this, it is said there was the expedition against Egypt and that
Egypt was subdued. (21) At this point, the Indian Ocean bounded his
empire to the east; the Black Sea to the north; Cyprus and Egypt to
the west; and Ethiopia to the south. The limits of these borders are
uninhabitable because of heat, in one case; by cold in another; by
water in another; and by lack of water in another. (22) Making his
habitation in their center, he himself spent seven months around wintertime in Babylon, for this place was warm. Around springtime, he

spent three months in Susa. The peak of the summer heat he spent in
Ecbatana, for two months. Acting in this manner, they say that he always spent his time in the warmth and the coolness of spring.

(23) Human beings were so disposed to him that every nation
thought they got less if they did not send to Cyrus whatever fine thing
either naturally grew in their land, was raised there, or was made by
art; and so too with every city;[31] and every private person thought
that he would become wealthy if he could gratify Cyrus in something.
For Cyrus, taking from each whatever the givers had in abundance,
gave in return what he perceived them to be lacking.

∾ CHAPTER 7 ∾

(1) With his lifetime having advanced in this way, and Cyrus being
very old, he arrived in Persia for the seventh time during his reign.
Both his father and mother had long since died, as was to be expected.
Cyrus made the customary sacrifices, began the dance for the Persians in accord with the ancestral ways, and gave gifts to everyone,
just as was his habit. (2) After going to sleep in the king's palace, he
saw a dream like this: Someone more than human[32] seemed to him to
approach and say, "Get ready, Cyrus, for you are soon going away to
gods." On seeing this dream, he woke up and thought he almost certainly knew that the end of his life was at hand. (3) So he immediately
got victims and sacrificed on the mountain peaks, as Persians do, to
ancestral Zeus, to the Sun, and to the other gods, and he prayed as
follows: "Ancestral Zeus, Sun, and all gods, accept these gifts for the
completion of many noble actions and these gifts of gratitude because
you gave signs to me in sacrificial victims, in heavenly signs, in birds,
and in omens, both as to what I must do and what I must not. Let my
gratitude to you be great because I knew your care and never began
to think thoughts higher than a human being should over my good
fortune. I ask you to give happiness now to my children, my wife, my
friends, and my fatherland, and to give me an end of a sort similar to
the life you have given me."

(4) Having done such things and gone home, he thought that he
would rest pleasantly, and he lay down. When it was time, those so

assigned approached and bade him wash, yet he said that he was resting pleasantly. Others so assigned, when it was time, put his dinner beside him, but his soul was not inclined to food. Yet he did seem to thirst, and he drank pleasantly. (5) When these same things happened to him on the second and third days, he called his sons. They happened to have accompanied him and to have been in Persia. He called also his friends and the Persian magistrates. When all were present, he began a talk like this: (6) "My sons and all my friends who are here, the end of my life is now at hand. I know this clearly from many things. When I die, you must say and do everything about me as about one who was happy, for when I was a boy, I think that I enjoyed the fruits of what is believed to be noble for the boys;[33] and when I was a youth, those for the youths; and when I became a mature man, those for the men. As time went forward, I thought that I recognized my power to be always on the increase, so that I did not ever perceive even my old age to be weaker than my youth, and I do not know that I undertook or desired anything that I did not obtain. (7) And I beheld my friends becoming happy because of me, and my enemies enslaved by me. And my fatherland, which before lived privately, I leave now as foremost in honor in Asia. Of what I acquired, I know of nothing that I did not preserve. And throughout the past, I fared just as I prayed I would, yet a fear accompanied me that in the time ahead I might see, hear, or suffer something harsh, and it did not allow me to think so very highly of myself or to take extravagant delight. (8) Now, if I die, I shall leave you alive, my sons, you who the gods granted to be born to me. I leave my fatherland and my friends happy. (9) Consequently, how should I not justly obtain for all time the memory of being blessedly happy?[34]

"I must now bequeath the kingship, and do so clearly, lest from being ambiguous it bring you trouble. Now I am similarly fond of you both, sons; but to deliberate and to lead, toward whatever may seem to be opportune, I assign to the one born earlier and, as is to be expected, more experienced. (10) I myself was educated like this by my fatherland and yours, to defer to my elders, not only to older brothers but also to other citizens, whether walking, sitting down, or speaking. And as for you, sons, I educated you like this from the beginning, to honor those who are older and to be honored ahead of those who are younger. So accept this, on the grounds that I am saying what is ancient, habitual, and lawful.

(11) "And you, Cambyses, have the kingship, since both gods and I, as far as I can, give it to you. To you, Tanaoxares, I give the satrapy over the Medes, the Armenians, and, thirdly, the Cadusians. In giving these things to you I believe that whereas I bequeath a greater empire and the name of king to your elder brother, to you I bequeath a happiness more free from pain. (12) I do not see in what sort of human delight you will be lacking; to the contrary, everything that seems to delight human beings will be at hand for you. As for loving things that are hard to accomplish, for being anxious over many things, for being unable to be at peace because you are goaded to compete against my deeds, for plotting and for being plotted against, these things must of necessity accompany the king more than you, and these, be assured, provide many interruptions to the leisure needed for taking delight.

(13) "You also know, Cambyses, that this golden scepter is not what preserves the kingship; rather, trustworthy friends are the truest and safest scepter for kings. Do not believe that human beings are born trustworthy by nature, for the same people would then be apparent as trustworthy to all, just as other natural things are apparent as the same to all. But each person needs to make people trustworthy to himself. The acquisition [of trustworthy people] is in no way possible by force, however, but rather by benefaction. (14) If you try to make any others fellow guardians of your kingship, do not begin from any place sooner than from one born from the same source. Human beings who are fellow citizens are more familiar than those from other places, and those who eat together are more familiar than those who tent separately.[35] As for those who have been begotten from the same seed, have been nourished by the same mother, have grown up in the same house, are cherished by the same parents, and have called upon the same mother and the same father, how are they not the most familiar of all? (15) Let the two of you never make pointless those goods to which the gods lead for the sake of familiarity among brothers, but immediately build other friendly deeds on top of them. In this way your friendship will always be unsurpassable by others. He who takes forethought for his brother takes care of himself. For whom else is a brother who is great so noble as for his brother? Who else will be so honored because of a great man's power as his brother? Whom will someone fear to treat unjustly so much as the brother of one who is great?

(16) "Do not then let anyone obey him more quickly than you, or report with more enthusiasm. For what is his, whether good or terrible, is closer to no one than to you.³⁶ Consider this too: By gratifying whom rather than him could you expect to obtain greater things? By helping whom could you receive in return a stronger ally? To whom is it more shameful not to be friendly than to a brother? Whom is it more noble to honor over all others than a brother? It is only when a brother is foremost for his brother, Cambyses, that the envy from others does not reach him.

(17) "By ancestral gods,³⁷ my sons, honor each other, if you care at all about gratifying me, for surely this, at least, is something you do not think you know clearly, that I will no longer exist when I end my human life, and not even now have you ever seen my soul, but you beheld it as existing through the things it accomplished. (18) Have you not yet considered what fear the souls of those who have suffered unjustly inflict upon those who are stained with their blood, and what avengers they send upon the impious? Do you think the honors to the dead would still continue if their souls were not lords of anything? (19) I, at least, my sons, was never persuaded of this, that the soul is alive as long as it is in a mortal body, but whenever it becomes free of it, it is dead, for I see that for as long a time as soul is in mortal bodies, it makes them alive. (20) Nor have I been persuaded that the soul will be senseless when it becomes sundered from the senseless body. But when mind is separated, unmixed and pure, then too it is likely to be most prudent. When a human being is dissolved, his several parts are evident going away to what is of like kind with them, except for the soul. This alone is not seen either when it is present or when it goes away. (21) Consider that of things human, nothing is nearer to death than sleep; but then, surely, the soul of the human being appears most divine and then it has some foresight of things to come, for then, as it seems, it is especially free.

(22) "So if these things are just as I think, and the soul leaves the body behind, do what I ask also out of respect for my soul. If they are not so, but if instead the soul remains in the body and dies along with it, then out of fear of the everlasting, all-seeing, and all-powerful gods, who hold even this order of the whole together unimpaired, without age, without defect, indescribable in both beauty and size, never either do or plan anything unholy or impious.

(23) "After gods, respect also the whole race of mankind, whose posterity is forever being born, for the gods do not hide you in the dark, but of necessity your deeds always live on, visible to all. If they appear pure and free from injustice, they will show you to be powerful among all human beings. But if you plot some injustice against each other, you will destroy your trustworthiness among all human beings, for no one would still be able to trust you any longer, not even if he were very enthusiastic to do so, after seeing him who is closely related by friendship treated unjustly. (24) Now if I am teaching you sufficiently how you ought to be toward one another, [fine]; but if I am not, learn also from what has happened in the past, for this teaching is best. Many parents have gone through their lives as friends to their children, and many brothers as friends with their brothers, but some of these have acted toward each other also in the opposite way. So in whichever of these ways you perceive actions that were advantageous, you would of course deliberate correctly in choosing it. (25) But perhaps there has now been enough of this.

"As for my body, children, when I die, do not put it in gold, silver, or anything else, but return it to the earth as quickly as possible. What is more blessedly happy than being mingled with the earth, which both gives birth to and nourishes everything noble on the one hand and everything good on the other? I was benevolent even in other ways, and I think I would now be pleased to be united as a partner with this benefactor of human beings.

(26) "But my soul seems to me to be leaving now, from the very point at which, as it seems, it begins to leave everyone. If one of you either wishes to touch my right hand or wants to look me in the eye while I am still alive, let him approach. When I cover myself, I ask you, children, let no human being see my body any longer, not even you yourselves. (27) Summon all Persians and the allies to my monument, in order that they may share in my pleasure, for I will now be in a safe place, since I cannot suffer evil any longer, whether I am with the divine or no longer exist at all. After doing such good things to those who come as are customary in the case of a happy man, send them back. (28) And remember this last thing from me, that by benefiting your friends, you will be able to punish your enemies. And farewell, my dear sons; report a farewell to your mother from me.

Farewell, all you present and absent friends." Having said this and shaken the right hand of each, he covered himself and thus died.

✦ CHAPTER 8 ✦

(1) Cyrus' kingship in itself bears witness that it was the most noble and greatest of those in Asia, for it was bordered on the east by the Indian Ocean,[38] on the north by the Black Sea, on the west by Cyprus and Egypt, toward the south by Ethiopia. Despite its size, it was governed by one judgment, that of Cyrus, and he honored and was attentive to those under him just as to his own children, and his subjects venerated Cyrus as a father. (2) When Cyrus died, however, his sons immediately fell into dissension, cities and nations immediately revolted, and everything took a turn for the worse. That what I say is true I shall teach beginning with the divine things.

I know that earlier a king and those beneath him would remain firm in their oaths, if they swore them, and would remain firm in their agreements, if they had given their right hands, even with those who had done the most extreme things. (3) If they were not of this sort and did not have a reputation of this sort, not even one person would have trusted them, just as there is now not even one person who trusts them any longer, since their impiety has become known. Thus the generals who marched upcountry with Cyrus would not have trusted [the Persian rulers] even on that occasion [if they had know of their impiety].[39] As it was, of course, they trusted in their former reputation, and handed themselves over, and being led up to the king, they had their heads cut off. Even many of the barbarians who joined the campaign perished, different ones having been deceived by different pledges.

(4) They are much worse now in what follows as well. Before, if someone should run risks on the king's behalf, or should make either a city or nation subordinate, or should accomplish any other noble or good thing for him, these were honored. Yet now, even if someone like Mithridates betrays his father, Ariobarzanes, and if someone like Rheomithres leaves his wife, offspring, and his friends' children as hostages in the hands of the Egyptian king, and after transgressing

the greatest oaths may seem to do something advantageous for a king, these are those who are rewarded with the greatest honors. (5) So seeing these things, everyone in Asia has been turned toward impiety and injustice, for of whatever sort those who are foremost may be, such also, for the most part, do those beneath them become. Now, of course, they have become more lawless than before in this way.[40]

(6) As for money, they have become more unjust in the following way: They round up not only those who have done many injustices but now also those who have done nothing, and they compel them to pay out money without just grounds. Consequently, those who seem to have many possessions are no less afraid than those who have committed many injustices. And they do not willingly get involved with those who are stronger, nor are they confident in joining the king's army. (7) It is possible for whoever may make war on [the Persians] to range about that country, without a battle, in whatever way they wish, and this is because of their impiety concerning gods and injustice concerning men. So their judgments are in this respect altogether worse now than they were of old.

(8) That they do not even take care of their bodies as they did before I shall in its turn now explain. It was of course customary for them neither to spit nor blow their nose. They had these customs, clearly, not to be thrifty with the body's moisture, but because they wished to harden their bodies through labors and sweat. Now it still remains the case that they do not spit or blow their nose, (9) but working up a sweat is nowhere practiced. Indeed, it was previously customary for them to eat but once a day, in order that they might use the whole day for actions and hard labor. Now it still indeed remains the case that they eat but once a day: Beginning their meal with those who have breakfast as early as possible, they spend the day eating and drinking from then until such time as the latest go to bed.

(10) It was customary for them not to carry pots into their symposia, for clearly they believed that not drinking to excess would result in fewer failures of body and of judgment. Now it still remains the case that they do not carry them in, but they drink so much that instead of carrying them in, they themselves must be carried out, whenever they are no longer able to stand upright and go out.

(11) But it was traditional for them when on a march neither to eat nor to drink nor to be evident doing any of the necessary conse-

quences of both. Now, in turn, abstaining from these things still endures [when on a march]; however, they make such brief trips that no one would still wonder at their abstention from things necessary.

(12) But they used to go out hunting so often before that their hunts sufficed as exercises both for them and for their horses. When King Artaxerxes and his circle became weaker than wine, neither did they themselves similarly still go out hunting nor did they take others out hunting. But even if any others were hardworking and often went hunting with their knights, [the king and his circle] clearly envied them and hated them for being better than they were.

(13) But the children's being educated at court still endures; however, the learning and practice of horsemanship has become extinct because of there not being anywhere in which they might become well regarded by showing it. And that the children before used to hear cases being justly adjudicated and seemed to learn justice, this too has been altogether undone, for now they see clearly that whichever side bribes more wins. (14) But before the children used to learn also the powers of the plants that grew naturally from the earth, in order that they might use the helpful ones and avoid the harmful. But now it looks as though they are taught these things so they can do the most harm. In any event, nowhere more than there are so many killed or ruined because of poisonous drugs.

(15) But they are also more delicate now than in Cyrus' time. Then they still made use of the education and continence they received from the Persians, as well as the dress and the luxury of the Medes. Now they look with indifference on the extinction of the Persians' perseverance, while they conserve the Medes' softness. (16) I wish to make clear their delicacy as well. In the first place, it is not sufficient for them that their beds be softly spread: They even set the feet of their beds on carpets, so that instead of a hard floor resisting, soft carpets yield. Moreover, as for foods baked for their meals, they have not omitted anything previously discovered; rather, they are forever contriving new ones. So too with sauces, for they possess inventors of both. (17) It does not suffice for them in winter that their head, body, and feet be covered, but they also have lined sleeves and gloves for their hands and fingers. Nor indeed in summer does the shade of either trees or rocks suffice for them, but people stand by and contrive additional shade for them. (18) Moreover, if they have as many cups

as possible, they preen themselves on it. If they have contrived to get them through a manifest injustice, they are not ashamed of it, for injustice and the sordid search for gain have increased a great deal among them. (19) But it was traditional for them even before not to be seen traveling on foot, for no other reason than to become as skilled as possible in horsemanship. Now they have more blankets on their horses than on their beds, for they are not so concerned with riding as with sitting softly.

(20) As for things military, is it not likely that they are worse than before in every way? In the past, it was a tradition for the landholders to provide riders from their territory (and they, of course, went on campaign if a campaign was needed) and for only those guarding the country's advanced positions to be paid for it. Now it is doormen, cooks, saucemakers, wine pourers, bathers, waiters to bring out dishes, waiters to take them away, assistants for going to bed, assistants for getting up, and cosmeticians who apply makeup, anoint, and arrange other matters—now all these are the ones the powerful have made to be knights, that they may be their paid troops. (21) It is evident that there is a multitude of them; however, there is no military benefit from them for war. Events themselves make it clear, for enemies range about their country more easily than do friends.

(22) Cyrus, of course, stopped the practice of skirmishing at long range. Putting breastplates on both his troops and their horses, and giving one spear to each, he made the battle be hand to hand. Now they neither skirmish at a distance nor come together and do battle hand to hand. (23) The infantry have shields, swords, and scimitars, just as if they were going to do battle in Cyrus' time, but they are not willing to fight at close range either. (24) Nor do they still use the scythed chariots for the purpose for which Cyrus made them. He, by exalting the drivers with honors and making them admired, had them hurl themselves against the heavy-armed line. But the present [rulers] do not even recognize the troops mounted on their chariots, and they think that it will be all the same for themselves with drivers who do not practice as with those who have practiced. (25) They do begin to charge, but before they are in the enemy's midst, some fall out voluntarily and others jump out, so that without drivers, the teams often do more harm to friends than to enemies. (26) Since, however, they themselves know how their military affairs are, they yield;[41] and none

of them will any longer enter into war without Greeks, neither when they make war on each other nor when the Greeks go on campaign against them. But they have decided to make their wars even against Greeks with Greeks.

(27) Now I think that I have accomplished what I proposed. I say that the present Persians and their associates have been demonstrated to be more impious regarding gods, more irreverent regarding relatives, more unjust regarding others, and more unmanly in what pertains to war than were their predecessors. If someone is of an opposite judgment, he will find on considering their deeds that they bear witness to my words.

Glossary

This short list of key words associates a family of selected English words with the Greek family that they translate. Although I list only one word from each family, it will often help to introduce its relatives. Hence "ambition" helps with "ambitious," for example, as does *philotimia* with *philotimos*. Similarly, the translation of words with meanings opposite to those listed often can be inferred from them. This list will help interested readers begin to follow a few Greek terms through the English translation, and it is also a convenient way for me to acknowledge some of the more important occasions on which a strictly consistent translation proved impossible. It is of course only a small step toward reducing the extra challenges that face the Greekless student of Greek texts.

"Able" and "capable" both translate *dunamai*. This family of words is based on the Greek word for "power," and "power" is thus also used to signal the presence of a Greek word related to *dunamai*. The noun *dunamis* is always rendered as "power."

"Advantage" is used to translate several different Greek words, all important especially for their relationship to what is good on the one hand and what is just on the other. Chief among them are *sumpheron, sumphoron,* and words related to *pleon echō* and *pleonekteō*. These last two phrases usually combine the notions of getting more than others and getting more than one's fair share. They usually suggest, that is, the disposition to get more, the techniques used to get more, or both. Forms of the last two Greek terms will generally be translated by "getting," "seizing," or "taking" the advantage. Key passages include 1.6.25–41 and 6.1.55.

"Aide" is sometimes used to translate *huperētēs*, but "servant" is my more common rendering. Service may be done at a high level, however, so "aide" is sometimes more apt. A wide variety of terms is used to describe those who associate with Cyrus, and these terms themselves often have a wide range of meanings. The others listed in this glossary are "friend," "companion," "comrade," "associates," "followers," and "chief aide." The full array of pertinent Greek expressions is too long and complex for consistent rendering into English.

"Amaze" and "wonder" both translate *thaumazō*. At 3.1.5 I use "admire," which is otherwise reserved for *agamai*.

"Ambition" translates *philotimia*, whose literal meaning is "love of honor."

"As is / was to be expected" translates *hōsper eikos*, a set phrase with which the narrator of the *Education* comments on its action. I use similar translations for the kindred Greek phrases, *hōs to eikon*, *hōs eikos*, and *kata to eikos*. Cf. 2.1.1.

"Associates" translates *sunontes*, a participle from *suneimi*, and, when possible, I use "associate" to translate the verb. However, I was not able to render *suneimi*, a common and important verb, with strict consistency (cf. 8.4.2, 6.1.36, 3.1.39).

"Be at a loss" translates *aporeō*, which has as its core meaning "to be without resources." Where intellectual matters are at issue, it indicates bewilderment. Cf. 3.1.6, 13–14.

"Beautiful" may translate *kalos*, which is more commonly rendered "noble." "Handsome" is used when the beauty of a man is in question. "Fine" may also render *kalos*, especially when in its adverbial form. No one of these three English words is used to translate any word except *kalos* and its cognates. See "Noble."

"Benevolent" translates *philanthrōpos*, whose etymology suggests the translation "friend of humankind." That Cyrus consciously cultivated a reputation for benevolence helps raise the question of how far he deserves it (Cf. 8.2.1, 1.2.1).

"Blessedly happy" is the rendering for *makarios*, which is to be distinguished from *eudaimōn*, "happy." These terms help raise and broaden the question of the effect of Cyrus' rule on his subjects as well as on how to assess Cyrus' own claim to be blessedly happy (8.7.8–9, 8.3.48).

"Care" is often used to translate *epimeleia*. Words with the root *mel*- occur very frequently in the *Education*, and it is impossible to employ a single word or phrase in the translation of all of them. "Discipline" and "training" (as at 8.1.43) are also used, and "neglect" is often used for the opposite quality.

"Chief aides" translates *epikairioi* on most of its appearances; "chiefs" does so on three. Its etymology suggests "timely ones," and it is especially Xenophon who uses this word to refer to men of authority, whether military or political.

"Companion" translates *hetairos*.

"Comrade" translates *parastatēs*, which occurs only at 2.1.13.

"Continence" translates *enkrateia*, many of whose cognates are translated by "control." Continence or self-control was a quality of special importance for the Persians in general (1.2.8). Cyaxares' amusing charge that his nephew is incontinent helps invite the reader to probe Cyrus' claim to possess this quality (4.1.14).

"Custom" and "law" are used to translate *nomos* and the adjective *nomimon*. *Nomizō*, the related verb, is generally rendered by "believe." Readers seeking to distinguish forms of *eiōthos*, for which I usually reserve "accustomed," will need to consult a Greek text. Cyrus' complex blend of exploitation and criticism of Persian customs forms one of the chief themes of the *Education*.

"Educate" translates *paideuō*, whose importance for the book is signaled even in the title.

"Endurance" and "steadfastness" both are used to translate *karteria*.

"Envy" translates *phthonos*.

"Fitting" translates forms of three Greek words, *harmottō*, *prepō*, and *prosēkō*. The first of these is used only in Book 1, Chapter 3. The other two terms occur elsewhere, but I could not distinguish them in translation. A fourth word, *eikos*, can be very similar in meaning. Except when used in the phrase "as is likely," I have rendered it "appropriate."

"Followers" translates *hoi amphi auton*, whose literal meaning is "those around him."

"Fortune" translates *tuchē*, although "misfortune" translates *sumphora* at 4.2.5.

"Free" is my usual translation of *eleutheros*. The Greek word may also mean "generous" or "liberal." "Independent" might better capture its meaning at 8.3.21.

"Friend" always translates *philos*. The verb *phileō*, however, may be translated either by a word related to "friend," as "to kiss," or as "to love." In the last case, I add an endnote to distinguish it from *eraō*. See "Love."

"Gain," when a noun, translates *kerdos*.

"Gratitude" translates *charis*, as does the noun "favor." See 1.2.7 for the importance of this quality in the Persian republic.

"Happiness" translates *eudaimonia*. Distinguish "blessed happiness."

"Holy" translates both *hosios* and *eusebēs*, as does "pious." A cognate of *eusebēs* is translated as "irreverent" at 8.8.27.

"Honor" is generally used in the translation of words related to *timē*. For the most important exceptions, see "Peer" and "Ambition."

"Human being" translates *anthrōpos* in most of its appearances. An *anthrōpos* is a human being without any claim to the special excellences or professed excellences of the male in particular. *Anēr* refers to the male and, often, to the male who possesses the qualities most admired by Greek males. The distinction between these two Greek words is evident in 1.1.6, for example, where Cyrus is called a man (*anēr*) and said to rule over human beings (*anthrōpoi*). See also 2.2.21. "People" may render *anthrōpoi* where "human beings" seems especially clumsy, but "the people" is reserved for *dēmos*. See "People."

"Insolent" translates *hubris*. At 2.4.5, however, a weaker "ostentatious" is used. *Hubris* indicates excessive pride or insolence and the actions, sometimes violent, that issue from it.

"Jealous" translates *zeloō*, which occurs only at 5.2.12.

"Judgment" translates *gnōmē*. It is related to the verb *gignōskō*, though this relationship cannot be indicated in translation. See "Know."

"Just" translates adjectives cognate with *dikaiosunē*, "justice." When the word "right" is used with moral connotations, it helps translate *axioō* (as at 7.5.45, 47, 78) or the sole use of *themis* (at 1.6.6).

"Know," as a verb, may render *gignōskō*, *oida*, or *epistamai*. I have not found a consistent way of distinguishing these words by their English translations, and it would become a distraction to try to solve this problem by endnotes. Indeed, in some of their uses *manthanō* and *suniēmi* are also difficult to distinguish from these more com-

mon words for "to know." For careful study of the several
Greek verbs that indicate cognition, one must know Greek. See
"Understanding."

"Knowledge," the noun, translates only cognates of *epistēmē*.

"Law" and "custom" translate *nomos*. The related verb *nomizō*, however, is generally translated as "believe." On several occasions it or
participles formed from it will be translated as "custom" or a related word, as at 8.5.3.

"Leisure" translates *scholē*.

"Love" is used whenever a form of *erōs* is in the Greek. "Love" may
also be used to render the verb related to *philia* (in which case I add
an endnote) and in the case of Greek compound words, such as
those translated by "lover of beauty" or "lover of labor" (and yet it
is a relative of *eraō*, which is translated as "lovers of praise" at 1.5.12).
Erōs and *philia* are the two main words for "love" in Classical Greek.
The latter often connotes friendship and friendly affection, the former sexual love. A third word, *agapaō*, I have generally translated as
"cherish." *Eraō* occurs with the greatest frequency at 5.1.10–18.

"Man" translates *anēr*. "Men" and "man" refer to adult males, and
they may imply the presence of the qualities Greek males admired
(cf. 2.2.21). See "Human being."

"Master" translates *despotēs* everywhere but in 4.5.40, where "poten-
tate" is used. *Despotēs* designates a master of the slaves who were
a part of many Greek households or, by extension, "despots," who
ruled like slave masters.

"Moderation" translates *sōphrosunē*. The roots from which the word
is composed suggest an original meaning of something like "of
sound heart or mind," and its meaning in Classical Greek ranges
from restraint in matters concerning bodily desires to discretion or
prudence. The Greek word implies more easily than its translation
that the moderate person is generally sensible or even prudent
(cf. 3.1.17). I have translated *aphrosunē*, the opposite of *sōphrosunē*,
as "immoderation" at 3.1.18 and 4.12.41 and as "folly" at 1.5.10.
Cyrus' view of the relationship between moderation, insolence, and
respect is reported at 8.1.30–31.

"Nature" is used to translate *phusis* as well as related words and
phrases. Exceptions are noted. Its importance emerges especially
in light of its distinction from law or custom.

"Necessity" is used to translate *anagkē*. I have used the adjective "necessary" to translate the Greek adjective *anagkaios*, though I hasten to stress that I have not generally been able to match parts of speech in translation.

"Noble" renders *kalos*, which has sometimes been translated also as "beautiful," "handsome," or "fine." See "Beautiful."

"Peer" translates *homotimos*, whose literal meaning is "of like honor." It refers above all to the small ruling class in the old Persian republic. Distinguish *entimos*, which is used of the upper classes in Armenia (3.1.8) and in the new Persian empire (8.1.6, 8).

"People" may translate *anthrōpos*, as it does at 6.4.11. "The people" translates *dēmos*, which serves as the basis for our word "democracy." At 2.2.22 *dēmos* is used by a member of the Persian upper class to refer to those many Persians who were without military training and political rights, and the word translated as "commoner" has *dēmos* as its root. "The people" is thus not the entirety of the political community but a particular political group, even if a very large one. In the eyes of this upper class, the *dēmos* may be but a mob (*ochlos*, 2.2.21).

"Power" is a translation of *dunamis* or a related word. See "Able."

"Praise" translates *epainos*.

"Provisions" or a phrase like "what is required" translates *epitēdeia*. "Sustenance" is used at 2.1.15.

"Prudent" translates *phronimos*.

"Relish" translates *opsa*. The Greeks—and Xenophon's Persians appear to have been Greeks also in this respect—usually ate bread as the main item of a meal and referred to its tastier accompaniments as *opsa* ("relish"). Meat was for them a favorite relish, and greens seem even then not to have aroused much enthusiasm. *Opsa* is translated as "meat" where meat is the relish in question, as at 2.2.4–5, 10.

"Respect" translates *aidōs*. It might also be rendered "reverence." Cyrus' view of its distinction from moderation is given at 8.1.31.

"Rule" is my preferred rendering of *archē*. It has a wide range of meanings, however, and its cognates may be translated as "command," "reign," "sovereignty," or "empire." When the reference is to those who hold office, I have used "magistrates" or, in a military context, "officers."

"Shameful" translates *aischros*.

"Soul" appears only when *psuchē* is in the Greek text, but on five occasions *psuchē* is translated as "life." These are at 3.1.36, 3.1.41, 3.3.44, 4.6.4, and 6.4.5.

"Steadfastness" and "endurance" are both used to translate *karteria*.

"Substance" translates *ousia*. Its primary meaning in the *Education* is "substance" in the sense of "possessions," but it can also mean "being." It occurs only at 8.4.25 (twice) and 8.4.32.

"Teach" is the consistent translation of *didaskō*.

"Understanding" translates adjectives based on the noun *epistēmē*, which is rendered "knowledge" in this translation, but its meaning might also be captured by "science" or "scientific knowledge." See also "Knowledge."

"Vile" translates *poneros*, as does "worthless."

"Virtue" translates *aretē* and only *aretē*.

"Visible" is used to translate *phainō*, as is "manifest." With a different grammatical construction, however, it may mean "appears" and is so translated. Although this word is important for helping to indicate that someone is putting on a show or is especially concerned with appearances, it cannot be translated with sufficient consistency to indicate to the English reader its presence in the Greek.

"Wonder" translates *thaumazō*. See "Amaze."

"Wrong" translates *hamartanō*, which may refer to mere mistakes, where a moral judgment is not implied, as well as to acts of injustice. It occurs only at 3.1.15, 27–28, 38.

Notes

NOTES TO BOOK I

[1] See Glossary, "People."

[2] See Glossary, "Human being."

[3] *Epistamenōs* is the adverb based on *epistēmē*. See Glossary, "Knowledge."

[4] There were two peoples called Phrygians, the Greater and the Lesser.

[5] As with many other aspects of his career, the conquests of Xenophon's Cyrus are not identical with those of the historical Cyrus. See Hubert A. Holden, *The Cyropaedia of Xenophon, Books I and II* (London: Cambridge University Press, 1887), 91–94.

[6] Other important mss. read "love of gratifying him" instead of "desire of gratifying him." See Glossary, "Love."

[7] *Basilikōs*, kingly; 1.3.18 suggests a distinction between kings and tyrants.

[8] *Thaumazō* is also translated as admire, as in 1.1.1. See Glossary, "Wonder."

[9] Perseus was the son of Zeus and Danae. His most famous exploit was killing the Gorgon Medusa, which he managed to do with help from Athena and Hermes. Xenophon does not show Cyrus being directly aided by his divine ancestors, but the belief that he descended from them was useful to him (4.1.24, 7.2.24).

[10] The three terms used to describe the public view of the main natural qualities of Cyrus' soul are superlatives based on the words *philanthrōpos, philomathēs, philotimos*. They might be more literally translated as "loving human beings," "loving learning," and "loving honor." The last of these words (and its cognates) will often be rendered by "ambitious" (and its cognates). The term used to describe Cyrus' bodily form is the superlative of the word *kalos*, of which this is the first use. See Glossary, "Noble."

[11] More literally, "in shape [*morphē*] and soul."

[12] Miller makes the most forceful statement of the common view that this Persia is based not on Persia at all but on Sparta. See Xenophon, *Cyropaedia*, ed. Walter Miller (Cambridge: Harvard University Press, 1968), viii–ix. For some of the evidence, see *Lacedaemonian Republic* 2.2ff. and Aristotle, *Nicomachean Ethics* 1180a24–30. And see Glossary, "Vile."

[13] See Glossary, "Rule."

[14] See Glossary, "Moderation."

¹⁵ The reference is not to the class of elders (*geraioi*) but to everyone older (*presbuteroi*) than the boys, as the possessive pronoun is meant to suggest here and elsewhere. I translated *presbuteroi* as adults in 1.2.2.

¹⁶ See Glossary, "Continence." Listing *enkrateia* (continence) separately from *sōphrosynē* (moderation) of course suggests a distinction. Cf. 8.1.30–32. For Aristotle's distinction, see *Nicomachean Ethics* 1145b8–20.

¹⁷ See Glossary, "Relish."

¹⁸ *Koinon.* Literally, "for the common," where a noun such as "good" or "interest" is understood. Greek readily uses an adjective to imply a noun, so that a more literal translation would be filled with such phrases as "a great," "the common," "this most wretched," "a beautiful." The translator is thus often obliged to select a noun from among several candidates that have different shades of meaning. I shall note only the most important of such cases.

¹⁹ The *kopis* was apparently a short sword with a curved blade. Though anachronistic, "scimitar" suggests the basic form of this weapon.

²⁰ See Glossary, "As is/was to be expected."

²¹ See Glossary, "Rule."

²² Perhaps this curious phrase emphasizes that men are not always what they are called. The adjective translated as "mature" in order to designate the previous age group is *teleios*, and it also means "complete" or "perfect."

²³ "Public" is a tempting translation of *koinon*, but I reserve it for *dēmosion*, which was used above at 1.2.10 and 12, and will be used just below. Perhaps this use of *koinon* also helps to show that what is common may not be common to everyone, but only to some. See note 18 above.

²⁴ The Greek could also be in the masculine. Faced with the ambiguity, I have translated in the neuter because Xenophon's initial interest in Cyrus was not primary but derivative from an interest in successful rule.

²⁵ *Kalos kagathos.* This common adjectival phrase is made up of words whose literal meanings suggest nobility or beauty on the one hand and goodness on the other. Others often translate it as "gentleman," which among other recommendations has the advantage of suggesting that the *kaloi kagathoi* as commonly perceived belonged to the upper crust. Xenophon's *Oeconomicus* is devoted in significant part to Socrates' investigation of the *kalos kagathos* (6.12ff.). Clumsy though it is, "noble and good" will be my rendering, and its very clumsiness may help to call attention to Xenophon's use of this important phrase.

²⁶ Translated as "affectionate," *philostorgos* may also refer to the desire to receive affection.

²⁷ See Glossary, "Beautiful."

²⁸ The Greek adjectives are *philokalos* (loving beauty) and *philotimos* (loving honor). See Glossary, "Ambition."

²⁹ Xenophon here begins to use indirect discourse. That is, the Greek implies that Xenophon is reporting the report of others, not himself vouching for its veracity. I have dropped most phrases such as "it is said that he said," for they are much clumsier in English than in Greek. I translate the last such phrase so the reader can see where the indirect discourse ends (section 12, at "it is said that he said").

³⁰ *Kallion*, the Greek word translated as "finer," is also the word for "more beautiful." More than does the English translation, the Greek thus links this beauty contest between Persian and Median dining practices with the one above regarding dress (1.3.2).

³¹ This name appears to be based on the servant's nationality. As was noted back at 1.1.4, the Sacians are among Cyrus' later conquests. Another important Sacian turns up in 8.3.25–50.

[32] *Hupoptēssō* refers more commonly to the cringing of an animal or the fear one feels in the presence of a powerful enemy. It is also used in 1.5.1 and 1.6.8.

[33] Literally, "This most wretched." I reserve "fellow," "person," and "troops" for use as nouns that are implied by masculine adjectives but are not expressed. See note 18.

[34] This speech and the others in sections 15 and 16 are in indirect discourse. See note 29.

[35] *Metron* will be translated with a form of the word "measure," as it was above at 1.3.14.

[36] *Pleonekteō*. See Glossary, "Advantage."

[37] *Eraō*. See Glossary, "Love."

[38] *Enthousiaō* is based on *entheos*, whose etymology implies possession by a god.

[39] For other instances of the oath, by Hera, cf. 8.4.12; *Memorabilia* 3.10.9, 3.11.5, 4.2.9, 4.4.8; *Symposium* 4.45, 4.54, 8.12, 9.1; *Oeconomicus* 10.1, 11.19.

[40] *Ek tou isou*. This might rather mean "on equal terms." A similar phrase occurs in 1.6.28.

[41] "In kingly fashion" might also modify "forbade," on which policy see 4.6.3–4.

[42] *Peltastēs* (targeteer) usually refers to such light-armed troops as carried small leather shields. Although many kinds of weapons and soldiers are referred to in *The Education of Cyrus*, the main distinction among foot soldiers is between light-armed troops who skirmished from a·distance and more heavily armed troops who came to close quarters with the enemy.

[43] The Assyrian prince divides his forces into three main parts, an infantry guard in the rear, a group of infantry to pillage the country, and a group of cavalry to discourage the Medes from attacking those doing the pillaging.

[44] Literally, "many Assyrian human beings."

[45] *Hippeus* will continue to be translated as "horseman" when the context refers especially to the ability to ride well. Either "knight" or "cavalry" will be used when the reference is to mounted troops.

[46] The word *theaomai* can refer to the mind's contemplation, to the watching of a play, to the reviewing of troops. In this context, it appears that Cyrus is gloating.

[47] *Timaō*, "to honor," can also mean "to esteem."

[48] *Paidikos logos*. The meaning of the adjective *paidikos* may be limited to what is merely boyish or playful, but here, as often, it has erotic overtones.

[49] This section, except for two of its statements, is in indirect discourse, so "it is said" is implied throughout. The two exceptions are when the Mede swears by the gods (27) and when he tells Cyrus that it is time to kiss him again, for he is going away (28).

[50] This character is finally identified by name in 6.1.9, but he appears next at 4.1.22.

[51] *To koinon*, which often means "the common [interest]," can also refer to the authorities who govern (as I have taken it here and in the next sentence), or to what might call the commonwealth in general. See note 18.

[52] *Homotimos* is made up of words that suggest the meaning of like honor, and Xenophon's use of it here makes it still more clear that the Persian regime is sharply divided between two classes, the *homotimoi* and the *dēmos* (see Glossary, "Peers," "People"). It is also implied here, and will be stressed below, that the two classes differed also in the weapons they used and the military training they received. The name, the powers, and the way of life of this tight circle have made it common to see the Spartan *homoioi* as their model, though important similarities should not obscure important differences.

[53] Greek phrases whose literal translations would be "with the gods," "with gods," and "with god" occur eighteen times in *The Education of Cyrus*. I have added an apostrophe and "[help]" for clarity in English, and for the same reason I have not been

strictly literal regarding the translation of the Greek article: I sometimes translate "gods" as "the gods" and "the god" as "god."

⁵⁴ *Pais* was translated as "my boy" when it was used by Astyages and Mandane in 1.4.

⁵⁵ *Themis* generally refers to fundamental laws or customs, especially those regarding or deriving from the gods.

⁵⁶ *Athemitos* refers to what is contrary to what has been set down (by the gods). *Themis* was translated as "right" just above, and *thesmos*, another related word, was rendered as "what has been set down."

⁵⁷ *Dokimōs.* This rare adverb means more literally "in a way that has been tested and approved."

⁵⁸ *Ta epitēdeia.* See Glossary, "Provisions."

⁵⁹ *Stratēgia* is usually best rendered "generalship," as in 1.6.14 just below. Here, however, it seems to have a narrower meaning, which Cambyses seeks to expand.

⁶⁰ One family of mss. reads "care" (*epimeleia*) instead of "arts" (*technē*).

⁶¹ There is disagreement about whether it is Cyrus or his father who speaks this sentence.

⁶² The Greek words for "love" in this section and the next are forms of *phileō.* See Glossary, "Love."

⁶³ *Pleonekteō* is the verb; the word translated as "heat" is actually *helios*, "sun." The words *pleonekteō, pleon echein, pleonexia*, and *pleonektēs* are all important for this part of the discussion, and together they occur seventeen times in sections 25–41. See Glossary, "Advantage."

⁶⁴ *Idiotēs.* Since the context is rule in the army, it might also be translated "private [soldier]."

⁶⁵ *Pleon echein* (literally, to have more). Like *pleonekteō*, it usually refers to getting an advantage over someone else. Here, however, Cambyses refers to the relative advantages of attacking as compared with not attacking. Cyrus uses the same phrase in his response, but he adds "the enemy" as its object and thus narrows the issue. See Glossary, "Advantage."

⁶⁶ As with the English word "simple," *haplous* can mean "uncompounded" or "uniform" as well as "plain" and "straightforward." Both meanings are in play here. See the word's next appearance, at 1.6.33.

⁶⁷ I have translated the emendation printed by Marcel Bizos in his translation of *Cyropédie*, vol. 1 (Paris: Belles Lettres, 1971). The mss. support this rendering: "I do not know whether you would leave any of your enemies [alive]."

⁶⁸ Literally, "the greatest." For other uses of this phrase and for Cyrus' view of the greatest subjects of education and the greatest things, see 1.5.11 and 1.6.24.

NOTES TO BOOK II

¹ The Greeks generally held that the good omens appeared from the right.

² A group of mss. reads "into the city" instead of "into Persia."

³ Editors uniformly print "thirty thousand" in order to make this figure match the numbers called for in 1.5.5. As Christopher Nadon points out (*Xenophon's Prince: Republic and Empire in the "Cyropaedia"* [Berkeley: University of California Press, 2001], 61), good statesmanship may require bad math. I have translated the text as we receive it from all manuscripts.

⁴ Another ms. reads "our work" instead of "your work."

⁵ The root of the word translated as "born" is "nature" (*phusis*). See Glossary, "Nature." Cf. 1.2.1.

⁶ *Ta epitēdeia* is here translated as "sustenance." See Glossary, "Provisions."

⁷ The prefix of the verb *hupotrephomai* hints that the lower class must do its nurturing of daring secretly.

⁸ See Glossary, "Fitting."

⁹ *Chōra*, translated as "station" here, was translated as "land" in section 15, just above.

¹⁰ Literally, "ruler of five." Although I have employed familiar terms for military units and their leaders, the size of the various units is not quite what contemporary usage might suggest. The military ranks and their translations here are as follows:

Stratēgos	General	Cyrus rules all.
Muriarchos	Brigadier general	Rules a brigade, 10,000 soldiers.
Chiliarchos	Colonel	Rules a regiment, 1,000 soldiers.
Taxiarchos	Captain	Rules a company, 100 soldiers.
Lochagos	Lieutenant	Rules a platoon, 50 soldiers.
Decadarchos	Sergeant	Rules a squad of 10 soldiers.
Pempadarchos	Corporal	Rules a squad of 5 soldiers.
Idiōtes	Private	Is ruled.

The passages that most suggest this scheme are 2.1.23–25, 2.3.21, 3.3.11, 6.3.21, 6.3.31–32.

¹¹ *Kratistos*, translated as "best" in this section, also often means "strongest."

¹² Or, with other mss., "greater hopes were held out," without Cyrus necessarily having raised the hopes himself. Cf. 1.6.19.

¹³ Translated as "less," *meionexia*, a rare word, is the opposite of *pleonexia*. See Glossary, "Advantage."

¹⁴ *Meion echein*, "to have less." See note 13.

¹⁵ Or, with a different ms., "So he took a piece, and what he took seemed to him rather small, so he threw down what he had taken with the intention of taking another. The cook, thinking that he no longer wanted any meat, passed the tray away before he took another [piece]."

¹⁶ I take *huper hou* to refer to the butt of each of the jokes. If *hou* is neuter instead of masculine, it would be better translated as "make a joke concerning what they are speaking and boasting about."

¹⁷ *Euphemeō* has a literal meaning of something like "speak well," but its strict use was to discourage speech that might be offensive during sacred ceremonies.

¹⁸ Most editors depart from the ms. and replace "lieutenant" with "captain" to make it correspond with sections 2.2.6 and 2.2.15.

¹⁹ Literally, "good learnings for their boys."

²⁰ This clause might also mean "There is consequently no excuse for us not to afford you a laugh." The next line is similarly ambiguous and could refer both to Aglaitadas laughing and to his causing laughter in others.

²¹ The appointment referred to might also be to Cyrus' appointment of officers more generally, rather than to overseers of contests. The word is *epistatēs*.

²² Translated here as "the community," *to koinon* is more literally "the common." See note 18 of Book I.

²³ Or, with another ms., "For of labors and other such things, I see him wishing very boldly to have less than anyone."

²⁴ Some mss. read "soldiers."

²⁵ Persia did not have good horses (1.3.3).

²⁶ One may infer that Cyrus refers to the goodness of his insistence that the army be purged, but he speaks in very general terms.

²⁷ *Suneimi* (to be together with) may refer to an intimate association, as in 6.1.32.

²⁸ The verb translated as "love" is *phileō*. See Glossary, "Love."

²⁹ Or, with other mss., "At least I see him more pleased when he gives them whatever he has than when he keeps it himself."

³⁰ *Dēmotikē agōnia* might also be rendered "struggle with the people."

³¹ Or, with a different ms., "many others from each of the two [classes] rose and spoke as advocates [of the proposal]."

³² There are thus four formations. The movement is from a single long column to a front that has the breadth of sixteen men and a depth of six (with either a corporal or a sergeant at the head of each short column; the sergeants both rule a squad of five and rule a corporal responsible for the second squad of five in each squad of ten). There are also four lieutenants and the captain himself, for a total of one hundred and one soldiers.

³³ See Glossary, "Aide."

³⁴ This is the first mention of a "squad of twelve" (as opposed to five or ten). If the corporal and sergeant are included in the count, a "squad of ten" would become a "squad of twelve."

³⁵ *Hubrizomai*, here translated as "be ostentatious," is based on *hubris*. To specify that Cyrus' dress shows no *hubris* could imply a contrast either with Cyaxares' dress or, perhaps, with Cyrus' own conduct. See Glossary, "Insolent."

³⁶ The kings of Assyria, Armenia, Hyrcania, and India will often be referred to simply as "the Assyrian," "the Armenian," "the Hyrcanian," and "the Indian." Greek may imply a noun without expressing it; I leave the noun to the reader's inference.

³⁷ More literally, "the just" (*to dikaion*).

³⁸ A parasang, according to Herodotus (2.6), represented a distance of thirty stadia. The stadion is estimated by some to be six hundred feet, by others to be as much as six hundred and twenty-four feet. Thus Xenophon's parasang would probably have been about three and a half miles.

NOTES TO BOOK III

¹ *Ta onta*, which in a philosophic discussion might be rendered "the things that are" or "the beings," in other contexts may designate one's material possessions.

² See Glossary, "Wrong."

³ Xenophon leaves it to the reader to judge which of the Armenian's two sons is here described.

⁴ One might also take *dikaia* as a predicate, which would suggest this translation: "these your [answers] are just."

⁵ Translated here as "wise man," *sophistēs* derives from *sophos*, which means "skilled" or "wise," and our word "sophist" comes from it. Although by the fifth century *sophistēs* could suggest either sham wisdom in general or the for-profit teaching of rhetoric in particular, it could also still be used to refer to someone wise or skilled.

⁶ *Sophrōn* is based on Greek words that mean something like "of sound wits." Its opposite is *aphrōn*, "senseless." See Glossary, "Moderation."

⁷ The two terms Cyrus opposes are the nouns *pathēma* and *mathēma*. The former might be rendered "something experienced," the latter "something learned." *Pathēma* is translated as "sorrowful event" at 7.3.6 and 8.

⁸ *Panta ta onta* in other contexts might be translated "all the beings." *Ta onta* occurs also in sections 32 and 35 (where it is translated "what you have"). See note 1 of Book III.

⁹ The verb is a compound based on *phileō*. See Glossary, "Love."

¹⁰ See Glossary, "Soul."

¹¹ Cyrus' first word here is an exclamation that can express grief, admiration, or both.

¹² I translate the text of Bizos, which is based on an emendation by Stephanus (see note 67 of Book I). One group of mss. would read "more lacking in learning," while another would read "more moderate."

¹³ *Tropos* might also be translated as "character" rather than as "manner." Perhaps this ambiguity is meant to help examine whether Cyrus has a generous manner or a thoroughly generous character. The issue is taken up more directly later, in 8.2.15–23.

¹⁴ See Glossary, "Chief aides."

¹⁵ The word translated as "desirous" is *erōtikos*, so a more literal rendering would be "after he had made them in love with doing something."

¹⁶ This could also be rendered, "if any of the other gods came to light ..."

¹⁷ A parasang was about three and one-half miles.

¹⁸ Literally, "Whatever is this?"

¹⁹ It is ambiguous in the Greek whether all three predictions are based on the sacrifices. Nor is it clear in the Greek to whom the gods have promised a battle, a victory, and safety.

²⁰ The Dioscuri were warrior heroes worshiped by the Greeks and especially the Spartans. Other mss. omit the reference to the Dioscuri and mention Cyrus by name as the one who begins the paean.

Notes to Book IV

¹ "You" is in the singular.

² Cf. 1.4.27–28.

³ The grammar of the Greek sentence is ambiguous as to whether the benevolence referred to is that of Cyrus or that of his grandfather. I infer the former.

⁴ This phrase could refer to the favor or gratitude they expect to earn from Cyrus by their support of him, as well as to the gratitude they feel for past favors received from him (which is the more obvious reading).

⁵ A parasang was about three and one half miles.

⁶ Instead of "something good," another ms. has "something soft."

⁷ Or, with a different ms., "But it does not seem to me to be a greater gain to take it than to purchase the result, by appearing to be just to them, that they come to delight in us still more than they do now."

⁸ Literally, "of the best women."

⁹ Or, with another ms., "with which we seem to turn our enemies...."

¹⁰ *Hōn pephykotōn dendrōn*. The phrase is curious; perhaps the primary thought is that trees are naturally incapable of attack or pursuit, especially because they are rooted and cannot move.

¹¹ *Ergon*. More literally, "were not at a loss for work."

¹² *Apronoētōs*, which occurred also in 1.4.21. Cyaxares' thought might also be rendered "so lacking in consideration for me."

¹³ Literally, "goods." According to historical sources, the Magi were a priestly class among the Medes.

¹⁴ Literally, "the common." See note 18 of Book I.

¹⁵ The word translated as "successes" would be more literally rendered as "goods."

¹⁶ "You" is in the singular throughout the entirety of Cyrus' remarks to the uncle he says has not been left alone.
¹⁷ Literally, "make them so they do not blame."
¹⁸ *Ta onta* might be rendered "the things that are" or "the beings."
¹⁹ Literally, "the best in looks" (*ta eidē*), rather than "those who looked best."
²⁰ *Doulos* might be translated here as "vassal" rather than "slave," for the person to whom it refers was himself a master of slaves. "Slave," however, does help emphasize the vast scope of sovereign power in Assyria, which is confirmed in the episode about to be recounted.
²¹ *Phileō* is here the verb for "love." See Glossary, "Love."

Notes to Book V

¹ The incident is described in 1.4.26.
² The Greek words for "man" and "woman," *anēr* and *gynē*, are the same as those translated as "husband" and "wife."
³ "Ties of hospitality" is used for *xenos*. Such ties were used as diplomatic channels.
⁴ "Looks" is here used to translate *eidos*, elsewhere rendered "form."
⁵ *Phunai* is rendered "begotten." It is based on *phusis*, the Greek word for "nature."
⁶ The manuscripts actually read, "Yes, by Zeus."
⁷ *Theaomai*, "gazing," was translated as "see" in the previous sentence and also at the end of the previous section. See note 46 of Book I.
⁸ The verb translated as "prepare" is *suskeuazō*. Its use at 3.1.43 suggests the translation "pack up and carry away."
⁹ When Cyrus says "I am grateful," he does not mean to settle the debt but to acknowledge it. One might thus translate, "I have an obligation to you."
¹⁰ Cf. 1.4.27–28.
¹¹ Cf. 1.4.25.
¹² Cf. 1.4.27.
¹³ "Stewards" would be more literally rendered as "those in the tents." Cf. 4.2.35.
¹⁴ Literally, "in a generation of human beings."
¹⁵ Literally, "whatever these things were," an echo of a Socratic question.
¹⁶ A Daric was a coin not minted until the time of Darius, a successor two generations after Cyrus. For an explanation of this anachronism, see Nadon, *Xenophon's Prince*, 86, note 56.
¹⁷ Cf. 4.6.8.
¹⁸ The main mss. seeming to make no sense in this phrase, I try to follow here the reading of a minor manuscript.
¹⁹ *Eleutherios* might also be rendered here with its more specific meaning, "generous" or "liberal," the adjectival form of the virtue Aristotle discusses in his *Nicomachean Ethics* at 1119b22ff. Its use at 5.2.16 helps to recommend "free" as its translation, however. See Glossary, "Free."
²⁰ Literally, "in thirty days," but the words were also more loosely used and hence may not have implied so definite a promise.
²¹ "Teach" is my regular rendering of *didaskō*, here translated as "explain."
²² Editors of the Greek text disagree about whether this clause is an interpolation and about where it should be located. E. C. Marchant ed., *Xenophontis Opera Omnia*, vol. 4 (Oxford: Clarendon Press, 1910) at 5.3.15.

²³ I have translated the mss., but several editors replace this reference to Gadatas ("him") with a text that reads "shall we invite some of them."

²⁴ Other mss. read "one thousand mounted archers," and still others read "twenty thousand mounted archers."

²⁵ *Oikonomia*, "household management," is here translated "disposition."

²⁶ If all the Commoners were indeed armed with breastplates, as was indicated in 2.1.19, and if there were no demotions, then this number should equal the total number of original troops minus the number turned into knights. Since 2,000 of the original Persian contingent have become knights, the infantry should number 29,000. Hence the front would be almost three times broader than the depth (290 versus 100). A broad front puts more troops into a position where they can engage the enemy, and a shallower depth would reduce the tendency for gaps to form during a rapid march at night. The next note invites one to question either or both of the first two hypotheses of this note, however.

²⁷ Since the light-armed Commoners were given the weapons of the Peers, it is not clear who these light-armed Persians are. One candidate is the reinforcements sent for in 4.5.16 (but whose arrival will not be mentioned until 5.5.3). Another is that the promotions of 2.1.9 were followed by demotions.

²⁸ Or, more literally, "when he knew the matter" (*to pragma*).

²⁹ Or, if the context were philosophical, "when they knew being" (*to on*).

³⁰ There is no possessive adjective in the Greek text, and one might infer "my friends" rather than the "your friends" printed here.

³¹ Here "harm," *adikein* is elsewhere translated as "to be unjust to."

³² Cf. 4.5.52, 4.6.11, 5.1.1.

³³ Cf. 4.5.16, 31.

³⁴ Cf. 4.5.31.

³⁵ Cf. 4.2.11.

³⁶ *Archē* is translated here as "command." See Glossary, "Rule."

³⁷ Cf. 1.5.4.

³⁸ Cf. 3.3.24.

³⁹ Cyrus' words to Cyaxares on this point are not recorded. Cf. 4.1.13.

⁴⁰ *Oikeiotatos*, the word translated as "most dearly," is based on the word for the household or family.

⁴¹ The verb here translated as "love" is *phileō*. See Glossary, "Love."

NOTES TO BOOK VI

¹ Cf. 1.4.27, 4.1.22, 5.1.24.

² Cf. 4.6.8.

³ *Dēmos* is the word translated as "bulk." See Glossary, "People."

⁴ Another ms. reads "weaker" instead of "stronger," which accords with the common view that the strong take the offensive. Cyrus seems to be suggesting that in the winter, it is better to be on the defensive in well-stocked forts. In extreme conditions such as have prevailed in more than one winter campaign in Russia, the defense may be favored even if the forts are not so well stocked.

⁵ One soldier fought from the chariot (or from near it, if he descended), and another drove it. If the best fighters fought from chariots and also chose good soldiers to be their drivers, 300 chariots would take away 600 good men from the main body of

infantry. As the next sentence indicates, Cyrus not only changes the design and tactics of the chariot, he also puts only one soldier on each.

⁶ A cubit (*pēchus*)was about 20 inches long.

⁷ This is the first of over twenty occasions on which Xenophon is explicit in looking beyond Cyrus and in referring to the continuation of certain of his policies after his death. (Since the last chapter of the entire book is devoted to the aftermath of Cyrus' rule, I do not include it in this count.) In these passages "the king" refers not to Cyrus in particular but to a king of the dynasty established by him. The Greeks referred to such a king as "the Great King" or simply "the King."

⁸ *Phileō* is the verb used here. Except where noted, it is *eraō* that is translated by "love."

⁹ *Parakatathēkē* is translated as "sacred trust" but means "deposit" more literally. It was used simply of monetary deposits, but it was also used of persons who were entrusted to guardians and of deposits at temples. It hence raised issues of piety as well as of justice.

¹⁰ These same lines occur at 6.4.2. Scholars incline to think they were written by a copyist rather than by Xenophon.

¹¹ Delebecque here departs from the manuscripts. His revision might be translated "... pull this most innovative platform of the siege engines" (Xénophon, *Cyropédie*, vol. 3, trans. Édouard Delebecque [Paris: Belles Lettres, 1978]).

¹² That is, about three times the length of one's outstretched arms. The "fathom" is thought to have been about or just under 6 feet.

¹³ If Xenophon means an Attic talent, which was about 56 pounds, each yoked team pulled about 1,400 pounds of baggage. When pulling the towers, each team pulled about 850 pounds. Since there were eight teams, the total weight of the tower would have been about 6,750 pounds. If Xenophon meant an Aegean talent, however,¹¹ different weights given here should be increased by about 40%.

¹⁴ *Euthumia* (delight) is related to *thumos*, translated as "spirit."

¹⁵ "Meats and side dishes" here translates *opsa*. See Glossary, "Relish."

¹⁶ Cf. 6.2.25.

¹⁷ Literally, "whenever the things of the gods are fine [*kalōs*]." See Glossary, "Noble."

¹⁸ Or, more literally, "in order that they might learn being [*to on*] more clearly." Cf. 5.4.7.

¹⁹ That is, about 7 miles.

²⁰ For "aides," see Glossary. It appears to refer to the group of knights mentioned in the previous section, those who were always with Cyrus, ready for instant use. Hence the "he" giving the orders at the end of this sentence would be Cyrus, not Hystaspas.

²¹ Literally, "learn the beings of the enemy" (*ta tōn polemiōn ta onta*).

²² 6.1.38 is the passage in which Cyrus comes closest to making a promise to Araspas in particular.

²³ The stadion is estimated by some to be 600 feet, by others to be as much as 624 feet. Forty stadia would thus be between 24,000 and 25,000 feet. Scholars agree that the soldiers had about 3 feet in which to stand. Thus the front would have been between 8,000 and 8,300 men across (and 30 deep). Still leaving apart the separate order of 120,000 Egyptians (according to 6.2.10), the total would be between 240,000 and 250,000.

²⁴ I have translated in brackets the emendations accepted and printed by Delebecque (see note 11 above). The mss. read "Then you, Araspas, take the right wing, since you have it." The mss. are suspected especially because Araspas has not yet been mentioned as having any command. The proposed emendations rest especially on 7.1.3, where Arsamas is mentioned as commanding the infantry on the left side and Chrysantas as commanding the cavalry on the right.

²⁵ "Hoplite" transliterates the Greek word for "heavy-armed foot soldier."

²⁶ The Greek word is *teleutaios*. The context makes its main meaning clear, just as section 27 makes clear the importance of such a rear guard.

²⁷ The "you" in this sentence is singular, whereas those of the previous section are plural.

²⁸ One reason for the difference is that the thigh pieces of the horses that were ridden were designed in part to protect their riders (7.1.2).

²⁹ It is apparently the case that linen could offer protection if multiple layers of it were first saturated with a solution of vinegar and salt and then compressed and dried. Mentioned also in Homer (*Iliad* 2.529, 830), these breastplates are only one of several links between this scene and the great tragic poetry that preceded its writing.

³⁰ *Kosmos* is elsewhere translated as "adornment."

NOTES TO BOOK VII

¹ The group in question was identified in 6.4.12.

² More literally, "were thigh pieces for the man."

³ Twenty stadia are about two and one-third miles.

⁴ In order to take advantage of his longer line, Croesus must halt the center and advance his wings so that these wings can attack the flanks of Cyrus' army at about the same time their front lines clash. Each side of his army will therefore have a right angle, or "hinge," like the Greek capital gamma or like our capital L. All troops on the wings will have to march in a 90° arc in order to face in against the flanks of the enemy, but those near the extremities will have to cover a distance much greater than those near the hinge. Even against a lesser opponent than Cyrus, this strategy requires good judgment about where to put the hinges in the line and when to halt the center. Nor would it be easy to keep the wings of a vast army in a straight line, since different parts of the wing must march at different speeds.

⁵ The metaphor is of a club or perhaps a group of banqueters each of whom contributes to the common fund. In the case of this most noble or most beautiful club or feast, the participants contribute good actions rather than money or food.

⁶ Cf. 6.3.36.

⁷ "Love of victory" literally translates the etymology of *philonikia*. It might also be rendered "competitiveness" and can have strongly negative connotations, such as "contentiousness."

⁸ Although the situation of Cyrus' army is clear, the metaphor used to make it clear is not. If *plinthion* can mean "roof tile," then the reference is to the way one U-shaped tile nests inside another. Thinking it cannot mean "roof tile" but must mean "brick," Delebecque amends the text so we have one Greek letter pi placed inside another. (See Book VI, note 11.)

⁹ That is, to Ares, the god of war.

¹⁰ That is, Cyrus not only attacks outward with his heavy infantry, against the face of the enemy's wing; he also attacks with his heavy cavalry from beyond the tip of the enemy's wing against its flank. He thus outflanks the wing intended to outflank him.

¹¹ This serves to remind readers that the enemy chariots served merely as transportation for a single infantryman. Cyrus' armored chariots were designed rather to crash into the enemies' lines and throw them into confusion.

¹² In a military context, the Greek word for "good" (*agathos*) often means "brave" above all else.

¹³ Cf. 6.4.17.

¹⁴ Another ms. reads "on behalf of those who betrayed you." It is certainly possible, however, that Cyrus means to imply that not his troops but the Egyptians' allies will bear the responsibility for their slaughter, so Xenophon may have written "by" rather than "on behalf of."

¹⁵ This fragment obviously requires one to understand a clause such as this: "You could save yourselves and your nobility, ..." Other mss. have Cyrus demanding that the Egyptians do surrender their weapons (while yet implying that doing so does not compromise their nobility).

¹⁶ For Herodotus' account of the curious tests to which Croesus subjected the oracle at Delphi, see 1.46–48.

¹⁷ The Greek word translated as "descended," *phuō*, is based on the root "nature," so Croesus tries to account for Cyrus' superiority on the basis of the threesome formed by gods, nature, and practice. Cf. 1.1.6. The claim that Cyrus was "born from the gods" is reported in 1.2.1.

¹⁸ That is, his ancestor Gyges had been a slave before he became a king.

¹⁹ The verb here translated as "love" is *phileō*.

²⁰ More literally, "to the suffering [*pathos*]." I here retain the "one thousand knights" of the ms. in preference to the "some knights" of Delebecque's emendation.

²¹ *Sphazō* is the verb, and it is most commonly used of the killing of victims offered up in sacrifice. A closely related verb is used in the next section in regard to the eunuchs' self-slaughter.

²² Satrap was the title given to the provincial governors of the Persian Empire.

²³ Cyrus is distinguishing this Phrygia from the Phrygia in the interior, which was between Lydia and Cappadocia. Cf. 1.1.4.

²⁴ "Rulers [*archontes*]" would be a more consistent translation than "officers." See Glossary, "Rule."

²⁵ Cf. 2.1.18.

²⁶ Cf. 1.1.4.

²⁷ Or, with a different ms., "he filled out the Persian knights to no fewer than forty thousand."

²⁸ Rather than have all his troops back away from the city and so become even more spread out as their circumference expands, Cyrus holds one part stationary ("the middle") and has the troops on the opposite side of the city peel back and so reinforce the depth of the ever-shrinking line. The result is a line of double depth around half the city. As the sequel indicates, when the front lines in heavy armor peel back, they go behind the inferior light-armed troops that had been stationed behind them, so the latter then become encircled and hence protected both from the enemy and from any temptation they might have to flee.

²⁹ That is, about 1,200 feet.

³⁰ The Greek word for "to grow" is *phuō*, and it is related to the noun meaning "nature" (*phusis*). See Glossary, "Nature." A plethron was about 100 feet.

³¹ One group of mss. omits the phrase "fearing nothing within."

³² *Prosēkousi*, the word for "relatives," could also be translated as "those fit [for the task]." See Glossary, "Fitting."

³³ On the connection between the seizure of the city and the offering of booty to the gods, cf. 7.5.73.

³⁴ Cf. 2.3.16, where the principle of reward on the basis of merit is established, with Cyrus as the judge of merit.

³⁵ Literally, "teach" (*didaskō*).

³⁶ Cf. 1.4.27.

³⁷ Cf 4.1.21–24. Artabazus performs another important service for Cyrus at 5.1.24–26.

[38] The verb *therapeuō* is normally rendered as "to serve," but it may refer to cases in which one serves, pays attention to, or even flatters in the hope of securing favors in return. In this sense its translation will employ the English word "court."

[39] Cf. 5.4.51.

[40] "All the world" is more literally "all human beings."

[41] The Greek word is *sunousia*, and it often has erotic connotations.

[42] This is the only place in *The Education of Cyrus* in which there is an oath to a Persian god. Cf. *Oeconomicus* 4.24.

[43] Cf. 7.5.46.

[44] Editors of the Greek text agree that it is here corrupt, but they offer different conjectures as to what it might have been. I have translated the text printed by Marchant, *Xenophontis Opera Omnia*, vol. 4, at 7.5.56.

[45] "No place on earth" is more literally "no place among human beings."

[46] *Pleonekteō*. See Glossary, "Advantage."

[47] *Hubristai*, "unruly," is an adjective related to *hubris*. See Glossary, "Insolence."

[48] More literally, "near his own body [*sōma*]." This Greek sentence does not require the reading that in making his servants eunuchs, he made the eunuchs that became his servants.

[49] *Archē* may mean "empire" in particular. See Glossary, "Rule."

[50] I have translated an emendation that appears to be accepted by all editors. The verb they reject is *mēnouō*, a rarely used word that may mean "betray" or "denounce." It is indeed easier to imagine Cyrus telling his troops not to "slacken in" their practice of virtue than to imagine him telling them not to "betray" or "denounce" this noble practice. But if Cyrus demands the show of virtue rather than its substance, the ms. reading can be defended.

[51] More literally, "labors and good things."

[52] *Ponerōs*, here translated as "worse," is an adverbial form of the word usually translated as "worthless" or "vile." See Glossary, "Vile."

[53] More literally, "for those who are always closest to their weapons, whatever they may wish for is most their own [*oikeios*]."

[54] *Agathois* may be either masculine or neuter. Hard work either makes the fruits of success ("the good things") more pleasant or increases the pleasures of the successful ("the good people"), or both.

[55] *Andragathia* is a compound of the words for "man" and "goodness."

[56] There is also good manuscript authority for reading "in honor [*entimoi*]" instead of "Peers [*homotimoi*]."

NOTES TO BOOK VIII

[1] Delebecque adds *philoi* to his text, so it would read "many other friends." (See Book VI, note 11.) I translate the ms.

[2] "Those in honor" translates *entimoi*. See Glossary, "Peer."

[3] Or "making the same things lawful."

[4] "Among the greatest things [*ta megista*]" would be more literal than "among the most important ways."

[5] *Ta kratista* might be more literally translated as "the strongest things" or "the best things." Previous uses of "the most important things" have translated *ta megista*.

⁶ Translated as "administrative matters," *oikonomika* is the adjective based on the noun *oikonomia*, "household management."

⁷ Noting that the captains (*taxiarchoi*) are omitted from the list, Delebecque amends the Greek text to include them. I have translated the ms.

⁸ *Ta oikeia* is here translated as "what belonged to." As with *oikonomia*, this word is related to *oikos*, "household."

⁹ Cf. 1.6.3–4.

¹⁰ The Greek word *aidōs* means not only "reverence" or "respect" but also "modesty."

¹¹ Cf. 8.1.10.

¹² The forms of the word "love" in this section, in the next section, and in the conclusion at 8.2.28 translate forms of the word *philein*. Cf. 1.6.24–25. See Glossary, "Love."

¹³ Or "differs in being [*tō onti*] and in the pleasure it affords."

¹⁴ This sentence, like the previous and the next, is in indirect discourse. Understand, "It is said that ..."

¹⁵ After "happiest" the mss. also have "and his money" or "also in respect to his money," but editors have bracketed or deleted it.

¹⁶ Cf. 2.3.7–15.

¹⁷ This was apparently a security measure to impede assassination attempts. Cf. Xenophon, *Hellenica*, 2.1.8.

¹⁸ Instead of "really," one might translate "in being" (*to on*).

¹⁹ Five stadia are approximately 3,000 feet.

²⁰ *Gennaiotes*, translated "gentility," means more literally "of high birth" and often refers to the upper classes.

²¹ The referent of this pronoun is ambiguous also in the Greek, though it seems likely that it is Cyrus and not Gadatas. If so, this statement of Cyrus' enjoyment in the company of another is unique.

²² This collection of proverbs is mentioned in 8.4.16.

²³ See Glossary, "Substance."

²⁴ *Eleutherios*: see Glossary, "Free." "Illiberality," as used just below, refers to the opposite quality.

²⁵ Delebecque here departs from the mss. I translate one family of mss.; the other reads, "are deceived."

²⁶ Delebecque accepts the emendation *pleonektēmata*. See Glossary, "Advantage."

²⁷ "Officers" is more literally "rulers," *archontes*. See Glossary, "Rule."

²⁸ *Titheneō* means "to nurse" or "to tend as a nurse." Cyrus' sojourn in Media is described in 1.3–4.

²⁹ "Subjects" is more literally "human beings."

³⁰ Literally, the Red Sea. Holden explains this as meaning the Indian Ocean with its two gulfs, the Persian Gulf and the Red Sea. See Hupert A. Holden, *The Cyropaedia of Xenophon, Books VI–VIII* (London: Cambridge University Press, 1887), 186. So too with the similar phrase in the next section.

³¹ *Meionekteō* "got less," is the opposite of *pleonekteō*. See Glossary, "Advantage."

³² Or, more literally, "better [or stronger, *kreitton*] than accords with a human being."

³³ *Karpaō* was translated as "to harvest" at 1.5.10 and elsewhere. The Greek allows that what is believed to be noble is his harvest rather than the source of his harvest, as my translation implies.

³⁴ One might also translate, "how should I, justly being blessedly happy, not obtain remembrance for all time?"

³⁵ *Oikeioteros*, translated as "more familiar," is based on the word for household (*oikos*). Cyrus' argument requires the inference, which the Greek encourages, that friendliness increases with familiarity. What the Greek encourages, however, it does

not necessarily require, and Cyrus himself did not entirely trust or respect ties of familiarity (1.6.8–9, 2.2.26).

³⁶ More literally, "is more familiar to" (*oikeios*).

³⁷ More literally, "by paternal gods" (*patroos*). The same adjective occurs at 1.6.1 and 8.7.3. I use the word "ancestral" at 8.7.1 for a different but related word.

³⁸ Literally, "the Red Sea."

³⁹ The reference is to the younger Cyrus, not to the Cyrus of *The Education of Cyrus*. See *Anabasis*, 2.6.1.

⁴⁰ *Athemistos* means "lawless," especially as regards laws held to be ordained by the gods.

⁴¹ *Polemistērion*, "military affairs," is commonly used with a narrower meaning and could refer simply to the war chariots spoken of in the context: "... how their war chariots are ..."

Index

The name of a place in the *Index* may stand also for the inhabitants of that place in the text, so entries under "Lydia," for example, may be for "Lydians." A more complete index may be found in Xenophon, *Cyropaedia*, ed. Walter Miller (Cambridge: Harvard University Press, 1968), vol. II, pp. 463–78.

Agora Editions

A Series Edited by Thomas L. Pangle
Founding Editor: Allan Bloom

CPSIA information can be obtained at www.ICGtesting.com
Printed in the USA
LVOW08s2117200916

505443LV00002B/290/P